THE PRAYER BOX

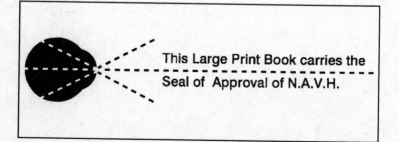

This Large Print Book carries the
Seal of Approval of N.A.V.H.

THE PRAYER BOX

LISA WINGATE

THORNDIKE PRESS
A part of Gale, Cengage Learning

GALE
CENGAGE Learning·

Detroit • New York • San Francisco • New Haven, Conn • Waterville, Maine • London

GALE
CENGAGE Learning®

Copyright © 2013 by Lisa Wingate.
Scripture quotations are taken from the Holy Bible, King James Version.
Thorndike Press, a part of Gale, Cengage Learning.

Thorndike Press® Large Print Christian Fiction.
The text of this Large Print edition is unabridged.
Other aspects of the book may vary from the original edition.
Set in 16 pt. Plantin.

LIBRARY OF CONGRESS CATALOGING-IN-PUBLICATION DATA

Wingate, Lisa.
    The prayer box / by Lisa Wingate. — Large print ed.
      pages ; cm. — (Thorndike Press large print Christian fiction)
    ISBN-13: 978-1-4104-6087-5 (hardcover)
    ISBN-10: 1-4104-6087-8 (hardcover)
    1. Large type books. I. Title.
PS3573.I53165P73 2013b
813'.54—dc23   2013023629

Published in 2013 by arrangement with Tyndale House Publishers, Inc.

Printed in the United States of America
1 2 3 4 5 6 7 17 16 15 14 13

To the two adorable boys
who have become incredible men:
I'd stand over your little beds
and brush kisses against your foreheads
again, if I could.
But since that would look strange at
this point,
I'll settle for leaving a kiss on this
paper, with only words.
Wherever the currents may take you,
Mom loves you to the end of the ocean
and back.

ACKNOWLEDGMENTS

If this book were a ship, it would have a very diverse crew. If you've been on that crew, I thank you from the bottom of my heart, just in case I forget to call one of you to muster here. So many people pour themselves into the making of a book before it is a book. First of all, to my treasured friend Ed Stevens, thank you for suggesting that the Outer Banks would be an excellent place to set a novel, and then for sending me pictures and information until I couldn't resist doing it. Thank you also to Shannon and Wick for opening your amazing Outer Banks home to our research crew during the development phase. What an amazing gift. Everyone should have the chance to walk the shores on the Outer Banks for days on end.

Thank you to my research crew, Sharon Mannion and Teresa Loman. There's nothing better than having just the right people

7

to canvas the town and stroll the beach with. Over five thousand pictures and one giant box of shells tell the tale. What a trip that was! To my amazing Aunt Sandy, what can I say to fully encompass what you've done for this book? Without you, there would be no Sandy's Seashell Shop. Thank you for lending your time and your talents, as well as your name. To all the local folks who helped us while we were in the Outer Banks — everyone from shop owners to members of the park service — we owe you a huge debt of gratitude and a massive hug the next time we visit. Thank you for answering all our questions and greeting us with the friendliness the Outer Banks is so famous for. I've never met nicer people anywhere.

My gratitude goes out, as always, to my beta reading crew. Aunt Sandy, we forgive you for clutching your heart and scaring us to death when you read the last scene of the book. You took a year off my life, but created an unforgettable moment . . . and a little inspiration for *The Sea Glass Sisters* novella. It's amazing how things end up working out.

To my sweet family, you are such a blessing to me. Thank you for all the help you always provide on these literary endeavors and the encouragement you give me. Your love is the current beneath the boat. Without you, it would wander the world, lost indeed.

If family-love is the current beneath an author's work, the members of the publishing crew are the riggers, climbing the masts and setting the sails and slathering pitch over all the leaky places. This project has been blessed with an incredibly dedicated, experienced, and hardworking crew. To everyone in the Ron Beers group who have not only taken such good care of this project, but encouraged me personally, I have no words to express what it means to have people come on board and instantly work so hard. Maggie Rowe, bless your sweet heart for opening your beautiful home for cover and video shoots. An immeasurable amount of gratitude also goes to Karen Watson, Jan Stob, Sarah Mason, Shaina Turner, and Babette Rea for believing so deeply in this project, for the hours devoted to it, and for being just plain awesome to work with. I never had a moment's doubt that you were the right people to sail with on this voyage.

To the Tyndale design team and the sales and marketing teams, who bring books into the hands of readers, you guys rock. Thank you for guiding *The Prayer Box* so gently and enthusiastically to distant shores. To my agent, Claudia Cross, at Folio Literary Management, thank you for manning the deck with me and helping to steer this ship over these many years and many journeys.

Lastly, to reader friends, librarians, and bookstore buddies far and near, including the awesome ladies of the McGregor Tierra Literary Society who read the book early for a book club premiere video, I do not even have words for how much you mean to me. Your encouragement is priceless. Without those who lovingly read, recommend, and share these stories, my ships would sail to uninhabited worlds and lie fallow on the beaches. Not that lying on the beach is a bad thing, but it's so much better when your friends are there too. Thank you for digging your toes into the sand with me for this story and many others over the years.

Beyond, beneath, and above all the other words of thanks to those who have sailed on this ship with me come a few last words that are the most important of all. Thank you to the Owner of the ocean. You are indeed a God of winds and tides. Thank you for the wind in my sails and the currents that have carried me to yet another story.

CHAPTER 1

When trouble blows in, my mind always reaches for a single, perfect day in Rodanthe. The memory falls over me like a blanket, a worn quilt of sand and sky, the fibers washed soft with time. I wrap it around myself, picture the house along the shore, its bones bare to the wind and the sun, the wooden shingles clinging loosely, sliding to the ground now and then, like scales from some mythical sea creature washed ashore. Overhead, a hurricane shutter dangles by one nail, rocking back and forth in the breeze, protecting an intact window on the third story. Gulls swoop in and out, landing on the salt-sprayed rafters — scavengers come to pick at the carcass left behind by the storm.

Years later, after the place was repaired, a production company filmed a movie there. A love story.

But to me, the story of that house, of

Rodanthe, will always be the story of a day with my grandfather. A safe day.

When I squint long into the sun off the water, I can see him yet. He is a shadow, stooped and crooked in his overalls and the old plaid shirt with the pearl snaps. The heels of his worn work boots hang in the air as he balances on the third-floor joists, assessing the damage. Calculating everything it will take to fix the house for its owners.

He's searching for something on his belt. In a minute, he'll call down to me and ask for whatever he can't find. *Tandi, bring me that blue tape measure,* or *Tandi Jo, I need the green level, out in the truck. . . .* I'll fish objects from the toolbox and scamper upstairs, a little brown-haired girl anxious to please, hoping that while I'm up there, he'll tell me some bit of a story. Here in this place where he was raised, he is filled with them. He wants me to know these islands of the Outer Banks, and I yearn to know them. Every inch. Every story. Every piece of the family my mother has both depended on and waged war with.

Despite the wreckage left behind by the storm, this place is heaven. Here, my father talks, my mother sings, and everything is, for once, calm. Day after day, for weeks. Here, we are all together in a decaying

12

sixties-vintage trailer court while my father works construction jobs that my grandfather has sent his way. No one is slamming doors or walking out them. This place is magic — I know it.

We walked in Rodanthe after assessing the house on the shore that day, Pap-pap's hand rough-hewn against mine, his knobby drift-wood fingers promising that everything broken can be fixed. We passed homes under repair, piles of soggy furniture and debris, the old Chicamacomico Life-Saving Station, where the Salvation Army was handing out hot lunches in the parking lot.

Outside a boarded-up shop in the village, a shirtless guitar player with long blond dreadlocks winked and smiled at me. At twelve years old, I fluttered my gaze away and blushed, then braved another glance, a peculiar new electricity shivering through my body. Strumming his guitar, he tapped one ragged tennis shoe against a surfboard, reciting words more than singing them.

Ring the bells bold and strong
Let all the broken add their song
Inside the perfect shells is dim
It's through the cracks, the light comes
    in. . . .

I'd forgotten those lines from the guitar player, until now.

The memory of them, of my grandfather's strong hand holding mine, circled me as I stood on Iola Anne Poole's porch. It was my first indication of a knowing, an undeniable sense that something inside the house had gone very wrong.

I pushed the door inward cautiously, admitting a slice of early sun and a whiff of breeze off Pamlico Sound. The entryway was old, tall, the walls white with heavy gold-leafed trim around rectangular panels. A fresh breeze skirted the shadows on mouse feet, too slight to displace the stale, musty smell of the house. The scent of a forgotten place. Instinct told me what I would find inside. You don't forget the feeling of stepping through a door and understanding in some unexplainable way that death has walked in before you.

I hesitated on the threshold, options running through my mind and then giving way to a racing kind of craziness. *Close the door. Call the police or . . . somebody. Let someone else take care of it.*

You shouldn't have touched the doorknob — now your fingerprints will be on it. What if the police think you did something to her? Innocent people are accused all the time, especially strangers in town. Strangers like you, who show up out of the blue and try to blend in . . .

What if people thought I was after the old woman's money, trying to steal her valuables or find a hidden stash of cash? What if someone really *had* broken in to rob the place? It happened, even in idyllic locations like Hatteras Island. Massive vacation homes sat empty, and local boys with bad habits were looking for easy income. What if a thief had broken into the house thinking it was unoccupied, then realized too late that it wasn't? Right now I could be contaminating the evidence.

Tandi Jo, sometimes I swear you haven't got half a brain. The voice in my head sounded like my aunt Marney's — harsh, irritated, thick with the Texas accent of my father's family, impatient with flights of fancy, especially mine.

"Mrs. Poole?" I leaned close to the opening, trying to get a better view without touching anything else. "Iola Anne Poole? Are you in there? This is Tandi Reese. From the little rental cottage out front. . . . Can you hear me?"

Again, silence.

A whirlwind spun along the porch, sweeping up last year's pine straw and dried live

15

oak leaves. Loose strands of hair swirled over my eyes, and my thoughts tangled with it, my reflection melting against the waves of leaded glass — flyaway brown hair, nervous blue eyes, lips hanging slightly parted, uncertain.

What now? How in the world would I explain to people that it'd taken me days to notice there were no lights turning on and off in Iola Poole's big Victorian house, no window heat-and-air units running at night when the spring chill gathered? I was living less than forty yards away. How could I not have noticed?

Maybe she was sleeping — having a midday nap — and by going inside, I'd scare her half to death. From what I could tell, my new landlady kept to herself. Other than groceries being delivered and the UPS and FedEx trucks coming with packages, the only signs of Iola Poole were the lights and the window units going off and on as she moved through the rooms at different times of day. I'd only caught sight of her a time or two since the kids and I had rolled into town with no more gas and no place else to go. We'd reached the last strip of land before you'd drive off into the Atlantic Ocean, which was just about as far as we could get from Dallas, Texas, and Trammel Clarke. I hadn't even realized, until we'd crossed the North Carolina border, where I was headed or why. I was looking for a hiding place.

By our fourth day on Hatteras, I knew we wouldn't get by with sleeping in the SUV at a campground much longer. People on an island notice things. When a real estate lady offered an off-season rental, cheap, I figured it was meant to be. We needed a good place more than anything.

Considering that we were into April now, and six weeks had passed since we'd moved into the cottage, and the rent was two weeks overdue, the last person I wanted to contact about Iola was the real estate agent who'd brought us here, Alice Faye Tucker.

Touching the door, I called into the entry hall again. "Iola Poole? Mrs. Poole? Are you in there?" Another gust of wind danced across the porch, scratching crape myrtle branches against gingerbread trim that seemed to be clinging by Confederate jasmine vines and dried paint rather than nails. The opening in the doorway widened on its own. Fear shimmied over my shoulders, tickling like the trace of a fingernail.

"I'm coming in, okay?" Maybe the feeling of death was nothing more than my imagination. Maybe the poor woman had fallen and trapped herself in some tight spot she couldn't get out of. I could help her up and bring her some water or food or whatever, and there wouldn't be any need to call 911. First responders would take a while, anyway. There was no police presence here. Fairhope wasn't much more than a fish market, a small marina, a village store, a few dozen houses, and a church. Tucked in the live oaks along Mosey Creek, it was the sort of place that seemed to make no apologies for itself, a scabby little burg where fishermen docked storm-weary boats and raised families in salt-weathered houses. First responders would have to come from someplace larger, maybe Buxton or Hatteras Village.

The best thing I could do for Iola Anne Poole, and for myself, was to go into the house, find out what had happened, and see if there was any way I could keep it quiet.

The door was ajar just enough for me to slip through. I slid past, not touching anything, and left it open behind me. If I had to run out of the place in a hurry, I didn't want any obstacles between me and the front porch.

Something shifted in the corner of my eye as I moved deeper into the entry hall. I jumped, then realized I was passing by an arrangement of fading photographs, my reflection melting ghost-like over the cloudy glass. In sepia tones, the images stared back at me — a soldier in uniform with the inscription *Avery 1917* engraved on a brass plate. A little girl with pipe curls on a white pony. A group of people posed under an oak tree, the women wearing big sun hats like the one Kate Winslet donned in *Titanic*. A wedding photo from the thirties or forties, the happy couple in the center, surrounded by several dozen adults and two rows of cross-legged children. Was Iola the bride in the picture? Had a big family lived in this house at one time? What had happened to them? As far as I could tell, Iola Poole didn't have any family now, at least none who visited.

"Hello . . . hello? Anyone up there?" I peered toward the graceful curve of the long stairway. Shadows melted rich and thick over the dark wood, giving the stairs a foreboding look that made me turn to the right instead and cross through a wide archway into a large, open room. It would have been sunny but for the heavy brocade curtains. The grand piano and a grouping of antique chairs and settees looked like they'd been plucked from a tourist brochure or a history book. Above the fireplace, an oil portrait of a young woman in a peach-colored satin gown hung in an ornate oval frame. She was sitting at the piano, posed in a position that appeared uncomfortable. Perhaps this was the girl on the pony from the hallway photo, but I wasn't sure.

The shadows seemed to follow me as I hurried out of the room. The deeper I traveled into the house, the less the place resembled the open area by the stairway. The inner sections were cluttered with what seemed to be several lifetimes of belongings, most looking as if they'd been piled in the same place for years, as if someone had started spring-cleaning multiple times, then abruptly stopped. In the kitchen, dishes had been washed and stacked neatly in a draining rack, but the edges of the room were heaped with stored food, much of it contained in big plastic bins. I stood in awe, taking in a multicolored waterfall of canned vegetables that tumbled haphazardly from an open pantry door.

Bristle tips of apprehension tickled my arms as I checked the rest of the lower floor. Maybe Iola wasn't here, after all. The downstairs bedroom with the window air unit was empty, the single bed fully made. Maybe she'd gone away somewhere days ago or been checked into a nursing home, and right now I was actually breaking into a vacant house. Alice Faye Tucker had mentioned that Iola was ninety-one years old. She probably couldn't even climb the stairs to the second story.

I didn't want to go up there, but I moved toward the second floor one reluctant step at a time, stopping on the landing to call her name once, twice, again. The old balusters and treads creaked and groaned, making enough noise to wake the dead, but no one stirred.

Upstairs, the hallway smelled of drying wallpaper, mold, old fabric, water damage, and the kind of stillness that said the rooms hadn't been lived in for years. The tables and lamps in the wood-paneled hallway were gray with dust, as was the furniture in five bedrooms, two bathrooms, a sewing room with a quilt frame in the middle, and a nursery with white furniture and an iron cradle. Odd-shaped water stains dotted the ceilings, the damage recent enough that the plaster had bowed and cracked but only begun to fall through. An assortment of buckets sat here and there on the nursery floor, the remnants of dirty water and plaster slowly drying to a paste inside. No doubt shingles had been ripped from the roof during last fall's hurricane. It was a shame to let a beautiful old house go to rot like this. My grandfather would have hated it. When he inspected historic houses for the insurance company, he was always bent on saving them.

A thin watermark traced a line down the hallway ceiling to a small sitting area surrounded by bookshelves. The door on the opposite side, the last one at the end of the hall, was closed, a small stream of light reflecting off the wooden floor beneath it. Someone had passed through recently, clearing a trail in the silty layer of dust on the floor.

"Mrs. Poole? Iola? I didn't mean to scare —"

A rustle in the faded velvet curtains by the bookshelves made me jump, breath hitching in my chest as I drew closer.

A black streak bolted from behind the curtain and raced away. A cat. Mrs. Poole had a cat. Probably the wild, one-eared tom that J.T. had been trying to lure to our porch with bowls of milk. I'd told him to quit — we couldn't afford the milk — but a nine-year-old boy can't resist a stray. Ross had offered to bring over a live trap and catch the cat. Good thing I'd told him not to worry about it. Letting your new boy-friend haul off your landlady's pet is a good way to get kicked out of your happy little home, especially when the rent's overdue.

The glass doorknob felt cool against my fingers when I touched it, the facets surprisingly sharp. "I'm coming in . . . okay?" Every muscle in my body tightened, preparing for fight or flight. "It's just Tandi Reese . . . from the cottage. I hope I'm not scaring you, but I was wor—" The rest of *worried* never passed my lips. I turned the handle. The lock assembly clicked, and the heavy wooden door fell open with such force that it felt like someone had pulled it from the other side. The doorknob struck the wall, vibrating the floor beneath my feet. Behind me, the cat hissed, then scrambled off down the stairs.

Picture frames inside the room shivered on the pale-blue walls, reflecting orbs of light over the furniture. Beyond the jog created by the hallway nook, the footboard of an ornate bed pulled at me as the shuddering frames settled into place and the light stopped dancing. By the bedpost, a neatly cornered blue quilt grazed the floor, and a pair of shoes — the sensible, rubber-soled kind that Zoey, with her fourteen-year-old fashion sense, referred to as *grandma shoes* — were tucked along the edge of a faded Persian rug, the heels and toes exactly even.

The feet that belonged in the shoes had not traveled far away. Covered in thin black stockings, they rested atop the bed near the footboard, the folded, crooked toes pointing outward slightly, in a position that seemed natural enough for someone taking a mid-day nap.

But the feet didn't move, despite the explosion of the door hitting the wall. I tasted the bile of my last meal. No one could sleep through that.

The bedroom lay in perfect silence as I stepped inside, my foot-falls seeming loud, out of place. I didn't speak again or call out or say her name to warn her that I was coming. Without even seeing her face, I knew there was no need.

Gruesome scenes from Zoey's favorite horror movies flashed through my mind, but when I crept past the corner, forced myself to turn her way, Iola Anne Poole looked peaceful, like she'd just stopped for a quick nap and forgotten to get up again. She was flat on her back atop the bed, a pressed cotton dress — white with tiny blue flower baskets — falling over her long, thin legs and seeming to disappear into a wedding ring quilt sewn in all the colors of sky and sea. Her leathery, wrinkled arms lay folded neatly across her stomach, the gnarled fingers intertwined in a posture that looked both contented and confident. Prepared.

The chalky-gray hue of her skin told me it would be cold if I touched it.

I didn't. I turned away instead, pressed a hand over my mouth and nose. As much as the body looked like someone had carefully laid it out to give a peaceful appearance, there were no signs that anyone else had been in the room. The only trails on the dusty floor led from the door to the bed, from the bed to what appeared to be a closet tucked behind the hallway nook, and past the foot of the bed to a small writing desk by the window. Whatever she was doing up here, she didn't come often. What was the lure of this turret room at the end of the upstairs hall, with its gold-trimmed walls painted in faded shades of cream and milky blue? Did she know she was approaching her last hours? Was this where she wanted to die? Where she wanted to be found?

Could I have helped if I'd checked on her sooner?

The questions drove me from the room, sent me into the hall, gasping for air. I didn't want to think about how long she'd been there or whether she'd known death was coming for her, whether she'd been afraid when it happened or completely at peace.

Truthfully, I didn't want anything more to do with the situation.

But an hour later, I was back in the house, watching two sheriff's deputies walk into the blue room. The deputy in back was more interested in getting a look inside the house than in the fact that a woman had died. For some reason, it seemed wrong to leave them alone with her body. I felt responsible for making sure they gave what was left of her some respect.

I waited in the doorway of the blue room, letting the wall hide all but the view of her stocking-clad feet as the men stood over the bed. They'd already asked me at least a dozen questions I couldn't answer: How long did I think she'd been dead? When was the last time I'd talked to her? Had she been ill that I knew of?

All I could tell them was that I was staying in her cottage out front. I'd used the term *renting* to make it sound good. The lead deputy was a thin, matter-of-fact man with an accordion of permanent frown lines around his mouth. He didn't seem to care much one way or the other. He checked his watch several times like he had somewhere to go.

"Well," he said finally, the floor creaking under his weight in a way that told me he

26

was leaning over the bed near her face, "looks like natural causes to me."

The younger man answered with a snarky laugh. "Shoot, Jim, she had to be somewhere up around a hundred. I remember when my granddad retired, Mama wanted to buy the altar flowers for church, to get his name in the bulletin, but she couldn't. The pastor had already ordered the altar flowers that week, on account of Iola Poole's birthday. She was turning eighty then, and that was back when I was in middle school. Mama was mighty hot about it all, I'll tell ya. Granddaddy'd been a deacon at Fairhope Fellowship for forty years, and Mama wasn't about to be having him share altar flowers with the likes of Iola Anne Poole. Our family helped move that old chapel here to start the church. Iola was just there to play the organ, and they paid her for that, anyway. It's not like she was a member, even. Mama figured, if Iola wanted altar flowers for her birthday, she could put some at a church down in New Orleans, where her people come from."

Deputy Jim clicked his tongue against his teeth. "Women."

His partner laughed again. "You haven't been down here long enough to know how things are. Stuff like that might not matter

27

much up in Boston, but it sure enough matters in Fairhope. Believe me, if they could've found anybody — and I mean *anybody* else who knew how to play that old pipe organ over to the church, they would've. That's half the reason my mama pushed for that new band director at the high school in Buxton a few years ago; he said he could play a pipe organ. I never saw the church ladies so happy as the week the band director took over at Sunday services and they sent Iola Poole packing."

"Okay, Selmer, we might as well get the right people out here to wrap this up." Deputy Jim ended the discussion. "Looks pretty cut-and-dried. She have any family we should call?"

"None that I'd know how to find. And that's a can of worms you don't wanna open either, by the way, Jim."

"No next of kin. . . ." The older man drew the words out, probably writing them down at the same time.

Sadness slid over me like a heavy wool blanket, making the air too stale and thick. I stood gazing through the blue room to the tall bay windows of the turret. Outside, a rock dove flitted along the veranda railing. What had Iola Poole done, I wondered, to have ended up this way, alone in this big

28

house, laid out in her flowered dress, dead for who knew how long, and nobody cared? Did she realize this was how things would turn out? Was this what she'd pictured when she placed herself there on the bed, closed her eyes, and let the life seep out of her?

The dove fluttered to the windowsill, then hopped back and forth, its shadow sliding over the gray marble top of the writing desk. A yellowed Thom McAn shoe box sat on the edge, the lid ajar, a piece of gold rickrack trailing from the corner. On the windowsill, half a dozen scraps of ribbon lay strewn about. As the dove's shadow passed again, I noticed something else. Little specks of gold shimmered in the dust on the sill. I wanted to walk into the room and look closer, but there wasn't time. The deputies were headed to the door.

Hugging my arms tightly, I followed the men downstairs and onto the front porch. It wasn't until we'd reached the driveway that I looked at the cottage and my stomach began churning for a different reason. With Iola gone, it would only be a matter of time before Alice Faye Tucker came to evict us. I had less than fifty dollars left, and that was from the last thing I could find to pawn — a sterling watch that Trammel had given me. The watch was only in my suitcase by accident — left behind after a trip to a horse event somewhere, undoubtedly in better times. If Trammel knew I still had it, he would have taken it away, along with everything else of value. He made sure I never had access to enough money to get out.

What were the kids and I going to do now?

The question gained weight and muscle as the afternoon passed. The coroner's van had just left when Zoey and J.T. came in from school. I didn't even tell them our new landlady had died. They'd find out soon enough. At nine years old, J.T. might not make the connections, but at fourteen-going-on-thirty, Zoey would know that the loss of the cottage spelled disaster for us. The minute we reemerged on the grid — credit card payment at a motel, job application with actual references provided, visit to a bank for cash — Trammel Clarke would find us.

I slipped into bed at twelve thirty, boneless and weary, guilt ridden for not being honest with the kids, even though it was nothing new. Outside, the water teased the shores of the sedges, and a slow-rising Hatteras moon climbed the roof of Iola's house, hanging above the turret like a scoop of vanilla ice cream on an upside-down cone.

How could someone who owned an estate

like this one end up alone in her room, gone from this world without a soul to cry at her bedside?

The image of Iola as a young woman taunted my thoughts. I imagined her walking the veranda in a milky-white dress. The moon shadows shifted and danced among the live oaks and the loblolly pines, and I felt the old house calling to me, whispering the secrets of the long and mysterious life of Iola Anne Poole.

CHAPTER 2

It's amazing how endless a week can be when you're wondering if you're about to be living in your car. Iola Poole's house had been quiet for days — no sign of Alice Faye Tucker, sheriff's deputies, or any family members or friends. I'd slipped into Bink's Village Market on Fairhope Inlet twice now and looked for a funeral flyer among the notes taped to the front of the counter, but I hadn't seen Iola's.

It was as if she'd never existed at all, but of course I'd found her in the blue room, and that meant that sooner or later our time in the cottage would end. I had no idea what I'd do when it happened. After weeks of looking for work around the Outer Banks, I'd figured out that between the hurricane damage and this being the off-season, no place was hiring, and even if they were, a woman with no references and no past history to offer isn't too tempting. The last official job I'd had was riding Trammel Clarke's show horses, and that was before one of them hooked a toe on the top rail of a jump at a grand prix event and cartwheeled to the ground with me on board. A botched surgery and a long recovery had led me down a dark hole I was still trying to climb out of.

No matter what it took now, I had to keep moving forward. I might've fallen short in the mothering department over the years, but I'd always promised myself that Zoey and J.T. wouldn't have the kind of life my sister and I had. If it came down to scrubbing streets with a toothbrush, I was going to find a way to take care of us and keep Trammel out of our lives for good. He'd already done enough damage.

If worse came to worst, Ross had said that we could move into his place, as soon as he was back in town. He had a saltbox house on Ocracoke, but most of the time he stayed in beachfront rental homes his father owned. He did light repair work and maintenance on them when he wasn't gone delivering long-haul orders for the family lumber company. Meeting Ross at Frisco Pier was one of the good things that had happened since we'd been here. But I'd picked up on the fact that Ross wasn't too much on kids in general. Zoey and J.T. would grow on him over time, but I knew better than to rush things.

It was probably too much to hope that we could keep Iola's cottage until a job came through, but as each day came and passed, I grew slightly more optimistic.

When I heard car doors shutting outside on the seventh day, I felt the ax tipping over my head again.

We were going to end up at Ross's, like it or not. He was due back from a long haul tonight. I'd have to pack what we had in the cottage and be ready when the kids came home from hanging out at the beach with a boy Zoey had met at school.

Anxiety hit me like a wave striking shore, dragging me out to sea in bits and pieces. More than anything I wanted to pop an OxyContin to tamp it down. But when we left Texas in the middle of the night, I'd made a promise — no more pills and no more Trammel Clarke. So far I'd held true on both.

I stepped out of the cottage with a greeting and a big smile, to make it look less like we'd been squatting there on purpose. Growing up in the family I had, I'd learned so much about delivering the kind of smooth story that could hide all sorts of ugly truths underneath. The lines I'd been crafting all week rehearsed themselves in my head. *After she passed away, poor thing, and I didn't hear from anyone, I wasn't sure what to do. I hated to just leave the place unsupervised and her cat with no one to take care of it. We've been keeping an eye on things — putting out food and water. The cat comes and goes from the house, so there must be a pet door somewhere, but I couldn't find it. The night after she died, I was worried because the cat was locked inside, but then the next day, he was out in the yard again. I thought we should look after him anyway, poor thing. I hope that's all right. . . .*

I really would miss this place. Nestled between the towering Victorian and an old horse corral that stretched to the parking lot of Fairhope Fellowship Church, it seemed protected from the things that were chasing us, its routines a sort of salve on wounds that were still bleeding. I would miss the sounds of fishermen readying their gear in the dim hours of the morning and boats rumbling out of Fairhope Marina. I'd even miss the church bells marking the time of day, over and over and over.

In the driveway, a man was unloading a riding lawn mower from the back of a pickup filled with yard-care equipment, chain saws, and ladders. I stopped at the top of the porch steps, craning sideways to get a better view around the crape myrtles. He seemed young, in his twenties or maybe even a teenager. He was wearing orange tennis shoes and red-flowered swim shorts, topped off with a lime-green Windbreaker with palm trees and lizards on it. A floppy fishing hat cast a shadow over his face and hid all but the endmost curls of his hair, reddish blond. All in all, he looked like he'd raided Jimmy Buffett's closet and then gotten dressed in the dark.

He didn't seem to be searching for anyone in particular, and my hopes flitted from the muck, taking flight like a marsh bird. Maybe he was just here to mow. Maybe we were safe for another day.

No sense giving anyone a reason to ask questions. I'd just tiptoe back inside and stay away from the windows until he left. . . .

"Afternoon." His greeting stopped me as I reached for the door. I paused midstride, a trespasser caught in the act.

Be calm. Be calm. Don't look guilty. Remember the story about keeping an eye on the house and the pet cat.

Smoothing my T-shirt over the old, holey jeans that I loved but Trammel would have frowned on, I turned slowly and flashed a smile. "Hi. I'm sorry. I didn't mean to get in your way. You look like you've got a job to do."

He shooed a carpenter bee away from his tools, his face still concealed by the shadow of the paint-spattered fishing hat. "Just finished mowing at the church." A shrug indicated Fairhope Fellowship next door. He walked closer to me, carrying a weed whacker. "Had the mower all loaded, and then I noticed how bad this place looked. Thought I'd do the church a favor and knock down the grass a little. Looks like I'll need a hay cutter and a baler, not a lawn mower."

I chuckled, still playing it low-key, yet friendly. "Too much rain lately." The yard had been a swamp most of the time we'd been here. When we moved in, there'd been some mention of a lawn service, but with all the moisture, no one had shown up. This guy didn't look like he was from a lawn service, though. I hoped he didn't try to give me a bill when he was done with the work.

He'd said something about doing this as a favor, hadn't he? Why was mowing Iola's yard a favor to the church? Just because the overgrown grass looked bad next door? Or was the church caretaking the house now?

He wandered nearer, and I felt obliged to come down the porch steps. We stopped on either side of the oyster-shell driveway. Up close, he looked older than the horrendously mismatched outfit made him seem. Somewhere in his thirties, maybe close to forty. The deep laugh lines around his caramel-brown eyes gave the impression that he smiled a lot, but something about him, maybe the reddish hair, reminded me of a smart-mouthed kid who'd put me through freshman-year agony in a high school near my third foster home in seven months.

"You staying in the bungalow?" His question seemed casual enough.

Bungalow . . . What a funny word for it. For some reason, I thought of reruns of *Fantasy Island.* "Yes. Just renting short-term." A blush crept up my neck. I hoped he couldn't see it in the thick pine shadow. When he was finished mowing here, would he go check with someone to make sure I belonged in Iola's cottage?

He nodded as if that made sense enough, and we hovered in an awkward silence for a moment before he shifted the weed whacker so he could shake my hand. He wiped his palm on his shorts before offering it. "Paul Chastain."

"Tandi Reese."

"Sad about Miss Poole," he commented after the introductions.

He was the first person I'd heard mention Iola in days. I'd almost started to feel like her death wasn't real. "Did you know her?"

Shaking his head, he squinted at the house. "My mom was from Fairhope, but I never spent time here, except visiting my grandparents on vacation. Didn't really know the old-timers. I heard she left this place to the church, though. That's pretty awesome."

My jaw stiffened at the memory of what the deputy had said about the church ladies and Iola. I'd watched Fairhope Fellowship since we'd been here. The old white chapel with its lighthouse-style steeple did a brisk business with brides looking for a picturesque wedding spot and tourists seeking a quaint place to go for Sunday morning service. Judging by the collection of high-dollar cars coming and going, they weren't hurting for money. On top of that, I hadn't seen one person from that church darken Iola's door. I couldn't imagine why she would leave anything to those people.

"I'll get out of your way." I turned and started back into the house before what I was thinking could come spilling out. The less information I exchanged with Paul

Chastain, the better.

Inside, I tried to read a copy of a Tom Clancy novel from the bookshelf, then gave up and turned on an old episode of *I Dream of Jeannie.* But nothing keeps the attention of a guilty conscience for very long. Every few minutes, I was up peeking out the windows, wondering what he was doing out there, how long he would stay, and whether he was calling anyone about me.

When the mower and the weed whacker finally went quiet, there were voices outside. Two people. Men. My nerves pulled clothesline tight, and adrenaline jangled through my body. Someone was walking up the porch steps, but it wasn't Paul Chastain. Paul had on tennis shoes. He looked like he'd be light on his feet, sort of wiry and quick. These were boots, heavy steps. Slow and purposeful.

I opened the door and found a stocky, middle-aged man poised with his fist in the air, about to knock.

"Well, my eye! I think you jus' took a good year off my life, young lady!" He staggered backward a few steps. The slight Cajun accent surprised me.

"I heard you coming." Pulling the door closed, I kept a death grip on the handle as he introduced himself — Brother Joe Guil-

40

beau — and explained that he was the music minister at Fairhope Fellowship Church. He smiled and said he'd enjoyed visiting with my kids at Bink's Market a few times, which wasn't good news at all. I'd told the kids to stay close to home and not to tell people in Fairhope anything about us. We'd rehearsed the story — newly divorced mom, two kids, just looking for a job and a new place to be. Nothing interesting that anyone would want to pry into.

After this conversation, it probably wouldn't matter what the kids had let slip about us. As soon as Brother Joe Guilbeau finished with the small talk, the ax would fall and we'd be moving on, though I had no idea how. After a week of waiting for it to happen, I wanted to break down and cry, blurt out our whole story, beg this stranger for help. But I couldn't. There was no way to know who to trust. Aside from that, bilking a church was far too much like something my mother or my big sister would've done. I wasn't going to be someone's charity case. I'd find a way out of this mess myself.

"You know what's the situation with the house, I guess?" The question slipped off his tongue in a roll so smooth and pleasant-sounding, I barely heard it coming. His accent reminded me of old Pat, who lived next to my Pap-pap's little tidewater farm on the North Carolina mainland near Wenona. Pap-pap's was the only place I remembered where things were calm day in and day out when I was little, but we only spent time there in bits and snatches — usually whenever my mother left my father.

"We've just been renting by the month." My voice quivered, and I swallowed what felt like a cocklebur. "I was hoping to stay . . . a little longer . . . if that's possible. The kids and I just moved to the island, and I've been looking for a job. Once I get something, it'll be easier to think about relocating."

Brother Guilbeau studied the porch ceiling rather than me. "Alice Faye rushed outta town when her daughter birthed that grandbaby premature. Granny Jeane, she takin' care of the real estate office, but jus' to keep up wit' the phone calls and the mail. They got enough to worry about, so you find any problem wit' the cottage, you come on by my office next door. Gonna take some time to get all the paperwork sorted out, but Iola had it planned to leave this ol' place in the hands a' the church."

I nodded, my mind racing ahead. The real estate lady was out of town for a family emergency? That explained why no one had come knocking when the rent was due. "Okay . . . well . . . I'll let you know if we have any problems, thanks."

I was hoping he'd leave, but he lingered there, surveying the rafters.

"Lil' seekahsah, he got 'im a nest up there. Better take you some spray and knock it down." He motioned to a lacy paper wasp nest in the corner.

"I'll do that."

"You be interested in doing some cleanin' in the big house? Get the food and trash outta there, pass a broom around the floors, few things like that? Maybe we pull it off in rent here?"

I should've been overjoyed, but it took me a moment to answer. I had a feeling that Brother Joe Guilbeau knew a whole lot more about me than I wanted him to. I wondered what my kids might have told him in Bink's. This felt way too much like a handout. But when it's a choice between feeding your kids and watching them go hungry, you do what you have to do. "Sure. I might be interested in that."

He nodded, the sun glinting off his large, round head, making it seem more dispro-portionate in size than it already was. "Nine tomorrow mo'nin', you come by the church office. We'll see, can we work up some-thin'?" Then he exited the porch, studying Iola's house as he crossed the yard.

In the driveway, Paul Chastain was load-ing the riding mower into his pickup truck. Brother Guilbeau stopped to help. Then the two of them shook hands, and Brother Guil-beau strode off across the field in front of the tumbledown stable, headed back to the church parking lot.

The pickup was finally leaving when the kids pulled into the driveway in the decked-out ragtop Jeep belonging to Zoey's new crush. Paul Chastain pointed a finger at them, I guess to let them know they'd made the turn too fast. Zoey's date waved back like he didn't get the point.

Rowdy Raines fit his name, from what little I could tell about him so far. He was built like a tank and filled with high school swagger. Being the new girl in school, Zoey was excited that he liked her. She'd had to leave a boyfriend behind in Texas without even saying good-bye. Now that she'd made friends in Fairhope, I was hoping she'd see that leaving Dallas without a word to anyone was our only way out. If Trammel knew what I was planning, he would have found a way to stop me.

Oyster shells crunched under the Jeep's

tires as it rolled up in front of our cottage. J.T. hopped out as soon as he could, and Zoey followed, her flip-flops scuttling across the shell gravel. Rowdy waited in the vehicle, leaving it running.

J.T.'s oversize shorts flopped around his skinny legs as he hurried toward the front door, his stick-straight blond hair bobbing. "You have fun?" I asked, snaking an arm out to stop him. He dodged it and went on up the porch steps. "J.T., did you have fun?"

One hand was clasped on the screen door handle when he finally stopped. "Yeah." The usual one-word answer, with a side of nine-year-old disinterest.

"Did you play with Rowdy's brother?"

"Yeah." His nose wrinkled under the freckles.

"Did you tell Rowdy and his brother thanks?"

"Yeah."

"Can you say anything but *yeah*?" I wanted to dig down inside J.T. and find the chatterbox who used to talk about dinosaur bones and snails he discovered in the dirt outside the riding arena and zoo animals he learned about on TV and how earthworms eat. These days, he didn't say anything unless he had to, and he didn't do anything but sit in front of the TV with his video

45

games. Somehow during these last few years, he'd learned to make himself invisible, and I hadn't even noticed the change. Between trying to keep things on an even keel with Trammel and the haze of pills that had started after the accident, I'd missed a lot.

"Mom, I was supposed to be on Zago Wars twenty minutes ago. I'm missing the battle!" J.T.'s favorite thing about the cottage wasn't the beach just blocks away or the hiking trails of Buxton Woods nearby. It was the wireless Internet installed for vacationers and the video game system he'd crammed into his backpack when we left Trammel's house.

"Oh, well, *excuse* me. I hope the zombies didn't attack while you were gone."

He smirked then, his big blue eyes twinkling with a hint of the little teddy bear he used to be. "It doesn't *have* zombies."

"I knew that," I joked, and he rolled a doubtful look my way.

Zoey glared at him and huffed, "He hardly even did anything with Rowdy's brother, he was so worried about stupid Zago Wars and whoever he's playing with online. There's a party down at the pier, but we had to leave to run the dorkface home. Next time, I'm *not* bringing him with us. Anyway, we're go-

46

ing back down to the beach."

"Who's having a party at the pier?"

Zoey's eyes flashed wide. She wasn't used to me asking questions. She pretty much ran her own life, like another adult in the house. Zoey had been taking care of herself since before she was old enough for school. There was a deep-down part of me that knew it was because there were so many times she'd had to.

"Rowdy's friends, okay?" A nervous look flicked toward the car, and she shifted her hips to one side to let me know she didn't have time for this. She was already mad at me for not telling her when Iola Poole died. Three days had passed before she'd heard about it at school, and then she'd come home in a panic, worried that we'd be moving in with Ross. I'd lied to her and told her I had enough money for another month's rent.

"Maybe y'all could just hang around here. . . ."

Her eyes went cold. When Zoey looked at me like that — like everything in her that cared about me had turned to mortar and stone — I wondered if I'd already lost her for good.

"We'll be back later." She started toward the car. "I've got a stupid biology test tomorrow, and dorkface there screwed up his math homework too. I'll help him redo it when I get home." She left without bothering to ask me to help J.T. with his math, and even that hurt a little. She knew I'd always been good with numbers.

Rowdy's car pulled out of the driveway, and J.T. opened the screen door, his shoulders rounding forward as I followed him inside. He hated it when Zoey was mad at him.

"I could help you with your math."

"Zoey knows how to do it." The bits of driftwood decorating the cottage walls rattled slightly as he ran to the enclosed back porch, where he'd been sleeping on an old foldout sofa bed. It was the only room in the house with an extra TV where he could play his video games to his heart's content.

"You want something for dinner?" My stomach was growling. I'd been skipping lunches to save a little on groceries. "A hot dog or mac 'n' cheese or something?"

"I'm not hungry too much. We ate at the beach." His answer came with the closing of the door.

I sat down on the flowered chair in the living room, let my eyes fall shut, and felt the walls closing in around me. Sometimes

48

it seemed like no matter how far away we went or how much I tried, Zoey and J.T. would never let me back into the world they'd built, the place where the two of them huddled together as the storms went on around them.

The phone rang while I was sitting there trying to decide whether to get something to eat or just skip it for the night. I answered and Ross was on the other end, home from a week of delivering processed, pressure-treated Carolina pines. I loved it that he always called as soon as he was back home. Guys like that don't come along every day. Especially guys who look like Ross. On top of the fact that his parents owned a lumber company and vacation rental houses all over the Banks, he was a competitive amateur surfer in his off time. What girl wouldn't have her head turned by a guy who took on massive waves and made it look like art?

"So, c'mon over." His invitation was smooth like the purr of a kitten. "I'm at one of the houses in Salvo for a couple days while it's empty. It's lonely around here." The thick, seductive tone pulled a delicious, warm feeling from deep inside me. It felt good to know that a man like him could want me. After listening to Trammel for six years, I'd started to believe no one could.

I was off the sofa and on my way to the kitchen, giddy inside, before I even had time to think. The sound of laser guns and explosions in J.T.'s room caught my ear as I crossed the hallway. I groaned, "Ohhh . . . J.T.'s here and Zoey's gone."

"So what. He's got his face in a video game so much, he probably won't even notice you left. The kid's old enough to stay by himself." Ross's answer was sharp enough that I stopped moving toward my shoes.

Ross was right, of course. J.T. kept to himself whenever he could. He'd probably be right there in front of Zago Wars all evening.

"I know, but there's the whole thing about the cottage. If somebody shows up here and tells him we have to get out, he'll be scared to death. He won't have a clue what to do."

"Bring him with you. He can watch TV here, same as home." His tone conveyed that it was a big sacrifice. After just getting back, he probably wasn't in the mood to have a boy underfoot. The video game noise drove him nuts, anyway.

"He has some kind of math homework to do tonight."

"Well, I'm not helpin' him with that." Ross let out a rueful laugh. "I get enough math all day, dealing with orders and invoices. I just wanna kick back, crack open a cold one, and get close to my baby." A low moan sifted through the phone, like he was already stretching out on the sofa in some rental house that was probably eye-popping gorgeous. I pictured him combing his fingers through his dark hair, his coffee-colored eyes falling closed. I wanted to be right there with him, curled up in his arms, knowing I didn't have a thing to worry about because he would take care of me. Ross made me feel that way.

"Come on, darlin', it's been a long trip. Come hang out in the hot tub with me. Ocean view, and I need me some welcome home."

A heady feeling wound around me in a way I couldn't resist. Ross could fix so many things for the kids and me. He had a house, a family with money. At thirty-nine, he was only six years older than me, so unlike with Trammel, we had things in common. He made me feel good about myself, attractive and wanted. He'd come along like a knight in shining armor, just when I needed one.

Looking down the hall at J.T.'s door again, I tried to decide whether to take him along to Ross's or leave him here to wait for Zoey. Ross would like it better if I let J.T. stay behind, and so would J.T. Evening was setting in. Surely no one would stop by about the house anymore tonight. . . .

The sound of boots on the porch outside broke up the thought. Maybe Brother Guilbeau had changed his mind.

"Ross, I have to go. Someone's here." I started toward the door.

"You know what, Tandi? If you don't wanna come over, just be straight about it." Ross was strangely touchy this evening, mad right away. "I'll go down to Captain Jack's and hang awhile." Captain Jack's was one of his favorite dives, a nothing-fancy place where local boys went to get a cold beer and shoot pool. One of Ross's ex-girlfriends worked there. He knew I knew that, of course.

"Listen, I'm not making it up. There's someone here. I have to —"

He didn't even wait for me to get the rest of the sentence out. He just hung up.

I set the phone down and pulled in a breath, smoothing my hair back before going to the door. When I opened it, no one was there.

CHAPTER 3

A baby's cry woke me. I blinked into the
darkness, thinking I was in Nebraska and
the kids were still little — Zoey, a five-year-
old with eyes that were summer-sky blue,
and J.T., just a few weeks. Zoey had been
such an easy baby, and thank goodness for
that, because when she'd come into the
world, I was a nineteen-year-old college
dropout, on my own after a literature
professor, who swore he loved me, dumped
me at the doors of an abortion clinic with a
wad of cash in my hand.

Where Zoey had been the perfect baby,
her brother was colicky and hard to handle.
J.T.'s daddy was getting restless about family life. I could feel it. He was tired of working every day to pay the bills. He missed
traveling and rodeoing the way he had
before we met and I got pregnant. . . .

I stood on the deck and waved good-bye
as he left in his pickup, but when the dust

cleared, Iola Poole's big house was there. The front door hung open, the soft glow of a lamp seeping across the salt-weathered porch, bleeding through the railings, tumbling into a spray of overgrown white roses.

A figure moved past a window along the porch. Someone was in there. But it couldn't be Iola. I'd found her lifeless in her blue-flowered dress . . . hadn't I?

Had I only dreamed it? Was that real, or was this real?

I tried to make out the face of the woman setting a teapot and cups on the little table in the bay window. Was it Iola? Through the wavy glass and the lace curtains, I couldn't tell.

I wanted to walk closer, to cross the lawn, but my legs were like lead, refusing to take me even as far as the driveway.

Suddenly I was in the towering white house, walking from room to room. "Hello? Is anyone here?" Lamps burned bright and fires crackled in hearths as if the house had been prepared for guests. Yet each shadowed corner, each hallway, was empty. "Hello? Iola Anne Poole? Iola? Who's in here?"

The question was answered only by timbers groaning and wind whistling through window sashes. The baby was crying again, but farther away this time, somewhere outside. Whose baby? Was it wandering toward Mosey Creek or the sedges, in danger of falling into the water?

I was in the upstairs hall, but I couldn't remember how I came to be there. I stood among the bookshelves, reached for the door to the blue room. The one-eared cat jumped from a shelf, hissing. The bedroom door fell open, and a warm light radiated into the hall. The light grew brighter, blinding, mesmerizing. Compelling. Someone was standing within it.

"Iola?" The word was little more than a breath. "Iola Anne Poole?"

"Mama?" The answer seemed wrong. The wrong voice.

J.T.'s voice. Was he in the house with me?

"Mama?"

Something grabbed my shoulder, tried to pull me back from the door. I raised my arm, felt my elbow strike flesh and knock the hand away. I wanted to look into the room, to see who was inside the light.

"Mama!"

The light, the room, the door — everything faded. I was in bed in the cottage.

J.T. stood over me, a silhouette against the glow of an old night lamp featuring the Virgin Mary clasping her hands in prayer. He rubbed his arm. "You hit me."

"What?" My mouth was dry, my throat filmy and swollen. "What time is it?"

"I dunno."

The small pearl-cased alarm clock read three in the morning. "Why are you out of bed?" J.T. hadn't gotten up and wandered around the house like this since we'd moved into Trammel's enormous home after the accident. Trammel had taken up residence on a cot beside my bed, seeming devoted to my recovery. It wasn't long before he let J.T. know that he was too old to be coming into my bedroom at night. Trammel and I disagreed about it at the time, but Trammel had insisted that there were things women just didn't know about how to make a man out of a boy.

It never even crossed my mind that Trammel wasn't the kind of man I wanted my boy to be.

"You were talking," J.T. whispered, still rubbing his arm. "I tried to wake you up." Shivering a bit, he squeezed his elbows in tight against his body. "You said that lady's name. The lady from the house. I think she's out there."

"Who?" The window heating unit kicked on, puffing out an initial gust of cold night air, wet with fog and salt spray. A chill ran over me.

Glancing toward the yard, J.T. kneaded his elbows with his fingers. "The old lady. Iola Poole. She's a ghost now. I think she's out there. She wants us to get away from her house."

The sting of interrupted sleep cleared slightly from my eyes. I started to pull the covers down and let J.T. slide into bed with me like the old days. But in the back of my mind, there was Trammel complaining that Zoey and I babied J.T. too much. Ross said the same thing. He thought J.T. should be out duck hunting or throwing a football instead of hanging around in the house playing video games, reading books, and drawing animated superheroes with magical powers.

"J.T., no one's out there."

He inched closer to the bed. "I heard the cat screaming in the yard." His eerie whisper raised the fine hairs on my skin. "They do it when there's a ghost. I saw it on the sci-fi channel."

"J.T., ghosts aren't *real*. Zombies aren't real. Vampires aren't real. It's all just TV stuff. You know that." Sighing, I sank back against the pillow. In the morning, I had to go over to the church first thing, and if it all worked out, I'd get started cleaning early, before the sun fell behind the vine-tangled oaks, melting long shadows over Iola's house. The last thing I needed before going in there was a little boy filling my head with crazy ideas about ghosts. "Go back to bed, okay?"

He shifted from one foot to the other, ducking his chin like he was trying to make himself as small a target as possible. His hands fiddled with the hem of his T-shirt. "*Some* people turn into ghosts when they die."

"No, they don't."

"Do people turn into angels sometimes?"

"I don't know." On nights like this, I felt weary and empty, like I had one foot in the grave at thirty-three. I didn't want to be the person who was supposed to have all the answers, who was supposed to handle everything, to figure out where we'd live and how we'd live. I wanted an OxyContin so bad I could taste it on my tongue, feel it sliding down my throat with a gush of water, my body relaxing in anticipation.

"It's three in the morning, J.T. Go to sleep."

A shiver and a little shake of his head, an almost-involuntary act of defiance, answered. "What if she's mad nobody found her before she died? The kids at school said she stayed locked up in her house because she went crazy."

I thought of my dream, of seeing Iola inside the house. An uneasy feeling seeped through me, stirring up nerve endings. "When people die, they go to heaven, all right? Especially people who played the church organ like Iola Poole. They don't wander around the yard at night." Sometimes you'll say anything to end the questions — even something you don't really believe. It wasn't that I didn't believe in heaven. Pap-pap's little white church was a refuge where we were loved and saved, but bouncing around from place to place with Mama and Daddy, I'd learned that the people you meet aren't necessarily good just because they darken a church door every Sunday.

J.T. glanced at the window again. "Am I gonna die pretty soon? A kid drowned last summer. I heard people talkin' about it at the beach. I dreamed that I drowned, and then they found me in my bed, like the lady in the house. Do you think I'll ever drown?"

I felt a stab in the tender place that mothers have, even lousy ones. "What? No, of course not. You're just nine years old, J.T." Pulling the covers back, I scooted toward the middle of the big bed. "You're not going to drown. Here, climb in."

J.T. was beside me in two seconds flat, his legs tucking under the covers. His feet were cold from the floor, and he made a satisfied sound as he pushed his frozen toes my way. I closed my eyes, enjoying the feeling of him snuggled in, enjoying the comfort of not being alone. So much for making a man out of him.

"Mama?"

"Ssshhh."

"But what's heaven like? Do you have to be a ghost a long time before you go there?"

"There *are* no ghosts. Go to sleep." I let my arm fall over my eyes to block out the glow from the night lamp, hoping sleep would come.

But when it did, I was in Iola's tall, white house, whether I wanted to be there or not. The light in the blue room was bright and blinding. I couldn't see past it or into it, but it was all around. It was so beautiful, I could only stand and stare.

By morning, I felt like I'd been run over by a bulldozer. Sleeping in a bed with J.T. was like trying to catch forty winks in the monkey cage at the zoo. He'd somehow turned sideways, and even though I was all the way at the other end of the queen-size mattress, he'd been chasing rabbits and stomping ants on my back for an hour before Zoey came and woke him for school. They were so quiet, I barely heard him slipping out and following her to the kitchen. As usual, Zoey took charge. One thing about Zoey, she was reliable. Easy. She took care of everyone around her. Where she got that from, I couldn't imagine. Gina and I were never like that when we were kids.

I drifted back to sleep, and when I woke again, a drowsy glance at the clock sent a bolt of panic through me. Eight forty-five! I was supposed to be over at the church at nine.

Within twenty minutes, I was dressed and rushing out the door while trying to dig a hair clip from my purse. My foot collided with something metallic, liquid splattered everywhere, and before I knew it, I was tripping and stumbling over a mass of spitting, growling black fur. *J.T., cat, dish, milk* ran through my mind in no particular order, and I did the tomcat tango, the contents of my purse spewing everywhere before an old metal porch rocker finally broke my fall. I flopped facedown over it, letting out a loud "Ooof!" From the corner of my eye, I caught an upside-down view of the one-eared cat running through a spill of milk and straight into the cottage.

"No, no, no!" The door swung shut and

the lock clicked just as I was realizing that the cottage key with the plastic card attached was nowhere in the spattering of purse clutter on the porch floor.

"No!" I scrambled forward, but there was no key under the mat where we usually kept it in case I wasn't around when the kids came home. "Please, please, please no." But *please* doesn't fix things when you've *pulled a stupid,* as my daddy would have put it. There was nothing on the porch but pens, a hairbrush, and a random assortment of makeup, all floating in a shallow pool of milk next to a blue enamelware mixing bowl.

Seconds ticked by as I stood with my arms held out, looking down at the sticky white stains on the T-shirt and jeans that were now a disaster. *Who in the world's going to give you a job?* The thought came in Aunt Marney's voice. My father's sister had a way of making you feel worthless with only a few words.

"Well, good mo'nin', good mo'nin', good mo'nin'!" Brother Guilbeau's voice surprised me, and I spun around. He was crossing the yard at a good clip, moving like a man in a hurry.

On my way down the steps, I apologized for being late in getting over to the church and folded my arms self-consciously over my milk-spattered T-shirt. I hadn't found a hair clip either. *You look like trailer trash. I wonder why that is?* Trammel was hanging out with Aunt Marney in my head, but Brother Guilbeau only smiled and waved off my apology. A strange sense of comfort washed over me. Something about Joe Guilbeau made me feel like everything would be all right.

For a short man, he was surprisingly quick. He moved fast and talked fast. Within a few minutes, he'd commented that it was a nice walk through the stable yard in the morning mist, so he really didn't mind coming over. He'd told me he remembered visiting the Outer Banks on vacation years ago when there were horses there, asked me what brought the kids and me to Hatteras, and given me some instructions for cleaning out Iola's house — throw away the trash, anything perishable, and stuff that might attract bugs and mice. "We'll get to decisions about everythin' else after the paperwork's settled wit' the house," he added, and I felt a pinprick of worry.

I started to ask about the unsettled paperwork, but then I thought, *Why rock the boat?* Brother Guilbeau seemed to know what he was doing.

"Can't offer you any money for the job right off, but you got the cottage and all the paid bills. I get a chance, I'll see can I come up wit' a few dollars out of the discretionary fund wit'out havin' to pass it round church council. Best just keep your work quiet over here till everythin's settled wit' the house."

That was the second time he'd said it — *settled with the house.* This time, it rang in the corner of my mind like a smoke alarm detecting a fire not far away.

I glanced at the cottage and saw the one-eared cat sleeping happily on the windowsill in the front room. Luckily, there were several keys on that ring Brother Guilbeau was holding. Hopefully one of them opened the cottage.

"Okay," I answered as a breeze wafted by, wrestling a few loose leaves from the trees and raining them silently down around us. One landed on Brother Guilbeau's head, but he didn't seem to notice as he handed me the keys and reminded me again to clean out all the perishables. I was welcome to keep whatever food I thought I could use. If I needed any cleaning supplies today, I could get them at Bink's Village Market and charge them to the church account. As soon as he had the chance, Brother Guilbeau would drop off some cash I could use to buy supplies at the Food Lion or Burrus Market, where there was more selection.

"No tellin' what's in the kitchen there." He motioned toward the house. "Last year or two, Iola had a worry somebody'd try to move her into the old folks' home, so she stopped havin' anyone pass through the front door. She didn't mean to make nobody the misère, but she wanted to be in her house when the death angel come to call. Guess she got her way."

A heebie-jeebie ran over my body. I didn't want Brother Guilbeau to think I couldn't do the job, but the less I heard about Iola and the death angel, the better. Working alone in that house would be bad enough without remembering that someone had just died there.

Brother Guilbeau slid a business card from his shirt pocket and handed it to me. It had his name on it, but it was for a zydeco band, not for the church. Underneath the name, the card read, *As seen in* Reme's Bayou. Even I had watched the movie *Reme's Bayou.*

"My other job, when I'm not doin' the worship music over to Fairhope Fellowship. Only Louisiana-bred zydeco band on the Banks," he told me and winked. "There's

65

the number to my cell phone. You got any question, you call me up, okay?"

"Okay." The keys felt weighty in my hand, but I tried to make it look like I didn't have a worry in the world. I'd managed to successfully plot an escape from the well-guarded lair of Trammel Clarke. How bad could one strangely creepy house be? "I'm sure I can handle it."

Brother Guilbeau gave me an enthusiastic nod, and we parted ways. Standing alone in Iola Poole's front yard, I gazed up at the house with its wraparound veranda and intricate railings. Ribbons of peeling paint and crumbling plaster shivered in the breeze like bridal veils, mimicking the uneasy quiver in my stomach.

There was no sense putting it off. As soon as I got the cat out of the cottage, grabbed a little breakfast, and put on some dry clothes, I'd have to get started.

Whatever was inside that house, it wasn't going anywhere, and in some strange way, I felt that the place was holding its breath, every nail, board, and batten watching through time-weathered eyes, just waiting for me to come inside.

Whether it was stalking me or inviting me, I had absolutely no idea.

CHAPTER 4

In the fourth grade, a girl named Isha asked me home with her after school. I went, even though I knew Aunt Marney would have a fit if she found out. It wasn't like any of the other kids were going to invite me over — not with the reputation my parents had. They'd just been through another humdinger of a breakup. This one got hot enough to include dishes flying and the police showing up. CPS had dumped Gina and me with my father's sister in Texas again, and Aunt Marney had made it clear that this was the last time she was taking us. Having us around my father's old hometown was an embarrassment to her, and even at just ten years old, I could see why. It's never good to be in a place where your daddy's bad deeds walk through every door before you can even get there. Gina wasn't helping matters. At twelve, tall and blonde, she looked sixteen and was already a whole lot like Mama and Daddy.

Isha's mother was from Sierra Leone — *black as the ace of spades,* as my father would've not-so-nicely put it. Isha's daddy was a local boy who'd gone all the way to Africa to oversee production in bauxite and platinum mines. They lived on a corner lot in a big blue house with antique rosebushes outside and all the things I'd always wanted inside. There were sweet rolls, milk, and a smiling mama waiting in the kitchen when we walked in.

When Isha's daddy came home, he swept his daughter up like they hadn't been together in a month. I just stood there watching from the upstairs hallway with my arms wrapped awkwardly over the princess clothes we'd made from safety pins and old bedsheets.

"And who's this?" her father asked, smiling. He had kind eyes. Soft and warm and friendly.

Isha introduced me as *Princess Tandinajo the Brave.* When I snaked out my hand, trying to be on my best manners, he bowed low and pretended to kiss my fingers the way Robin Hood did with Maid Marian. His lips never touched my skin, but I jerked my hand back anyway. After a stint in emergency foster care, I'd learned a few things about being too friendly with men I didn't know.

Isha's father just smiled and said, "Well, welcome to our kingdom, Princess Tandinajo the Brave," and I *felt* welcome, as if the air in their home were so fresh and so sweet, I couldn't get enough of it.

The name and the memory came back to me as I let myself into Iola Anne Poole's house and made my way to the kitchen. "Tandinajo the Brave," I whispered, chuckling at the echo off Iola's high ceilings. It felt good to laugh after almost an hour of chasing the one-eared cat around the cottage. I now fully understood the saying about herding cats. That scabby old thing was not only wily and ugly, he was as mean as an acre of alligators.

There was a scent in Iola's kitchen that reminded me of the temporary realm of Tandinajo the Brave. Cinnamon . . . or ginger. Maybe both. A pumpkin pie smell, like the sweet rolls Isha's mother made. Despite the clutter of storage boxes and canned food around the edges of Iola's kitchen, it smelled like she'd just been there, baking a pie.

The effect was unsettling. I had the urge to walk through the house, ensure that she was really gone. The place didn't *seem* empty, and I felt like a houseguest who'd breezed in without taking time for all the proper niceties. It wasn't a sense of being unwelcome exactly, more like I should be acknowledging something that I hadn't yet, as if the house were one big question, and the answer had nothing to do with cleaning the food out of the kitchen. As if the place *wanted* something from me.

Silly, of course. Houses don't want or think or wonder. They don't bake pumpkin pies when no one's home. They don't love or hate or hope. They just *are.*

They don't *know* anything.

Yet this house was telling a story, even now. Iola's story. She'd eaten something on a blue-rimmed china luncheon plate for her last meal, washed the dish, and set it in the draining rack with a single fork and a stoneware coffee mug. The cup had a faded pink heart on the front, printed with the words *Love is . . . knowing you love me!* Next to the heart stood a sunbonneted Holly Hobbie girl in outdated shades of brown and harvest gold.

The companions to the blue-rimmed plate waited in a neat stack behind glass, their golden edges glinting in the morning light. The cabinet hinges complained as I opened the door and stood on my toes to run a

70

finger across the shelf, parting the dust. When I lifted one of the matching teacups, a perfect circle of clean space appeared. No one had used these in a while.

Was that her routine every day — to drink her coffee in the faded Holly Hobbie mug, then wash it and leave it to drain? Was the mug her favorite? Had someone given it to her a long time ago, someone she loved?

Where was that someone now?

The buzzer on the oven sounded, and I jumped at least a foot before crossing the kitchen to turn the little white pointer firmly to the off position. My fingers were trembling when I pulled my hand away. So much for Tandinajo the Brave. I was shaking like a poodle being hauled in for annual vaccinations.

"Okay, listen, the food needs to be cleaned out of this kitchen because there's nobody here to eat it." I braced my hands on my hips and looked around the room. No one could hear me, but somehow it seemed right to acknowledge the fact that this house had an owner, and she hadn't been gone very long. "Brother Guilbeau sent me. Someone's got to sort out this mess before the mice take over. I know about mice, believe me. I lived in some ragtag places growing up. One cat isn't going to cut it with all this food sitting around."

The cat was as strange as everything else about this house — a puzzle I couldn't put together, no matter how hard I tried. He had me *ferhoodled,* to put it in Pap-pap's words. I could not, for the life of me, figure out how he came and went from the house, but he did.

At night I'd see him sitting in the turret window. Same black tomcat with eerie gold-colored eyes and half of one ear missing. Just sitting there, still as a stone, staring over the treetops toward the marina and Pamlico Sound, a faint glow casting out from behind him. Someone must have left a lamp on after they took Iola's body away.

The next day, the cat would be sitting on the roof of the stable or prowling the irises in the flower bed or cautiously sniffing around our porch to see if J.T. had left anything.

There was definitely no cat door in this house. I'd looked more than once in the past week. How to explain an animal seemingly walking through walls, I had no idea.

Now the pumpkin pie smell was a mystery too.

I tried to put it out of my mind as I moved around the kitchen and the adjoining wash-room, gathering up cleaning supplies, some of which were so ancient that the containers had rotted through.

Upstairs, something fell off a table or a shelf and hit the floor above the kitchen. I jumped again, slapping a hand over my collarbone. "I know that's you up there!" After our run-in at the cottage, the cat was probably messing with me on purpose. "Stop knocking her things over. Iola wouldn't like it, I'll bet."

Blood prickled into my cheeks, and the next thing I knew, I was laughing at myself. Talking to a cat. Really?

"Time to get to work." I went looking for trash bags and came up with enough to get started for a while. There was an envelope on the counter with fifty dollars inside. I folded it and tucked it into my back pocket. I'd have to go get more bags soon, at least. Brother Guilbeau must have stopped back by the big house and left a few bucks for supplies while I was over in the cottage changing clothes and chasing the cat around. All the better, because I wasn't nuts about the idea of charging expenses at Bink's Market. Bink's was information central around Fairhope, and I was trying hard to stay off the local grapevine.

A sliver of temptation needled me as I made a shopping list in my mind. *You could add a few extra things to the supply list, then return them and get the money back. Nobody would know the difference. . . .*

I shook the plan off as soon as it found a voice.

I'd been listening to Trammel's form of logic too long. That kind of thinking oversaw the operation of dozens of medical and dental clinics that performed unnecessary procedures on Medicaid kids, then bilked the system for millions of dollars. I was married to Trammel by the time I'd started to really understand what paid for the massive house, the acres of white-fenced pastureland, the horse barns, the staff, the guard at the front gate, the upscale social engagements where women with the right pedigrees made snooty comments to let me know I was good enough to hire as a rider for horses worth hundreds of thousands, but not good enough to marry into their circle.

If they had any idea where Trammel's money came from, they looked the other way. For far too long, I had also. You'll make a lot of excuses for yourself while you're letting your life tumble down a well. It's not until you hit bottom that you see what a deep hole you're in.

"Okay . . . trash." I pulled a Hefty bag off

the roll and snapped it open, but what I really needed was a flamethrower. What was Iola waiting for here? The apocalypse? An old woman living alone couldn't possibly eat all this food. Not in ten years. And on top of that, there was a box of groceries on the counter that looked recent. A delivery from Bink's Market, judging by the yellow ticket. Eighty dollars' worth of groceries the day before she died.

I thought about the way I'd found her there in the bed — peaceful, as if she'd known her time was coming. Maybe she hadn't. Why else would she have ordered groceries?

Still, as mercenary as it sounded, the food would be nice for the kids and me to have. There were even some mini MoonPies. J.T.'s favorite.

As I went back to work, bells jingled somewhere in the house, the sound high and light, barely audible, but it was there.

"Stop that, or I'll haul you off to the pound. The *dog* pound!" If that cat didn't quit, I was going to tell Ross to bring his live trap after all. Seriously.

Outside, the church chimes rang, adding bass to the melody. The music drowned out the cat, and I started sorting through the box of groceries on the counter, counting the church bells as they sounded and faded. Eleven. The old clock on the kitchen wall was fast. I stopped to adjust the hands. I wasn't sure why.

Mice had been in the box on the counter. Bits of pasta and cereal lined the bottom, and a multicolored confetti of chewed-up packaging decorated the food containers inside. It was as good a place to begin as any. Might as well tackle the most recent stuff first and work my way down.

After the church bells quieted, there was no more noise in the house. The cat had settled in somewhere. I finished one box and moved on to another, sorting out ruined food, checking expiration dates, saving things the kids and I could use. It felt good to be working, to be moving in some direction after weeks of basically just scrambling to survive. Compared to wondering if you'll have a roof over your head, boxes full of nibbled-on cornflakes and black mouse droppings mixed with white rice don't seem like a problem at all. The job here was much bigger than I'd thought, though. I wondered if Brother Guilbeau had any idea. After an hour and a half of hard work, almost everything still looked the same. I'd filled four bags and packed a big box of food to take to the cottage, but I'd barely made a dent in Iola's mess.

In the pantry, a mouse scampered over the cans and cans and *cans* of food that flowed onto the kitchen's black-and-white hexagon-shaped tiles, a sort of card castle gone wrong. I counted the wax paper rolls stacked beside the cans. Thirty-two. Some of them were so old that the boxes looked like they belonged in an antique mall. Who knew what was in this house that might be valuable to the right people?

I had the temptation to explore the place and see what I could find. Nobody would even know the difference. . . .

The idea slid up my arm like the sleeve of an angora sweater, soft and pleasing at first, then itchy. Uncomfortable.

Unlocking the window over the kitchen sink, I let in a spray of cool spring air and thought of that one perfect summer on Hatteras. The scents outside were the scents of that summer, the air of that twelve-year-old girl who walked in Rodanthe, hand in hand with her grandfather.

You know things about yourself when you're twelve, before your body changes, your hormones surge, and in the space of six months the whole world seems to be looking at you differently.

That summer on Hatteras, I knew I was

made for something good. I knew the world was limitless. I knew that in spite of all my parents' problems, and the things they said to me, two people in this world thought I was something special. Meemaw was sure I had the prettiest blue eyes and long brown hair she'd ever seen, and Pap-pap had always liked the fact that, whenever we visited, I went with him to his job inspecting properties for the insurance company instead of running around like Gina. I liked learning about how to repair houses after a storm and hearing Pap-pap's stories of the old days in the Outer Banks and the Tidewater region of North Carolina. Stories about the people I came from — sailors and shrimpers and pioneers. Courageous people. I loved the story of the Lost Colonists, who'd been deposited on the Outer Banks years before the Pilgrims landed on Plymouth Rock. Unlike the Pilgrims, the Lost Colonists had vanished, no sign of them remaining when their ship had returned again with supplies. When Pap-pap told me that story, the mystery of it ran over me in delicious shivers.

Maybe it wasn't too late for me to dig around and find some piece of that summer girl who still believed the honey-sweet things Meemaw and Pap-pap said about her. Maybe there was a bit of her left here on Hatteras Island. Maybe there was a bit of her left inside me.

"What do you think, Iola?" I snatched the last trash bag out of the box and popped it open, letting it drift through the light like a filmy white parachute. It crackled softly, its mouth lapping up swirls of dust as I started toward a tower of newspapers with two leaking boxes of instant oatmeal atop. "Is it too late? Too much water under the bridge? It's too late for this oatmeal, that's for —"

I heard water running upstairs and tipped my head back, tracking the sound through the pipes.

"Ohhh-kay . . . cats don't turn on the water. . . ." Someone *was* in this house. Maybe Iola had a roommate nobody knew about — a recluse or a mentally handicapped child who was afraid to come out. Maybe someone really had broken in here last week, and Iola's death wasn't an accident after all. Maybe there were secret passageways within the walls, concealed rooms. Perhaps someone was still hiding in them.

A rush of crazy possibilities whirled in my mind, the stories fleshing out over the bones in ways that almost seemed to make sense.

Slipping a hand into the pantry, I wrapped

my fingers around the closest thing that felt like a weapon and came out with a wooden-handled feather duster. Lot of good that would do me. I could tickle the intruder to death.

I tossed it aside and rummaged through the pantry mess, finally ending up with a wooden rolling pin and a can of wasp spray. The mental picture was distractingly funny as I started down the hall, cringing each time the floorboards creaked underfoot.

Overhead, the sound of water was so clear, it seemed like liquid would surely push through the ceiling any moment. I envisioned one of those spreading, seeping stains people see in horror movies. One that starts faint and clear, then darkens into blood or a black ooze, slowly feeding a tangle of clutching vines that sprout snakelike from the plaster, grab the unsuspecting woman who's been hired to clean out the house, and drag her into the wall, where the plaster quickly closes up and goes back to normal, swallowing her whole. . . .

Maybe there was a reason Brother Guilbeau hadn't hired someone he already knew for this job. Maybe he wanted someone . . . expendable.

A nervous laugh bubbled up, and I didn't know whether to surrender to it or swallow it. If there was someone upstairs, he or she already knew I was here . . . and clearly did not want to be found by me.

My stomach squeezed into a pulsating knot the size of a walnut, and I considered making a run for the front door as I passed by the piano room again. The woman in the portrait seemed to be watching me, her tumble of strawberry-blonde hair shifting in the light, her green eyes curious. That wasn't Iola in the picture. Iola's skin was darker, more of a buttery olive color. The woman in the portrait had skin as pale and smooth as the china cups in the kitchen.

Maybe there had been two old women living here — cousins or sisters — but for some unknown reason, one of them hadn't been out of the house in so long that everyone had forgotten her. Maybe she'd kept herself hidden during all the commotion when Iola died. Maybe she was the one who'd been letting the cat in and out and turning on the lamps at night.

If I had to believe the house wasn't empty right now, I liked that scenario better — a helpless old woman. Someone frail and weak. Someone who would be intimidated by a five-foot-four-inch house cleaner with a rolling pin and a can of wasp spray.

Each stair creaked as I made my way up,

stepping, then listening, then stepping again. I took the final three stairs right in a row, going for the rush tactic, then stopping in the hallway, swiveling both ways, pointing the wasp spray ahead of me, NYPD style.

The hallway was empty, deep and shadow-filled, quiet. Not a sound except for the running water. The doors to other rooms hung ajar, just as they had been on the day I'd found Iola's body, but the door to the blue room was closed. Either the men had shut it after they'd taken her out, or it had closed on its own.

Or someone had closed it since.

I moved toward the sound of the water, pointing the wasp spray as I went, my finger trembling on the trigger, the rolling pin wavering above my shoulder. If someone came at me, I was going to start spraying and swatting without asking questions.

I peeked into doorways as I passed. The dark-walnut floors in the rooms were dusty, and even in the hallway, a thin layer of silt had started to settle over the random pattern of tracks left behind by the men who'd come for Iola's body. There was no evidence that anyone had been moving around up here since then.

That wasn't as comforting as it might've

been. It brought up the question of who could possibly turn on the water in the upstairs bathroom without leaving footprints in the dust.

Maybe the faucet was old, and it just . . . sort of slipped on by itself?

The door was open only an inch or two.

I hiked up the rolling pin, readied the wasp spray. The humor of that vanished like a whiff of smoke as I moved closer. Nothing was left but a wild pulse thrumming in my ears and the rush of quick, shallow breathing, my lungs refusing anything more than tiny puffs of air.

"Who's in there? Whoever you are, get out here. You're not supposed to be in this —"

The door pulled back slowly, and I froze, the blood draining from my face, seeping downward through my body, leaking through the soles of my feet, pooling on the floor and leaching through. My heart rapped in an empty shell.

Everything in me was screaming, *Run!* But I couldn't move.

Beyond the door, a slice of the bathroom came into view. White pedestal sink, water running from an ornate brass faucet, a clawfooted tub with green glass orbs clutched in the brass talons, a leaded glass window . . .

No one standing in the doorway, even now

that it was almost halfway open.

No one . . .

A whisper of movement slid past the baseboard.

I forced my gaze downward, an inch and then another, another, until finally I could see.

Not a shadow.

The cat.

A crooked black tail snaked around the corner as the furry intruder escaped into the library nook, leaving a trail of wet tracks in the dust on the floor.

Stumbling forward and collapsing against the bathroom entrance, I laughed, then gulped in air, then laughed, then gulped in air. Sometimes there really was a simple explanation. With the old lever-style faucets, it wasn't impossible that a cat could turn on the water. Just to prove it, I stepped into the room and batted the faucet with one finger, turning it partway off, on again, then all the way off. It had to be the cat. He was smart, like one of the animals on Letterman's Stupid Pet Tricks.

Bells jingled softly somewhere down the hall, playing a strange, sweet music against the silence. I followed the sound, expecting to find a black fur ball skulking among the bookshelves, but instead, the library area was empty. At the end of the corridor, the door to the blue room stood ajar now. Not open, not closed, but halfway between. The music was coming from inside, the high, distinct notes drifting into the hallway as random and alluring as luna moths flitting through space on a quiet summer night.

The roots of my hair tingled, and a shiver convulsed my shoulders. I remembered the door falling out of my hand and slamming against the wall the day Iola died. The impact had rattled the entire second story. Even if the cat could operate doorknobs as well as water faucets, how could the door be resting quietly a foot or so from the wall?

Maybe this was all some strange dream, and I'd wake up any minute, laughing about it. *Cats opening doors and using water faucets! Really?*

Yet the feeling that something was waiting for me in that room was overwhelming.

Not just waiting . . . but insisting that I come in.

Inviting me, drawing me closer, until I could see the slice of the room that the opening allowed.

Under the turret window, the marble-topped writing desk basked in the sunlight. There were birds on the windowsill again. Two. A cardinal and a robin. They watched but didn't flit away as I touched the door-frame, craned sideways to see the foot of the bed. Part of me expected Iola to be there, looking perfectly at peace atop the wedding ring quilt in her blue-flower-basket dress.

She wasn't, of course. In taking her away, the men had rumpled the quilt so that now it hung askew, even the impression of her body gone. Behind the door, one of Iola's black shoes sat perpendicular to the wall, the toe propping the door open. Someone must have kicked it during all the coming and going when she died. The other shoe was still sitting beside the bed, neatly placed, exactly where it had been the last time I'd seen it. It looked lonely now, slightly forlorn.

The bells jingled again, and I swiveled so fast that I stumbled sideways and caught the cool crystal of the doorknob to steady myself. On one of the small walnut night-stands, the cat was walking in slow circles, arching to scratch its back against the scal-loped edges of a Tiffany lampshade. Each time it passed the window, the shepherd's hook of its tail touched the fringes of a stained-glass suncatcher with little brass bells dangling from the bottom.

"So that's what you're doing." I pointed

at the cat, pleased with myself for figuring out the secret.

He looked at me, his head tilting slightly as if he were coyly smiling back. Despite our love-hate dance all morning, I almost felt sorry for him. The scars of a long and difficult life were evident up close. The old tomcat had been through more than a few scrapes.

His look turned wary, and he quit circling in favor of keeping an eye on me.

"You're just full of surprises," I told him as his tea-colored eyes studied me up and down. "I'll find out how you're getting into this place, you know. I'll figure out the answer sooner or later."

He yawned in a way that said, *Go ahead and try, kitchen-cleaning woman. You'll never discover my secrets.* His eyes met mine for a moment before he jumped from the table and whisked underneath the bed, disappearing beneath the dust ruffle and a patchwork of blue wedding rings.

Crossing between the bed and a closet doorway, I straightened the quilt. It seemed like Iola would want it that way.

The suncatcher was beautiful up close. Hummingbirds and passion vine. Patchy sunshine flickered through, spreading colored light over my outstretched fingertip as

I swept it along the bottom of the three brass bells, listening to their music, then stopping to capture the one closest to the bed. There was a small gold sticker on the back. Turning the bell over, I cocked my head sideways to read the words.

Sandy's Seashell Shop
An Ocean of Possibilities

The sticker wasn't sun-dried or faded, and the green ribbon attached to the fringed window shade was still shiny and pliable. The tiny work of art hadn't been hanging here overly long. Apparently, even though Iola didn't leave her house, she still bought things somehow — at Sandy's Seashell Shop, wherever that was.

The bell jingled as I let it fall into place again before finishing with the quilt, giving the room the picture-perfect, if dusty, look of the first time I'd seen it. I reached for the single black shoe behind the door, then thought better of it. No sense letting the knob crash against the wall repeatedly. The shoe almost seemed to belong there, as if Iola might have used the same trick herself.

I wondered if she liked this room, with its sunny windows and framed prints of ladies in turn-of-the-century gowns, hiding their smiles coyly behind lace fans, sharing tea in a garden, greeting beaus dressed as huntsmen on horseback, playing croquet with smiling, cherub-faced children. Over the bed, a majestic collie posed in lush green grass, overlooking a pastoral scene with sheep grazing on a hillside. Everything in this room spoke of a beautiful life, a perfect life.

But in the back of my mind, there were the things the deputy had revealed. Her life hadn't been ideal. She'd been rejected by the good people of Fairhope. I knew exactly how that felt.

Outside, the breeze caught a nest of pine branches, spilling a beam of unfiltered sun through the turret windows. The spray of glitter and ribbons on the sill danced in the glow, and I was there beside it before I even realized I'd moved.

The curtain of light withdrew slowly, surrendering the old shoe box to shadow again as I leaned over it, took in a tangle of gold rickrack lying atop a pile of ribbon scraps and wallpaper shreds. The craft supplies had been weighted down with a bottle of Elmer's glue and a pair of scissors.

The corner of a floral stationery sheet peeked from underneath the box, a few words in blue ink visible at the bottom of the page.

   . . . in our own time.
Your loving daughter,
Iola Anne

The writing trembled uphill, the final *e* in Anne disintegrating into a curved line that slipped across the page and ran off the margin. The letter couldn't have been written very long ago.

But . . . *Your loving daughter?* Iola had been in her nineties. There was no possible way her parents could still be alive.

I slid the box back a hair, read the rest of the last line.

We are all warriors in our own time.

What in the world?

Maybe Iola had been confused, suffering from dementia, hopelessly trapped in the past and living in a world that didn't exist anymore. That might explain why she kept herself locked in this house and why some parts of it were in perfect order while others were cluttered with thirty-two rolls of wax paper and food stacked to the ceiling.

My skin tingled with the sense that someone was watching. It forced me to glance back to check, but the room was empty, of course. No one there to see me lift the box, slide the letter from beneath it, and begin to read.

Dearest Father,
I had thought there would be no more of these letters. It seems rather silly, doesn't it, that I would write to you when penning words requires such effort now? These old hands. They don't tell stories as they once did, send words into the world with abandon, the lines bleeding forth as if there will forever be more words, more paper, another pen filled with ink in all the hues of life.

How odd, isn't it, that in the end, life comes to surviving more than living. But these things I do, this melody of an ordinary day, keep the hours in order. I have lived my way into this music, note by note, and now I know no other.

Strange to think of that. The song of an ordinary life. Mine would be in these letters to you.

A rain song, these months since the storm. A song of placing buckets and emptying buckets, and placing-emptying-placing-emptying-placing-emptying. A melody of drip-drop-drip-drop-drip-drop. I suppose I should try again to have a carpenter come to fix the roof, but it seems too large a task. If they see the shape of things, I'll find myself in the county home, and then who will empty the buckets?

But still, it is a wearisome task. You have left this big house in my charge for so long. I wonder if there may have been another way.

I took time with the newspaper today, other than just to sop water with it. There was a boy on the front page in a photo. I knew him. He brings the groceries every week in the rusty blue truck that sounds like an ailing farm tractor coming up the drive.

I write to you because of this boy. The newspaper told of families on Hatteras struggling in the aftermath of the storm. The boy's father lost his employment when the bridge was out and no commerce could come to the island. The father left to find work and never returned. Now there is only the boy, a mother, a little sister, a brother, and a grandfather. The boy's name is Jeremy. Sad to say that I have exchanged the payment for my grocery bill with him each week for six months now since the storm and never asked. He colors his hair an unnatural black and wears rings in both ears and one pinched in his nose, like the warriors in a photo from *National Geographic.* I suppose this is my reason for never having inquired.

I've tucked fifty dollars into an envelope and left it on the kitchen counter to remind myself. Before he comes next, I will write his name on it and set it out with the bill. But I wonder if you might do something for him as well? My ways of helping are small, but your resources are boundless.

I am left to ponder what else I could have done, had I looked sooner, had I opened my door and seen not a boy, but a warrior with his fearsome hair and his rings of gold. I, more than most, should know that the most difficult battles are not the ones fought outside the armor, but the ones within it.

Those like Jeremy will breathe life into these scraps of land cast among sea. Theirs will be the task of repairing the damage wrought by the storm, rebuilding what lies in tatters. My time for fighting is running dry. I feel it.

I pray that this boy might have strength for his battle. A warrior's strength. I pray also for the Mulberry Girl. We are all warriors in our own time.

Your loving daughter,
Iola Anne

CHAPTER 5

Bink's Village Market was quieter than usual. The midday air was warm and pleasant, the fishing boats still out. Old man Bink looked up from the counter and squinted, trying to place me as I came in the door.

Usually, if I had to go into Bink's, I tried to slip in when the place was busy so I wouldn't be noticed, but after a day and a half of scrubbing dirt and piling up trash at Iola's house, I needed more supplies, and I couldn't go over to Buxton to get them. I'd burned up a quarter tank of gas last night, driving around to see if I could track down Ross, so using more fuel for a shopping trip was out of the question. I hadn't even thought of picking up cleaning supplies while I was out, because my mind was on Ross. At this point, I was seriously nervous about the fact that he hadn't called back since he'd hung up on me and headed for Captain Jack's. If I hadn't been busy with

Iola's house, I would've been in a complete panic by now.

"Afternoon." Bink rested his elbows on a counter covered with taped-on yard sale flyers, along with advertisements for lost dogs, live music, and free kittens.

"Hi." I hurried to the half-dozen aisles of groceries near the meat counter. The few times I'd stopped in before, the store smelled like fish and salt water, but today the air was a rich mix of spices, peanuts boiling in a Crock-Pot of brine, and food frying on a griddle behind the meat counter. The scents reminded me of something, but I couldn't quite place it. The feeling was warm, though. Soothing, like knowing that your favorite comfort food is cooking on the stove.

Behind the counter, Bink's wife, Geneva, was tending the griddle.

As I passed by, she waggled a gloved finger, sloppy with what looked like raw meat. "Try that sausage."

I glanced over my shoulder, but there was no one else around.

"See if it's good," she added, again without looking at me. "It's always a guessing game, getting the mix right. If I ask Bink, he'll have it so hot it'll fry your noggin."

I knew now why the aroma in Bink's was

familiar today. It reminded me of Pap-pap and Meemaw's house.

I tasted one of Geneva Bink's sausage patties, and it was as good as it smelled. "It's wonderful," I told her. "Really good."

"Super. Go ahead and eat up the rest of it. Lord knows, my rear end doesn't need it." She gave the plate of sausage a backhanded wave. When I reached for another piece, she was watching me, though. "You're little J.T.'s mama, aren't you?" The meat-covered finger wiggled again, and behind her glasses, hazel eyes lit with a look of interest that struck off a warning in my head.

Apparently J.T. had been hanging around town even more than I thought. He and Geneva Bink were well acquainted.

"Tandi," I said, by way of not confirming or denying anything.

Geneva seemed to like the sound of me. "That boy of yours is somethin' else. What a sweetheart. Stronger than he looks, too. He's been hauling my trash for me after he gets off the school bus every day. I imagine he told you that."

"Oh . . . sure." I tried not to seem completely dumb to the fact. Our first couple weeks in Iola's cottage, I'd been too sick to know what the kids were doing. Getting off painkillers isn't a smooth process. Since I'd met Ross, I'd been with him or out looking for a job so many afternoons that I wasn't sure what time J.T. was actually supposed to get home from the bus.

"He can clean out a doughnut case too, I'll tell you!" Geneva laughed, her cheeks rounding into two plump red globes that pressed against her eyeglasses. "I'm amazed what he can eat. But that's kids. They're starving after school."

The sausage coagulated in the back of my mouth, and my throat went dry. I tried to swallow, but I couldn't. Now I knew why J.T. never complained about the lack of food in the cottage anymore.

"But it works out, because by that time of day, I've got a lotta trash built up, and whatever's left in that doughnut case is history, anyhow. Pretty fair trade — trash hauling for leftover doughnuts." She turned away long enough to flip several sausage patties on the electric griddle but kept right on talking. "Bet by now, y'all are tired of all those doughnuts coming home, though. I asked him about that, and he said you didn't mind him having them."

I could feel blood creeping up my neck and washing into my cheeks. I forced the sausage down in one big gulp.

Bink joined in the conversation from across the room. "He's been helping some of the guys wash decks and cull out junk fish on the dock too. I think you've got a natural-born fisherman there. That boy's got a love of the water. Hung around here half the day, couple weeks ago Satur-dey, just workin' on the boats. Got himself a free lunch for it."

"Oh . . ." A couple weeks ago Saturday, I'd been in Raleigh with Ross. We ate at a steak house and went dancing at a place he liked. J.T. was with Zoey. I'd thought. Did she tell him he could come down here?

"I'm glad he hasn't . . . been any trouble," I choked out.

"Oh no, ma'am," Geneva assured me. "He's a cute little rascal."

Bink nodded in agreement.

I thought about leaving without even buying cleaning supplies for Iola's house. I just wanted to get out of here.

"So you're in the rental at Iola Anne Poole's place." This time, Geneva gave me more than a shootin'-the-breeze look. "So sad that she passed away alone like she did. She's been a good customer a long time."

Bink made a disgruntled noise under his breath and pushed off the counter, watching as a skiff motored to the dock out back.

99

"I heard you found her," Geneva pressed. "Poor old thing."

Bink spit air through his teeth and crossed his arms over his belly.

"For heaven's sake, Bink. The woman laid there in the bed for who knows how long and passed away all alone."

Bink adjusted his cap lower and slouched over his belly bulge, turning his face away.

"That's not very charitable." A few visual daggers flew in Bink's direction. "There's history," she whispered to me. "But some people need to get over it."

I glanced at my watch, deciding that a three-dollar roll of trash bags would do for now. I'd figure out the rest later. No way I was charging cleaning supplies on the church's bill here. I could just imagine the round of questions that would bring on. As much as Iola deserved to have someone defend her, I was not the one. If word got around that I was working in that house, these people would be all over me.

"Nice talking to you." I grabbed a box of trash bags off an endcap, then hurried to the front counter.

Bink was in no rush to ring me up. It took him forever to slide off his stool. "Tell that young fella of yours, if he's around in the summer once the rental places fill up on the island, there's work for him here." He was all smiles again. "When the tourists move in, Jeremy can always use help filling orders and getting boxes packed for deliveries. Those people like their groceries waiting on the steps when they get to their cottages, don't they, Jeremy?" Bink nodded toward a teenager coming in the door — tall, thin, with his hair dyed black. Two gold earrings and a gold nose ring glimmered in the sunlight.

"Yeah," Jeremy answered without really looking at either of us. His shoulders slumped as if, given the choice, he wouldn't be noticed at all.

The boy with the black hair. The one whose father had left the family after the storm. The envelope I was just about to reach for, the fifty dollars I'd been trying to convince myself it'd be okay to keep because the kids and I needed it, was for him.

I knew what it was like for a family when the father walked out. There were bills to pay and no one to pay them.

I opened my wallet and handed Bink the money for the trash bags. All I could think was, *There goes a gallon of milk. Six boxes of macaroni and cheese. A jar of peanut butter . . .* But with the food I'd carried back to the cottage on my way to Bink's, we'd be

101

okay for a while.

I had the strangest urge to touch Jeremy's arm as he slipped by, quiet and dark like Iola's house cat. I wanted to look into him and say, *I know. I know it's hard, but hang in there. I hope your father wakes up one day and sees how much a kid needs his daddy. And when your high school English teacher says you're smart enough to really do something with your life, listen to her, okay?*

I didn't tell him any of that, of course. One thing I'd learned growing up was to mind my business and let other people mind theirs.

But for some reason, today, as I passed by Jeremy's vehicle out front, it seemed right to slip that envelope from my back pocket and drop it onto the seat of the rusted-out truck that Iola had described in her letter.

Maybe that money would do whatever she hoped it would do.

Maybe, if she was watching right now, she'd be happy that her envelope had been delivered after all.

I felt good as I started across the parking lot — like the day was worth it, beyond just putting food in our bellies and keeping a roof over our heads. Beyond just surviving. I pictured Jeremy finding that envelope, opening the flap, looking around, and wondering if an angel had dropped it into his car.

Maybe an angel had. I guessed I had Iola and her crazy old house to thank for that. It's not every day you get to be someone's angel.

A smile pulled from deep inside me for the first time in recent memory — the real kind of smile, not the kind you paste on to keep up a front. The sky was clear, just the barest upsweeps of white clouds rising over the sound. *Hen scrat,* Pap-pap had called them. *Hen scrat and fillies' tails make lofty ships carry low sails.* I remembered that now. He'd pointed out the wispy, low-hanging clouds to me all those years ago when we were here on Hatteras. I could feel his whiskery chin on my hair as he leaned down and stretched an arm over my shoulder, aiming a finger and tracing the contour of the vapor in the sky. *When they come early in the day like that, it means there's wind and weather ahead. The hens are scratchin' up little dust puffs in the sky and the fillies are on the run, so their tails are long, see? My granddad used to tell us that on the shrimp boat.*

I saw the hen scratches and fillies' tails then, and I thought of the wild Spanish mustangs that still ran free up north in

Corolla, their tails trailing behind them as they bolted down the beach. I imagined my grandfather on a shrimp boat with my great-great-grandfather, who knew the sea and lived by it.

They're pretty, I said. I thought Pap-pap would like that, and he did.

Yes, they are, Tandi Jo. He stood beside me then, bracing his hands on his overalls, smiling at the sky and watching the clouds. I felt like *I* was pretty too. Like I was special because Pap-pap took the time to teach me things.

"Looks like you're having a good day."

The voice caught me by surprise, and I glanced down to see the guy who'd mowed the lawn at Iola's house. He was walking from Mosey Creek with mason jars full of murky water sloshing in each hand. *Paul . . .* The last name wasn't coming to me right off. *Ch . . .* something. *Chastain,* maybe.

A boat passed by in the marina behind Bink's, the motor vibrating the air, so I didn't feel the need to come up with something to say until the sound had died.

By then, Paul was at the edge of the parking lot with his jars of water. He lifted one so I could get a better look. "Science class," he explained. "I teach part-time at the school and do contract work for the park service in the afternoons." He set the jars on the tailgate of his pickup. He had a kayak instead of lawn mowing equipment in the back this time. "Few drops of that stuff, you'll find all kinds of things to look at under a microscope. Bacteria, viruses, protists. Things that fundamentally influence the ocean's ability to sustain life."

"Well, when you put it that way, it looks like more than just dirty water." I flashed a smile, and then I wished I hadn't. I didn't want him to think I was coming on to him. With the divorce papers left behind for Trammel, and Ross in my life now, I wasn't looking for any complications. Aside from that, a guy wearing camp shorts and a shirt covered with flamingos playing jazz instruments doesn't exactly scream, *sexy.* Still, I felt so good today I couldn't contain it. I felt clearheaded and like I'd done something really . . . right, for once.

He quirked an eyebrow underneath his floppy fishing hat, as if he wondered what I was thinking, then adjusted the stampede string that ran through a wooden bead under his chin. "Dirty water doesn't get enough respect."

"It's good that it has you to defend it, then." I laughed as he turned to put the lids on the jars, his long, thin fingers twirling the rings into place with surprising finesse. The man could handle a mason jar. Maybe that came with the territory, science teaching.

"I didn't realize you were J.T.'s mom the other day until I saw the kids drive up in Rowdy's Jeep." Setting the jars in a crate stuffed with hay, he hooked a leg over a corner of the tailgate. A flip-flop dangled loosely from his foot as he threaded his hands together and rested them, like we were going to have a sit-and-whittle together. "I have J.T. in class. He told me you were living in a rented place, but he didn't say where. He doesn't talk much."

Guilt needled, poking little holes in my blue-sky day, letting in the gray behind the paper-thin good feeling. There was a time when J.T. was such a chatterbox, I'd send him to the store with Trammel's housekeeper just so I could pop a pill and sleep the day away. I wasn't even sure when the surgery pain stopped or when J.T. changed or when the pills became a mechanism for dulling a different kind of pain. That was the worst part of it — I just woke up from the haze one day and realized I'd been elbowing the kids away for so long, I didn't even know who they were or who I was.

"He's in a phase," I told Paul. What else

can you do but make an excuse when you can't tell the truth?

"He does his work," Paul said, and I was relieved. I was afraid he would ask me to explain J.T., and I couldn't. "While he's back there drawing dragon slayers and Pokémons, or whatever those things are he doodles in the margins of his papers, he is getting the material."

"He's into Zago Wars." That much I did know.

"Has some interest in oceanography, too," Paul offered. "He was down here the other day when I was cast netting, and he had quite a few questions about the things I pulled out of the water. That's more words than I've gotten out of him in a month and a half of class."

"Oh . . . well . . . that's good."

"There's a summer camp for kids who want to work with the sea turtle nests. They help monitor the sites, keep track of the incubation days, maintain spreadsheets, watch for depressions in the sand that might indicate a nest is getting ready to hatch. If they're lucky, they get to be there for a hatching or two, count hatchlings, chase the foxes away, and that kind of thing. Might be something he'd enjoy. You never know what will ignite an interest in a kid. I could send some information home with him, if you like."

"Sure . . . okay." I wasn't used to teachers coming to me about the kids, bad or good. Usually Zoey kept a lid on things for both her and J.T., so there wasn't any need for teachers to call home. Zoey's excuses were nothing new — I'd used them all myself, years ago. *Oh, my mom has to work. . . . She's out of town — she said to tell you she's sorry she missed open house night. . . . She's down in the bed. Her back gives her trouble. . . .*

It crossed my mind that this was a new place, a new start. Things didn't have to be the way they were before. I wanted the kids to have a home life they didn't have to hide from everyone. I wanted to know what they were doing in school.

"That'd be nice. Thank you." Then I was sorry I said yes. What if J.T. got all excited about some summer camp? I couldn't pay for that kind of thing. "You know, on second thought, it might be better if you didn't. I'm not sure where we'll be by summer. I hate to get his hopes up." Sooner or later, something would happen with Iola's place, and we'd have to move out. I'd be lucky if the kids could even finish the school year on Hatteras, much less be around for summer camp.

It hit me full force now, how much of this plan of mine depended on luck. I was making promises I probably couldn't keep. I'd told the kids we were staying here. This was it. Our new place.

The science teacher's brown eyes studied me, narrowing. He had nice eyes — a warm honey-tea color, framed with lashes that were surprisingly dark for someone with a redheaded complexion. "The opposite of getting your hopes up is not harboring any," he said softly, and I had the uncomfortable sense that he'd read my mind. For a moment, I couldn't do anything but look into his eyes and wonder how much he knew.

A white bucket in the back of his truck rattled on its own, and I jumped.

"The prisoners." Winking sideways at me, he nodded toward the bucket, offering me a look.

My curiosity was piqued, and aside from that, I was glad to be off the topic of hopes and summer camp. "What've you got in there?"

"Take a gander." Reaching into the bed of the truck, he hooked his fingers over the edge of the bucket and dragged it closer, but I couldn't see the bottom.

I inched in, leaning over my crossed arms, the grocery bag dangling against my elbow.

I caught the faint scent of sand and seawater.

Paul shook the bucket a little, and something squirmed inside. I jerked back again, and he chuckled. I knew he was messing with me. "Hold it still," I squealed.

"What?" He sounded like a little boy in the school yard, hiding something in his fists and saying, *Betcha can't guess what I've got behind my ba-ack.* "You don't trust me?"

"Depends on what's in that bucket. If that's a snake or something, I'm outta here. You live in Texas awhile, you learn to hate snakes with a passion. The first time you step out the door and find a rattlesnake sunning, you're cured of the good-snake-bad-snake myth."

"No, ma'am, this is dinner."

"Well, that leaves out snakes, I guess."

I set the grocery bag on the tailgate and the two of us leaned closer, our shoulders brushing. "Not necessarily," he joked, finally tipping the bucket far enough that I could see crabs in the bottom, four of them.

"Oh, man," I breathed. I remembered going crabbing with Pap-pap and Meemaw. We helped Pap-pap tie chicken necks to lengths of twine, then tossed the bait in the cove and drove little metal stakes into the ground. Gina and I built drip castles on

110

shore and chased ghost crabs while we waited.

There was a small hoop-shaped crab net lying in the bed of Paul's truck. I reached for it without even thinking to ask. "My pap-pap had one of these. We used to drive down a road someplace around Kill Devil Hills. . . . I can't remember exactly where that was."

An image flashed through my mind: Pap-pap's weathered, sunspotted hands pushing bait into a green mesh bag and tying it in the center of the homemade net. *But they'll just climb out,* I'd protested, and he'd smiled at me.

You watch, sis. I remembered his face now — every detail of it. Over the years, I'd let it go, let him go, and Meemaw. It was too painful to remember how good those times were, how peaceful and sweet. How much I wanted Pap-pap and Meemaw to be able to keep Gina and me forever. How angry I was when my mama made sure they couldn't.

"I can't remember how it works." I was talking to myself more than Paul now, the whisper a drift of breeze from the past.

Paul let the bucket rest. "And here I had you pegged for a landlubber." His fingers settled over mine, and he moved one of my hands to the center of the net, then gripped

111

the lines on either side of the rim. "Like this." He pulled, and the frame bent at the hinges, folding into a half-moon shape, trapping my hand inside, the metal closing loosely over my wrist. "There. You're caught."

A truck turned in to the parking lot, the rumble of the diesel engine echoing off the weathered wood and concrete block of Bink's store. Something in the sound of it — the grinding of the knobby tires or the soft groan of a leaf spring — caught my attention, plucking a familiar thread. I looked up, and I knew who it was even before the shadow of Bink's roadside sign blocked out the glare that hid the driver.

Ross.

CHAPTER 6

I jerked away quickly enough that the crab trap tightened around my wrist, the salt-encrusted edges leaving red marks on my skin as the lines pulled taut in Paul's hands.

"Whoa, hey, hang on a minute," he chuckled, grabbing the metal rim to open it. "There you go. Relax. I wasn't going to toss you into the dinner bucket with the captives, I promise."

"Sorry." I stepped backward, putting distance between Paul and me. I could feel Ross watching as his truck crossed the parking lot, but I didn't turn to look. I didn't want to seem like I'd been caught at something. "I hope I didn't break it."

Paul bent to wrap the lines around the net, his face disappearing beneath the fishing hat. "Nah, this old thing's tougher than that. I found it with some of my granddad's fishing rods when I moved back here to look after Gran. It's been around the block a few times." I had a feeling he was talking about more than just the net, but I didn't have time to wonder. I could hear Ross getting out of his truck. Inside, a part of me cringed as the door slammed shut. I felt like I'd been doing something wrong, and now I'd pay for it. Old habit.

Not that Ross had ever treated me that way, but there were a couple times when guys got friendly on the beach, and Ross had already let me know he didn't like it. He thought I was doing something to bring it on. *You're pretty, Tandi. You look at a guy, he's gonna look back.* When he said things like that, I soaked it up as a compliment. Everywhere we went, women from seventeen to sixty checked Ross out. Chicks he knew smiled and hugged him when we went into surf shops and restaurants and whatnot. He could have pretty much any girl he wanted, and he wanted me.

Paul was completely oblivious to the change in the air around us. He whistled the theme from *Jeopardy!,* his head bobbing back and forth as he shook out the tangles in the lines and wound them around the net.

"Well, thanks for telling me about J.T.," I said, loudly enough that Ross could hear every word as he approached. What was he doing here, anyway? Had his friends at Captain Jack's told him I'd come looking for him last night? "I'm glad J.T.'s doing so well in science."

Paul quirked a brow at me, probably wondering if I thought he was deaf all of a sudden. He didn't know we had company until Ross was right there on top of us.

Ross didn't say anything — he just stopped and stood with his hands on his hips, his fingers spreading into his jeans pockets, the muscles in his arms flexing around the hem of a short-sleeved Western shirt that fit just right.

He looked like a dog bristling when another dog comes sniffing around. "What's goin' on, Tandi?"

"Hey, Ross." I blinked at him like I hadn't noticed him driving in. "Where'd you come from? I figured you were still crashed out after your last trip."

"Yeah, I can see that." His jaw tightened, and he nodded toward Paul, making it clear that there would be no polite introductions and he wanted Paul to exit the scene.

Paul looked from me to Ross and back, his forehead wrinkling against the dorky hat, the leather stampede string catching on his ear and hanging cockeyed beside his mouth so that he looked like Gilligan. If Ross was the mad pit bull in this stare-down, Paul was the clueless Labrador retriever with no idea that he was about six inches from a bad situation.

"Thanks again for telling me about J.T.," I repeated, then snagged my grocery sack off the tailgate.

"Sure. Anytime. He's a good student. Whenever I see him drawing those . . . things he draws, I'll know it's Zago Wars, not Pokémon." Paul grinned amiably. "No wonder he's been giving me the lame-oh look every time I say that."

"That's good. Well, have a great afternoon." I reached for Ross, intending to catch his arm and turn him toward his own vehicle. I could feel the testosterone radiating in the air, like steam off a boiler.

"This the guy that was at your house when I called the other night?" Ross shifted his weight to one leg, bracing the other in front of himself, slightly bent so that his posture had a forward slant, a silent challenge to it.

A familiar rush of queasiness swirled through me. Since I was little, I'd known the feeling of a conflict working toward a flash point.

Apparently Paul didn't have a clue about things like that. He smiled and jutted an open hand toward Ross. "Paul Chastain."

The greeting was relaxed and casual. Ross gave him the eye, and Paul just stood there with his hand hanging, like he didn't even notice that he was failing to read the international man sign for *back off.*

Finally Ross shook Paul's hand. "Ross." He followed with a head jerk in the direction of his truck. "C'mon, Tandi. Wind swell's got the surf pumping waist-plus off Pea Island. Gotta fix a faucet at one of the rentals, and then I'm headed that way to meet the crew." His lips squeezed tight over the last word in a way that made it more than a casual invitation. This was a test.

"Sure." I knew Paul was watching me. He rubbed his chin with the backs of his fingers, sliding the stampede string over his ear as his gaze fluttered past mine, a question in it.

Ross was already striding across the parking lot to his truck. I could feel the distance growing, the pressure increasing like a rubber band tightening. If I didn't give, it would snap, and Ross would be off to the beach without me. There was a good chance he wouldn't be coming back again after that.

"Well, enjoy your crab dinner," I said awkwardly, then turned and trotted after Ross. He was already settling into the driver's seat and starting the engine as I stepped onto the running board. For a minute, I thought he'd decided not to unlock my door, but then the button clicked and I slid in just before the truck lurched forward.

All four wheels spun, spitting out a shower of gravel that pinged against the metal on Bink's store. I imagined Paul ducking out of the way, protecting the bucket of blue crab, but I didn't look back to check.

"Geez, Ross. Bink is probably taking down your license number so he can complain to the police the next time they come in for doughnuts."

Ross rolled his eyes and snorted. "I don't give a rip about Bink." The edge in his voice pushed something heavy through my stomach again, and what was left of Geneva Bink's sausage created a hungry-sick feeling that took me back to Dallas. I hated it when Trammel talked to me that way — like he was disgusted by so many things about me, and I'd just reminded him of every little flaw.

Ross rolled down his window, and the breeze swirled my hair away from my face, cooling the burn in my cheeks. It wasn't right for me to hold things against Ross just because I'd been stupid enough to get myself involved with a man like Trammel

Clarke. Ross and Trammel weren't anything alike. Ross made an honest living, for one thing. He worked hard. He was entitled to be in a bad mood if he wanted to, and he *had* come by Fairhope to find me, which meant that I mattered. He could've just headed for the beach without me. Of course, then he and his friends wouldn't have anyone to run video cameras while they surfed, which was usually my job.

Ross looked me up and down, taking in the holey-kneed jeans and the T-shirt that was dirty from working all morning at Iola's. "Where've you been, anyway? I stopped by your place looking for you a minute ago."

"I went up to Bink's to get some trash bags. I'm doing some cleaning work for the church. That'll take care of my rent for a while, I hope." I left it at that. I had a feeling that if Ross knew I had the key to Iola's big white house, he'd expect to take a look inside. He was curious, just like everyone else.

We passed the driveway, and he pulled off into the ditch. "You need anything from your place?"

A mixture of guilt and curiosity nibbled at me as I looked through the trees at Iola's house, and for a fraction of a second I wished that Ross hadn't come by. I needed to be working, but more than that, I wondered what other pieces of Iola's life I might find in there. After reading her letter on the desk yesterday, I'd started peeking in drawers and looking in cabinets when I didn't need to. I hadn't found anything else like the letter — or much of anything personal at all. It was almost as if Iola were only a visitor in the house, keeping her life in containers rather than moving in. What would cause her to do that? Was she afraid of something in there?

"Tandi, you need anything from your place?" Ross repeated, wrapping his fingers over the gearshift impatiently.

"Sorry. I zoned out for a sec." Actually, I was trying to remember whether I'd locked all the doors at Iola's before walking over to Bink's for trash bags. I couldn't go away and leave the place open, but I didn't want Ross to see me with the keys, either.

"You know what?" I turned to him and smiled. "Why don't you just drop me here and come back after you fix the faucet?" As much as I liked wandering the decks and checking out the view at the rental places, I couldn't take the chance that Brother Guilbeau might come by and find Iola's house hanging wide open. "That way I won't be holding you up. It's not too far for you to run back by for me, is it?"

He shrugged. "Yeah, I guess not. Whatever. I'll be back in forty-five." He frowned and checked his watch — a fancy titanium Lodown with some feature he could use to check the tide on two hundred beaches around the world. "Less if I can patch the stupid thing back together good enough to hold for a while. Be ready."

"I will." I slid out the door and started toward the cottage, then turned in the direction of the main house when Ross was out of sight.

The water was running upstairs when I stepped through Iola's front door. It sounded like a flash flood might cascade through the plaster any moment.

"Oh no!" Kicking the door shut behind me, I ran up the stairs two at a time.

Luckily, when I reached the bathroom, the sink was keeping up well enough that the basin was only half-full. As soon as the faucet was off, the drain slurped away the remaining pool, then went silent. In the quiet, the sound of bells pressed through, the music high and soft, drawing me down the hall and into the turret room. This time, the cat was standing in the window with one paw braced on the glass and the other toying with the bells on the suncatcher. *One, two, three* in succession, then *two,* then *one, one, three, two, one,* as if he were listening to the tone of each bell and putting together a melody.

"What are *you* doing up here again?" My voice disturbed the dust in the air, and the cat paused to look at me, his topaz eyes blinking slowly beneath the bitten-off ear. The shepherd's hook tail twitched slightly.

"You know, you're about the ugliest cat I've ever seen."

His nose lifted a little, the gesture conveying that he really had no use for my opinions. Turning soundlessly, he crossed the walnut night table, then circled Iola's resting spot before rolling over in the center of the quilt and stretching his front paws into a patch of indigo fabric.

"What, you're not going to run and hide this time?"

A twitch of the broken ear and a yawn answered my question.

"Yeah, well, don't go turning on the water anymore either." Chewing my lip, I glanced at the tangle of rickrack and ribbon near the box on the writing desk. "In fact, I think I'll take care of that issue right now. There's a bowl in the kitchen, you know. You can go down there for a drink if you're thirsty." Since I couldn't figure out how the cat was getting in and out, I'd set up food and water dishes yesterday before I left the house. I couldn't find any cat chow, but Iola's kitchen was loaded with Beanee Weenee cans with varying expiration dates. As long as the cat liked Beanee Weenees, he'd be in good shape. If he knew how to use a can opener, he could survive here forever.

"You have turned on your last faucet, buddy." I pointed a finger at him, a declaration of war, of sorts. I knew just how to make sure there was no more danger of unexpected flooding inside the house.

Twenty minutes and some of Iola's ribbon and rickrack was all it took to tie every available faucet firmly into place, making them kitty-proof. I almost wished the cat would follow me so I could see the look on his face when he encountered my handiwork. The urge to find him and officially lay down the gauntlet before I left became overwhelming, so I trotted up the stairs with the last of the rickrack dangling between my fingers.

He was still lounging in the blue room.

"Okay, if you can get those faucets to turn on now, you're more than just a normal cat, and I'm not coming back in this house," I joked. "But since I'm the one with opposable thumbs and control of the can opener, you might want to think twice about running me off."

I twizzled a piece of rickrack along the edge of the bed, and the cat looked at me like *Do you really think I'm going to fall for that old kitty-kitty-kitty trick? Go find some fluffy little thing named Fifi if you need a patsy to chase your ribbon around.*

His disinterested look made me laugh as I balled the rickrack into my palm. A slice of colored sunlight fell across it, giving the gold threads a glow, and I turned slowly toward the suncatcher in the window beside the bed. In the corner beyond, the closet door was open, a crack revealing the fathomless darkness of the space behind the library nook.

"That door wasn't open yesterday," I whispered to myself or the cat or the house. Perhaps all three. I'd come to the point where it almost seemed natural to talk to the walls here.

A strange warmth slid over me as I walked toward the closet. I thought of the dream that had haunted me after I found Iola's body — the blue room, the light, someone standing within it, the comfort I'd felt and the way it drew me in, made me want to know more, to come closer.

The reflection of hummingbird and passion vine caressed my skin, melted across it as I walked to the closet, slowly opened the door, let in a spill of light, caught a breath of dust and stillness and wonder.

In the area near the door, clothes hung on wooden hangers — a fur coat, a man's suit, something that looked like a long black cape with a red satin lining, a pink dress and a matching pillbox hat, both encased in plastic.

My gaze skimmed past, drawn instead to a patchwork of color and shape against the back wall. Cloaked in shadow, clothed in fabric and wood, adorned with ribbon, rickrack, buttons, multi-colored bits of beach glass, and tiny shells with glitter sprinkled on like sand, they waited.

A diorama of boxes, upon boxes, upon boxes, neatly stacked from floor to ceiling. Judging by the layer of dust, they'd been hidden there, keeping their secrets, for a very long time.

CHAPTER 7

I heard the car horn only dimly at first. I was crouched in Iola's closet, looking at the boxes. I'd slid another one off a shelf, a wooden box this time, the varnish old and yellowed, a faint image still visible on the lid. I touched the crackled paint, traced the sails of a galleon on a storm-filled sea.

I'd figured out the organizational system of the boxes, peeked inside a few long enough to look at the dates, deduced that they ran left to right in rows, bottom to top like the imitation hieroglyphics outside the Luxor hotel in Las Vegas. Floor to ceiling, next to what must have once been a built-in ladder that provided access to an attic hatch high in the eaves — fourteen feet, at least. Far out of reach now, since the ladder steps had been pried off the wall at some time in the past.

Every box seemed to be filled with Iola's letters to her father, written on stationery and scrap paper of all types, the edges yellowed, the ink faded, the corners dissolved by time or eaten through by the tiny creatures that find their way into sealed boxes.

Had her father stored them here, building a collection as the numbers grew? The shelving was as random as the boxes it held — created out of boards that ranged from oak table leaves to bits of plywood to the flattened remnants of a La Motte oyster crate. The oyster-crate shelf was held together by more bent nails than straight ones. On the sidewalls, brackets had been made out of everything from metal cracker box lids to what looked like two broken bits of broom handle nailed on horizontally.

My grandfather would've been appalled at the carpentry, and actually so would my father. Daddy had only taken on construction work when he couldn't make enough money buying and selling horses, but he was surprisingly good at building things. He kept me home from school and made me come along if he needed an extra pair of hands or a sober driver. I'd shuttled him to jobs since I was old enough to reach the pedals, so it never really occurred to me that it wasn't normal for a ten-year-old to drive across town. The upside was that I'd learned things that had come in handy later at some of the fixer-upper places I'd lived in before Trammel. I could have built better closet fixtures than these with a blindfold on and six fingers tied behind my back.

It was a lucky thing Iola's shelves were holding no more than paper-filled boxes, some decorated with fabric and trims, some the salvaged packaging of days gone by — a wine carton, a bamboo tea container with Chinese characters printed in red, the shellac blackened and crazed. The wooden box in my hands looked ancient, like it might have traveled around the world in some sailor's chest before it came into Iola's collection. On the top shelf — the one far out of reach and supported precariously by broom-handle brackets — a stained-glass container sat last in line, looking far too heavy to be where it was.

The car horn blared long and loud outside, and I fell off-balance into the wall, realizing with a quick note of panic that I'd been so mesmerized by the boxes, I'd forgotten all about Ross. High on its shelf, the stained-glass container trembled, then settled into place again as I returned the sailing-ship box to its correct position and hurried from the closet. Downstairs, I rushed through checking locks, then left via the back door by the kitchen, crossed behind an overgrown bayberry hedge, and came out from behind the cottage. Ross had exited the truck and was on the cottage porch, trying to find me.

"Where've you been?" He looked me over, taking in the disheveled hair and the same clothes I'd had on when he left. Then he peered around the corner of the cottage like he expected to find someone there.

"Finishing up some stuff for the church. I lost track of time, sorry. Let me grab a couple things, and I'm good to go."

Ross licked his lips, holding the bottom one between his teeth and looking from me to the backyard again before he turned and walked back to his truck. I let myself into the cottage, grabbed what I needed, locked the door, and was in the passenger seat in under two minutes, which wasn't fast enough. Ross gunned the engine on the way out, his chin stiff, his eyes focused straight ahead.

"So who's the guy?" he demanded as we pulled onto the narrow, tree-lined street that led from Iola's house to Highway 12.

"What guy?"

"The guy at the store." A hard look came my way. "The loser in the flamingo shirt."

I was afraid to ask why Ross was bringing Paul up again. "He mowed the lawn the other day. . . . well, and he's J.T.'s teacher. I just bumped into him at the store when I went for trash bags."

Ross leaned back in his seat, one arm resting atop the steering wheel, his thumb sliding across the pads of his fingers. "He come back by just now while you were at the house?"

"No." The word puffed out in a little cough. "Nobody was over there but me, Ross. He's J.T.'s teacher, and he introduced himself when he saw me at Bink's. That's all."

"Yeah, well, maybe you shouldn't hang around the store letting your kid's teacher hit on you." Considering that he was headed out to surf, Ross was in an intensely foul mood. I'd never seen him quite like this. No doubt he was irked that his daddy had him out fixing faucets while the waves were good. He hated working for his daddy.

"He wasn't hitting on me. He was showing me a crab trap. He'd been out crabbing." Suddenly wishing I'd stayed at Iola's, I pushed closer to the door as we swung onto the highway. I wanted to know more about the boxes, but after turning Ross down the night he got home, I was lucky he wasn't hooked up with that girl from Captain Jack's, taking *her* to the beach. She could probably run a video camera too.

It crossed my mind that I should've left a note for the kids, to let them know where I was. When Ross hit the water, there was really no telling how long he'd be there. I would've thought of that if I hadn't been in such a hurry. Fortunately Zoey would look after J.T. this afternoon, whether there was a note or not. She'd gotten in the habit of not assuming anything.

"Yeah, right. He invite you over for a little crab dinner?" Ross was still sniffing down the same rabbit trail. The question had a sharp edge to it.

"Geez, Ross. No, he didn't invite me over for dinner. I remembered my pap-pap having a crab trap like that, and I wanted to look at it, that's all. I'd been there, like, a minute before you came."

Ross whipped past an SUV with kayaks racked on top, then ducked back in so late that an oncoming delivery truck had started moving over. A gasp sucked backward into my throat. I swallowed it soundlessly, my fingernails clutching the armrest. Ross wasn't usually wound quite this tight.

"So . . . tough time at work last week?" I tried to change the subject.

"What? Now I'm the one who's got a problem? I come home from a trip, you make excuses not to come meet me, then I drive up and find you flirting with some loser in a howlie shirt."

"I tried to call you back. You wouldn't answer. I tried to find you yesterday, too." No matter what I said now, it wasn't going to make a difference. On the one hand, it felt good that Ross cared enough to be jealous. On the other hand, it was frustrating. Maybe we weren't as solid as I thought we were. The idea scared me. Without Ross, we had no security here, no one to help us if we needed it.

"Yeah, whatever. That's why I've got all *two* of those missed calls from you on my phone. That's why I called your place, like, six times yesterday, and you weren't there." He grabbed his cell phone and held it up like it was proof of something.

"I told you I got a job finally. I was working yesterday. And I called you more than two times. You wouldn't answer."

"Whatever," he said again.

I gave up talking and just looked out the window, letting Ross have some time to cool off. On a path toward Buxton Woods, a group of tourists on horseback plodded along. I'd seen riders go by on the trails along Mosey Creek a time or two.

"That looks like so much fun. I've never

ridden on the beach." I didn't even realize I'd said it out loud, at first. The most carefree moments of my life had been spent on the back of a horse. When I was young, there were usually horses at home that needed riding, although we were lucky if any of them were actually fit for kids to be around. Daddy liked to buy horses with bad habits, ride the hair off them for a few weeks, then take them to the auction barn when they were dead-dog tired and put Gina or me in the saddle. We knew better than to act scared, even if we were. Buyers paid good money for something that seemed gentle enough for kids. We also knew that, by making a horse look good, we were probably saving a life. If the saddle-horse buyers didn't outbid the slaughter buyers, those horses were headed for a dog food can. Either way, Daddy got his money.

"Yeah, well, maybe you can find *some guy* to take you out riding," Ross snapped. "You want me to let you out?"

I rubbed the little drumbeat between my eyebrows and wished Ross hadn't found me today after all, at least not when he was in a mood like this. It was hard to believe that not so long ago I was dropping the envelope into Jeremy's truck and feeling like the day had magic sprinkled over it.

133

I tried to leave off analyzing things as we passed through Buxton and continued along the Cape Hatteras National Seashore, where the beach houses gave way to wild, unspoiled country, the land so narrow at times that the sound peeked through on one side, placid and glassy, while the blue-green waters of the Atlantic churned against the dunes on the other. Ross chilled a little and turned on the radio as we passed by Avon, then drove the narrow strip to Salvo, Waves, and Rodanthe. The farther north we went, the more intense the leftover hurricane damage grew. Neighborhoods that had been filled with mansions on stilts now sported empty spaces next to massive beach homes that teetered uneven, the pilings splayed out like the legs of a new colt, the property owners unable to come up with the money for repairs. Caution tape and Condemned signs spoke the fate of homes now permanently off-kilter. Balconies dangled forlorn, and outside stairways had been removed, leaving the houses unreachable.

In my mind, I heard my grandfather complaining about people building multistory homes right on the beach. To him, the only things that belonged there were saltbox cottages like the ones in Old Nags Head, the nothing-fancy kind that were fully expected to die a death at sea sooner or later. *What do they think — the storms will never come? You build a house on the sand, the sand shifts eventually, Tandi Jo. You remember that.*

When we'd come here after the storm all those years ago, I'd thought Pap-pap could fix anything, including my parents. Now I knew that sometimes life is like those flooded houses. You can keep driving yourself crazy fighting the sea, or you can leave the past behind, find dry ground, and build somewhere new.

Somehow or other, I'd find a way to do that.

Ross's mood took a turn for the better when we pulled off the road in a spot already packed with boards and cars with wet suits hanging on them. He was smiling from head to toe as he stepped out of the truck.

"Hey . . . Cowboy!" some surfer chick called to him as we crossed over the dunes. The surf crew all called him *Cowboy,* and you didn't have to hang around with Ross long to know that even if he didn't go for long hair and surfer duds, the other guys admired his skill with a board. He had *soul,* as they put it.

Within a few minutes, he was out of his

jeans and shirt and into a Hurley wet suit over his swim trunks. He handed me the camera bag and a folding chair, knuckle-bumped with a couple of his bros on the beach, and then stood with a group of them talking over the conditions, their hands moving in surfer sign language, mimicking the shapes of the waves and reenacting some epic wipeouts.

I set up my beach chair, pressing the back of it into the sand until it was level, then settled in and took a big breath. The sun on my hair and the thrum of the tide made me feel good again. Compared to most of the guys who hung out on the water, Ross was more intense, less mellow than the surfer vibe called for, but even he couldn't help getting relaxed out here.

The sand swirled around my toes, sun-warmed on top and cold underneath as I rolled up my jeans. You couldn't have paid me to get in the water this time of year, but on the beach it was glorious today. A friend of Ross's, a skinny, loose-jointed kid the guys called *Gumby* because he wore a lime-green wet suit, lifted a hand and waved at me. "Hey, Cowboy-girl. You gonna run video? You tape for me?"

I nodded and shot him the high sign, and he trotted off to get his camera. Ross's friends had taken to calling me *Cowboy's girl* at first and then just shortened it to *Cowboy-girl* when they found out I used to show horses. They thought that was cool, and they liked having someone around who could run a camera, check weather reports on an iPhone, operate a stopwatch, and mentally calculate the average period between waves by timing the frequency as they struck a pier or buoy.

The breeze combed my hair, and I closed my eyes, listening to the water. At the edge of the sea like this, it was hard to believe anything could be wrong. I loved being part of the surf crew, feeling like I had friends here after so many years of trying to fit in with Trammel's social circle and still being labeled a gold digger, someone who'd used her horrific accident to worm her way into his life and his finances. That couldn't have been further from the truth, but it didn't matter anymore.

By now, Trammel's friends were probably hearing about him on the news. I'd made preparations before I left town — printed a stack of private e-mails between Trammel and his business partners and sent them to an investigative reporter on Channel 8. With a little digging, the reporter would be able to uncover everything. No more of those young patients Trammel referred to as *government charity cases* would be subjected to unnecessary medical treatments or strapped down in a dental chair while healthy baby teeth were filed off and a mouthful of silver crowns were crammed into place, in rapid succession.

Considering all the things Trammel criticized about me, all the things he held over my head, you'd think he would have remembered that I'd *been* one of those childhood charity cases. I remembered what it was like to have people you barely knew take you into a medical clinic, distort a few truths, and walk out with prescriptions for drugs to keep you placid and easy to manage — as if it's abnormal for a child to be emotional when home life is a roller-coaster ride with occasional holes in the track. I knew what those kids in Trammel's medical and dental clinics were going through. They were more than numbers in a Medicaid file.

But here by the water, Trammel and all the rest of it seemed far away. There wasn't a thing to worry about. There couldn't be. The outside world didn't exist here. With any luck, the story had broken and Trammel was in jail, where he belonged.

A tiny ghost crab scuttled a few feet from its hole, then rushed back in as I grabbed a pair of Ross's spare sunglasses and waited for Gumby to bring his camera. Once everything was said and done, I had five cameras and five guys to tape, plus one guy's surfer girlfriend.

The afternoon went by in a rush. As the sun slid low over the water, the wind quieted and the breakers flattened out. Some of the guys built a fire and hung a kettle over it. I helped dump in corn, potatoes, and a couple pouches of Old Bay crab boil spices before grabbing the camera to catch Ross on his last trip of the day. The wave was small but clean, and he stroked it like an artist, cutting smooth curls, teasing the frothy tip. I zoomed in and watched his face, studied his intensity. Ross was never just having fun. He was always perfecting his art.

The breaker collapsed, and he rode the momentum in, his body silhouetted against the blushing sky, a magazine cover image. For an instant, I wished Trammel could see me now, dating someone like Ross, sur-rounded by friends who actually liked me, just hanging out on the beach, enjoying everything this place had to offer. Trammel was wrong when he'd said that if I left him, I'd be sorry — that I was nothing without him and the pills. He'd used them to keep a thumb on me, told me I needed them to get past the leftover nerve damage from the accident and the emotional side effects of no longer being able to ride competitively. I'd trusted him in those confusing first months — he was a doctor, he should know. He had become the source of medications, money, security, everything I thought I needed to survive. But the truth was that I didn't need any of it. This place was healing me, giving me a new life. Cleansing me, body and soul.

Ross paddled back out with a couple of buddies and they sat on their boards awhile, their hands once again speaking the silent language of breakers and tubes. Finally they rode in, and he jogged up the beach as a few of the guys pulled the boiling basket from the pot, dumped the vegetables on a pad of newspaper spread over a beach towel, then put shrimp, crab, and sausage in the basket before submerging it again. The water frothed over the edges of the pot, droplets hissing into the fire, gone in an instant.

Ross slid a damp hand over my shirt, leaned close, and kissed me, then shook out his short dark hair, the spray pelting both me and the fire. The flames complained, finding a voice again.

"Ross!" I squealed, shielding the video camera.

He laughed and wicked water off his wet suit, flicking it at me. "You get good video?" The wet suit made rubber noises as he unzipped it. He looked good in it. He looked good without it.

"I got good video," I said.

Smiling, he reached for the camera, his dark eyes dancing in the light. "I knew you were good for somethin'." He gave me a look that smoldered with hidden invitations.

"Funny," I sneered playfully at him. The fight was over. Ross and I were good again.

Gumby trotted up with a small blue cooler. "Dude, you forgot these." He opened the lid and dumped another pile of blue crab and sausage into the pot.

Watching the crab tumble in, I thought of Paul Chastain and wondered if he was all by himself somewhere, having his fresh-caught dinner. I felt bad about the way we'd just left him standing there in the parking lot at Bink's.

Thinking of Bink's reminded me of the kids and the fact that it was getting dark. At home, Zoey would have everything under control, of course. She'd be fixing dinner, making sure J.T. got his homework done, eventually hollering across the house that if he didn't get off Zago Wars and go to bed, she was going to come in there and rip the cord out of the stupid thing . . .

They'd both be psyched about all the food I'd brought over from Iola's this morning, especially the microwave popcorn and the tinful of Belgian waffle cookies. They'd probably have a snackfest all evening.

Still, I should borrow Ross's phone and call to be sure everything was okay.

A good mother would have thought of that before night started to settle in.

CHAPTER 8

I knew something was wrong the minute we turned into the driveway. The cottage was dark, no TVs on, no signs of activity. Iola's house loomed large and silent in the background, the only light a faint glow from a lamp downstairs.

"They're not here. Where could they be?" The past rushed through me, wild and unbridled, and I saw my mother staggering out of some guy's truck, yelling down the road as a CPS caseworker drove away with us in the backseat of his car.

The idea of that nightmare repeating itself crowded my mind now. Had Trammel found us, maybe tipped off the police here? Or had he come here himself and taken my kids, to prove that we would never be free of him?

If you ever tried to leave, I'd find you, Tandi. He'd always promised that.

Nightmare scenarios spun in my mind,

one right after another. What if something else had happened? What if J.T. had walked over to the marina and gotten in some kind of trouble? What if he'd fallen off the dock, hit his head, sunk beneath the water without a soul around to notice? What if he'd been lured into a car with a stranger? He was still so little. . . .

Could Zoey be out looking for him, trying to find him?

"Chill out, Tandi." Ross was somewhere between supportive and irritated that we'd had to leave the beach boil. "The kids're probably with that punk football player Zoey's so hot about." For whatever reason, Ross didn't like Zoey's boyfriend. I could never quite tell whether he was looking out for her or just jealous because Zoey liked Rowdy a lot better than she liked Ross.

"They never turn the lights off when they leave." Unhooking my seat belt, I reached for the door handle before we were completely stopped. "They haven't *been here* since school got out, Ross. Something's wrong. Zoey wouldn't take off until almost nine o'clock at night without letting me know. She has your cell number, and Rowdy has a phone." I'd been trying to call Rowdy's phone for thirty minutes now. No answer.

144

Ross scoffed, a suggestive chuckle rolling under his breath. "You even *watch* her with that Rowdy kid, ever? I can pretty much tell you where *she's* at. She probably dropped her little brother off at the arcade or some-place, and she and Romeo are out in the backseat of the Jeep right —"

"Stop it!" Halfway out the car door, I wheeled on him. "Don't talk about her like that."

Ross blinked slowly, his head cocking to one side. "Well, don't go all *Jerry Springer* on me. I told you that you oughta get her away from the kid, though, didn't I? You don't look out, Tandi, you're gonna be a grandma, and I'm not interested in raisin' a baby. . . ."

I slid out of the truck and slammed the door hard behind me. The cottage was deathly quiet when we stepped inside. Call-ing the kids' names, I checked the rooms. No one there. No sign that anyone had been. No note. They were just gone.

"Well, they've gotta be someplace." Ross was standing in the living room, and even he looked a little concerned. "When that girl gets home, you need to bust her chops, I'm tellin' you. You better get her under control before she ends up in real trouble. I've got a little sister, and she —"

"Ross, please!" My hands were shaking, my entire body a rush of blood and fear. My voice echoed against the close-set walls of the cottage, high and shrill.

"Geez, calm down." He reached for me, pulled me against his chest, and I pressed my hands over my face. His voice rumbled near my ear. "Here. I'll call a buddy at the sheriff's department if that'll make you feel better."

Nodding, I took in his salty scent, the comfort of his arms, the muscles circling tight, encasing me in the assurance that I had someone to rely on, someone who cared. He reached into his jeans pocket, pulled out his cell. "You know, we need to get you a cell phone."

His fingers slid into my hair as he paged through his contacts, then talked to a friend at the sheriff's department — not surprisingly, a woman.

"Well . . . nothin' to report." His motion was relaxed and casual as he tucked the phone back in his pocket. "See, I told you they're just out . . . doing whatever. They'll show up. Relax." He stepped away from me, and my skin went cold where his warmth had been. In the tiny living room of the cottage, Ross seemed out of place, his bulky, six-foot-four-inch frame dominating the space as he looked around, trying to decide what to do next.

"You got anything to eat in this place?"

"Eat . . . huh?" Nothing had been reported to the sheriff, but still, my kids were missing. Zoey wouldn't do this, especially not when they had school the next day. "I can't think about food. I have to know where my kids are."

Ross's sigh communicated his frustration. "You're gonna have to relax, Tandi. They'll show up when they're ready, and then you can whip some tail. Till then, there's no sense starving to death. Man, I could go for some of that beach boil right now. . . ."

He wandered off to the kitchen and started rummaging through the box of goods I'd brought home from Iola's house. "What's with all these cans of Beanee Weenees? Haven't you got any meat around here except hot dogs? No wonder that kid of yours looks like he's a baby anorexic. A man needs meat."

Ross's voice faded into the background as I wandered out the front door and stood gripping the porch railing. Tears pressed again. "Please . . . *please,*" I heard myself whisper. I wanted Rowdy's car to come rolling up the driveway. "They have to be all right."

Beyond the old stable yard, the church bells rang, then stopped.

"Who're you talking to?" Ross passed by the door with a spoon in one hand and a can of Iola's Beanee Weenees in the other. "Standing out there won't make them show up any sooner." He scooped a bite from the can, swilled it around his mouth, and swallowed. "These aren't half-bad. It's not crab legs and corn, but it's food. You want me to fix you a plate?"

I didn't answer but walked to the steps, searched the yard, and listened to bullfrogs croaking in the sedges, the hush of wind across salt meadow hay, the seemingly endless trill of a nightjar calling. A fog rolled off the sound, creeping through the bayberry hedges, filling the low places first, stringing upward in ribbons that hung suspended, silver-bright in the moonlight.

I wanted to take J.T.'s hand in mine, steal through the fog, whisper, "Ssshhh," as we moved closer to the bird's call. I would translate its song for him the way my grandfather had for me: *Chuck-will's-widow, Chuck-will's-widow, Chuck-will's-widow* . . .

The cat mewed, the sound mingling with the bird's call, their voices coming in rapid succession, a song in two parts, performed in perfect time. *Chuck-will's-widow. Meow.*

Chuck-will's-widow. Meow. Chuck-will's . . .

Slipping around the corner, I found the one-eared cat sitting in a spill of moon glow, his fur blue-black in the light, his gaze focused through a thin streamer of fog into the live oaks overhead, as if he were conversing with the nightjar.

The bird stilled, and the cat looked my way, meowed, then swiveled toward the old stable.

There was something in the fog, a faint light. Squinting into the darkness, I focused on it, lost it in the mist, then found it again, nearer this time. The cat took a few silent steps, maintaining the distance between us as I moved closer.

What was that? . . . What was out there?

I blinked, tried to see. Light reflected against the vapor, outlining an image that faded into a bank of condensation, then re-appeared again, took on a human shape. A person, seeming to hover in the mist . . . someone small . . . a woman with long hair . . . carrying a lantern.

The image pinned me where I was, left me mesmerized and terrified at once, unable to find my voice. "R-Ross!" I croaked finally.

"Mama?" the specter answered.

"J.T.?"

The lantern stopped, the shadow figure coming no closer. A whiff of breeze stirred, lifted the long, thick hair, rippling it, flag-like. I had the sense that this was all just another dream. None of it real.

The cat yowled and darted away.

I thought of J.T.'s words after his night-mare a couple days ago. *I heard the cat screaming in the yard. . . . They do it when there's a ghost.*

"J.T.?" I called out again, louder this time. "Is that you? If that's you, you come over here right now, you hear me?"

The kitchen window slid open in the cottage. "Tandi, what the . . . ?"

I didn't hear the rest of whatever Ross had to say. Next door, a car circled the church parking lot, the headlights strafing the stable yard, pressing over the veils of fog just long enough that I could see J.T.'s scrawny form — shorts, skinny legs, tennis shoes with reflector tape, a light of some kind in his hand. He had a cloth wrapped over his head.

Before the car had pulled away, I was running through the yard. I caught him by the bayberry hedge, scooped him to me, sobbing and gasping. He was here. He was safe. Trammel didn't have him. No one had him.

"Where *were* you?" The words tumbled out. "Where's your sister?"

150

Vaguely I was aware of Ross leaving the cottage, his boots echoing on the porch, his footsteps crunching against the oyster-shell path. "You scared your mama half-outta her mind," he complained as he approached. "Where've you been?"

J.T. stiffened in my arms, pulled away, then reached up and snatched the thing from his head, a Windbreaker hanging on only by the hood. His backpack slid on his shoulder, and he hiked it into place again.

"Where's Zoey?" I looked toward the stable, expecting her to materialize as well. What could J.T. possibly have been doing over there? That building was one step short of falling in. Why would they go there in the dark?

Folding the jacket against his body, he hugged it close. "I dunno." His voice went high, then cracked. "Her and Rowdy went someplace after school got out. I saw her at Bink's when I got off the bus. She told me to just go on home, so I did, and she left with Rowdy."

"Yeah, who guessed that one right?" Ross pointed out.

I turned back to J.T., grabbed his shoulders. "Why weren't you at the cottage? Why didn't you let yourself in and wait like you're supposed to? I've been going crazy."

151

"The key was gone." J.T.'s voice was barely audible. His shoulders crumbled beneath my fingers, shrinking inward. "When I got home, the key wasn't under the mat, and Zoey didn't come, and you didn't come, so I went back down to Bink's and helped the guys for a while, and then, so it was getting dark, and Brother Guilbeau came to the store, and he said they were havin' spaghetti dinner and a family movie night at the church and did I like spaghetti? And I said I did, so I had spaghetti, but it tasted so good I ate too much spaghetti and popcorn, and my stomach hurt, so then I went to the bathroom for a while after the movie was goin'. By the time I came out, the hallway was dark and everybody was headin' home. I saw the windows were lit up in our house, so I got my key chain light out and —"

"Yeah, well, I'm glad somebody got to eat." Ross braced his hands on his belt, towering over J.T. "*We* missed out on a good beach boil because *we* had to come look for your little butt. If I ever did that to *my* daddy, he would've whipped me till I couldn't stand up straight, and then I would've known not to do it again."

J.T. backed against me, and I slid an arm around him. "It's my fault for not putting the key back." While I was rushing off with Ross earlier, I'd forgotten to make sure the extra key was under the mat. For the past two days, I'd been using the one on the ring Brother Guilbeau had given me. "It's okay now." I turned to guide J.T. toward the cottage, holding tight to his shoulders, feeling the little points of bone beneath my fingers. "There's no real harm done."

"Yeah, except it screwed up our whole night." We passed through the light from the kitchen window, and I could see Ross glaring at me, expecting me to take his side.

"Let's just go in the house." My body was quickly turning to mush, awash with relief as we made our way back to the cottage and closed the door behind us. I was ready to let the tension wane, not keep the fight going.

"It's no wonder they don't listen worth a flip," Ross complained. The can of Beanee Weenees hit the trash half-full, and the spoon sailed across the kitchen and clattered into the sink.

J.T. stopped. Froze. He looked up at me, his eyes two brimming pools of ocean blue, the freckles over his nose trembling. "I woulda come home before, but it was dark in here, and I was afraid of the ghost," he whispered, ducking his chin. A nervous glance flicked toward Ross, then back to me.

I shooed J.T. toward his room, then leaned against the corner of the hallway wall, my body still shaking, the nerves vibrating leaf-like and fragile under my skin. "I just need to . . . catch my breath a minute, okay? I'm sure Zoey will show up soon."

"Yeah, we'll see," Ross grumbled. "Guess I should go get the cooler out of the truck." He walked out the door, and I sank down on the edge of the sofa, vacillating between being angry, being worried, and being confused. This just wasn't like Zoey. Where was she?

She'd come in soon. Of course she would. And she'd have a good reason for going AWOL tonight. She would be here any minute. Home. Safe.

But hours ticked away as I waited on the sofa, alternately calling Rowdy's cell number and checking the driveway. By midnight, Ross was like a fighting rooster chained to a peg, and I couldn't take it anymore. Whenever Zoey *did* finally show up, things were going to be a mess, I could tell.

One of Ross's friends called, and I was glad for the diversion. They'd moved the party from the beach to a house. They were jamming on guitars and hanging out, planning to crash for a few hours before hitting the water again in the morning. Tomorrow's forecasts called for waves hip to waist.

I urged Ross to go join the party and then was strangely disappointed when he took me up on it. After he left, all I could do was let my head sag against the sofa and try to focus on the TV rather than the disaster scenarios in my mind.

J.T. staggered up the hall, drowsy and clumsy, dragging the sleeping bag from his room. He curled up next to me, and I sat finger-combing the silken strands of his hair, trying not to think all the worst things.

Sleep slipped over me sometime after midnight. When I woke, Zoey was sneaking past, trying to keep the worn plank floorboards from making noise as she crossed to the sand-crusted carpet runner that ran down the hallway.

"Zoey?" I whispered.

"Sssshhh." She pointed at J.T. The two of us had collapsed into a heap, and I couldn't move without disturbing him. After the long day, my mind was slow and sluggish.

"What time is . . . ? Where were you?" I blinked hard, tried to sort out the muddle in my head. J.T. stirred in my lap.

"Go back to sleep." Zoey shifted from one foot to the other, rubbing her hands up and down her arms like she was half-frozen. "We got Rowdy's truck stuck at the beach. I need to get some sleep. There's a stupid science test tomorrow." She didn't wait for an answer but disappeared into the bathroom, closing and locking the door behind herself.

I slipped out from under J.T., started toward the bathroom door, but decided to leave it be for tonight. Instead, I tucked J.T. in tight on the sofa, then stumbled off to my room. A heavy moon hung outside the window, its soft glow soothing me into sleep almost before my head hit the pillow.

In the morning, Zoey was trying to get quietly out the door when I woke up. She had J.T. in tow and her backpack slung over her shoulder. "Where's the key?" she demanded when she saw me in the bedroom doorway. She looked tired and red-eyed, her long brown hair hanging in tangled wet strings around her face. "The dork said he got locked out yesterday because the key wasn't there."

"Yes, and he was wandering around after dark by himself because you weren't *here,*" I snapped, my anger fresh and potent this morning.

Zoey's jaw squared, her eyes flaring, revealing an odd mix of bloodshot red, dry pink, and sky blue, a miniature sunset in reverse. "You know what — *you* weren't either. *You're* his *mother,* remember? You do whatever you want. Why can't I? Rowdy and me went to the beach. We got the truck stuck when we started to head home. His phone was dead, so we had to walk." She spotted the key on the windowsill and snatched it up, then pushed J.T. out the door. He stumbled on the stoop and took a couple of running steps across the porch before catching his balance.

Zoey slanted a narrow glare at me, her fingers closing over the knob. "We've gotta go. We'll miss the bus." The panes of glass rattled as the door slammed behind her.

Fury flared in me, and I yanked it open, yelled into the yard, "You come home after school today, you hear me!"

She didn't answer, just kept walking toward the marina with J.T. trotting along after her, shooting concerned looks back and forth. I stood watching, tears of frustration blurring the outlines of the kids as they reached the trail through the salt meadow and slowly vanished into the morning fog.

The silence closed in hard and fast as soon as they were gone. It crossed my mind that Ross hadn't checked on us since he left last night. For all he knew, Zoey could still be missing — or worse. We weren't even on his mind.

I wanted something medicinal to take the edge off that realization.

But there were no crutches around, and that was for the best. It was easier to leave the pills behind when no one was handing them to me and watching to make sure I took them day after day.

I showered, dressed, and went to Iola's house, leaving the cottage unlocked, just in case Zoey lost track of the key. Not that I planned to go anywhere today. When Zoey showed up after school — and she'd better — she would listen to what I had to say. I refused to let my baby girl repeat my history. She was better than that. She deserved better. My parents might not have found much to like about me, but I loved my daughter, even if I wasn't good at showing it. I had hopes and dreams for her. Somehow I had to make her see that.

Iola's house was quiet and cool inside, the damp, foggy night still clinging in the corners.

"G'morning, Iola," I said, my voice echoing through the house. Today I liked the feeling that I was not alone here, the sense that I was coming to spend the day with a friend who'd awaited my arrival.

Setting my things on a little table in the vestibule, I looked toward the stairs. In the excitement last night, I'd forgotten all about Iola's boxes.

CHAPTER 9

January 1, 1933

Dear Father,
Sister give this box to me. She say, "Iola, you write to Father when you got the sadness in this place, and Father, he gon listen." Sister tell me, put my letters in this box and hide it in my clothin chest where no one else gon know of it. This box a secret between Sister and me. "Not all secrets are sin," say Sister. She make the box beautiful. "Not all beautiful things are sin," she say. "Were not the gifts of the magi beautiful?" I like the way Sister talk, all proper like Isabelle.

"Beauty is created with purpose," say Sister. She hold my chin in her hand and lower her face close to mine, her eyes round and green like a fresh growth of daffodils. "Beauty is created. It's intentional." She give extra voice to them big words, *created* and *intentional,* to be sure that I know they matter. I ask her just how the ABC's supposed to go in them words, so I can write them good in my letter to you. They important words.

"We do not choose the vessel we're given, Iola Anne, but we choose what we pour out and what we keep inside," she say.

This box a vessel for my letters to you, Sister tell me. I got to put in all the things I keep inside me, get them out in my words. "This is good for the soul," Sister say. "Tell Father your worries. He will understand. He knows you so well."

I don't like the way I look.

I don't tell this, even to Sister.

They make me come stay here cause of my look. I ain't stupid. I know it.

I wish I look like Aurelia. She got long hair in braids, black as a dead coal.

I pray this prayer ever night, but in the mornin I wake up and run myself to the mirror in the water closet down that long hall and still, there the same girl lookin back at me. She got a bad look.

My heart so empty for Mama Tee and Maman and Isabelle.

If I look a different way, I can go home again.

I got to believe even harder. I got to believe you gon hear me, Father.

I want to go home.

Your lovin daughter,
Iola Anne

Letting the letter rest, I ran a finger over the words, carefully written in a child's slow, uneven print. My fingernail grazed the edge of the paper, slipped off onto the quilt, and snagged a stitch of white thread along an aster-blue square. I hadn't even realized I was sitting on the bed, rumpling Iola's resting place. The oldest of the boxes — one that had been almost hidden among dust bunnies, stray fur, and cast-off ribbon scraps in the bottom left corner of the closet — lay upside down on the bed beside me, the contents in a neat pile, still shaped like the interior of the box.

The uppermost shelf had me worried today. High out of reach near the attic hatch, it had slipped off its rickety broom-handle bracket overnight, as if I'd disturbed the balance of things when I'd come into the closet yesterday. One side now rested on the shelf beneath it, the boxes compacted like train cars in a pileup. The heavy stained-glass container was teetering with the others, one corner hanging in air.

I'd looked for a stepladder, but so far I hadn't found anything taller than a kitchen stool. No way to reach the glass box.

Finally I'd tiptoed into the closet and started at the bottom instead, with a shoe box–size container covered in a faded brocade fabric and decorated with bits of colored lace that had faded to pale shades of lilac and peach. The corners were smudged and worn. Now, with the first letter resting on the wedding ring quilt, I touched the box, thought of Iola's small hands holding it close to her body, opening and closing the lid, hiding her letters to her father inside.

Had she ever sent them to him? If so, how had they ended up back in her box, neatly stacked?

They make me come stay here cause of my look. I ain't stupid. I know it.

Could her father have been dead already when she wrote the letters? Maybe that was why she was sent away from her family — because she was a reminder of him, because she looked like him?

Maybe her mother had remarried, and her stepfather didn't want her around? I knew how that would feel. All my life, it had seemed like Mama and Daddy didn't really want Gina and me cluttering up their lives. They didn't want us, but they didn't want to give us up to Pap-pap and Meemaw for good either. We'd run from CPS more times than I could count too. As a child, I mistook those wild flights for evidence of love, but as I got older, I didn't know what to call it. Possession isn't the same as love.

Maybe Iola's family simply couldn't afford to feed and take care of her — 1933 was the Depression. People were starving, standing in bread lines. Kids were sent away. During my ill-fated freshman year of college, a history teacher had shown us photos of destitute families fleeing the dust bowl. The vacant, weary expressions on the women's faces brought back memories of my mama when she woke up hungover and worn-out.

Could Iola and her sister have been in an orphanage when Iola wrote the letter? Maybe it was the only choice her family had.

Who was Aurelia, and why did Iola want to look like her? Why did she believe that would make things better? Was it a child's unrealistic fantasy, like all the times I'd convinced myself that if I could just be a better girl — smarter, prettier, quieter, more helpful with the house, less trouble to have around — my parents would stop fighting, my daddy would come home every night, and my mama would be like the other moms at school, up and dressed each morning, waving good-bye to the school bus?

My heart ached for Iola, alone in a strange place in 1933. She must've been only about ten.

In a few years, she would realize that there was nothing she could do to change the world around her, to repair the people she needed most. The missing pieces were out of reach of her tiny hands, the broken places not hers to mend. In my adult mind I understood that, but deep inside me there would always be the girl who wondered if she could have fixed things.

Iola's letter reached into that little girl in a way nothing else ever had. I found myself spinning a web that intertwined Iola's story and mine, my thoughts running over the silky threads on nimble spider legs, creating intricate patterns.

A little girl trapped and helpless. Afraid. Waking each day to find her prayers unanswered . . .

I'd prayed the most desperate prayers of my life here on Hatteras. For a while, they'd seemed to be working. Finally after so many chaotic, uncertain years, God had heard me and repaired my family, patching up all the broken places with sun and sand, ready construction jobs, easy money, the magic of this place, and Pap-pap and Meemaw nearby. They'd promised to help my parents out, give them part of the farm to build a house on if Daddy would keep himself sober and take on construction work and Mama would stay home to take proper care of Gina and me. Pap-pap's job as an insurance adjuster gave him an in for lining up all the work my daddy could handle. It could be a new start for all of us. Life would finally be good. Stable day after day.

And then the post-storm construction boom was over, the repair work done, the tourists returning to grab up the available spaces, the rental prices rising. It was time to move to the farm across the sound on the mainland and start building our house. But Daddy missed Texas. He was tired of having to live by someone else's rules. He missed rodeos and horse auctions and trying to turn a quick buck so he wouldn't have to take as many construction jobs. The night he came home with a bottle in a paper bag, I knew my prayers hadn't been answered after all. The lopsided carousel of our lives had only been stopped for a while, and now it would resume its cockeyed motion — up, down, around. High and low. On and off.

Iola's prayers wouldn't be answered either — at ten, she probably had no way of realizing that. Sooner or later, she would figure out that she was never going to wake up looking like Aurelia.

I reached for the pile, slid my fingers over the next letter, lifted it free without disturbing the rest.

The cat, sitting on the far corner of the bed, twitched an ear, then stretched lazily against a pillow sham latticed with blue granny circles and tatted lace. His raspy pink tongue curled as he yawned and blinked, seeming to already know the stories in these boxes.

The half ear twitched again, reacting to the sound of old paper, as I unfolded another letter.

January 20, 1933

Dear Father,
Mama Tee say prayers only a dust of words that blow away. Her maman had the voodoo. She come from Haiti Isle on a tobacco ship, Mama Tee say, a slave woman to the tobacco man up in Caroline. He tell her not to do no voodoo.

He tell her she gotta be a Christian now. Mama Tee, she born a farm slave, but she don't remember that. She live her life mostly in the Quarter here in New Orlean, not in no tobacco field.

But she still believe in the voodoo.

Mama Tee say don't speak bout none of that. Monsieur, he don't like that kind of talk, Mama Tee say to me. His family got a bad history with the voodoo from long time ago, before Mama Tee come to work for Monsieur's folk and live in they big house by the Quarter. My own Maman just a little girl then, and I ain't even a dust speck yet.

Benoit family give us everythin. Always have. House to live, food to eat. They pay Mama Tee good, and then they pay Maman, when she old enough. Treat us good. They love us like family, let me learn my numbers and letters with Isabelle. Let me learn that big piano, jus like Isabelle.

I wonder, do Isabelle miss me now? Do she ask Monsieur, "Papa, why you send Iola Anne away?"

Did Isabelle hear Madame say, "Just look at her! I won't have it. I won't have her here, do you understand me? There are places a child like her can be sent.

Places where she will be educated, taken care of, given her catechism properly. It isn't cruel. She'll be better off, and so will Isabelle."

Everythin different since Monsieur marry again and bring Madame to the big house. Everythin shiny and proper and careful. Isabelle don like it neither.

Do she pray that I gon come home? Do we say the same prayer when we up in our beds at night, hers so far apart from mine now?

Maybe her prayers better than mine. Maybe she do it right.

Maybe you mad about the voodoo, Father. But I don't never do it. I don't believe it none, neither.

Sister Marguerite say you gon answer all prayers in they own time. I keep prayin my same prayer, gon keep writin it too, keep putting it in my prayer box Sister Marguerite give me. Keep waitin on you to answer. Keep wonderin if you been hearin these prayers.

You gon bring me home soon?

Can you find me in this place where they got so many?

Your lovin daughter,
Iola Anne

A mist of tears crowded my eyes. I knew how Iola felt, what she was thinking, what she was feeling. She was trapped in an orphanage or a school, some sort of warehouse for children whose families didn't want them around. Sister Marguerite wasn't her sister, but a nun — a teacher or a caretaker.

The letters were Iola's prayers, her private thoughts. That's why they'd never been mailed. These letters weren't meant for earth, but for heaven. Not for her biological father, but for God.

Iola's mother had sent her away . . . to please an employer? What kind of mother would do that? What kind of mother would abandon her little girl to make someone else happy?

There are places a child like her can be sent. . . . It isn't cruel. . . . What did that mean, *a child like her*? Was Iola handicapped? Deformed? I hadn't noticed anything when I'd found her body, but back in the day, there were superstitions about problems like that. I'd seen a little girl on the news who'd been nearly starved to death in an African orphanage because a mutated gene had caused her to have mottled skin. A couple from New Jersey had adopted her and saved her life.

Could something like that explain why Iola's mother would agree to send her away? Did she really believe it was best for Iola, or was it just convenient — a compromise made in order to keep a job, to maintain a life that was comfortable?

Was her ten-year-old daughter the price she had to pay to please Monsieur and Madame? Would a mother sell her child for so little?

My mother had given us up for less than money — for liquor, for parties, for one-night stands, for her constant need to feed on the chaos and drama of relationship upheaval — anything that kept the momentum going. If life calmed and settled into a pattern, like it had during those months on the Outer Banks, she eventually couldn't stand it. She'd conjured false accusations to insure that Pap-pap and Meemaw couldn't seek custody of us. She'd told horrible lies and made everyone believe them.

Folding Iola's second letter, I set it atop the first one, slowly re-creating the collection from the box, the timeline of a life that wasn't easy, at least in its beginnings. Yet Iola had ended up owning this beautiful house, having money, gorgeous things.

Bracing a hand on the quilt, I looked around the room, took in the pastoral prints on the walls.

Was that the kind of life Iola had ended up living? Did I really want to know? It hurt to read the words of the little girl who'd been sent away, who was alone and afraid that the people who were supposed to love her had instead forgotten about her. It dredged up too many memories, unearthed feelings I didn't want to remember, scenes from my life that I'd been trying to bury for thirty-three years, pain that was pointless now. My parents were both gone, victims of self-destruction.

A drop of moisture slid down my cheek, leaving a trail that was warm and itchy. I closed my eyes, wicked away the salt water with my thumb.

This was stupid. I needed to put the letters back in the box and leave them alone. There was no point rambling around in Iola's life. Reading her thoughts was like dipping a ladle into the toxic waste of my life and pouring it all over myself. It burned as it oozed along fresh skin and old scars.

What good could possibly come of walking through all that pain again?

Swiping the moisture on my jeans, I reached for the stack of letters, slipping one hand on top and one hand underneath, preparing to lift the stack all at once, turn it over, and wiggle it back into the box. It was wrong to invade someone else's prayers. I shouldn't have been looking. These things weren't meant for human eyes.

But why had she kept them? Why had she left them here, carefully stored and boxed all in order?

Did she want *someone* to see, to understand? Did she want to leave behind a record of her life, of all the things she'd prayed for? Did she know someone was coming — someone who would feel this girl's words in the deepest parts of her own soul?

She couldn't have known, of course. There was no way Iola could have predicted that I would come here.

She hadn't left the letters for me.

The best thing would be to gather all the boxes, take them next door, and toss them into the church Dumpster with the rest of the trash from the house. Surely Iola wouldn't want her private thoughts to end up being bargained off in some estate sale, possibly distributed all over the island, a freak show for those who were curious about her, who'd whispered behind their hands while she was playing the church organ.

Those people didn't deserve to see what

was inside these boxes, to have Iola's private life exposed for them to examine, to ridicule, to criticize.

I could empty all the boxes, take the letters to the trash, and put the containers back on the shelves. No one would ever know the difference. When the house was cleaned out or auctioned off or torn down — whatever eventually happened — Iola's private life would remain private. It was the least I could do for her, considering that she'd sheltered us when we had nowhere to go. A final favor for a woman who took the time to think of the grocery delivery boy, even when she was struggling to save her house from rainwater pouring through the roof.

Setting the stack of letters on the bed again, I rose so quickly that the cat sat up, arching his back, startled.

"Good thing I bought trash bags yesterday," I said. "Wonder how many it'll take to empty all those boxes." I could start with the lower ones, but I'd still have to figure out how to get to the upper shelves. Maybe I could stack a couple chairs on top of each other. It might take three to reach the collapsed shelf near the attic hatch. Climbing that high on a tower of chairs didn't sound like the most brilliant plan. If I fell and broke a leg, the kids and I would be in worse shape than we were now.

Where in the world could I get a ladder?

If I asked Ross, he would want to know why I needed it. I'd have to admit that I was working in Iola's house. Knowing Ross, he'd tell the whole surf crowd. Word would get around, and people would be pushing me to let them see. And considering what the deputy had said, and Brother Guilbeau's request that I keep things quiet, asking at the church didn't seem like a great idea either.

I'd just have to start cleaning out the boxes at the bottom and figure out the rest later. Something would come to me. I'd always been good at finding a way to make do with what I had. Pap-pap taught me that. He created the most beautiful things from scraps of wood he picked up here and there. Somewhere in the moves from foster home to foster home those last few years, I'd lost a little driftwood treasure chest he made when we were on Hatteras. I'd helped him cut the wood and hollow out the space inside, not knowing that it was for me. I'd seen him make the boxes before and sell them at the roadside stand where Meemaw peddled vegetables and canned goods from their farm. Tourists loved the boxes as much as they loved Meemaw's blackberry jelly.

While I was sleeping, Pap-pap had created the little treasure chest, pressed shell hash, bits of mother-of-pearl, and chips of softly colored beach glass into the cracks and knotholes, then suspended it in place with clear lacquer so that his creation became a work of art, a piece of the ocean I could hold in the palm of my hand. He'd given me the treasure box on the morning of my thirteenth birthday. Something made from nothing. Inside was a little piece of blue beach glass on a silver chain. *A mermaid's tear,* he called it and patted me awkwardly on the shoulder as I slipped the chain over my neck.

The mermaid's tear. I'd lost it along with the treasure box.

But I hadn't lost the lessons I'd learned, scrambling around construction sites. I knew how to build things. If I had to, I'd gather up some scrap wood and make a ladder.

For now, I'd take care of what I could reach.

I hurried downstairs for trash bags. A sliver of guilt needled as I glanced past the piano room toward the long hall, where the kitchen doorway loomed, the light in there bright and cheery, a slice of black-and-white tile and blue-rimmed china showing. So much work was waiting for me, and I wasn't making enough progress on it. I'd spent too much time messing around upstairs and running off with Ross. The trash bags I'd bought were still on the table in the entry hall, not a single one used to contain the refuse in the kitchen. Now I was headed upstairs again.

What if Brother Guilbeau stopped by to check on me?

I'd just have to be quick. Before anyone else could find it, I was going to bury Iola's junk — and my own — where it would never come up again.

My footsteps echoed through the house as I grabbed the trash bags and ran back up the stairs, taking them two at a time. When I reentered the blue room, the tomcat was lounging in the center of the bed, lying broadside over the letters, the stack now flattened and spread out.

"Get off of there!" I pulled out a trash bag and shooed him with it. "Those aren't yours to . . . lay all over. Go 'way. Shoo."

He hissed and held his ground, his tongue curling behind sharp yellow teeth.

"Shoo!" I batted at him with a pillow, and he arched like a tiny panther, moving to the corner of the bed and growling, the primal sound raising short hairs on my neck. "You keep talking to me like that and I won't feed you anymore." The show of bravado was as much for me as for the cat. "I'm doing her a favor. She wouldn't want those people putting their hands all over this stuff, okay? It's private. You might not know that — well, of course you don't. You're a cat. But I get it. I understand, believe me."

He growled again, his gaze narrow, steady, and eerily bright.

Monitoring him from the corner of my eye, I set the bag nearby and reached for the letters, raking them into a pile with both hands. "You've probably got rabies. Or you've been in so many fights, you're not *all there,* if you know what I mean. That would explain a few things about you."

The cat didn't answer, which was a good thing. When he started talking back in full sentences, I'd know I'd been in this house too long.

A sense of relief slid over me as I pressed the now-disorganized batch of letters between my hands and tried to maneuver the trash bag with one elbow and one pinkie finger. "You wouldn't want to . . . help open this. Would you?"

Something slipped from the papers, snaked over my skin cool and slick, then fell. It landed on Iola's single black shoe and slid to the floor, the sound a metallic tap, then a series of tiny taps — *tap, tap, tap, tap, tap.*

I leaned over, looked down.

A small silver cross was lying on the floor, its surface dark with tarnish, a string of black glass beads slowly slipping from the toe of the shoe onto the floor. *Tap, tap, tap, tap, tap . . .*

"What in the world . . . ?"

Setting the letters atop the trash bag, I reached for the piece of jewelry, avoiding Iola's shoe, as if a single touch might somehow conjure up an unwanted ghost.

A rosary. One so tiny it fit easily in the palm of my hand. It must have been tucked inside the papers, shaken loose when the cat scattered them around or when I scraped them back together.

Turning it over in my hands, I studied the image, the outline of a man barely pressed into the thin metal. I ran my finger over it, felt the arms and legs. The tiny bump of the nails, the ribbon of the crown of thorns, the banner above the head.

My fist closed around it, and I swiveled toward the closet, toward the boxes. Other things might be hiding among the letters. Things that shouldn't be thrown away . . .

"No," I whispered, bringing my hand to my face, breathing the words over silver and tarnish and glass. "All those boxes . . ."

Each would have to be checked, sorted, taken care of one by one.

"Okay. Okay, I see."

Disposing of a person's history wasn't so simple, not as easy as gathering it up and packing it into bags. Valuable things hid among the scraps of a life. They could be anywhere. This job would take time, care.

Whether I liked it or not, I'd been chosen to do the work.

Lowering myself slowly to the edge of the bed, I reached for one of the letters, opened it, took in the uneven print, and turned my attention to the words, to the life of Iola Anne Poole.

Nearby, the cat began to purr.

CHAPTER 10

I was deep in the fourth box on the bottom row, the letters from 1936 painting a world I'd never known existed. Iola was thirteen, still living in the mission school in downtown New Orleans, where nuns cared for and educated children of color. That was Iola's crime, I'd figured out. She was a mixed-race child in a society that only wanted black and white.

Iola was better off than many of the charges at the orphanage, however, as her board and education there were paid for, unlike those of the orphans found on the streets or dropped off by desperate families who couldn't feed them as the Depression raged on. Children with families to sponsor them received packages and letters in the mail, were given lessons in music and foreign languages, and were sent home to visit on holidays if their families could transport them.

At thirteen, Iola had come to realize that her prayers of waking up to look like Aurelia, another girl at the school, would never be answered. She had adjusted to life with the nuns and the other children. But she still missed home, where her mother and grandmother managed a large house near the French Quarter for Monsieur, whose daughter, Isabelle, had grown up alongside Iola. Iola went home once each year when Monsieur and Madame, Isabelle's stepmother, were away vacationing in Charleston. Iola hadn't seen Isabelle in the years she'd been at school, and she still missed her friend. In her prayer letters, Iola repeatedly pleaded with God to persuade Monsieur and Madame to allow her to come home, particularly when life was difficult in the school, when the other children were cruel or the nuns were harsh.

I understood Iola's feelings, her yearning, her fear. Life with strangers isn't easy when you're just a child yourself. You can try your best to be good, to be perfect, to look at those people with eyes that say, *Love me, please. I need it.* But love doesn't always come your way. Eventually you learn to stop taking the risk. By the time I'd finally ended up with a foster family who really wanted me, at sixteen, I couldn't open myself up to them the way they needed me to.

The Lathrops were empty nesters with their daughters' show horses standing in the pasture, and they loved the fact that I was a good rider. They taught me everything I needed to know about riding show jumpers and helped me get a scholarship at a little college with an equestrian team. I repaid them by believing my freshman English professor when he told me I was special, talented, and that he'd never met anyone like me. I didn't even go home to the Lathrops again after I got pregnant. I knew how disappointed in me they would be. Instead, I tracked down my sister and moved in with her. Like most things with Gina, it didn't last very long.

Reading Iola's letters, I wondered if she'd ever had the chance to go home again or if she eventually traveled off into the world on her own, as I had.

Iola enjoyed learning at the orphan school. Her writing had changed from uneven print to artful cursive, her thoughts slowly transforming from those of a child to those of an adolescent. The nuns had discovered that she was exceptionally bright, talented both in music and language. In the four years she'd been there, she had learned to speak proper French, begun instruction in Latin, and studied music. She'd been selected for a choral group that performed at various events around town, where ladies' societies and audiences at all-white churches were delighted with the angelic singing of colored children who had been lifted from their lowly stations by the compassion of nuns and generosity of benefactors.

During her snatches of contact with the outside world, Iola had learned two things about herself. She revealed them through the final letter in the box, written just before Christmas, 1936.

. . . hear them whispering, the ladies behind their hands. I catch bits and pieces as we file past after our singing. I see them watching me, craning beneath their broad-brimmed hats, fanning their sweating chins. Their voices buzz by my ear like the hum of a dragonfly, whirling along a riverside among the cattails. ". . . at that one, how pale she is. No surprise that she's been sent away. . . . Someone's bastard . . . will be quite a beauty . . . Wouldn't want her around my home, either. Too much temptation there . . . an anathema, really . . ."

Anathema. When we are back in school, I find Sister Marguerite so that I might ask her, what does this word mean? Her baby-leaf-green eyes twinkle as she looks up from scrubbing the floors in the bathroom. She sings, even as she cleans the mess from too many children in so small a space. I ask, why does she sing when the work is hard? "All labor is joy," she tells me. "It is not washing dirty floors, but the feet of Jesus, Iola. All we do for others, we do for the One Most High."

I think of this for a moment. Is it possible that all service is worship?

I do not ask her this but instead I ask about the word I have heard today, *anathema.*

"My, my, Iola Anne, but you do come to me with the most interesting questions," Sister Marguerite says. "You've the intelligence of a girl much older than thirteen. Where did you hear that word?"

"At the Women's Aid Society. A lady looked at me and said it," I tell her.

Sister Marguerite's smile fades. When she pauses to turn my way, moisture clings along the bottoms of her eyes, like dew in a trumpet vine. "It is a complicated word," she answers. "Not one our heavenly Father would be pleased to have us dignify with thought or conversation. We are his children, each knit together as we should be. We must go by the name our Father has given us — Beloved — not by the names which others might seek to place upon us." She brushes a wrist across her cheeks as she returns to her work. She sniffles softly. I see that I have hurt her, and I should not ask about this again. I would never wound Sister Marguerite. She is kind to me.

I suppose it matters little, Father, as I heard Sister Agnes whisper yesterday when we filed out of choral practice, "It's time we must replace Iola Anne. She's developing." There was an emphasis on the final word. I felt her frowning at me, her wrinkled mouth like the navel of a Christmas orange. At first, I did not understand. I have learned so very much in the choral group. I have even begun to master the organ, not so different from Monsieur's piano. I strained to hear the whisper, as Sister Agnes went on with her thought. "The audiences prefer children who are young, too young to be out working for themselves. It pleases them to feel as though they're donating to the helpless. Keeping urchins off the streets, you know."

"Certainly," said Sister Mary Constantine. "It is a shame, though. Iola Anne has such a beautiful voice. . . ." Sister Mary Constantine is pleased that she chose me for the choral group, and I have done very well. Just yesterday, she promised a new hymn for me to sing, a difficult one.

I will not be learning the new hymn now, Father. I know it. I wonder, what will they do with me instead? Were I an orphan, they would be looking to place me in a cotton mill or tobacco house, but of course I am still here because Monsieur has paid my keep. I wonder, will I be here forever?

I pray that soon you will bring me home to Mama Tee and Maman and Isabelle, Father. I pray that you will ever remind me to answer only to the name you have given me, not to the words men may offer.

I am your child. My Father has named me. I am Beloved.

Your daughter,
Iola Anne

A sound broke the silence. Something ringing . . . an alarm clock, maybe. It faded, then came again.

A hot, sharp lightning of panic rushed through me. The doorbell. I scrambled off the bed, bouncing the mattress and causing the cat to jump to the ground and run for cover.

"Oh no! Oh, shoot-shoot-shoot." I froze with my hands in the air over the quilt. If that was Brother Guilbeau or someone from the church, I was dead. I had stuff strung everywhere, and I wasn't even supposed to be up here. Anyone seeing the kitchen would think I was either lazy or a complete liar. I'd said I could handle the job, no problem. Instead, I'd allowed myself to be sidetracked over and over.

Or what if it was the sheriff's deputies, back to . . . investigate something? If I opened the door, they would bulldoze their way past me like they owned the place. They'd paw through everything and find the letters. . . .

Think, think, think. Think, Tandi. Think of something. The contents of three boxes lay scattered in unkempt piles on the bed. I hadn't even been trying to fold the letters or prepare to fit them back in the boxes. I hadn't put one box away before getting out another. I'd just grabbed one letter and then the next, one box after another, reading hurriedly, hungrily, anxious to discover Iola's story, to learn how life had brought her from an orphanage in New Orleans to here.

"Okay, be calm. Be calm." I could finesse my way out of this. Somehow.

Moving to the window, I took a peek at the driveway, but if a car was out there, it had been pulled through and parked near the old garage building. Between the thick growth of trees and the porch roof, I couldn't see a thing. A passing glance in the dresser mirror confirmed that, on top of everything else, I was a wreck. My hair hung in a frizz-ball ponytail, my eyes were red and puffy, and my cheeks were streaked with dried tear trails. I'd been through a meat grinder of emotions this morning, and it showed. I'd promised myself I would only stay here with the boxes a few more minutes, but instead I'd been here for hours.

My heart pounded as I smoothed back my hair, slapped and pinched my cheeks, then hurried to the stairs. The old rotary bell clanged again, the visitor thumbing the trigger, then letting it free. Once, twice, a third time. Whoever it was had no intention of going away.

"Hang on," I called from the midlanding, then winced as the treads popped and creaked underfoot, the noise ridiculously loud. What if the visitor heard it and knew

189

I'd been upstairs?

A story began spinning, part fact, part invention.

The cat. I heard the cat up there and then the water running . . .

It's all taken care of now, though. Nothing to worry about. No, no reason to go up there. The faucets are old and they must have slipped on a little. I tied the handles closed so it wouldn't happen again.

The tapestry wove itself, threads intertwining with impressive speed.

Behind the veiled glass sidelights in the entryway, a human outline shifted back, then forward, disappearing as the visitor reached for the bell, then reappearing.

Someone tall . . . a man . . . dark clothes. Too thin to be Brother Guilbeau.

Wrong kind of hat for a sheriff's deputy. This guy had on a ball cap.

I reached for the knob, flipped the ornate-looking brass slider that secured the lock from the inside, pulled the door open.

A UPS man. The man in brown. Middle-aged, friendly looking, clean-cut, with a gray-dusted mustache. He had a box under one arm and a plastic grocery bag dangling from the other. We stood staring at each other for a moment while I caught my breath, thinking, *Seriously? All that panic for a UPS delivery? Whew, thank God . . .*

He blinked. "Where's Miss Iola Anne?" He lifted the grocery bag in an unconscious way that told me it was for her. The outline of a flour sack, two cans, and several bananas showed through the thin layer of plastic. "I brought her something."

It dawned on me that I was about to be the bearer of bad news. "She passed away a little over a week ago. I'm sorry. I guess you didn't know." I stepped out and peeked around the corner of the house. He'd pulled his truck in by the old garage. He probably knew from experience just where to stop so that he could back up and turn around without hitting trees or the weathered concrete hitching posts with the iron mermaid finials.

"Old Mrs. Poole." He let his head fall forward, looking crestfallen. The dry river of a sweat stain drew a faint, uneven line around the rim of his hat. I focused on it a moment, thinking that it probably wasn't easy schlepping packages in the thick summer humidity here. "I'm gonna miss her. She was one of my favorite stops."

I felt a surprising backwash of grief. It seemed strangely sad that I was trying to understand Iola now, after my chance to meet her was gone. "Did you know her well?"

I shouldn't have asked, I guess. The question made it obvious that I was a stranger here.

"She was one of my *Gutennannies.*"

"Your *what?*"

Lifting the grocery sack again, he gave me a sheepish look. "*Guten* nannies. That's German for 'sweet little ladies who can really cook.' I'd bring a few supplies by here if the grocery store was clearing out over-ripe fruit, and when I'd come back this way for a delivery in a day or two, she'd have beignets or cookies in the freezer waiting for me. Put Iola's banana beignets on the dashboard, let 'em warm up in the sun a couple hours, and mmm-mmm-mmmh." His eyes closed, and he shook his head back and forth, as if he could taste them now.

"That's nice." So Iola hadn't been the hermit that everyone thought. She was friends with the UPS man. "I guess she got deliveries quite a bit, then?" What could she possibly have been receiving, and where did she put it? The downstairs was cluttered with boxes and belongings, but most of it seemed to be old stuff.

"Yeah, fairly often." The wrinkles deepened around his eyes, and I had the sense that there was something he wasn't telling me. "Especially since she quit driving a couple years ago. The first year I was on this route, she had a little red Dodge Dart she ran around town in. It was vintage, but slick as a whistle. She must've been in her late eighties by then. Then one week I came and the Dart was gone. She'd backed into a post by Burrus Market down in Hatteras Village, and she got rid of the car the next day. Said she was afraid she'd have an accident and hurt somebody."

I nodded along, indicating neither that I knew the story nor that I didn't, but it sounded like the Iola I'd begun to know from the letters upstairs.

"Felt sorry for her after that." Setting the box down for a minute, he whisked the cap off his head and wiped his brow with a tan hankie, then stuffed it back into his pocket. I hadn't seen a man carry a hankie in years. "She was lonely. Kept my number right there on her refrigerator. I'd pick things up in town for her if she needed them. I'll miss that high, squeaky voice coming over my cell phone. 'Mr. Mullins? I do so hate to trouble you at home, but if it isn't too much bother, when you're out in your truck . . .' She never could quite grasp the fact that the phone was traveling *with* me in the truck. She always thought she was calling me at home. I guess when you've been around since the days of steam trains and milk wagons, some things just don't seem possible."

"Guess not." I couldn't help thinking about all the evolutions Iola had seen in her life — the changes in the world, the events, the cultural shifts. Dictators, wars, men on the moon. She'd been born in a different universe than this one. Her grandmother was a slave. My mind couldn't quite grasp that. . . .

Were all those things recorded in the boxes upstairs, her thoughts about the world carefully chronicled in prayer?

I wanted to know her, to understand her. To solve the mystery of her.

I felt the blue room tugging at me again, but I wasn't going up there, other than to put away the mess I'd made. Not today. I'd lucked out when this visitor was only a delivery driver, but I couldn't make that mistake again. I needed this job.

The UPS man glanced at his watch and thumbed over his shoulder. "The mailbox is stuffed full outside. It's hanging open a little. I can run and grab it for you, if you want. I used to do that for Miss Iola Anne from time to time, especially this last year or so. She got to where she didn't come out of the house much. I think it was hard for her to make it down the porch steps." He indicated the eight wooden steps that led to the front walk.

I squinted at them. Iola didn't seem to have any problem climbing the stairs in the house. She was capable of hauling drip buckets back and forth to the bathroom. She could've made it down those outside steps if she'd wanted to. There was a reason she had kept herself locked away here. Maybe it was just that she was afraid she'd be taken to a rest home.

Maybe there was something more.

Her boxes might tell me. . . .

"No, that's all right. I'll pick up the mail."

The driver nodded, then handed over a package the size of four shoe boxes put together. Surprised by its weight, I shifted it to my hip, and both of us hovered there on Iola's porch, not seeming to know what to say.

"Someone probably ought to open that up," he suggested finally. "Usually when she bought stuff, she had it billed to her. She didn't believe in credit cards — she told me that once. She had accounts with shops all up and down the Outer Banks. A couple times she gave me cash, and I dropped off payments for her, but mostly she paid through the mail, I think. Anyway, there's probably a bill in that package. Whoever's looking after her affairs might want to take care of it. The stores on the island are operating on a shoestring since the last hurricane. What stores made it through, that is."

"Sure . . . I'll see that it's taken care of."

"You a family member?"

"No. Just a friend." I did feel like one at this point. A friend.

Clicking his tongue, he surveyed the Confederate jasmine and climbing roses pressing through the railings, ripe with the determined growth of a new spring. "She was a pretty lady, even at ninety years old. Had the brightest silvery-colored eyes. One time when I came, she brought out an old black-and-white photo. She told me she'd been sorting through some things and came across it. I'll never forget her handing that thing to me and saying, 'I was a looker, wasn't I?' And she was. That was quite a picture. She was posed like Jane Russell in the hay, and there was a big ol' palomino horse nibbling on her ear. She looked like a pinup girl. I gave it back to her and said, 'Miss Iola, you're still a looker.' She laughed and told me if she was forty years younger,

I'd have to watch out. She was something else. I think she had stories she never shared with anyone. There was a lot that folks around here didn't know about her."

I set the package by my feet and leaned against the doorframe. "Did she ever tell you where she came from? How she ended up here in this house, I mean?"

He shook his head. "No, she didn't. Every once in a while, she'd mention something — a certain kind of car she had at one time or another, or someplace she'd been, but that was about it. She always wanted to make sure she wasn't holding me up from my work. That's the way she was. She thought about other people first — just like getting rid of that car. She didn't want to hurt anybody with it. She . . ." He stopped, reconsidered whatever he was about to say, then changed the subject. "I'll sure miss Iola Anne and those banana beignets. Melt in your mouth. Like little bits of heaven." He extended the grocery sack my way as if he'd suddenly remembered he was holding it. "Here, do something with this stuff, okay? I don't want to look at it today."

"Okay." I understood, really.

After he was gone, I scooted the box farther into the vestibule so I could close the door. Then I peeked into the grocery

197

sack, letting the scent of overripe bananas waft out.

There was an old metal recipe box on Iola's counter. Maybe I would see if the recipe for banana beignets was inside. I'd never been much of a cook, but I'd watched Meemaw make beignets years ago, helped her squeeze the dough through the cutoff corner of a plastic bag into hot oil. I could cook them while I was cleaning in Iola's kitchen.

Maybe I would. It couldn't be that hard. When the kids came home, I'd have something special waiting in the cottage. Something homemade, smelling of cooking and love. We could sit down and eat the sweets, laugh and lick the powdered sugar off our fingers. Zoey and I could talk without yelling, the three of us acting like a family for once.

I could freeze a batch for the UPS man, call him and let him know to stop by when he had a chance — I had a surprise for him. A last little gift from Iola.

I'd turned toward the kitchen before I remembered the package. I'd promised the driver I would make sure the bill was taken care of. Aside from that, I was curious about what was inside.

The keys in my pocket worked well

enough to slit the tape, and I folded back the thick cardboard flaps, revealing layers of soft white tissue paper with glitter infused. Underneath, the box was divided into a beehive of small cardboard cells, two dozen in all, and in each one, something strangely familiar.

Tiny wings of colored glass, a soft twist of ribbon, a gold ring, brass bells. I slid my fingers into one of the cells, pinched the tip of a wing, wiggled the tiny hummingbird into my hand. Cupped in my palm, it was surprisingly heavy, the body made of molded metal, the wings and the passion vine formed from delicate stained glass.

"What did she plan to do with you?" I whispered, holding the bird up and looking at it eye to eye. "Who needs two dozen suncatchers?"

The paper price tag twisted back and forth on a string, a flash of gold alternating with white. Forty-five dollars . . . times two dozen suncatchers . . .

"Over a thousand dollars' worth of stained-glass doodads." I caught the tag with my fingers, turned it over so that I could read the gold label on the other side, but I didn't need to. I knew what it would say.

Sandy's Seashell Shop
An Ocean of Possibilities

CHAPTER 11

I dawdled in the field of salt meadow hay, watching a pair of river otters frolic in a slough lined with saw grass and spike rushes. In the parking lot at Bink's, the cab of Paul Chastain's truck was empty. I was hoping to catch him as he came out — to just *happen* to be passing by with the ladder problem in mind and *happen* to see him there and *happen* to ask if I could borrow one of the ladders that I'd seen in his pickup the day he came to mow.

I looked down at the bundle in my hand. The beignets, still warm, had soaked through and made three round grease stains on the napkin I'd wrapped them in. Bringing them was a stupid idea. They were a dead giveaway that I wasn't strolling by Bink's at random. But it also seemed like, given the ugly parking-lot scene with Ross, some sort of apology was due. Paul was a nice guy, and he didn't deserve to have Ross giving him the stiff arm just for talking to me about J.T. and turtle camp.

The front door opened at Bink's, and the bright colors of a Hawaiian shirt caught the sunlight beneath the overhanging porch. I hurried on to the parking lot as Paul exited the store backward, still talking to someone inside. When he turned around, there I was, passing by his truck.

"Well, hey!" he said, his lips spreading into a smile as he came closer. He had something pinned between his teeth — the stick from a sucker — and he was talking around it, a bulge in his cheek. If he thought less of me after our last meeting in the parking lot, it didn't show.

"Hey." I was smiling back before I knew it. Something about a grown man not ashamed to carry on a conversation with a sucker wadded in his cheek was funny. "How's the crab hunting?" There were buckets in the back of his pickup again — at least a dozen this time. "You planning on feeding an army or just doing science experiments on a larger scale?" I pointed to his cargo.

He shook his head. "Working today." Setting his drink on the tailgate, he tipped one of the white plastic pails so I could see into it. There were plugs of grass inside.

"Weeding gardens?" I took a guess. He didn't look like he was dressed for garden work. Today, he had on a pink-and-green shirt with frogs on it, camp shorts that might have been camo-colored once but were bleached to pale tones of cream and peach, and heavy rubber hiking boots. His freckled legs were sunburned in streaks where he'd apparently missed with the sun-block, and a foldable camp-style shovel hung over his shoulder on a nylon strap. All in all, he looked like a cross between a mountain climber and a *Captain Kangaroo* character.

"Stabilizing frontal dunes and valuable boundary areas." He cleared his throat and deepened his tone to give the words an exaggerated importance. "The park service doesn't pay me to crab hunt."

"Oh, I see." I pressed a hand to my chest, pretending to rethink my earlier question. I remembered now. He'd said he worked part-time for the park service.

Shrugging, he lifted his palms into the air. "If a crab trap or a fishing line *happens* to fall into the water *while* I'm in the perfor-mance of my duty, well, I can't exactly help that, now can I?" One of the buckets rattled, and he cast a wry, one-sided smile my way, a little twinkle in his caramel-brown eyes.

"Well, I suppose not." I stood on tiptoe, and he reached for the bucket to show me. "I guess you keep the crab traps and fishing lines all baited, just in *case* one slips into the water . . . *accidentally.*"

"They work better with bait on them."

I peeked into the bucket. Crawdads. "Looks like there's a problem with crawdad seines slipping out of the truck too, huh?" I knew all about seining crawdads. We'd lived on a canal in east Texas once. I remembered walking along the bank with Daddy, helping to pull the seine, netting up dinner.

Paul lifted his hands, palms up, his shoulders rising. "Darnedest thing, really. What slips out usually depends on where you're working. I was over in the Tidewater today, just down from a crawfish farm, and those seines get rowdy when there's a mudbug hole nearby. When a net wiggles off into the water, what can you do but pull it back out? Learned that from my dad. He was a county sheriff down in Alabama, so he rambled around in the backwoods a lot."

"I take it there were also a few fishing poles and a crawdad seine or two in the back of the sheriff's car." I caught a whiff of banana beignets and noticed that Paul was giving the napkin a curious look.

"I do come by it honestly," he admitted.

"You know what they say about the seines of the father . . ." He blinked slowly, holding back his lopsided Tootsie Pop smile, waiting for the pun to work.

"Ohhh . . . that was bad." The joke pulled a groan from me, but I found myself thinking about Paul's father, wondering what kind of man he was and trying to imagine him. Was he redheaded and fair skinned, like Paul? I pictured him a little like Andy Griffith, with little boy Paul in the Opie role. I had the strangest urge to ask Paul about it — to sift out a scene of boy and man walking down the levee in the summer grass.

Instead, I somewhat awkwardly handed over the napkin with the beignets.

"Ooooh," Paul appraised appreciatively as he unfolded the napkin and examined the sugar-dusted contents. "These look a whole lot better than crawdads. Can we work a trade?"

"I wanted to thank you for being so good to J.T., and . . . I have a favor to ask."

"Okay . . . shoot," he replied, as in, *Whatever it is, I'm there,* but he didn't look at me. He was busy comparing the beignets and deciding which one to eat first. I wondered if he'd forgotten that he had a lollipop in his mouth. The thought seemed to occur to him at the last minute, and he quickly extricated the Tootsie Pop, then dropped it into one of the buckets.

I got around to my original reason for being there. "I was wondering if I could borrow that tall ladder you had in your truck the other day." He gave me a curious look, and I quickly added, "There isn't anything like that around the cottage, and I need one for a day or two."

"Don't imagine Iola did much ladder climbing at her age." He sampled one of the beignets, closing his eyes and smiling as he chewed. "Ohhh, man, these are heaven. I've had some good beignets, but these are top-notch. What's in there? Bananas?"

I nodded, an unexpectedly light, airy sensation fluttering through my chest. I couldn't remember the last time I'd cooked anything that wasn't from a box, but it'd felt good to take the supplies from the UPS driver and create something warm and fresh. Sort of a new beginning from an old ending. A rebirth.

I had a feeling Iola would've liked that. Maybe she was rubbing off on me a little. Iola . . . and Sister Marguerite. It felt good to do something good for someone else. To add a few deep-fried droplets of kindness to the world. A little act of service. *Is it pos-*

sible that all service is worship? The words were still in my head.

"It was Iola's recipe." I slanted a glance toward the store, thinking of the last time I'd been in there, the way Bink had sneered and crossed his arms when Iola's name was mentioned. How could anyone dislike the sweet little woman who made beignets for the UPS driver?

"I thought I'd heard she was from down in New Orleans, so I guess it makes sense — beignets," Paul mused. "When I passed through the church office a few days after she died, they were talking about her final arrangements. That was how I knew she'd left the house to the church and what gave me the idea of dropping over to do the mowing."

"Is that where she was buried — New Orleans?" It bothered me that I didn't know. That I still hadn't heard a thing about her funeral. It seemed like she deserved something more than to just . . . disappear.

"I think so. Brother Guilbeau said she wanted to be buried in some kind of family plot."

"Oh." A sense of loss struck me suddenly, and the scent of beignets, beach grass, and crawfish turned cloying. I had the urge to tell Paul about the closet, the boxes, the shelf dangling fourteen feet in the air. By my count, the glass box teetering on the broken shelf had probably been placed there just last year. By a woman in her nineties, with no ladder.

I backed away instead of sharing the story. "Anyway, a ladder loan would be great."

Paul pinched a beignet between two fingers, held it up, and admired it from all angles. "Sure. I'll stick the ladder in the back of the truck tonight, then drop it by tomorrow after I'm done at the school. I only have classes through the morning — helping to fill in for a teacher who's taking care of a sister with cancer. Anyway, ladder deliveries are no problem. Is noon soon enough? Otherwise, I'll run it by in the morning." He toasted me with the beignet, then popped it into his mouth. Smiling, he murmured, "Mmmm."

My blue mood lifted like a cloud rolling offscreen in fast-motion video. "I'll bet your mama loves you." I imagined a dinner table scene — the happy mom, the friendly fishing dad, and redheaded Paul, all gathered around a big platter of crawfish, rice, and garden-fresh vegetables, a little dog sitting patiently on the floor waiting for someone to toss a crumb his way.

"Yes, she does." He nodded, then popped

the last beignet into his mouth and noisily licked his fingers. His mama hadn't emphasized manners. He seemed like the type who would've grown up with brothers, a family filled with men, where table manners and fashion choices meant nothing.

He was giving me a curious look now, probably wondering what I was thinking.

"Well, okay, thanks. Noon's fine for the ladder. I appreciate the loan. If I'm not there when you come by tomorrow, could you just leave it on the porch?" I needed to keep the schedule loose in case Ross called, and I also had the box of suncatchers to return to Sandy's Seashell Shop. If Iola's estate ended up suspended in some kind of legal battle, they might never get paid for that box.

"Sure. No problem. You mean the porch of the main house or the bungalow?"

There was that funny word again, *bungalow*. And why had he mentioned the main house? Did he know I was working there? Maybe Brother Guilbeau had told him. . . .

The school bus whirled around the corner, then stopped at the edge of Bink's parking lot and let off kids. J.T. wasn't among them, and neither was Zoey. I hoped that meant they'd ridden home with Rowdy, but still, we needed to talk about the two of them running all over the place without letting me know. That talk probably wouldn't go well even with the beignets, but last night, thinking even for a few hours that I might never see my kids again had awakened me from the sleep of my own life. Something had to change between Zoey, J.T., and me. The more time I spent with Iola's boxes, the more I could see what a mess we were.

I answered Paul's question, then said good-bye and hurried off across the salt meadow to get back home before the kids made it there with Rowdy. With any luck, I'd still have time to lock Iola's house, bring the beignets over to the cottage, and set us up for an afternoon snack and a family conversation, instead of a shouting match.

But when I reached the cottage, Zoey was on her way out the door with her backpack over her shoulder and a towel under one arm. She had on short shorts and a flowered tank top I'd never seen before. She was all legs and curves. At a glance she could've been eighteen instead of fourteen.

I recognized the MO of a little girl trying to look way older on the outside than she was on the inside. When I was Zoey's age, I'd figured out that the right clothes could get you all kinds of attention, and I liked it. It felt good to know that someone could desire me, want to be with me. Want me.

Zoey gave me a deer-in-the-headlights look, and then her eyes turned hard. Icy. Rowdy was sitting in his Jeep out front, his head bobbing to music amped so loud that the bass was creating a minor earthquake.

"I've gotta go." Zoey made a preemptive strike, telling, not asking.

"Wait . . . hold on a minute." Several quick steps brought me to the bottom of the porch stairs, blocking her exit path unless she wanted to hop over the railing. Which she looked like she might.

"What?" A flash of lashes and a quick tilt of the head. Her hips jutted to one side. I knew the posture. Right now, Zoey looked too much like Gina. My big sister could give attitude like nobody I'd ever known. No matter how wrong she was, she was right. Zoey huffed and jerked her chin toward the house. "The dork's inside. I brought him home, okay? I made sure he's all safe in there, since it's not like *you're* ever here to —"

"Stop calling him that." What was wrong with her lately? She'd been the little mommy since J.T. was born. He adored her, always had. "And all I did was walk over to Bink's for a minute. I've been here all day, waiting for you to come home so we can *talk.*"

211

"Whatever." Zoey fingered the thick silver chain holding an oversize class ring suspended over way too much cleavage. When had my little girl gotten cleavage? When had she become so comfortable showing it? "I figured you'd be gone with *Ross* again."

Suddenly I was on the defensive. "Yesterday wasn't Ross's fault, Zoey."

"Of course not. Nothing's ever *his* fault." She rolled her head to the other side, hair skimming over a bare shoulder in a silky curtain. "But don't worry about it, okay? We're fine on our own. We're *always* fine." She blinked hard, her dark lashes matted with moisture.

The words sliced through all the soft places, and I saw my sister again, saying the cruelest things, knowing right where to aim to cause the most pain. "What, like those clothes?" I swept a hand in the air between us, indicating the new outfit. "You know what those clothes say, Zoey? Did he buy those for you?" Rowdy must have bought the clothes. Zoey didn't have any money.

"Like mother, like daughter." She trotted down the steps and shoved past me, striding toward the car.

"Zoey, get back here!" I hollered, but she just circled the Jeep, slipped in, and closed the door hard.

Rowdy stretched a hand across the seat and strung his fingers into her hair. He didn't even turn the vehicle around but backed all the way to the street at high speed like he was afraid I'd jump in their exit path. I could imagine the things Zoey had told him about me. He probably thought he was saving her from the claws of a she-devil.

Frustration drove me back and forth across the porch, furious, sad, helpless. I wanted to tie Zoey to a kitchen chair, lock her in her room, force her to listen. She was better than this. Somehow, I had to find a way to show her, to make her see, like Sister Marguerite had with Iola, that she was beautiful, that she was worthy.

Standing here with Iola's prayer boxes so close, I wanted to be better than I was. I wanted to stop running blindly down all the same paths. The thought nipped and bit, hungry and angry, painful and unnerving. I didn't know how to be anything except what I had always been.

A car pulled in soon after Rowdy's Jeep squealed away. I gathered my wits and walked down the steps, meeting the vehicle as the driver turned off the engine and opened his door. He was middle-aged, balding on top, dressed in black pants and a

white jacket with some sort of emblem on
it. His round-cheeked face made him seem
likable enough, but a ripple of concern
inched upward inside me. "Can I help you?"

"I just came by to look the property over."
He grabbed a clipboard off the dash.

"Oh . . . are you from the church?" Thank
goodness I'd put the prayer boxes away after
the UPS driver had surprised me.

The embroidered label on the man's
jacket was from an investment company. He
tucked the clipboard under one arm and
twirled a pen from finger to finger like a
tiny baton, then pointed it at the cottage.
"You staying in the rental?"

"Yes." Up close, he didn't seem so nice. It
was an old horse trader's trick, not giving a
direct answer to a question, and right now
he wasn't really looking at me, but *through*
me, like I was getting in the way of his
agenda, whatever it was. I thumbed over my
shoulder toward Fairhope Fellowship. "You
might want to go by the church because
Brother Guilbeau —"

"Just taking a gander at the place for the
county commission." He cut me off, nodding along with his own words as if he
wanted to make sure I swallowed them
whole. "Looks like the hurricane damage
was never fixed. Imagine the place is a

health hazard by now. Water through the roof, mold all over the place, no doubt. Terrible to lose a historic home like this one, but it's obviously listing toward the west. Too bad the owner didn't keep it up properly over the years. Shame when these aging houses have to be torn down. Do you have a lease on the rental, and for how long, if I might ask?"

"Torn dow — what?" I was possessed with a sudden, fierce defensiveness of Iola and her home. Who was this man? He had some nerve, standing here talking like that when the woman was barely in the ground. I was no expert in social niceties, but I'd been on the receiving end of a down-the-nose look too many times not to recognize one. *Her name was Iola,* I wanted to yell. *Iola Anne Poole. She went to sleep in the blue room and never woke up.* Instead, I said, "But I thought I was supposed to clean . . ."

"You have a key to the main house?" He started toward it as if he was accustomed to people following at his heel. I recognized the drill. Trammel treated people this way.

I liked this guy less by the minute.

"No. I don't. And I have somewhere I need to be, actually. I'm sorry. Maybe Brother Guilbeau can help you. His office is next door." I pointed to the church again.

215

The man swiveled at the waist and peered over his glasses.

"I have to go. I'm sorry." I hoped I wasn't making a mistake, but something told me to stay as far away from this guy as possible. Without waiting for an answer, I rushed back to the porch and stepped inside.

I nearly collided with J.T., who was clearly on his way out. Like Zoey, he stopped stock-still, blinking as if he'd been caught.

"Where are you going?"

"No place." A guilty look.

"To Bink's, so you can hang around, maybe?"

He shrugged, the answer clear enough.

"J.T., listen, I know you like it there, but we don't need everyone in our business right now, okay?" In view of our latest visitor, that was doubly true. If that man knew we didn't have a lease and were overdue on the rent, I had a feeling we'd be out quicker than you could say, *Pack your suitcase.* "We just . . . the three of us have to stick together. We don't want people checking up on us, understand?"

"But can I still go carry out their trash?" His enormous blue eyes pleaded for me to say yes, to let him continue his trips to Bink's.

I rested a hand on his head. "What are

216

you doing with all those leftover dough-nuts?"

He squirmed under my fingers, looked down at his feet, and kicked a rock across the porch. "I take 'em to school."

"Why?" Zoey had been packing PB and J sandwiches for lunch each morning because that was all we had around. They could get water free at school. It was hard to believe things had come to this, but they had.

Slipping his hands into his pockets, he shook his head.

"Why, J.T.?"

" 'Cause."

"Because *why?*"

"Because then we don't use all the bread, and you don't have to pay for more." His eyes rolled upward under a knot of blond brows, watching for my reaction.

I felt sick. I'd been fussing at the kids about every bit of wasted food since we'd come here, especially early on when I was still getting off the pills and wondering if I'd make it through.

Now my little boy was surviving on stale doughnuts so I wouldn't have to feed him.

"Well, there's plenty of food now." I swallowed the tears. How in the world had we ended up here? I was better than this, smarter than this. How many times had I promised myself that I would never be like my mother and Gina? I'd be the one who held down a job, made a living, didn't take charity from anyone, made a life instead of just an existence.

But this wasn't a life. This was desperation. We could be kicked out of the cottage tomorrow, end up on the street. Maybe the church didn't really own this place after all. Maybe it really was about to be torn down. If Ross changed his mind about taking us in, we could end up sleeping in the SUV, and there wouldn't be a thing I could do about it.

I had to find a job. A real job — something better than just cleaning out Iola's house. And I had to do it now.

CHAPTER 12

In the morning, I was on the porch of the Hatteras Village library, waiting in the lingering morning mist when the librarian opened the door. Three minutes later, I was on a computer, poring over web listings, looking for any place new that might take a chance on hiring someone with no references. I couldn't exactly put Trammel's name down as my last employer, and over the Internet, it was hard to successfully deploy the story that I was a recently divorced stay-at-home mom just reentering the workforce. Growing up, I'd learned that the more you stick to one story, the easier it is. Gina never figured that out. When things were bad at home, she invented one wild tale after another, letting out so many lines that she eventually hung herself in them.

I was finished on the library computer and heading for the door before I really wanted to be. There wasn't anywhere else to apply.

Stopping by the front alcove, I considered my next move. If a job didn't magically come through soon, I'd have to leave Iola's place and Hatteras Island behind. The idea hollowed me out in a way I wasn't prepared for. I felt like I'd failed, like there was something I was supposed to unearth here, something I was meant to find in that big house, but I hadn't been looking in all the right places.

"The builders positioned that so it points true." The librarian motioned to a compass rose built into the tile floor of the alcove. "Follow the north arrow and you'll be heading due north." She gave the tile work a fond look as she moved past me with a bottle of Windex and a rag in hand.

I studied the compass rose for a minute, waiting for the librarian to clean the glass door. If only true north were so easy to find in real life. I needed someone to show me which way to go, what to do now.

The librarian must have read the desperation on my face. "Can I help you with anything else?" She offered a kind, accommodating look.

I took the opportunity to ask for directions to Sandy's Seashell Shop. Nothing was too hard to find in Hatteras Village, but I couldn't afford to waste gas wandering around, and I hadn't noticed the store during previous trips down the island with Ross. I wanted to drop off the box of hummingbirds while I was here. If Sandy's Seashell Shop's financials looked anything like mine, they'd probably appreciate it.

The librarian pointed out the door. "Just keep on going around the corner. It's on the sound just up from the ferry landing. The storm took out their sign, but you can't miss the place if you know what to look for. Cute little I-style house with yellow siding. It was built around the turn of the century by a Dr. Parnell, but it's a shop now, of course. Blue Adirondack chairs out front and a wraparound deck with ice cream tables. I'm not sure they're officially back open yet. It's been a nightmare around here, dealing with insurance claims, FEMA paperwork, and then . . . well, just try to find someone to do construction work who's not booked six months solid, and *if* you can get all that done, you've got all the inspections to deal with for your occupancy permit and whatnot." She shook her head, sighing and looking out the window. "Sorry. I guess that's more than you needed to know. Are you visiting the island?"

"Just moved here," I said, shifting toward the door a step. "How far is the shop? Can

I walk?" The SUV was on empty, and I had five dollars in my pocket.

"It's around a mile. You could walk it, but you might want to drive." She smiled pleasantly and finished wiping the door.

I thanked her and made my way out, then debated the gasoline issue for a minute before finally deciding to drive. I'd be running on fumes by the time I made it back home, but there was work to do at Iola's house, and aside from that, I wanted to find some time for the prayer boxes today.

But first I had one last errand to do. A little hummingbird mission of mercy. Today's good deed. The idea of it lifted my sense of impending doom as I drove past the shops and weathered houses of Hatteras Village. It's hard to feel bad about your own life when you're helping out someone else.

Iola would like this one too, I had a feeling. I felt like she was right there in the car with me, watching the sound through the bright, silvery eyes the UPS driver had described. She was smiling, her gnarled hands folded in her lap, resting against the blue-flowered dress.

Paul's ladder would probably be waiting when I got home. I could get the glass box off the top shelf and see what she had hidden inside. The UPS driver would be stopping by on his route also. I'd called and told him I had a surprise for him, from Iola.

Sandy's Seashell Shop melted into view as I rounded the corner. It was just as the librarian had described — yellow lap siding, a front porch with blue Adirondack chairs, a wraparound deck where ice cream tables and twisted-wire chairs waited in the shade of live oaks that looked scrappy after the last two storms. The tables and chairs were lying on their sides, as if a sudden wave had swept from the placid waters of Pamlico Sound and toppled all the furniture.

As I climbed the steps, a black-and-white Boston bulldog wearing a bandanna and doggy swim trunks yipped at me and dashed through the open front door. I followed, stopping on the welcome mat to let my eyes adjust.

Inside, the place was definitely in a state of construction. Store fixtures and shabby-chic tables sat stacked against the wall by the door. Two overstuffed sofas and a mismatched collection of lamps had been pushed together with display cases in the center of the room, and bamboo stools sat legs-up atop a rough-hewn wooden bar on the left side of the room. Overhead, a chalkboard advertised coffee and free Wi-Fi. Other signs here and there offered wisdoms such as *Life is better in flip-flops. Wake up and live. You can shake the sand from your clothes but not from your soul. If your ship doesn't come in, swim out to it. Sandy feet always welcome. May you always have a shell in your pocket and sand in your shoes.* And my favorite of all: *Sand castles or seashells? That is the question.*

The wall opposite the bar had a hole in it where someone had torn down the Sheetrock and exposed the studs. Pieces of wallboard lay on the floor, the mildewed lines of water damage drawing a landscape of mountains in black and brown. It looked sadly familiar. I'd driven my father to many a construction job involving flood damage and repair. Usually people didn't know they had a lingering problem until mildew started coming through the Sheetrock months later.

"Hello?" I craned first to one side and then the other, searching for anyone working in the adjoining rooms. They were darker than this one, no lights on and the blinds drawn. A set of double doors hung open along the back wall, offering a view of the rear deck and the water. The remains of what must have been a tree big enough to shade the entire area stood barren, the limbs sawn off. Storm damage, no doubt.

The dog hopped onto a stool behind the

bar and barked at me, standing up and resting his paws on the counter like a miniature Starbucks barista. His nub tail wagged through a split in his swim trunks, indicating that his bark was all bluster.

"Did they leave you alone to run the place?" I asked, and he sneeze-nodded in response, his overbite creating an upside-down smile.

Now what? I wondered. I couldn't just dump the box of suncatchers without any explanation. Someone had to be working here. There was shop merchandise all over the place — stained-glass pieces hanging in the bay windows, jewelry in the case beneath the cash register, shell sculptures in the front display area, a cubbyhole case of beads and strings for making necklaces, a rack of colorful sun hats and sarongs with fringe along the edges. Beach shoes, blingy flip-flops, coffee mugs, shellscapes in bottles. Small glass globes that looked like snow globes, except they had beach sand and shells inside. The sign leaning against the box read:

BYOB
(Build Your Own Beach)
Turn over, shake gently, and see what
surprises sift to the top.

Take home and enjoy a day at the beach anywhere!

I rested the box of suncatchers temporarily atop a display case built from an old writing desk with crackled green paint. Inside, the viewing area had been filled with sand, and clamshells lay here and there, serving as mother-of-pearl cups for jewelry made from beach glass and silver wire. I leaned close, reading the paper tags.

Mermaids' Tears. Treasures from the deep, which sailors once believed to be the tears of mermaids. The color of the glass was thought to match the color of the mermaid's tail. Original art jewelry by Sandy and Sharon.

A pendant caught my attention. Made from a heart-shaped curl of wire suspending a smooth bit of blue sea glass, it reminded me of the necklace Pap-pap had tucked inside my treasure box so many years ago — a beautiful thing that promised me I was beautiful as well.

I wanted to buy it for Zoey, bring it home, and say, *I know I haven't always shown it the way you needed me to, Zoey, but I love you. We're mother and daughter. We always will be.* The glass was salt-frosted and fragile, a product of struggle and uncertainty, a treasure, just as the sign said. If only a magic piece of jewelry could fix everything. When Zoey and I were together lately, words were arrows and shields, meant to wound or to defend. I wondered if it would always be this way.

The price tag on the pendant read seventy-five dollars. Not so long ago, that would've been nothing, but now it seemed impossibly far away.

A woman's voice drifted through the rear doors. The conversation was one-sided, a phone call.

"No, we didn't pass. This Fletcher guy is impossible. If there's any way he can make things hard for us, he will. You know, that's just what we don't need around here — one more thing muddying up the waters. As if we haven't had enough problems. If it weren't for our online sales, we'd be in the tank already."

She was on the back deck now, coming closer.

I pretended to be engrossed in looking at the jewelry so she wouldn't think I'd been listening in.

"Well, he's some sort of relative of Lucy Grimes, and you know she's been wanting my building for years. They're trying to run me out of business. Now we've got quote-unquote *a structurally unsound wall.* Fletcher found water damage we didn't know we had and some old termite destruction he says we also have to fix. He tried to tell me the roof was probably bad, and there's no way. *But* the Sheetrock is wet in the north wall and so is the wainscoting, so now I've got the trim ripped off and massive holes in the Sheetrock. We're back in a holding pattern until we can get this thing fixed. You know I was counting on being up and running for the music festival, and if we're going to survive at all, we have to be going full steam before beach week hits. I can't believe that after everything we've been through, we're still closed down. George is out of town again, taking care of another crisis with his mother, and I'm not even going to tell him because there's nothing he can do about it from there. I want to grab Fletcher's scrawny little neck and . . ." She stopped midsentence, coming in the door. "Hey, ummm . . . call you back later, 'kay? I've got someone in the shop right now."

I turned around, pretending I hadn't just heard the threat to Fletcher's life. The woman crossing the room was in her sixties, perhaps, with short blonde hair, a friendly face, and a fan of wrinkles around her eyes like she smiled a lot. She had on an apron, and she was carrying a stained-glass box like the one in Iola's closet. I couldn't see the top of the closet box, but this one had a sea horse atop, frozen within a tangle of driftwood.

I had the strangest feeling that Iola might have stood right where I was now. Did she come here to buy boxes and other things? Had she lingered over this very display case and studied the necklaces made from mermaids' tears?

The woman set her stained-glass creation on the coffee counter and shooed the dog off his stool. "Technically we're not back open yet, but if there's something in that case you'd like to see, I'd be happy to show it to you." She shielded her mouth with one hand and winked conspiratorially, and I decided right away that I liked her. "Just don't tell anyone. Officially we're only taking orders through the website right now."

I considered asking her to open the case so I could look at the blue glass pendant, but there wasn't much point. Still, it felt good to pretend that I could still buy something, that I was just a tourist out for a day of decadently frivolous shopping. "No, that's okay. I just stopped by to bring you this." I grabbed the case of suncatchers and handed it to her, then explained why I was returning them. Her reaction was much like the UPS driver's.

"Oh, Iola," she sighed, setting the box on a plush chair. "She was such a sweet, sweet soul. One of our best customers since we opened the shop. I'll never forget the day I first met her. My gosh, that's been nineteen years ago now, I guess. George and I came to the Outer Banks for an empty-nest getaway, and we fell in love — with the place and with each other again." Bracing her hands on her back, she stretched her shoulders and gave the decimated north wall a disheartened look. "This little sandbar will do that to people — so watch out, if you're not from here. You can never really leave the Outer Banks."

She pointed to a sign on the wall that echoed the words she'd just said, then chuckled and went on with her story. "George and I drove down to Hatteras Village to catch the ferry to Ocracoke Island on the last day of our trip, and we passed this cute gray house, right on the highway not far from the ferry landing. The whole thing just came on me like a vision as we drove by. I saw the deck out back, the workshop in the old garage building, the tables on the porch. *Yellow,* a voice in my mind kept saying. *That house ought to be yellow.* I pictured a coffee bar inside, a little sandbox for kids to play in while their moms shopped, and the comfortable old sofas so people could step in from the heat, relax, have coffee, visit, and feel at home. I didn't say a word about it to George, other than to point out that there was a sign up for an estate sale on Friday."

She gazed toward the sound's quiet waters, and I shifted a little closer, the story pulling me in like a magnet tugging a compass needle.

"I thought it was a crazy whim, but that night I even dreamed about it." Her eyes were far away now, lost in the memory. "In my dream, I walked into the yellow house, and it was filled with light. There was just this bright, bright light everywhere — so bright I couldn't see into it."

So bright I couldn't see into it. My dream. My dream about Iola's house, after she passed away. The blue room filled with light.

Sandy's gaze met mine, her eyes the gray-blue of a quiet summer storm. "The next morning at the breakfast table, George set down his newspaper and said he'd been thinking about the house we went by yesterday, the one with the estate sale sign. He

231

had this idea that maybe we could buy it and put a store in, live out this kind of crazy fantasy we'd always had but never thought we'd have the guts to go after for real. And then he said the funniest thing. He said he thought the house ought to be a brighter color. Yellow maybe.

"Right then, I knew. That dream of mine was a sign from heaven. We canceled our return flights and bought the place the next day. Sold two mini-storage businesses and rented our house in Michigan to a nephew, then drove ragtag across country with a motor home and a Ryder truck, like *O Pioneers!* We'd barely started on this place when the cutest little candy-apple-red Dodge Dart rolled up one day. Out stepped this tiny woman in lace gloves and a sun hat. She walked right up the porch steps like she owned the place."

Sandy laughed, and I laughed with her. I pictured Iola — not the silent, unmoving shell from the blue room, but animated, a spunky little woman filled with life. The UPS driver's friend who'd once posed in a haystack like Jane Russell.

Sandy reached down and scooped up the dog, then gave him a head noogie as he snorted happily. "It was the funniest thing, too. The first words she said were, 'I'm glad you're painting the home yellow. It was always yellow.' She'd been on the island since the late thirties, and she remembered a doctor who'd originally had a medical practice downstairs and lived upstairs. She wanted to know all about what we were planning to do with the place. We sat right there on the porch, and I described this dream we had and how I was going to work on my stained glass in the old carriage house out back. How we were planning to have the shop in here, sell pieces by local artisans, and provide a space where people could come on vacation and make a craft of their own. Folks my age remember when families used to do things together on vacation, instead of everyone just wandering off to watch separate TVs and use their cell phones."

Sandy frowned at me, and I thought of J.T. and his video games. Even when we were in the house together, we weren't really together.

I focused on the story as Sandy went on. "Iola sat there and listened to my whole dream. That was one of the special things about her — she was a great listener, interested in people. She never talked much about herself, just listened." Reaching across the space between us, Sandy laid a hand on my arm. For a moment, I felt Io-la's touch there. "I guess you know that about her. Are you a granddaughter or a niece?"

I blinked, surprised. "No . . . just . . . well, a friend, sort of. My kids and I happened to be staying in her rental cottage when she passed away. I'm helping with some things."

Sandy studied me as if she were trying to piece something together in her mind. There was a strange look of recognition in her eyes. I wondered why, but she didn't offer an explanation. "Well, life has a funny way of working out, doesn't it? You've brought my little birdies back, and I do appreciate that. After these last two storms, every dol-lar counts, I can promise you that. There's so much damage the insurance companies won't cover — all this malarkey over what's wind damage and what's flood damage. Don't even get me started. Water is water, no matter where it comes from."

A truck rattled by outside, and the dog started barking, his high-pitched yips echo-ing off the walls. "Chum, stop that!" she scolded, then set him down. We watched him run zippety-dog circles around the shop, his feet spinning out as he rounded the corners, toenails clicking wildly on the uneven wood floors.

"Iola was my first customer, you know," Sandy added when the dog finally disappeared out the back door. "A week after she first walked onto our porch, she came back with a glass box that had been in her family. Some of the panels were cracked, and she wanted me to repair it, so I did. The next thing I knew, she was ordering an eight-thousand-dollar stained-glass window for an old Catholic boarding school in New Orleans. I thought I was going to fall down and faint right there. I'd never even attempted anything that big, but we did it. George and I drove it down to New Orleans personally and presented it to the Mother Superior. That was quite a moment. The window was a replacement for one that had been destroyed by vandals. The nuns had been living with a piece of plywood over the opening for sixty years. Iola wouldn't even let us tell them who'd commissioned the work. They sent us pictures after it was installed, along with some bits of glass from the original piece. The photos of the altar with the light coming through that new window were something to see, I'll tell you. I made two cute little shadow box frames from the scrap glass and gave one to Iola. The other one used to hang on the shop wall that's such a mess now. I guess the frame is somewhere out to sea right now, taking a world tour. You wouldn't believe how much water came through this place during the hurricane two years ago."

"I'm really sorry." I meant it. I understood, in more ways than I could possibly say, what it was like to have your life floating in pieces.

"Well, you know what, you just pick up and go on," Sandy offered cheerfully, taking a hummingbird from the box and letting it dangle on a string. "Everything happens for a reason. We'll put these little guys right there in the bay window, and they'll bring customers in like they always do. People love our hummingbirds." She measured the suncatcher against the window, her lips pursed to one side. "That is, if we can ever get this place past inspection." Casting a glance at the damaged wall, she rolled her eyes heavenward. "Lord knows how we're going to accomplish that in the next week, with George tied up in Michigan. If we don't get the wall fixed, according to the inspector, it'll be another month before he can make it back down this way."

Words went through my mind and found a voice before I even had time to think about them. "I could fix it for you. The wall, I mean." It wasn't normal for me to blurt out something like that. I'd always been careful of what I said to people, and after years of having Trammel correct everything that came out of my mouth, I was even more so. "My father was a finish carpenter — well, he did all kinds of construction, really — and my grandfather was an insurance adjuster. He inspected a lot of places with storm damage and flood damage. I helped him write up estimates for repairs and that kind of thing. I went on jobs with my father, too, whenever he needed an extra pair of hands. And I've fixed up quite a few houses over the years. I know drywall."

I waited for her to nicely thank me and send me on my way, but instead she threw her hands in the air, sending the hummingbird on a wild circular flight. "I knew it! I knew it. I knew there was a reason my little birds ended up in your hands, and you ended up here today. Praise be! You tell me what you need in tools and materials, and I will either gather it up or go buy it at Home Depot tonight. When can you start and what do you charge?"

Within five minutes, I had become the new official handywoman at Sandy's Seashell Shop. I walked out the door stunned and a little scared, minus the weight of the hummingbirds and the weight of the world.

Suddenly, unexpectedly, the carpenter's daughter had become a carpenter herself.

CHAPTER 13

The house was eerily quiet as I carried the stepladder and the broom upstairs. There was a sense of anticipation. It floated on the air, a dust suspended. I breathed it in, exhaled, felt it swirl around my skin.

The ladder had been waiting on the porch when I'd gotten home from Hatteras Village. Paul had dropped it off earlier than I'd expected, but it was only a six-foot stepladder. A note had been tucked beneath the hinge, apologizing for the fact that Paul's grandmother had loaned out the taller ladder to a neighbor. He would try to get it back in a couple days and bring it to me, if the short ladder wouldn't do the job. He'd also included an offer at the end of the note: *I'm not exactly a Wilt Chamberlain, but I've got a longer reach than you. Call me if you think I can help.*

He'd written his number at the bottom. I couldn't call anyone, of course, so after the

UPS man stopped by for his beignets, I'd grabbed a broom from the utility room, hoping against hope that I could somehow tip the glass box into my hands, catch it, and come down the ladder without . . . well, killing myself, for one thing, and shattering the box into a million pieces, for another. I could picture several ways this could go wrong. The *dumb idea* meter was already going off in my head as I climbed the stairs.

The feet of the ladder scratched the wall as I turned on the landing midway up. The plastic caps over the metal corners left a tiny red streak on the paint. I winced, suddenly aware that I was off task again. Now that I'd gotten the work at Sandy's, I would have to finish up in Iola's house. I couldn't keep spending hours in the blue room rummaging through boxes, reading her letters.

But this house, the turret room upstairs, had a hold on me, and I couldn't shake it. Iola's boxes, her stories, that singular glass box, the dream about the light, wouldn't let me go.

I wasn't looking for Iola in those boxes, I knew. I was looking for myself, for the answer to the question I'd been asking and avoiding for years now. *How do you finally move beyond the past? How does anyone?* Would I always be, deep inside, that little girl hiding behind the sofa while bottles broke against the walls and voices thundered and fists flew and doors slammed? Would I always feel that, if others looked at me — really looked — that's what they'd see? Someone worthless? Someone who couldn't fix anything, including her mama and daddy? Would I always be suffocating inside the mask of trying to find proof that I was good enough, that I was worthy of loving?

But Iola seemed to have found peace within herself, despite the rejection in her childhood and the pain in her life. How do you cast aside a word like *anathema,* instead of slipping into it like second skin and living in it forever?

The blue room was impossibly quiet as I entered, the only noise the creaking of the closet hinges, the awkward bumping of the ladder against the sidewall, the rustle of the dry cleaner's bags. The ladder caught the sleeve of the fur coat and lifted it as if there were an arm inside, waving.

The rubber-tipped legs wobbled as I climbed upward, passing rows of Iola's boxes, feeling the pull of each one. What might be inside the wooden tea box from China, the cigar box from Cuba, or the heavy wooden one with the faded imprint of a ship on top? What other treasures, like the little rosary that was now sitting on the night table beside the bed? What secrets? What stories?

A slip of cold air came from nowhere and teased the back of my neck, trailing like fingers over my skin. My shoulders shimmied, causing the ladder to dance on uneven feet. I caught my balance on the third step from the top, bracing the broom against the wall. Overhead, the glass box rested precariously, still well out of reach. The ladder was shorter than I'd thought, in comparison to the ceiling. I had a bad feeling this wasn't going to work.

Before I rethought the wisdom of it, I was all the way up, my feet splayed on either side of a paint-spattered label that still clearly read, *Danger! Do not stand on top step.* If I fell from here, I'd knock myself silly, and no one would ever find me. I'd become the stuff of local lore and haunted legend — the doofus house cleaner who went where she wasn't supposed to go, fell to her death, and still walks the floors to this very day.

The idea stirred a giggle, and I snorted softly. "This really . . . is . . . ridiculous, Tandi."

Taking one hand off the wall, I stretched the broom handle toward the glass box, now dangling overhead. The lid was ajar, its sharp corner burrowing into the plaster, a letter trying to slip through the opening.

"Okay . . . now . . . hold on a . . . minute . . ." The ladder wobbled and squeaked as I shuffled, trying to get into box-catching position. "This is . . . probably not . . . such a good . . ." It crossed my mind that I had a broom in one hand, which meant that I'd be catching the box with one-and-a-half hands, unless I could drop the broom fast enough . . .

The cat growl-meowed from somewhere below, and I jerked back, the weight of the old straw broom pushing me off-balance so that for a moment I thought I was headed down the hard way. Instead, I ended up crouched on the top of the ladder like a monkey on a branch, the broom clamped against my feet. My head swirled. Heights had never been my thing. I'd always hated it when my father did roof repair work. He almost seemed to enjoy the wildness of it, the risk, the fact that I clung to the flashings as I carried tools up and down. I hated being up there with him. If he was in a good mood, he'd grab me and pretend he was going to toss me off, just for the fun of it.

I glanced under my arm, and the cat was in the closet doorway, watching me with a bemused expression. "You're right." I let my head fall forward and wiped beads of nervous perspiration from my forehead. "This is nuts. It's never going to work." Like it or not, I wouldn't be getting the glass box off the shelf until I had a taller ladder. "Well, if I can't get it down, at least I can make sure it stays there, I guess."

The cat didn't answer, of course. He just stood watching, his broken ear flicking toward the sound as I moved down a step to get a better balance, then extended the broom handle upward, hoping to hook the lid just under the hinge and push the box back onto the shelf. "If this doesn't work, you'd better look out," I said to the cat. At this point, the box had to be hanging more or less by the soldered-lead corner that had carved itself into the wall. It resisted as I moved the broom handle into place and tried to push upward. I applied more pressure, and the corner popped free, knocking me sideways as the lid snapped against the handle and plaster rained down like a sprinkling of pixie dust.

The cat sneezed.

A slip of paper seemed to come from nowhere, sliding off the shelf, from underneath one of the cockeyed boxes, perhaps. It floated downward slowly, zigzagging back and forth like a sailboat tacking against the wind, until it found a vanishing point in the bottom of the closet. Things settled into place on the broken shelf, and I prodded gingerly with the broom handle, just to make sure. The pileup of containers seemed stable enough for now.

By the time I finally set my feet on solid ground again, the cat was sniffing around underneath the fur coat, seemingly looking for the letter, as if he'd caught the scent of his mistress there. A puff of dust wafted out, hanging in the air as I retrieved the slip of paper, then moved to the bed to read it. In a way, it was a good thing that I hadn't been able to extract the glass box from the shelf. I didn't need the temptation. After spending the morning in town, I only had a few hours left to work in the kitchen before the kids came home. Double employment meant that I'd have to be more efficient now, but it also meant bringing in some money on top of getting to stay in the cottage. I would work my fingers off if I had to. These jobs could be our way out of desperation.

The letter from the top shelf was new and pliable, the paper seeming recently purchased. Pastel-printed images of sea oats and lighthouses adorned the margins of the page, and along the bottom, in Old English script, the caption read, *Lighthouses of the Outer Banks.* All the lighthouses were there — Currituck, Bodie Island, Cape Hatteras, Roanoke, Ocracoke. Beneath the caption was a quote in soft blue letters that almost seemed a part of the ocean waves: *"Inside my empty bottle, I was creating lighthouses while all the others were making ships." Charles Simic.*

The quote reminded me of Pap-pap's stories of accidents at sea. It was a dangerous life. The ocean floor around here was a graveyard, a watery resting place littered with the bones of ships and men.

I turned my eyes to the familiar handwriting on the page. The words trembled and ran uphill, like those on the final letter left on the desk with the unfinished prayer box.

Dearest Father,
Forgive me for not coming to this sooner, this writing to you. Time goes by in the storm-washed days, unpredictable moment to moment, a pouring in and then a washing away. The ocean is calm today, beautiful, sunlit, and placid all around. How difficult to imagine that it has rushed ashore, washed through buildings and cars, and wrestled boats

loose from their mooring lines. But what is left behind tells the tale. Trees down in the yard, mud against the pilings, and driftwood lining the sedges nearby. On television, the news of businesses destroyed and families waiting in line at the Salvation Army canteen trucks. Camping trailers prostrate in the surf, beached like the carcasses of great whales. Rubble on curbs. Houses that sit dark at night. No lights. No air. No families.

Yet amid all this, there is the water of grace. It flows in all directions, seeping into the hidden crevices, the darkest spaces. It comes with the stranger who rows by in a kayak when the water is yet high. "Just checking. Do you need anything?" he asks. The grace water moves in meals from hand to hand, in blankets, in trucks filled with supplies, in young men wearing military uniforms, in old men carrying chain saws, in lamp oil and candles. Light passed from hand to hand.

The water of grace. A sponge to thirsty lips. A trickle and then a flood.

Hope.

The river moves a mountain stone by stone, slowly widening its path, flowing over each of us, cutting into each of us, washing through the places that are hard, that would separate us from one another, from you among us and within us.

After the storm, all are equal. All wanting. All needing. All in need of the water of grace from one another and from you.

I think on these things, and the tides are multiplied. They flow over me, stronger and more potent than the tides of destruction. The debris of anger, of desperation, seeps away, little by little. A tiny stone and then another. A mountain moving. Moved by all that is right.

There is so much good. So much grace. So much pouring into the river. A quiet water, this river of grace. Its work done in ways that do not seek attention. Yet it is there. Always there.

A shrimp boat rests in a parking lot not far away. You have seen this, of course. Such a strange thing. I would ask your help for the shrimper. His home is lost. There is a family to feed, the humiliation of moving children to a public shelter, meals taken from a canteen truck. The starting of a new school year, the holidays just months away, and they have nothing.

You know this man, I am certain, as you know each of us. You are always mindful.

And then I wonder, am I to think of a way to aid this neighbor? Is this why I have seen him today? Can these tired old hands still cup the water, pour it out? This old body that creaks and groans with small efforts, can it yet serve?

I think to myself, *What can I do?*

Then I look at this bit of paper, the one I have grabbed up because it was close at hand when I set about writing to you. I run a finger over the margins, touch the printed images. *What does a lighthouse do?* I ask myself. It never moves. It cannot hike up its rocky skirt and dash into the ocean to rescue the foundering ship. It cannot calm the waters or clear the shoals.

It can only cast light into the darkness. It can only point the way.

Yet, through one lighthouse, you guide many ships.

Show this old lighthouse the way.

Your loving daughter,
Iola Anne

I stared at the page, my finger tracing a path over the lighthouses and back. I skimmed the last words again.

Outside the window, the sun slid behind a cloud. A chill walked through me, and I felt someone over my shoulder, watching as I intruded again on Iola's private things — thoughts that were never meant to be shared with the world.

I couldn't imagine her kind of life — the kind in which there was an underground river, the water of grace beneath even the most horrible events. The kind of life in which she saw the divine in everything.

Maybe I'd never seen it because I'd never looked. Maybe there was grace here, now. Maybe it was in simple things like banana beignets and a sturdy cottage waiting empty in the off-season. A box of suncatchers with a return address and a shop wall that goes rotten and a carpenter's daughter who happens through the door. Maybe there was grace in a letter-filled shoe box.

Maybe grace was all around me, bubbling through, passing under my feet, and I'd never seen it because I'd never tried to see.

Pressing my hands to my lips, I breathed out and in, smelled dried ink and aging paper and dust.

Outside, the day was clear, the sky an endless blue, dotted with the sort of fluffy, flat-bottomed clouds that roll off the sea. The yard needed mowing again. There were tiny wildflowers blooming in it. I'd walked right past them and never seen.

The sun reemerged, and for an instant, the water of grace glimmered everywhere.

Nothing that had happened since I'd been on this island had happened at random. I'd been given shelter for my family, food to eat, work to do.

Given.

Gifts. I'd wanted to earn my own way, to do this myself, to form a new life on my own, but instead, this had been given to me. This life. This place. These letters.

This revelation.

Prayers are answered in ways we don't choose. The river of grace bubbles up in unexpected places.

I closed my eyes, and tears pressed hard, seeped through, traced hot and sweet over my cheeks. I tasted their salt, like the tip of an ocean.

"Thank you," I whispered. "Thank you for this." Zoey and J.T. could be sitting in a foster shelter right now, in a home with strangers. I could be in jail, caught up in Trammel's mess, or dead beside a bottle of pills, gone just like my mama, while my kids still needed me. I could be living in Trammel's house, existing in a fog, in the prison of believing everything he told me about myself.

Instead, I was here.

Thank you. I wanted to write it on paper and fold it up in a box to remind myself, the next time I couldn't see anything but mountains ahead, that where there's a mountain, there's always a river flowing nearby.

Ultimately the river is the more powerful of the two.

CHAPTER 14

My nerves were flapping like a sheet in the wind when I pulled into the Seashell Shop parking lot for my first day of work. Overhead, what was left of a pair of cabbage palms fanned lazily in the breeze, and behind the shop, Pamlico Sound's gentle current teased the shore, the water shimmering peacefully. Despite the welcoming scenery and the fresh shade blanketing the iron tables and the sea-blue Adirondack chairs, I felt out of place. Doubts had started to creep into my mind during the drive over, inching in the way the first bit of water breaches the walls around a sand castle. Now the waves were tumbling full force, washing out bits of my confidence with every swipe.

Ross had called before I'd left this morning. After being on a two-day beach bender, he was kicking back in one of his dad's rental houses. This one was tucked in a little neighborhood in Duck. Three stories of porches and decks, hot tub, view of the beach over the canopy of pines. Today was perfect for sitting on the beach and watching the breakers roll in. Ross wanted me to join him, and of course I'd had to tell him why I couldn't.

"You're gonna hang drywall and do *carpenter work?"* He said it like it was some excuse I'd pulled out of a hat of completely stupid excuses.

I felt the need to defend myself. "I told you that my daddy did construction work. I helped him a lot. The shop owner is supplying the tools and materials. The job will take a little time. I have to figure out where the water came from, then get rid of everything I can that's holding moisture, then dry out the rest so they don't have a problem again after the work's done."

"*You're* gonna hang *drywall.* What, all hundred pounds of you? How much do you weigh, anyway?"

His point was that I wasn't strong enough to do the job, I guessed. That irked me. I'd been working since I was seven years old. Sometimes I wondered if Ross could imagine a life where daddies didn't give their kids hot cars and surf lessons and vacations in nice beach houses and other good things.

"I *know* how to hang drywall, Ross." I grabbed the keys and my purse and tried to decide whether anything else was necessary. "Besides that, the pay is good."

"You know, if you need money, all you've gotta do is ask," he said like I should be aware of that already. "You don't have to go trying to schlep drywall in someone's shop."

I heard Trammel in my head. *Let me take care of you, Tandi. You and the kids need a friend right now. . . .*

I'd ended the phone call before I could say something that was aimed more at Trammel than at Ross.

Now, as I sat in the parking lot of Sandy's Seashell Shop, Ross's questions repeated in my head. What if I really couldn't do this? What if Sandy didn't have all the right tools? What if she turned out to be picky and demanding, and I wasn't able to satisfy her?

Ross might be right. I'd never done this kind of thing, other than helping my daddy or fixing up houses I was living in. I didn't have any experience making sure that my work was up to someone else's standards. Most of the houses my daddy worked on weren't anything special. As long as the end product wasn't atrocious, nobody cared, including my father.

Sandy, I had a feeling, would care. Her shop had the aura of a well-loved place. A special place. It was a historic building. Maybe I didn't have any business working on it.

The front door was locked today, a Closed sign hanging crooked in the window. I had a half-second urge to bolt for home, but I'd driven here on fumes and nineteen quarters' worth of gas. I'd found the quarters in a cracker tin in Iola's kitchen yesterday afternoon while I was working like a banshee, cleaning and stuffing trash bags before the kids came home. I would put the money back as soon as I could, but for now it was a godsend. Zoey had needed to buy a loaf of bread last night so she could make lunches. I'd given her the last few dollar bills in my stash.

I was already trying to figure out how to ask Sandy for an advance on this week's pay without sounding like a charity case. The likelihood of finding more coins wasn't that good, and somehow I couldn't help thinking of the jar Trammel tossed his pocket change into when he undressed at night. Every few days, he emptied it into a larger jar that he kept locked in a gun safe with his hunting rifles. He didn't want to tempt the housekeeper. Or me.

Taking a deep breath, I walked around the back of Sandy's shop. The garage door was open on the long, narrow building attached to one side of the original house.

"Hello?" I called, stopping at the edge. "Anybody in here?"

Chum answered with a wary yip, and then Sandy came out of a back room, wiping her hands on a towel. "Hey!" She smiled as she walked into the light, her cheeks round and red, shiny with sweat. "You came back! I thought you might've realized what you'd gotten yourself into and decided to run away screaming."

Little did she know . . .

Before I had time to react, she was hugging me like I was her long-lost sister. We bounced back and forth while Chum yipped and did happy-dog calisthenics, jumping up and down, then dancing on his hind legs. When that didn't get attention, he tried the opposite, walking on his front legs with his rear in the air, his nub tail wagging.

Sandy held me at arm's length and smiled the way a kid smiles at a new toy. "I'm so glad you're here! After you left yesterday morning, I started thinking of all kinds of things I could have you do." She had the quality of Alka-Seltzer just hitting a glass of water, bubbling up and up and over. She looked a little like a mad scientist, too, dressed in a white baker's apron, yellow dishwashing gloves, rubber rain boots, teal pedal pushers, and sea glass earrings. A pair of goggles formed an odd hair band on her head, pulling her short blonde strands away from her face and making them stick straight up.

Chum licked my shoe, and she nudged him away. "Chum! Stop that. No eating the help." She patted my arms, the gloves flapping. "So here you are."

"Here I am." I lifted both hands, as in, *Just point me toward the tools and watch me solve all your problems.* The first step in being confident was looking confident. That was one good thing I'd learned from watching Trammel.

Sandy pumped a fist. "Let's get going."

"Let's!" I was caught in her wave of enthusiasm now.

"Sharon, come out here and meet Tandi," she called, taking me by the arm and weaving me through piles of boxes, store fixtures, wooden crates, and stacks of mud-covered terra-cotta pottery. "My workshop is back here — my sister's in there laboring away on some store stock right now. Of course, we had such a mess after the first storm, and then we rode out the one last fall in our house. We packed the glass and everything we couldn't take with us and put it on shelves up high. Glass is expensive, but if it gets broken, you can still use the pieces for lots of things. Now, my workshop tools, my glass grinders, solder irons, saws, and all of that went with me. No way the storm was getting that stuff. Anyway, when they finally let us back on the island after the first one, there'd been three feet of water in the shop. We had windows and shutters blown out and driftwood everywhere and all kinds of wet papers and debris inside. When the last one came through, it was just floodwater and surge, and the shutters held out, but then I had a heart attack and my niece, Elizabeth, had to save my life. But that's a whole other story. My son, Brad, took a lot of time off work to come down and help with repairs. So did my niece and her sweet husband. But they can't take any more time now. Which is why you're such a blessing."

She left me in the doorway while she and Chum went into the smaller room, where a woman wearing soundproof earphones was leaning over a bench grinder. I gathered that this little hole-in-the-wall workshop lined with Peg-Boards, shelves, and plastic storage drawers must have given birth to Iola's hummingbirds. On the left, a long, narrow countertop dipped slightly under the weight of power tools, scattered pliers, soldering irons, and hair dryers. Above the rainbow-spattered workbench, a tangle of power cords stretched upward like the limbs of the legendary sea kraken that Meemaw told bedtime stories about. Behind the cords, a long picture window overlooked the workbench. Now I realized that it fronted the sidewall of the store, allowing customers to watch the work in the glass shop or the glassworkers to monitor the shop. On an ordinary day when the store was open, it would've been pleasant back here, working and creating, watching moms in sundresses and sarongs as they shopped for baubles while their kids played around the little sandbox in the center of the store.

It looked like Sandy had a good life.

I envied the fact that she and her sister worked here together. When I was little and things were bad, Gina and I would cuddle in her bed while she invented stories about the future. One day she would have a store with tons of pretty dresses in it. I could work in her store and wear the dresses. Sandy's reality seemed pretty close to the dream that was light-years from the life my sister had actually ended up with. The last time I'd had more than a passing conversation with

Gina, Trammel had finally kicked her out after she'd shown up for a surprise visit, then stayed six months, enjoying all that life at Trammel's had to offer.

Sandy shoulder-hugged her sister as she introduced us. Sharon was a petite, pleasant woman who looked like she could be anywhere from fifty to seventy. Other than the auburn hair, she reminded me of Sandy.

"Sharon's been helping me to get the inventory built up again," Sandy explained. "Between the storms and the Sandy's Seashell Shop website taking off so well, we're sort of cleaned out on our handmade items, especially the sea pearl jewelry . . . well, and the boxes and the hummingbirds, thanks to Iola, but now we can reinventory those. I'll tell you, so many things were ruined when the water came through. You really can't imagine. Everything we didn't take with us had to be either gutted or dried out and cleaned up. Thank God for friends from church, volunteers, and all the Internet orders, or our emergency fund never would've been enough to get us through."

"And family," Sharon reminded with a sideways smirk. I had that strange sense of yearning I sometimes felt when I saw sisters the way they were supposed to be.

"Well, of course, *family,*" Sandy agreed,

and the two of them toppled sideways, off-balance. Fortunately the room was small, and they caught themselves against a plastic organizer full of what looked like doorknobs and bits of colored glass. Through one of the hazy plastic drawers, I recognized the body of a hummingbird. No wings yet.

Why in the world did Iola want all those sun-catchers? The question was strangely on my mind as I talked with Sandy and Sharon about the shop, the repair problems, their future plans, and the stores in the area. Sandy's friends, Greg and Crystal, owned Boathouse Barbecue, in a rustic, weathered-looking building next door, and several other friends ran shops nearby.

By the time we finished the tour, checked supplies and tools, and looked at the damaged wall again, I felt at home in the place. Unlike Iola's house, the Seashell Shop was an open book. There were no secrets here, just two women determined to cling to what had begun long ago as Sandy's vacation fantasy.

As I started work on the wall, Sandy moved to the space behind the coffee bar, pulled out a mud-covered box with glass lighthouses on top, and began washing it off. "It's the strangest thing, what survived the storm and what didn't. Like this little box. The ones with the adornments on the lids are fragile, but when we came back, there this box was, sitting in the muck, fully intact. It'll be a fun story to tell to whoever buys it."

"Sounds like it," I said without looking at her. I had a feeling she wanted to watch me work for a while, to see if I knew what I was doing. Chum curled up in an empty bookshelf, tracking me with drowsy eyes.

I studied the wall and took a deep breath, then reached for the moisture meter, a carpenter's pencil, and a drywall knife. It was now or never. Time to put up or shut up. The first thing I had to do was find out how far the water damage went and where it came from. The answer to that question would tell me what kind of job I'd taken on.

I could feel Sandy quietly monitoring me as I moved along with the meter, testing the drywall on the top half and the old beadboard wainscoting on the bottom, which was no doubt original to the house. The meter went crazy, and the drywall had the consistency of chewing gum when I probed it with the knife. Even the old beadboards were so soggy, I could bend them slightly with my finger. No wonder the inspector found this so quickly. There were wicking stains everywhere, showing that the water had been working its way up the wall, not down.

"It's been wet for a week, maybe ten days. With any luck, it won't be moldy yet," I said because she was clearly waiting for a report. "A few of these stains are old and might have come from the roof at some time in the past, but those are actually dry. The wet stuff is recent, and it's generating from inside the beadboard."

"You can *tell* all that?" She seemed shocked and no small bit impressed. "It's not from the roof? And here I thought that I was going to have to hunt down the company we paid to air the place out after the flood damage and then read them the riot act. They brought in these massive dryers, sprayed for mold, and promised us that the place was sealed up tight."

I pressed the knife through the drywall, started cutting. "Well, water wicks through drywall about six inches a day. Usually you can look at where the stain is coming from and how far it's traveled and know about how long the wall has been wet. Are there any pipes in this wall?"

"The bathroom's on the other side," Sandy breathed. "We just turned the water back on in this building a couple weeks ago.

There were some broken pipes outside after the storm, and we didn't worry too much about it right away, since we weren't open for business. It was easier to just keep the water turned off."

"I guess that explains a few things. At least it's clean water and it hasn't been here all that long."

"So then we've found the bright side." Sandy leaned on the counter, giving me a wry smile. "I didn't think it made sense that the moisture in the Sheetrock had anything to do with a roof leak. That new inspector is a dope. Either that or he's just trying to get us to give up on the place. But he won't win." She brandished a long-handled bottle brush in the air, then pointed it at me like a sword. "Because we have a secret weapon. We have you."

I turned back to the wall, a hot flush pressing in. I'd never been a secret weapon before. In fact, it had been a long time since anyone had expressed that kind of confidence in me — a long time since I'd done anything to deserve it.

I studied the problem again, trying to come up with a plan. Stripping off the wet drywall on top would be easy, but the lower half, the original beadboard, would be really tough. I'd have to take it off a piece at a time, labeling the pieces and saving as many of the old square nails as I could, then dry it out and work it back together like a puzzle. I'd never done anything like that. Ever. But losing anything that was original to the building would practically be a crime. I had to make sure all the parts were dry before I started rebuilding the wall, or they'd have more problems in the future. Mold. Mildew. Wood rot.

I laid out a tarp for the soggy drywall, probed, cut, checked with the moisture meter.

"Was this wall redone after the storm?" I knew it must have been. Some of the drywall work was recent, but they'd done a lousy job. The old studs with termite damage should've been replaced, for one thing.

Sandy made a disgusted sound. When I glanced over, that round-cheeked face didn't look so friendly anymore. Seashell Sandy had a feisty side. "Yes, and by a contractor who pretended to be a good person. When he showed up with his crew not long after the storm, I thought he was the answer to a prayer. I even let him and his crew headquarter their trailers here at the shop, plug into the electric, all that. Their end of that deal was that they were supposed to do the work on my shop. What

I got was last place on their list and shoddy results. By the time we started trying to get our occupancy permit, they were long gone, and there were complaints about them all over the island."

"Oh." The whole drywall knife went through the wall, along with my hand. "I'm really sorry." I pulled it out of the wall and looked down at my fingers, sighed. What a mess.

"Don't be sorry." Dishes rattled and the water turned on in the bar sink. "Just figure out where the leak is coming from, and I'll get a plumber in here, and then you'll fix my wall, and all will be right with the world again."

I chuckled and moved on. "I'll do my best."

"I'm not even worried. Only the right sort of person would've bothered to bring back that box of hummingbirds." She held up a coffeepot, checked it against the light, then lowered it to wipe off a water spot. "There, that's ready to go. Now all we need is a wall, a plumbing fix, an occupancy permit, a food service permit, stock for the shelves, and hordes of customers coming in the door before we go totally broke." For the first time since I'd met her, Sandy sounded a little depressed.

267

"Well, you know how a river moves a mountain." The words surprised me at first, but I knew where they were coming from.

"Stone by stone," she finished. "Iola told me that on the phone when she called to order those hummingbirds."

I felt Iola there in the room with us. "I wish I'd known her better." It was still so strange that I knew the intimacy of her private thoughts, that I felt at home in her house, but in reality we'd never been face-to-face.

"Well, she was a sweet person. Friendly, but hard to get close to in a way too. Back when she was driving, she would usually show up in the late afternoon. She'd figured out that was when the girls from the other stores around here stop over for coffee. We've got a little sisterhood that hangs out here at the Seashell Shop. You'll meet them later. Iola liked to come sit with us. Every once in a while, she would share a story or two about some place she'd been in the past or some event she remembered, but mostly she just listened. She was private like that.

"I remember one time, she'd ordered fifteen of our glass boxes — the large ones, a size bigger than the ones on the shelf over there. A load of fifteen boxes is heavy and hard to transport. Anyway, I wanted her to let me bring them to her house, but she just wouldn't. She had me ship every single one of them to her by UPS, packaged separately. She planned to send them out for Christmas gifts, she said, but she didn't want to just give me the addresses to mail them to. That was usually how she did things. I never did quite figure it out, except that she must have sent a lot of gifts to friends and family out of state — either that or she just liked to buy things, and there's a houseful of our glasswork at her place."

Sandy paused, the statement rising into a question. She was wondering if I knew what was in Iola's house. I thought about the clutter of boxes and plastic bins on the lower floor. Most of it seemed too old to have come from Sandy's. "I've seen one glass box and a suncatcher, but that's about it." I left it at that.

"Guess I may never know what happened to all of our treasures. Anyway, I'd better stop bothering you and let you work." Sandy moved from behind the bar. "You look like you've got everything under control over there."

I sensed that I'd just received the nod of approval. "You might want to wait until the wall is finished to decide on that." I regretted the comment the minute it slipped out.

Habit. I'd learned long ago that bragging about yourself would bring a smackdown. Around Mama and Daddy's house, you didn't come home with your A-plus papers and wag them in someone's face. *Well, little miss smarty-pants, you just think you're too good, huh? That right?*

"Don't sell yourself short. I know a competent woman when I see one," Sandy replied, then exited the room and left me to contemplate whether the queen of the Seashell Shop saw something in me that I didn't see in myself.

By midafternoon, I didn't feel competent or contemplative. I was too tired to feel anything. I hadn't been so physically exhausted since my days of living in a little house next to a stable, exercising show horses, trying to work my way up in the business and raise my baby girl on my own after I dropped out of college.

When Sandy's shop friends came in for coffee and she and Sharon invited me to sit with them at a table on the back deck, I didn't argue. I'd done all I could with the project for the day. The wet drywall and craft-paper backing were off the studs on the top half. I'd uncovered the leak in the pipes from the back side, and now it needed a plumbing fix before I started the painstaking process of taking off the old beadboard, drying things out, and replacing studs. Sandy had a plumber friend coming by after hours.

"It'll help if that thunderstorm doesn't come in," I said as I sat down with Sandy, Sharon, and Crystal from the Boathouse Barbecue, along with Teresa and Elsa, who owned the ice cream stand down the street, and Teresa's eighty-eight-year-old mother, Callie.

"Well, that's the one thing we can't control, sweet pea." Callie leaned over and patted my knee. "You learn that, livin' eighty-odd years on a sandbar. It's all in God's hands." She smiled at me, her eyes a cloudy brown. "Now where did you say you're stayin', exactly?"

The other ladies at the table gave me apologetic looks. Callie repeated the same questions over and over — I'd already noticed. My grandmother had started to do that the last time we were allowed to visit her and Pap-pap. Alzheimer's had been setting in.

"She's taking care of Iola's house, Mama," Teresa answered patiently. "Remember, Sandy told us that a few minutes ago? Iola passed away."

"Oh." Callie nodded, her hand still resting on my knee. "She was a WAC during the war. She told me that once. I was a WAC too. That's Women's Army Corps, if you didn't know. I was a pilot. Ferried supplies and antiaircraft artillery around. A WASP, they called us girls. Did Iola Anne ever tell you about those days?"

"Mama, *you* were a WAC, not Iola," Teresa corrected.

Callie glanced at her daughter, then turned an entirely lucid look my way. "We, *both* of us, were. Or maybe that was USO. . . . She was at Camp Davis in Holly Ridge, I think. Yes, that was it. I was there too. I don't think we saw each other. Maybe I went to her wedding. I can't recall now. . . ." She drifted off, pulling her hand away and scratching her head. "Oh, it's all such a muddle. . . ."

"I do remember Iola saying something about dancing with the soldiers." Sandy sweetened her coffee, then passed the dish around. "I had some cute embroidered hankies in the store once, and Iola said they reminded her of the ones the soldiers gave to the girls when they danced. I don't know that she was ever married, though. She never mentioned a husband in all the years I knew her."

272

Callie lifted a finger into the air. "I think she left him after the war. . . . Yes, that's what it was. I . . ." Her finger curled slowly, and she lowered her hand, pressing a knuckle to her lips and sighing. "I don't know. . . ."

"It's okay, Mama." Teresa leaned over tenderly, holding a teaspoon of sugar. "Do you want your coffee sweet today, or just plain?"

"Oh, sweet is best." Callie turned her attention to the cup. "And with cream. That kind that tastes so good. Yes, yes, that's it." She supervised the alteration of her coffee, then lifted the cup to her lips, the liquid trembling inside. Setting the cup back on its napkin, she took a breath of the salt air, smiled at me, and said, "Now, tell me again who you are, sweet pea?"

Teresa changed the subject, and the talk at the table turned to shop issues and insurance forms. I excused myself after a while. All of a sudden, I wanted to hurry back to Fairhope and see if I could sneak over to Iola's house for a little while before the kids came home.

CHAPTER 15

The storm I'd seen brewing over the sound when I'd left the Seashell Shop passed with little more than a sprinkling of rain, leaving the sky clear again. The sun was streaming through the kitchen window of Iola's house when I walked in.

A new worry had started nagging me on the drive home, competing for space with the fact that I hadn't worked up the guts to ask Sandy for an advance on my pay. The new problem was more complex than the question of how to come by some gas money. The soggy mess at Sandy's had only made me realize what was probably happening inside the walls and ceilings in Iola's house. Mold, wood rot, deterioration. The annoying guy from the county had been more spot-on than he knew. The place needed attention, and soon, if it was going to be saved. It was only luck that a heavy rain hadn't fallen in Fairhope since I'd been watching the house. Unusual luck, for the Outer Banks.

The roof needed to be repaired or replaced. Walls need to be opened and dried, mold sprayed or removed. How soon before the church would be looking at those issues? Should I point it out to Brother Guilbeau? Bringing in other people would mean giving up the house for myself. I hated the idea of interlopers almost as much as Iola seemed to have hated it. What if they found the boxes? What if there were other secrets here — things I hadn't discovered yet?

What if, given the issues, the church decided to just lock up the place and let nature take its course? What if, by pointing out the problems in the house, I actually helped to bring about its destruction?

You've gotta do what you've gotta do to take care of you. Advice from my sister, a few days after she'd finally turned eighteen and left behind a group foster home she hated. *Nobody's gonna do you any favors, Baby Sister . . .* Gina couldn't stand the fact that, by then, the Lathrops had brought me into their empty-nest home. I didn't want to leave their little horse farm to move into an apartment with my big sister, and Gina found that irksome.

I needed to come up with a solution that

would make things better in Iola's house, not worse, that would honor her devotion to this place. There had to be a way.

But for now, I had no choice other than to think as I worked. It was time to summon up some energy and attack my second job for the day.

In the last hour before the school bus was due, I cleaned like a crazy woman, filling trash bags with expired food, old bread wrappers, bits of used foil, and hurriedly piling them by the bayberry hedge out back. When I finished the food, I attacked the stack of periodicals beside the pantry, grabbing a handful off the top of the four-foot pile.

A newspaper slid off the stack and landed by an empty plastic tub at my feet. I glanced at it, caught a photo of a shrimp boat marooned broadside in a parking lot. A family posed in a picture next to it. A tall, coatrack-thin man, a woman, five kids — little stairsteps, each carrying something. A new backpack for school, a bright-pink winter coat, a stack of children's books, an art pad and pencils. The oldest boy was sitting on a new bicycle with the tags still hanging from the handlebars. School supplies were piled in the parking lot around them.

I squatted down next to the plastic tub, set my handful of newspapers in it, picked up the one from the floor.

Below the photo, the caption read, *Outer Banks Hope Auction swells, thanks to anonymous donor.* The article was about an online auction that had raised over a million dollars for storm victims in the Outer Banks. An unnamed benefactor had contacted the producers of a cable television show, *Attic Treasures,* and offered to donate a rare Tiffany Magnolia lamp if an auction could be arranged to benefit the families displaced from their homes. I read the local coordinator's description of the online auction:

"In particular, she requested that a portion of the money be used to provide school supplies and clothing for the children, and that part of the money be used to help families like the Dawsons, whose shrimp boat was deposited in a parking lot during the storm. Like many families, the Dawsons are having difficulty with insurance claims following the storm, and they lack the resources to hire legal help. With the funds and publicity from the auction, we will be able to help the Dawsons and several other local families to settle with their insurance companies and begin rebuilding their lives.

"It just shows how many people out there really care. From the time the producers of *Attic Treasures* contacted us asking if we would provide a local base for the project, it grew like wildfire. People were donating things from all over the place — family heirlooms, weeks in time-share vacation homes. A car dealer in Michigan donated two new cars. A group of Mennonite women in Texas donated a half-dozen handmade quilts. And the bidding was phenomenal. I couldn't get things on the auction site fast enough.

"Because of the publicity, we've had numerous legal firms come forward and offer to represent insurance claims for Outer Banks families, pro bono. It's all thanks to that original Tiffany lamp. When something that rare and valuable suddenly comes onto the market, people sit up and take notice all over the world. It was a fantastic newsmaker. The lamp itself raised almost $500,000. The funniest thing about it is that it arrived here on a UPS truck. I thought the UPS driver was going to pass out the next day, when I told him what was in that package he'd delivered."

The article ended with a photo of the

lamp's buyer, a businessman from Japan, holding his new treasure. I recognized the lamp immediately. In the blue room upstairs, there was an empty night table, and just across the bed sat the mate to that Tiffany Magnolia lamp.

"The cat scratches his back on that thing," I breathed, and all I could think was, *Five hundred thousand dollars, five hundred thousand dollars. Anonymous donor . . .* "Holy cow." I sank onto the floor, let the newspaper rest against my legs, and looked up at the ceiling. "That was you. You did this."

Outside, a bird trilled, the sound cheerful and bawdy and raucous. I heard Iola chuckling, pleased with herself for having pulled it off.

Through one lighthouse, you guide many ships. Iola's words whispered in my mind.

Was she thinking of the Tiffany lamp, even as she wrote the letter, even as she poured out her thoughts on paper and tucked it into her prayer box?

Show this old lighthouse the way.

Or was the idea an answer to the prayer?

"You found a way," I whispered, and I felt Iola there in the kitchen with me. The woman Sandy had described. The one who drove to the Seashell Shop in her little red car and marched up the steps — vital, alive, a hand pressed over a mischievous smile, her eyes twinkling. "You found a way," I said again and laughed along with her.

The rivers of grace swelled around me, rushing wild, filling me with strength, with determination. If a ninety-one-year-old woman could rally support all the way from Japan to save a North Carolina shrimper's family, I could find a way to save this house. I *would* find a way.

"It's not impossible," I said and then blushed a little, but the words were sincere.

I took the newspapers out of the bin and set them back on the stack, flakes of instant oatmeal floating down like snow. Maybe Iola had kept those papers for a reason. Maybe there were clues in them. Bits of her story.

Chewing my lip, I considered the problem of what to do next. Maybe tomorrow I could pack the newspapers into the empty plastic bins and store them upstairs in the closet with the prayer boxes. It wasn't really a solution — I was supposed to be removing clutter, not just relocating it — but at least it would make the kitchen look better.

Right now, I needed to lock things up and haul the bags of trash stacked by the bayberry hedge over to the church Dumpster next door. The kids could show up anytime, depending on whether they rode home with

Rowdy or took the school bus.

The bus rumbled by a few minutes later as I was crossing the yard, moving like an overloaded pack mule, with one bag slung over my back and another dangling from my arm. I'd stuffed them full, and they were getting longer by the minute, the plastic stretching and growing translucent. "Please don't break." If they did, I'd have moldy SpaghettiOs and rotten apples all over me. I had cleaned out the refrigerator, while trying not to gag up my lunch, and the bins were drying on the counter now.

"My eye, it looks like Santy Claus is a-comin'!" Brother Guilbeau's voice was easy to recognize, even without looking up. Rather than run the risk of stopping, I continued my trudge toward the Dumpster.

"You don't want these presents, trust me!" The next thing I knew, I was smiling under my pack, my ribs convulsing in withheld laughter. I could just imagine what I looked like.

"You don' got a mess'a fried crawfish in that pack for a hungry man?" Brother Guilbeau teased, his tone as casual as if we were old friends who talked every day. His feet moved through the grass with a shuffling *swish-swish*.

"There's some stuff in there that might've

been crawfish once." I made it to the Dumpster — thank goodness — and rolled the heavier bag off my back. "But I'm not making any promises. You can dig for it if you want."

He grinned, craning his neck forward and pretending to consider the bags of trash. I pulled my hands away, offering to surrender them. I liked Brother Guilbeau, despite the fact that my experiences with church people in the past hadn't always been the best. He seemed different. Maybe there came a point in life where you had to quit categorizing whole groups of people by a few bad experiences.

I grabbed a bag, pitching it into the air with a Hail Mary swing. It sailed over the Dumpster rim and landed inside with a gushy plop. Brother Guilbeau reached for the second bag, but I snatched it up and threw it in as well. "My hands are already dirty."

"Sha, you pretty strong for a little thing." Brother Guilbeau was impressed.

"I've schlepped a few hay bales and feed sacks in my day," I said, feeling strangely pleased with myself.

Brother Guilbeau nodded. "Your boy, he was tellin' me his mama was a horse rider. Jumpin' horses, was it?"

A pang of surprise hit me, sudden and sharp like when my daddy would flick a finger and thump me in the head for not obeying quickly enough. "Yes, but not for a long time now." The answer was intentionally vague. Had Brother Guilbeau been pumping J.T. for information?

He seemed to guess at my thoughts. "Couple horse riders went by in the woods the other day while we were sharin' us an Icee out back of Bink's store. He mentioned his mama rode jumpers."

"He likes animals," I said blandly and then turned the conversation to the need for more trash bags, finally finishing with "I really didn't want to come by the church and ask since you'd told me to keep my work here kind of quiet. I don't know any of the history involved, but I get the impression that some people didn't like Iola . . . and that there may be some issues about ownership of the house." I was the one fishing for information now. That still, small voice in my head was insisting, *Tell him the roof needs attention. Now.* What might happen if I did? "I just didn't want to get in the middle of things and have everyone asking me questions about it. I won't know what to say to them." A load of guilt was quickly settling on my shoulders. I knew I was wimping out on getting help for the house, opting for self-preservation instead.

Brother Guilbeau pulled out his wallet, thumbed through bills, and handed me a fifty. "Yes, mmm-hmm, I see that point. I do, sha. Less said, better till we got all the legal mumbo jumbo cleared up."

My first thought as I took the money was that I'd be able to buy gas to get to work tomorrow. Then I wanted to bash my head against the Dumpster. I would *not* do that. I wouldn't. I'd find some other way to get gas money. Like being honest with Sandy and admitting that I needed an advance.

"Now, you do any drivin' around for the supplies, you use some a' that to pay the gas," Brother Guilbeau instructed, and my mouth fell open. "My mistake, I didn't get some cash money over there to you sooner on. Been a busy week round here."

"Oh . . . that's okay," I stammered, goose bumps pricking over my skin.

Brother Guilbeau checked his watch. "Got potluck and music t'night here at the church." He was already angling in the direction of his car, on his way to somewhere. "C'mon join us, bring that boy. Bring his big sister, too. Haven't had much chance to talk to her, but that boy loves his big sister."

284

"Oh . . . well, we'd better not, but thank you." The excuse spun off my tongue like silk. "I have a new job — just temporary, but I think I'll be crashing early tonight. I'm doing some drywall work at a shop down in Hatteras Village."

"Drywall?" Brother Guilbeau's eyes bugged. "Well, my foot! You didn't tell me you knew how to put up drywall."

I explained to him that I'd been working with my father on construction jobs since I was little. I almost cycled around to bringing up the problems in Iola's house, but fear won out again.

"Lotta folks round here need that kind a' work right now. You decide you want to do more, you make me some signs wit' your phone number, I'll share them in town, tell ever'body we got a new home handywoman." He was walking backward now, checking his watch again.

"Thanks . . . oh, okay . . . thanks!" I waved at him, the fifty-dollar bill still dangling from my fingers.

He spun around and hurried off to his car, and I walked back toward Iola's house with a new wind in my sails. *Home handywoman . . . me?* I'd never, ever considered that all those times my father had kept me out of school to drive him to jobs might actually come in handy for something. Maybe I really could start some kind of business. Brother Guilbeau seemed to think I could.

The funny thing about having people believe good things about you is that, without even realizing it, you want to make those things true. I wanted to be the person Brother Guilbeau saw, the person Sandy saw. I wanted to be worthy of their trust. This place, this house, everything about it was changing me. The prayer boxes, the grace water was slipping inside me like vapor, the life water of a different person, of someone completely new. The more I breathed it in, the more it filled me. The more I dipped my toe in Iola's river of grace, the more it washed away the stains of the past.

Laughing, I threw my head back and my arms out and drank in the day as I walked back to the house. I wanted to savor this feeling, to keep it.

A horn honked and I opened my eyes, my poetry moment shattering all around me.

Ross's truck was rolling in. Behind the wheel, he was grinning ear to ear. I blushed, picturing myself standing there in the yard in my old jeans and T-shirt, my arms thrown out and my head tossed back. I must've looked like some kind of a drunken ballet dancer.

Ross hopped out of the truck still laughing, and my heart fluttered upward at the sight of him. It was almost impossible to remember from one time to the next how good-looking he really was. He was a magazine photo in the flesh — the cover of *Sports Illustrated.*

"Hey, babe!" He crossed the yard and swept me up with one arm, his broad smile telling me that, whatever he'd been doing, it had been a good day. He looked tanned, rested, and happy. "I've got eighteen hours and forty-two minutes before the old man sends me off to Natchez with a load. Let's go have some fun."

He set me on my feet and kissed me, and for a minute I lost track of where I was — and everything else.

CHAPTER 16

Ross was trying to talk me into going down to Ocracoke Island for the night. There was a party brewing at one of his favorite dives, and then he was crashing overnight at the little saltbox house he seldom used.

His fingers toyed with the ends of my hair as he smiled down at me, his eyes twinkling. "Man, you haven't *seen* a beach until you've seen the one by that house. You'll like it. You can meet my dog. Mama said if I didn't come get him out of her yard, she was gonna call the pound, so I put him at the Ocracoke house. Anyway, you'll love the place, and the sunrise is awesome there."

"Like you'll be seeing the sunrise after playing pool all night." I'd been out with Ross enough times to know how the evening would go. He would play pool, gather an audience, and entertain everyone with epic stories from his two-day bender in Salvo. In the morning I'd wake up on Ocracoke, a forty-minute ferry ride away from Hatteras and my new job at Sandy's.

The strange thing was that not so long ago, I would've been jumping at the chance, a giddy feeling fluttering up, my body warm with the fact that Ross didn't want to leave home without me. Being his arm candy had been a confidence booster like crazy, and I'd craved that. But today, all I could think about were the issues with Iola's house and the fact that Sandy needed me to show up in the morning. The Ocracoke ferry had been closed due to shoaling more often than it had been open lately. What if I got stuck down there?

I heard J.T. talking to Zoey as they crossed the salt meadow, and I pushed away from Ross. "The kids are coming."

Ross listened a moment. Then his lashes fell to half-mast, and he leaned close to me. "Sounds like *both* of them, so we're good to go. Tell Big Sister she's got to stay home and babysit tonight. We'll head out, catch the ferry, and hit happy hour at Rob and Roy's — get a bite before the round-robin pool tournament. You can watch me work my magic."

"Ross, I should . . ."

"C'mon," he teased. "You can have all the money. Everything I win. You're my good

289

luck charm. They're all too busy looking at you to pay any attention to the table. We'll hit one of the shops on the way, get you something really . . . distracting to wear. You need some new clothes, Tandi. You're way too hot for jeans and junk T-shirts."

The pull of old habits tugged hard. He made the evening sound a whole lot more fun than I'd pictured it.

"I can't," I said finally. On top of everything else, the clouds were rumbling somewhere off over the water. If more storms blew in tonight, I'd have to do my best to make sure the drip buckets were in all the right places in Iola's house. I thought about telling Ross the truth, but instead, I settled for "I have to work in the morning."

"Work?" He drew back, flashing an eyetooth. "What?"

"The drywall thing at Sandy's Seashell Shop?" Sometimes I wondered if he listened to me at all. "Remember, I told you about that?"

J.T. came through the hedge with Zoey behind him. I could tell from a distance that she wasn't happy.

"I thought you were kidding. You're hanging drywall? Really?" Ross was so clueless. "Well, let it wait a day, till after I'm gone. What're they gonna do about it? It's not

290

like they can find somebody else. That's why Dad's chapping me about all the rental houses. He can't get any construction help."

"I can't just . . . go off and leave the kids."

Ross braced his hands on his belt. "You leave the kids all the time, Tandi." He turned and started across the porch. "You know what? There's something goin' on with you lately, and whatever it is, I'm sick of it. You either want to be with me or you don't."

The panic place inside me cracked open. *You need to be nicer,* it warned. *You need to do what people want, or they'll leave.* "Ross, I do . . . I just . . ." Silhouetted there on the porch, Ross looked so much like my father, walking out the door again, leaving us behind. I felt sick. "I just can't this time, okay?"

"Yeah, fine, whatever." He brushed by the kids on his way down the stairs. Zoey ignored him.

"I'll call you tomorrow," I yelled after him. "Ross!" But he didn't answer.

"Why bother?" Zoey snapped as she skirted me. "He's a jerk. All guys are jerks." She continued through the door and dropped her backpack on the floor with a loud thump. J.T. slid in behind her and headed for his room. He didn't even hit the kitchen for food.

Zoey grabbed something out of the refrigerator, then slammed the door.

"What's the matter?" I wasn't ready to deal with more problems, but there they were, waiting in the form of an angry fourteen-year-old. "Did something happen with Rowdy?"

"Like *you* care," she shot back. "You just *wish* Rowdy would dump me. You're jealous because Rowdy's family has a lot more money than we do. Of course, *everybody* has more money than we do."

As usual lately, her venom was a splash in the face at first, a shock. Acid on bare skin. "Listen, I'm just asking because you came home by yourself and you seem mad. I thought you might want to talk about it or something."

"I don't." Tossing a waterfall of dark hair over her shoulder, she rounded the kitchen corner, her narrow hips swinging gracefully past it. She had on another shirt I didn't recognize. An Aéropostale. Expensive. It looked new.

"Zoey, stop. I don't have the energy for this, okay? What happened at school today? What's wrong?"

She whipped around, her lips pressed together in a hard line. "I want to go *home.*

I *hate* it here. I miss Karlie." Karlie was Zoey's best friend back in Dallas. She lived in the little groundskeeper's house on Trammel's place. She and Zoey had worn a path between the two homes. Anytime they could, Zoey and J.T. stayed the night at Karlie's. More nights than they should have, definitely, but things were easier that way. When I knew I had to leave, Karlie's mother had helped me get out. I hoped Trammel never discovered that she had anything to do with it.

"And Jake," Zoey added, softening for a moment. Jake was the boyfriend Zoey had left behind — sort of a nerdy, quiet kid who adored her, liked novels about dragons, and was nice to J.T. because they both played video games.

"I'm sorry, Zoey." I wished I could turn back the clock and give her a different life — not take the job showing Trammel's horses, not let myself be coaxed into moving my eight-year-old daughter and three-year-old son onto Trammel's place, not agree to ride exclusively for him. Not put myself in the position to be drawn in, completely dependent after the accident happened. There were so many things I'd do differently, if I could go back.

I wasn't sure what to say to Zoey. Who

was I to give advice? "Don't worry, okay? Things are going to be better for us here. They are. I know it."

"Yeah," Zoey muttered, then turned and walked down the hall. Surprisingly she went into J.T.'s room instead of her own. I heard them in there talking. It sounded like she was trying to get him to share his video game box. Life couldn't be too bad if she was doing that. Maybe after I left her alone awhile, she'd tell me what had happened with Rowdy and why she was suddenly homesick for Dallas.

While they were holed up in J.T.'s room, I slipped over to Iola's house and made sure all the drip buckets were in place. The air smelled like rain, and judging by the weather radar on TV, it wouldn't be just a sprinkle this time.

Back in the cottage, I rummaged through the boxes of food from Iola's house and came up with something for dinner. It would be good for Zoey if we could all sit down together for once, do the things that normal families do. Talk. Laugh. Share secrets.

The meal ended up being pancakes, leftover banana beignets, and frozen hash browns. It wasn't anything fancy, but I set the table with the old stoneware dishes from the cabinet. The colorful pattern of apples, leaves, and branches made the table look cheerful, despite the lack of meat or anything resembling a normal main course. The kids wouldn't care. They were always happy with pancakes. Before Zoey was nine, she knew how to make almost any kind of breakfast food she wanted. Looking at our supper now, I remembered the two of them, still innocent enough to watch me with expectation-filled eyes. They'd made a pancake meal, and they wanted me to come eat with them, but I was too hazed out to move. I could imagine their disappointment now, though I hadn't seen it then.

I hadn't even really seen *them,* I guessed. Not in years. Perhaps not in all of our years together. I'd been too busy gazing into the holes in myself and trying to find a way to fill them.

J.T. answered when I called down the hall. He poked his head out the door, his hand still tethered to a video game controller.

"Hey, come on, I fixed dinner."

His face squeezed around a confused frown. "I'm not real hungry, 'kay? I ate a doughnut at Bink's." A quick wince and then, "We didn't hang around there or anything." The video game was beeping behind him, demanding attention. "I gotta go. Snakefish wants me to fight him in the Hall of Doom."

He was already pushing the door closed as I started down the hall. "J.T., I *said* I fixed dinner. Tell Snakefish that the Hall of Doom can wait until later, and tell Zoey to come on too. What're you two doing in there?"

He fidgeted impatiently. "Zoey went someplace."

"Someplace?" I looked past him into the bedroom. "Where?"

His thin shoulders rose, then fell. "I dunno. She just said she was goin' someplace, then she gave me my PS3 back."

"Great." So much for my big plan. While I was at Iola's house, Zoey had flown the coop without saying a word. "She didn't say where? Or when she'd be back?"

Another shrug, another longing glance over his shoulder toward the game system, which sounded like it was about to levitate off the floor. "Mom, I gotta go. Snakefish —"

"Tell Snakefish you're busy!" I snapped, and J.T. jerked away, blinking at me. "Never mind. You know what, if nobody wants dinner, then . . . fine." Frustrated, tired from the day, I turned and stalked back up the hall.

A minute later, I was grabbing silverware off the little table by the window, yanking open the kitchen drawer, throwing everything in, knives and forks landing in an indistinguishable mix.

When I went back for the plates, J.T. was sliding into a chair, his chin trembling, his eyes two big, blue baseballs. "I think I'm hungry . . . kinda," he croaked out.

Tears flooded the spaces where anger had been. "Okay, baby," I whispered, grabbing a handful of silverware and bringing it back to the table, then leaning over J.T. to press a kiss into his hair.

"It looks good," he whispered, afraid to trouble the waters too much. "I like pancakes. A lot. Even better than doughnuts. A lot better."

Laughter pushed in over the tears. J.T. and I talked about Zago Wars and science class while we ate pancakes, undercooked hash browns, and perfect beignets. Afterward, we cleaned up and washed the dishes together. The only thing missing was Zoey.

There was a show about sea turtles on one of the cable channels. We watched it together, J.T.'s sharp shoulder blades pressing into me as I rested my chin on his head and strummed his hair. He mentioned that Mr. Chastain had brochures for turtle camp in his classroom. I didn't say no when he asked if he could go.

"We'll see. I hope so," I said instead. I was starting to see a future here . . . if I could get some money together . . . maybe buy some used tools of my own. . . .

The evening was dimming outside when headlights pressed through the windows. I stood, and J.T. fell limp against the sofa. I hadn't realized he was asleep.

A truck was turning in to the parking pad in front of the cottage when I opened the door. In the glare of the headlights, it was impossible to tell for sure, but it didn't look like Rowdy's Jeep. I shielded my eyes as the passenger door opened and Zoey slid out. Arms hugged tight, head tucked forward, she walked toward the house, underdressed for the cool evening air in shorts, sandals, and a T-shirt.

"Zoey, where were you?" I squinted toward the vehicle again. Something about it seemed familiar, but in the dark it was hard to tell. "Whose truck is that?"

"I went out w-walking." Her teeth chattered over the words.

"Walking?" The pickup driver cut the headlights, and the area in front of the house fell into the darkness. "For three hours?"

"I walked down to the p-p-pier." She stopped beside me, her body folding in on itself, her voice thick with tears.

"That's miles from here."

"I wanted to s-see if Rowdy was there . . . with . . . with somebody else. I wanted to check, okay?" A violent shudder shook her body, and her teeth rattled so hard that I winced. It was cool out here, but not that cold.

"Oh, Zoey," I soothed. It was the kind of stupid thing I would've done — go running around town, checking up on some guy who, in the end, would turn out to not be worth the effort. "Zoey . . ." I reached out to lay a hand on her hair. She pulled away, the porch light sliding over fresh red welts dotting her skin. "You're eaten up with mosquito bites."

"I'm okay." She started up the steps, then paused and turned. "Thanks for the ride, Mr. Chastain."

"Sure. No problem." I recognized the voice, and now I knew why the truck was familiar. It was Paul's. He turned off the engine and got out as Zoey crossed the porch. "Next time, either don't go so far or start out earlier. You shouldn't be out walking by yourself at dark."

"Okay," Zoey muttered, then went into

the house.

I walked down the porch steps as Paul came up the path.

"Sounds like there's trouble in paradise," he said, his tone offering a listening ear. "She didn't tell me much, but you work around kids awhile, you learn to read between the lines. I found her walking along the side of the highway, about two miles down."

I sank onto the porch step without asking if he wanted to stay and talk. "I don't know what she was thinking. She was upset when she came home, but I had no idea she'd . . . do anything like that. Lately, I don't know what's in her mind from one minute to the next, and it doesn't matter what I say to her, it's the wrong thing. It's like . . . she's not even the same person she was a couple months ago."

"Welcome to the teenage years." Paul's comment was light but sympathetic. He took a seat next to me on the step. "They are their own creatures. You have to think of it like *Invasion of the Body Snatchers*. Eventually the real Zoey will defeat the invaders — you just have to keep yourself from killing the host organism while you're waiting."

His geeky scientific explanation pulled a miserable smile from me. "But she's not like

300

that. She's always been . . . perfect. And to be honest, she hasn't had the perfect mom. But she's always kept it together. She's never done anything like this." She couldn't have afforded to, I knew. If she'd let things fall apart, there would have been no one to pick up the pieces. Even before Trammel, I was always shuffling the kids here and there so I could ride in some horse event, make my name in the business, make a living, chase after some guy I thought would love me, love us, fill the gaps in our lives. All things considered, Zoey had done an amazing job of growing up . . . until now.

Paul shoulder-bumped me, a friendly, familiar gesture that felt strangely comforting. "Like I said, body snatchers."

A breeze swirled across the porch, fanning the crape myrtles and chasing off the mosquitoes. It looked like the storm might blow over again. "I just . . . I worry that this last move . . . maybe it's too much for her, you know? We didn't come here under the best of circumstances." Loose strands of hair teased my lips, and I gathered them with my fingers, holding a ponytail and resting my head against my wrist. I knew I was telling him more than I should. "I'm sorry. You really don't need to hear all of that. Anyway, thanks for bringing her home." Letting go of my hair, I shifted toward my feet.

"I don't mind." Paul didn't move, just stayed where he was, his elbows comfortably balanced on his knees. "It's my grandmother's domino night at the church. I usually just go fish or whatever until it's time to pick her up. She can't drive anymore, but you wheel her up to the table and she can play a mean game of chicken foot or forty-two. It's cutthroat stuff. If she loses, she's mad for days, and I'll hear all about who she suspected of cheating on the draw. I figure it's good for her. It takes her mind off missing Grandpa." He chuckled, and the sweetness of that picture slipped over me — Paul driving his grandmother to the church and wheeling her up to the domino table.

I found myself wanting to etch out more scenes, fill in the colors and the shapes of Paul Chastain. "It's good that you're there for her. It must help a lot."

"Well, there's only so much you can do for someone in that situation." He paused to rub crusts of dirt off his fingers. "A lot of it, you just have to work through on your own — figure out what life's going to look like after you lose someone. Find a new normal. It's hard after you've been together a long time."

"That sounds like experience talking." I

was probing, but I felt the need to understand. When you're caught up in your own issues, you forget that other people's lives turn blind corners too, and they figure out how to move past it. Paul seemed so upbeat all the time. How did he manage that?

"My wife died three years ago after a lot of years and a lot of doctors — myeloid leukemia. She'd had it when she was a kid and again in medical school, so we always knew it was a possibility."

"Oh, I'm sorry." A cold lump traveled through my chest and rested somewhere in my stomach. I threaded my arms around it, trying to soothe the feeling away. "I didn't mean to bring up something so . . . painful."

Paul glanced sideways, his lips curving into a patient smile, barely readable in the dim porch light. "I wouldn't have said anything if it were a problem to talk about. We crammed a lot into the eight years we had. We didn't come up with a cure for cancer, but we saw a lot of places, looked at a lot of alternative therapies. That's one of the things I learned from Julia — the most important thing, I think. You can't run from your past. You have to take it for what it is and realize that it's part of you. The disease was part of who she was, but she wasn't going to let it control her. She made it the thing that reminded us we didn't have time to waste. Some of the best things in your life come out of the worst. It'll be that way for Zoey, too. Just give her time. She's a smart young lady. She's just trying to figure out who to be."

"I hope so. I'm worried that she'll do something like this while I'm gone to work." My mind was spinning ahead. "I can't watch her 24-7."

"So you found a job. J.T. mentioned that you'd been looking for one." I gave him a surprised look, and he added, "Well, it was in reference to turtle camp. He saw the brochure in class, and he was talking about whether or not you'd still be here during nesting season. He said it hinged on finding employment."

"I'm working down in Hatteras Village right now, doing water-damage repair and drywall at Sandy's Seashell Shop. I just sort of . . . stumbled into it, actually. Right place. Right time. I've had some experience with that kind of thing."

"I know the Seashell Shop crowd. They're good people." Paul didn't seem at all surprised that I was doing drywall work, nor did he question whether I could actually handle the job. "And if you're open to doing light carpentry and whatnot, I know quite a few older folks who could use some help with that sort of thing. For some of them, it's as simple as replacing lightbulbs or climbing a ladder to take down window screens or fixing storm damage on hurricane shutters and brackets. Actually, the neighbor who's got my tall ladder right now shouldn't be climbing it, if you want to know the truth. Anyway, if you're interested, let me know. I'll spread your name around."

"Thanks," I said, and I had that feeling again. The feeling that, against the odds, all of this might work out after all.

Overhead, the clouds parted, this storm moving on like the last one. Paul pointed toward the blanket of night sky in the gap. "North Star," he said quietly, and I tried to follow the trajectory of his finger.

"Which one?" I thought of the compass rose in the Hatteras library and my desperate wish that I could finally find true north in life.

"Right there." He leaned closer to me, baby-fine razor stubble ruffling my hair. "In the summertime, you can just find the Big Dipper and go straight up from the side of the bowl, but in the wintertime, it's down too low — behind the trees. This time of the year, you need to look for Cassiopeia.

See the sort of sideways W right there?" He traced it with his finger, and I followed along.

"Oh, okay. Yes, I see it."

"Now track from the middle of the W. Down this way, see?" His hand moved, his arm brushing my shoulder. "And there's Polaris, the North Star. It always sits over the North Pole. That's why sailors used it to navigate. The rest of the constellations around it — the Big Dipper, Cassiopeia — they're transpolar. They move around as the months of the year change, but the North Star never moves. It's constant."

I saw it then. The North Star. True north. Not so impossible to find, once someone showed you where to look.

CHAPTER 17

The flash of light woke me. I dragged my head off the pillow, groaning. After three days of working in Iola's house and going to the Seashell Shop, every muscle in my body ached. Over-the-counter ibuprofen was no match for it, but strangely enough, the pain felt good. It was evidence of something. A life. A completely new, wide-awake life.

Thunder rattled the cottage, and I sat upright, blinking the room into focus. In the glow from the hallway night-light, the furniture took on strange shapes. I watched the reflections in the arched dresser mirror as water dripped from the tin roof, playing a soft melody in the overgrown gardens.

It was a good thing that Paul had come by to do the mowing last evening and cleaned the gutters while he was here. He'd brought crawfish, held it forward in a bucket when he'd knocked on the door, then smiled at me and lifted an eyebrow. "I haven't got time to cook this stuff tonight if I'm gonna get the mowing done before the storms come in."

"Been seining again?" I teased, smoothing a hand over the hair flying out of my ponytail. I was a mess, sawdust all over me and bits of insulation in my hair from my slowly progressing wall rebuild at Sandy's. Paul didn't seem to notice.

"Well, actually these came from the fish market. I brought Mrs. Meeks some plants for her water garden, and she wouldn't let me out the door until I took something with me."

J.T. jumped up from the sofa, leaving his homework behind to see what was in the bucket. He'd been spending a lot of time in the living room the last couple days. Since Zoey's crazy walk to the pier, she'd taken over J.T.'s room and his video game — a distraction, I guessed. She was heartbroken that Rowdy seemed to have dumped her completely, which meant that her new crowd of school friends had ditched her too.

J.T. peeked into the bucket. "Whoa, awesome! Are those for us?"

"Yeah, if you can talk your mama into getting out a boiling pot, there's some good eatin' in here." Paul set it on the ground so

308

J.T. could investigate further. "J.T., you think you can run over to Bink's and pick up the stuff for a crawfish boil if I give you some money? Just ask Geneva what you need. She'll help you out." Paul glanced at me then. "That is, if you guys haven't eaten yet?"

A few minutes later, J.T. was bolting through the yard with twenty dollars to buy the necessities. I didn't argue. The longer we were here, the more relaxed I felt about it. I'd even let J.T. go to the church ice cream party with kids his age. Fairhope was starting to feel like home now. Our old lives seemed a million miles away.

I was glad that Paul had come by with the crawfish. Zoey had even emerged from the bedroom for a little while. It was a nice evening, just peaceful. I'd gone to bed feeling good about things, hoping the storms would pass over again.

Now the thunder and lightning outside proved that they hadn't. The rain thickened to a downpour, quickening my thoughts and stealing them away from the crawfish boil and the memory of Paul's lawn mower whirling through the yard. A waterfall was rushing off the eaves between my bedroom and the front porch.

The clock on the nightstand read 1 a.m.

How long had it been raining? How much water? I'd gone to bed early, taking a shower and falling onto the mattress just after Paul left at nine.

The buckets in Iola's house. What if they had filled up, spilled over?

My body creaked and groaned in harmony with the cottage floorboards as I stood and moved to the window. A flash of lightning illuminated the towering white house next door, the blowing trees, the water running off the turret roof in a sheet, shimmering and strangely beautiful, diaphanous like the veil tumbling from the conical hat of a fairy-tale princess. If only a knight in shining armor would ride in on a white horse and empty the drip buckets. I really didn't want to go over there in the dark, in the rain, with lightning streaking and the smell of the sea close in the air, but there was no prince to rescue the bucket-emptying handywoman. No suave Rhett Butler to kiss me on the forehead and say, *Return to bed, Scarlett, dah-ling. That storm is no place for a lady.*

The cold crept up my legs, and I shivered as I slipped on sweats, tennis shoes, and the one jacket I'd brought from Texas, then grabbed J.T.'s mini lantern from the kitchen table, along with the keys. I didn't have an umbrella, but thanks to Brother Guilbeau, there were plenty of trash bags, so I ripped a peephole in one and pulled it over my head. The picture was funny even at one in the morning, if you didn't think about the possibility of being struck by lightning or flattened by a falling tree branch and later found dead, looking like a giant, armless SpongeBob SquarePants.

The rain soaked me from the knees down on the trip through the grass, and water ran in rivers from my new Halloween costume as I dashed onto the porch and skinned off the bag, tucking it behind a rocking chair. Kicking off my soggy shoes and socks, I hunched against the blowing mist, grumbling at the old lock's stubbornness and the dim light of the mini lantern.

When I finally turned the knob, the door blew open, dragging me with it. I stumbled over the threshold and landed on Iola's welcome mat, the lantern skittering across the floor and blinking out. Behind me, the wind snatched the trash bag, filled it, and animated it so that it sailed into the hallway on its own power. The door rebounded from the wall and smacked my arm before I crawled out of the way, gasping and shuddering, staring in morbid fascination as the bag floated in the dim light from the lamp in the front room. The white plastic apparition seemed to hover for a moment between the hallways and the grand staircase before the front door finally swung shut on its own. Lightning flashed outside, the double-globe lamp in the front room flickered and died, and I scrambled to my feet. Darkness enveloped me, and in spite of all the time I'd spent here, I didn't feel welcome now. The house that had seemed such a comfort by day was anything but at night.

"Please, please, please come back on." The power on the island wasn't the most reliable right now. The infrastructure wasn't back up to par. "Any chance you've got some flashlights, like, right around here . . . ummm . . . Iola?"

A low growl answered from somewhere downstairs, and my stomach fell through the floor. "Kitty?" I whispered into the inky blackness. "It's just me. Here, kitty, kitty, kitty . . ."

The cat replied with a mew, friendlier this time, almost desperate. I caught a breath. "Do you know where your mommy keeps the flashlights?"

Something tickled my ankle, and I squealed. My voice echoed up the stairway, darting randomly through the darkness on bat wings. The cat had never come that close to me before. Out of reflex, I held my arms out and felt the air around me . . . just to make sure it wasn't something . . . bigger.

The lamp blinked on. "Oh, thank you," I murmured. "Thank-you-thank-you-thank-you-thank-you."

The cat was less than a foot away, looking up at me. I watched his pupils contract in the flood of light. I could have touched him. The bitten-off ear twitched as thunder rumbled. Then he mewed, his amber eyes beseeching, the ear lowering and his head ducking into his body.

"What? Don't tell me you're afraid of storms. A big, bad tomcat like you?"

He mewed again. I extended my arm and lightly touched his head, careful to keep my fingers away from his mouth, just in case. His body arched around me, and he leaned against my hand, suddenly my friend.

"Okay, now I know this is some weird dream." Any minute now, I would wake up in the cottage, still bloated on crawfish, corn, and boiled potatoes. Surely the cat who had been carefully avoiding me for days now wasn't meekly trailing me as I tried to get J.T.'s lantern to work, then moved through the house, checking closets and cubbyholes in search of a flashlight, in case the power went out again.

Unfortunately, there were a million hiding places for a flashlight in Iola's house, and if the cat had any clues, he wasn't telling. I finally ended up settling for an oil lamp that was sitting on the fireplace mantel in the small, narrow room where Iola's recliner and console television resided. Along one wall, an old Queen Anne settee sat dusty with disuse, keeping company with a set of TV trays, a magazine rack, and the window heat-and-air unit that had gone on and off every day like clockwork when Iola was still living here. I lingered for a moment at the bookshelf by the door. Iola was a fan of romance novels. Go figure. Some of the paperbacks looked like they'd been read a million times, the spines creased white, the titles practically gone. A few well-worn classics sat among them as well. A booklet — the kind probably printed for tourists at some time in the past — perched sideways atop three copies of *The Old Man and the Sea.* I tilted my head to read the title: *Historic Homes of Hatteras Island.*

The cat clung close to my legs again as I slid the booklet from the shelf and looked at the montage of photos on the cover. I recognized the image in the bottom left corner. The artificially colorized photo had been taken in better days when the gardens around this house were carefully manicured, the climbing roses trimmed, and the gingerbread railings on the porch freshly painted. A man in a suit stood beside a fifties-model car in the driveway, his thumbs tucked into the pockets of a vest that fit tightly over his round stomach, his chin upright and stiff. He wasn't smiling but regarding the camera with an aristocratic air meant to indicate that he was someone important.

The lantern cast light over my shoulder as I set it on an upper shelf and opened the booklet, thumbing through until I found the same photo inside. An older picture and a newer one flanked it. The old photo was of a party on the lawn beside the house, perhaps in the early forties, judging from the cars parked in the driveway. The caption underneath read, *Benoit House shown during the collegiate graduation celebration of Isabelle Renee Benoit, May 1941. Isabelle and her daughter, Christina, would both die young, leaving Benoit House and the Benoit shipping empire with no heir. Rumors of voodoo curses placed on the Benoit family by Haitian slaves would haunt Benoit House and Girard Benoit Sr. until his death from liver cancer in 1963, shortly after the Herbert C. Bonner Bridge, of which he was a strong proponent, officially linked Hatteras Island to the northern Outer Banks.*

On the opposite side of the page, a color photo showed Iola's house, not in its present state of decay, but not in its full glory, either. The flower beds were neatly groomed, but the paint on the garage building was weathered, and the upstairs railings were already leaning outward. A red Dodge Dart was parked in the garage.

The caption read, *Benoit House in 1981, now owned by Mrs. Iola Anne Poole, remains an example of Gilded Age splendor on the Outer Banks. (House not open for public viewing at this time.)*

Moving so that I wouldn't cast a shadow on the book, I scanned through the one-page article, the lantern glow flickering over the words as the house lights blinked off, then on. The details in the article were largely about the history of the house.

. . . built by a Carolina lumber tycoon in 1898, eventually purchased as a summer property by Girard Benoit Sr., a shipping magnate from New Orleans whose family had long-held interests in the Outer Banks. Benoit's adult sons from his first marriage lived briefly in the house. Both sons died in separate shipping accidents, one occurring just off Cape Hatteras, in an area known as Diamond Shoals, where two major Atlantic currents collide. The ship sank within sight of the Cape Hatteras Lighthouse, but rescuers were not able to reach it in time. Benoit's daughter from a short second marriage, Isabelle Renee Benoit, similarly died young, giving fuel to the legend that Benoit labored under a lifelong curse, placed on the family when a slave midwife was forced to leave her own daughter to labor through a deadly breech birth alone so that the midwife could attend to a birth in the Benoit home. After a long illness and rumored bouts of mental instability, Girard Benoit left his fortune to his household help, rather than to extended family members, in a much-rumored effort to protect them from the curse and thus ransom himself in death.

"Whoa," I breathed, looking down at the cat. "Okay . . . well now, there's a story, right?" That explained, perhaps, how Iola had come to own this house. Her family members were the household help.

I studied the room in the dim light — the books on the shelf, the stack of plastic tubs in one corner with misty outlines of yarn balls, knitting needles, and swatches of fabric showing through.

Was this her story? Was this why she had lived the way she did, almost as if she were a guest here? As if the furniture and the fixtures were not hers to alter? Did that explain the belongings packed in containers, stacked in the hallway? Did she feel guilty about taking over ownership? Did she feel as if this place had never really belonged to her?

The cat stopped moving and sat with his body pressed against my leg. His crooked tail curled around my ankle like a furry leg iron, the tip brushing back and forth over my foot.

"Aren't you just my best friend all of a sudden?" Lightning flashed outside, illuminating the dark corners of the room and blinking the lights again.

The cat ducked his head and let out a low, miserable sound.

"It's just a thunderstorm." I scratched his head, then untangled my leg and put the book back on the shelf, making sure it was exactly as I'd found it. All this business of family curses and mysterious deaths had shifted me off center. The only good thing about the pounding rain was that, if the house was making any of its usual noises — popping floorboards that sounded like footsteps, wind moaning through window sashes, bells ringing — I couldn't hear them tonight. There was only the drumming of the rain, the rush of water from downspouts, and the crash of clouds colliding like titans.

The overhead lightbulbs browned out, the filaments barely casting a glow as I carried the lamp through the house, the flame circle dancing against the paneled walls, sliding over boxes, reflecting against plastic containers, casting into dark rooms, and slipping over the random arrangements of furniture. Upstairs, there were new sounds. In addition to the bass of thunder, the snap of lightning, and the rumble of rain, the drip of water into containers played a strange, random melody. *Drop, plink, splash, plink, plink, plink, drip.* I stopped at the top of the stairs, looked both ways up and down the dark hall as far as the lamplight would allow, listened. This was Iola's music at the end of her life, the theme song of her struggle to save this house, to protect it.

Why did she care so much, if she had no one to leave it to?

If only I'd known, during those first weeks we lived in the cottage, when the cold rains fell endlessly. If I'd had any idea that the tiny old woman here, frail and stooped, had been dealing with all this mess, I could've helped.

I would have, wouldn't I?

I was afraid of the answer, if I looked at it honestly. Maybe I wouldn't have. I'd been so messed up, chopping the last of the Oxy-Contin into tiny pieces, taking a little less and a little less, trying to come back to earth, to lose the haggard, foggy-eyed look so I could search for jobs. Counting the pennies as they dwindled. Worrying about whether Trammel would find us.

I hadn't given one thought to the old woman in this house. The trouble with drowning in the mess of your own life is that you're not in any shape to save anyone else. You can't be a lighthouse when you're underwater yourself. If Iola were still alive now, I'd walk across the yard and ask what I could do to help. We'd sit on the porch and share tea and have long talks. She would show me the photo she'd shown the UPS driver — the one of her posing as a pinup girl.

Lightning struck so close that I jumped away from the hallway window. The hurricane glass on the lamp rattled, threatening to fall off. The cat hissed and skittered off. I realized I'd stepped on his tail.

"Be careful." The breathless words broke the silence that lingered when the noise died. I imagined myself tripping over the

320

cat, dropping the lamp, oil and flames shooting everywhere.

The cat mewed, watching from underneath a bowlegged table as I set down the lamp and emptied buckets. A new drip had started in the hallway. I scavenged a red-and-white kettle and placed it under the leak near the door to the blue room.

"Enough rain already," I murmured. The cat sidled closer again, standing with me in the doorway, his tail swaying back and forth, a feathery whip against my skin. The thunder had quieted. Hopefully the storm was moving away, headed across Pamlico Sound toward the tidewater marshes on the mainland.

I walked into the blue room — the last one I hadn't checked for water. So far, the ceiling in there seemed pristine. The room smelled neither of plaster nor of rain. On the east side, the windows and the double glass doors to the balcony rattled gently, glass shivering against fingers of wood. The walls seemed firm and solid as I set the lantern by the Tiffany Magnolia lamp and crept to the closet, slipping past the short stepladder to take the next box in order, to find out what happened to Iola after she wrote the letter I'd read just this morning. With working at Sandy's, I'd only been able to allow myself one box each day, but after three more years at the orphan school, Iola had ended the prayers of her fifteen-year-old year, 1938, with four words in large, joyful script, a bird in flight sketched beside them.

I am going home.

Home, I'd learned, was Monsieur's grand house near the French Quarter of New Orleans. Did Iola later move permanently to the Outer Banks with the Benoits? Why the change of heart about letting her return to the Benoit home in New Orleans at fifteen, after so many years of keeping her away?

This box was heavier than the others — made of tin, probably a container for food or cigars originally. It was decorated with faded prints of palm trees and water and dunes, the sort of images that might have come from tourist postcards back when the wonders of the world were represented in artificially pure colors, blended with misty pastoral lighting. Tiny knobbed whelk shells lined the edges of the lid — *a mermaid's necklace,* Pap-pap used to call them. When we found the tubular, papery cases on the beach, he'd cut them open with his pocket-knife and show us the miniature whelk shells hidden inside their translucent casings like white diamonds.

The hinged lid groaned softly, protesting my opening it, seeming to momentarily consider keeping its secrets. As always, I slid my fingers beneath the stack inside, lifted it out all at once, and turned it over on the bed. Sand sprinkled the quilt, and several tiny shells fell from among the pages, landing soundlessly and rolling into a patchwork valley of sea colors.

The first letter crackled in my hands, the parchment dry and fragile and smelling of age. A piece of pink sea glass slid along the fold and came to rest in the palm of my hand. I brought it into the lamplight. It was thin, perfectly round, with a thicker rim circling the edge. The base of a very old bottle perhaps. I wasn't surprised that a young girl would pick it up and save it among her most valuable things.

Rubbing the sea-smoothed edges between my fingers, I turned to the letter.

Dearest Father,
Forgive me. Again, it has been long since I have written to you. How strange that when the hours are long with misery, when needs are many and my heart aches, I seek the solace of conversation with you. Yet when the day is sun-

drenched and calm, as peaceful as a milk-full foal splayed on the grass, I am silent, my needs quiet in their slumber.

You have brought me one step short of heaven after my years away. If there is a bit of the divine on earth, these pearls of land among endless sea are that place. If ever all the troubles of the world could be left behind, cast away and washed out with the tide, these islands would hold that magic. I feel you everywhere around me now. I see you in all things — in the vastness of the sky, in the endless roll of the sea, in strange and wondrous creatures washed ashore, in treasures and mysteries, and the flight of seabirds over the water. Here at the edge of land and sea, there is no space for denying you.

Only days are left now before Isabelle will leave for her first term at college in Richmond, so we rush to grab the last of this glorious summer by the sea, this summer of only the two of us, here in this island home. We know that soon enough, Isabelle will board the ferry to travel inland, and Maman and Mama Tee will arrive to take over care of this house and keep it for Isabelle to return to during her respites from school.

There will be cleaning and airing out

and dusting and scrubbing and laundering and weeding in the gardens, but for now we leave the dust to itself. We walk over sandy floors and let it gather in moats along the creases of carpets. We run to the stable in the early morning, and we climb onto the old horse bareback, a poke slung over our shoulders. We ride to the sea, along the shore, and the old horse snorts and paws in the surf, tossing his head as if he were young again. His lungs fill beneath our thighs, his skin shudders, and he nickers into the wind. Somewhere in the distance, the wild ponies answer, I think. He quickens with the call of freedom, and so do we.

We travel farther than ever before, first riding, then walking together in the surf, the old horse trailing behind us on his lead. We collect shells and bits of sea glass, holding our finds in our palms and admiring their beauty, their magnificence, their perfection. We clutch them tightly as if this will somehow imprison time itself. This day kept still, inside a whelk's chambers, an iridescent angelwing clam, a parchment-like casing filled with tiny shells.

We climb among the bones of a shipwreck and imagine its final moments. We find a diving suit washed up along the shore, and together we weave stories of what might have happened to the diver. Isabelle's mind is fancy with ideas.

When the afternoon has finally spent itself, we stroll along the tide line, leading the old horse. He snorts and cocks an ear as ghost crabs begin to scuttle from their holes. The sun sinks low over the water, kissing the clouds with amber. The day is at its end, and it is one less day, and sadness overwhelms me.

Isabelle notices, and she asks after my mood.

"You're leaving in six days," I say. "Just six days. Maman and Mama Tee will be here in three." This time is almost over, this time of just the two of us with our sandy feet and long walks by the sea. Maman and Mama Tee will arrive to pack Isabelle off to college. Isabelle's father cannot do it. He is far away, seeking medical treatment for Madame. Mama Tee says she will not recover. Maman has seen the consumption enough to know it.

It seems that it was only yesterday I came from New Orleans with Isabelle. I think for a moment of Sister Marguerite, who wept as she bade me good-bye and sent me off with Monsieur's driver, Old Rupert. Now I feel as if I am Sister Marguerite, being left behind by someone who is eager to go away.

"I'll only be across the ferry and a short train ride away," says Isabelle. "I'll be home for term breaks and summers. You can come and visit me too."

"At college?" I imagine the looks I would get. A colored girl, prancing through the halls of that school.

"Why not?" asks Isabelle.

My laugh comes with an angry sound beneath it. "I don't want to go to school. I've had enough of school. I'm finally home."

"They have colleges for colored girls."

"I don't want to go to college. I never want to leave this place. I wish nothing would ever change," I say, but the sun is sinking lower. The crabs scuttle toward the tide line to feed. The day is fading.

Isabelle scoffs. "Not me. I'll see things and learn things and travel around the world." The scent of freedom is ambrosia in her mouth now. Since Madame Benoit is stricken with illness, there is no one to confine Isabelle. She is free, like the wild ponies on these Outer Banks.

But the ponies won't swim out to sea when they cannot sight the opposite shore. Isabelle will.

I look over my shoulder toward the bones of the ruined ship in the distance. I think of Isabelle's dead brothers, those young men who were gone before Isabelle and I were old enough to understand it. I think of what can happen when one sets off into the world, seeking adventure. I yearn for her to remain. "If that ship yonder had stayed in harbor, it wouldn't be wrecked on the beach, now would it?"

Isabelle dips sideways in her step, her shoulder bumping mine so that I stumble into the tide. "If that ship had stayed in harbor, it couldn't serve its purpose."

We say no more about it. Isabelle throws the reins over the horse's withers and snatches a handful of his mane to swing on board like wild Indians at the picture shows. I swing up behind her, and when we give the horse his head, he canters homeward along the sand, eager for our day's adventure to end.

I think on Isabelle's words now, Father, as I sit at my window, watching the moon take the sun's place overhead. I suppose I thought that you had answered my prayers in bringing me here, but now my mind is filled with ships and bones.

You are not a God of endless harbors. Harbors are for stagnant sails and barnacled wood, but the sea . . . the sea is fresh rain and cleansing breeze and sleek sails. You are a God of winds and tides. Of journeys and storms and navigation by stars and faith.

You send the ships forth to serve their purpose, but you do not send them forth alone, for the sea is yours, as well.

Be close to the sailors, Father. Wherever your tides may lead them.

Your loving daughter,
Iola Anne

CHAPTER 18

I dreamed of Iola's life, of the things I'd read and the scenes I'd imagined. I'd learned so much about her the night of the storm and in the two days since. I'd barely slept, lying awake after I went to bed each night, then finally rising, tiptoeing from the cottage, and spiriting across the lawn, Iola's house seeming to wait for me, its peaks and chimneys an angular shadow wrapped in a blanket of moon and stars. The house was a prayer box in itself, the keeping place of a woman's thoughts and dreams and secrets. Of who she was.

Now, on this third night, my dreams were filled with letters, words on scraps of paper washing up with the tide as I walked along some distant shore. Mist-covered dunes hid prayer boxes of all shapes and sizes — wooden, silver, decorated, brown cardboard, glass. Tangled in strands of salt grass, treasures waited — a rosary, a bit of sea glass, a tiny bottle found nearby the carcass of a shipwreck, a small starfish, a photo of Iola and Isabelle taken standing by a miniature hippopotamus at the 1940 World's Fair. Along the frame at the bottom, the text read, *Billy, the famous pygmy hippo once owned by President Coolidge.* The story floated through the mist, a scrap of words. Iola spoke to me as I slept, her voice that of a seventeen-year-old girl slowly discovering the world outside the island and the orphan school, through travels with Isabelle.

. . . and such wonder all around us! There are no words for these many amazing things. I sat with Isabelle in moving chairs at the General Motors pavilion, as we slowly circled Futurama, a tiny vision of what is to come. The world of 1960 will be beautiful, communities carefully arranged for commerce, fine living, and ease of transportation. The tiny buildings in the City of the Future are sleek and white, joined by grand roads that run like ribbons from here to there, their transfer points fanning out in spirals like the leaves on summer clover. Atop the city buildings, landing pads await autogiros and helicopters. I try to imagine such a place as this one, people sailing the air like a sea.

"Look at the roads!" Isabelle gasps. "One day, we'll climb into an auto and travel all the way to California without stopping." She squeezes my hand, her eyes wide as we pass by a circular airport where a tiny dirigible waits at a hangar. "Imagine it, Iola! All of us driving autos wherever we wish to go. Even the women. A car for every house!" When Isabelle comes home to the island, she pleads with Old Rupert to let her drive the car. "We won't need a ferry! We'll ride a dirigible to the island and be there in the blink of an eye."

I lean close and whisper, "Even the coloreds, do you think?" In my mind, I hear Maman hiss, *Keep them bright eyes down, Miss High-Tone. You might talk like them convent sisters, but you still a colored girl.*

"Ssshhh, Iola Anne!" Isabelle's lashes flash wide. We both know that I've been passing on this trip. People see two college girls, Isabelle in her sweater and me alongside. No one is the wiser, but neither Isabelle nor I have spoken of it. Maman sent me along to watch after her, and back home, Maman and Mama Tee and Old Rupert are fretting up a storm that we'll make it back safe before Monsieur comes to Benoit House. With Madame dead and buried, he has no place else to be.

I fall quiet in my seat as we circle round and round that miniature city of the future. I wonder, Father, in that future city is there a tiny colored girl who no longer keeps her eyes down?

"Stand up straight, Iola Anne," Isabelle says as we stroll along afterward, past the pavilions of Poland and Czechoslovakia, which have not reopened this year due to the war in Europe. Isabelle looks the other way, hooks her arm in mine, and passes by a woman handing out leaflets about knitting sweaters for the British soldiers. "It's bad enough we have to hear of it in the papers over and over again," she complains. "If it weren't for the war, I could finish my art education in France this last term, but who knows when I'll ever go anywhere, once Papa comes home. I'll never learn to drive an auto now."

"You will. In 1960, everyone will have them," I say to cheer her. "Just think of all those roads!"

We laugh and go along, playing our game of Let's Pretend together. We are two college girls, cousins out to the fair. No one notices, but I wonder, Father, are you angry with me? Sister Mary Constantine taught the sins of omission, long ago. I have become an omission.

At a dance for European war relief, a blond-haired soldier boy purchases a paper rose and asks if I might dance with him.

Isabelle whispers in my ear, "Don't say anything. Just go," pushing me away, her face as buoyant as her tumble of strawberry curls. "Go dance."

The soldier boy will leave soon to join the war effort. His parents are French, his grandparents engaged in the struggle against terrible forces. When the first dance is over, he smiles and whispers, "Such a beautiful face." He asks if he may write to me. I tell him that my mother would never approve of it.

"Then we have tonight to dance," he says, and my mind swirls and my feet are winged. Never have I lived a moment like this one.

There is no anathema tonight. . . .

I dreamed of Iola dancing with her soldier, their images floating featherlight against the sky, around them a world running headlong from the horse-and-buggy era toward a society of family cars, commercial airlines, and cross-country interstates. Everything was changing, and as Isabelle's world opened, Iola's was opening as well. But she was playing a dangerous game. There were laws governing such things.

Guilt followed Iola on the train home the next day, the newly acquired weight growing heavier and heavier as the train steamed south.

I know the wickedness of temptation, its sly and clever ways, the sweet taste of what is forbidden. I think to myself, *What would Sister Mary Constantine say?*

I know I must never do this thing again.

I know I must not write letters to this soldier boy, pretending to be what I am not. No good could come of it.

But still, I wonder. Could he love me if he knew?

Forgive me, Father. Forgive my weakness. Forgive my wondering.

Bring me to those beautiful shores of home and let me content my feet in the soft sands of all that you have prepared for me. Let me be thankful for all that you have given, neither hungering nor thirsting for what is not my cup.

Your loving daughter,

Iola Anne

The dim awareness of waking pulled me from the dream of Iola's letters. I felt the kiss of hot tears on my skin, draining into my hair. I wanted to take that young girl's hands in mine, say, *Don't listen. Don't let them tell you who you are. You're just as worthy as Isabelle.*

I blinked and blinked again, my eyes grainy and rough from sneaking away again to spend time in the boxes. Between working at Sandy's, cleaning at Iola's, and reading the letters at night, I was running on fumes, but things were finally taking shape. Satisfaction rested like a cool, soft sheet over me as I lay in my bed. The kitchen at Iola's house looked so much better. I'd stored all the newspapers in a closet under the stairs.

So far I'd managed the work at Sandy's. The old beadboard wainscoting had dried out nicely and gone back together more easily than I'd thought it would. The repairs on the drywall were progressing now.

Even things at home had settled down. Rowdy and Zoey were definitely history. She didn't want to talk about it, but she was acting more like herself, looking after her little brother, spending long hours in the back room with him, playing video games and helping him with his homework.

Paul had stopped by to finish the weed eating, and he and J.T. had cooked a hot dog supper on the old stone grill behind the cottage. It was nice to have a friend who was just a friend, not a guy looking to get something out of it. J.T. liked him. They walked around the yard together, talked about arthropods and gastropods and other scientific things. With a few leads on future handywoman work already coming in, sea turtle camp this summer seemed like a possibility.

"Ma-maaah . . ."

The sound startled me, sitting me upright. Zoey's voice.

"Zoey?" I whispered, throwing the covers aside and standing. The floor was salty-damp and cool as if someone had left the windows open last night.

"Ma-ma . . . ," she whimpered again. I wondered if she might be dreaming. The voice had her little-girl sound to it — needy, sweet, afraid to make too many demands on anyone.

In the small room next to mine, she was lying atop her bed, fully clothed in jeans and a tank top, but curled into herself, her arms wrapped around her long, thin legs, her bare feet tucked tight. At first glance, it was obvious that something was very wrong.

The window was open, the air cold. Her hair wasn't just damp but wet around her head. I touched the sheet, found it warm and wet despite the cool air. "Zoey." Her skin was fiery hot beneath my fingers. "What happened? Where have you been?"

"Mmmmh-nowhere," she moaned. "I was ummmh-gonna go . . . a party . . . Rowdy . . . at the beach, but I didn't f-f-feel good. Ummmh-body hurts, Mama . . ."

"Zoey, you're burning up." A hint of frustration came out in the words, and I hoped she couldn't hear it. Worries were racing already. *We can't afford a doctor visit. I can't stay home today. How would we even go to a doctor? We don't have any insurance.* I had no idea how much a visit might cost these days. For six years, Trammel had taken care of us, prescribing everything we needed.

"Mmmm sor-ry," Zoey sobbed miserably. Burying her face in the pillow, she tried to push my hand away.

"When did you start feeling bad? Why didn't you tell me sooner?" I smoothed a tangle of hair away from her lips. "Why in

338

the world were you trying to sneak out in the middle of the night to go to a party when you're sick? Please tell me you weren't chasing after Rowdy again."

"I wanted to go see . . ." She rose from the pillow and tried to reach for a cell phone on the night table. I'd never seen it before. "I got . . . gotta . . . go."

I pushed her shoulders gently back, then picked up the phone. The case looked new. I could only assume that Rowdy had bought it for her during one of their shopping sprees before they broke up. "Don't worry about him. Are you hurting anywhere else? Are you sick to your stomach?" We went through a list of symptoms. It sounded like the flu. I gave her ibuprofen and waited, hoping she would sleep, hoping the fever would break.

By six o'clock in the morning, she was worse. I ran a bath to cool her down and helped her into the tub, then paced the house, trying to decide what to do next. What if it was really something serious? What if it was more than just the flu? I didn't have the money for a doctor visit, much less an emergency room call. Would they even see Zoey if I couldn't pay for it on the spot?

Sandy would help if I called her, but she

had no idea what a shambles my life was in. Neither did any of the Seashell Shop women. If they knew, I would be a hard-luck story, a charity case. I wanted respect. I wanted to earn my own way. I wanted to build a life I could be proud of, one I could live in front of my kids without setting all the wrong examples. It was finally happening . . . and now this.

Zoey called for me, and I found her halfway out of the bathtub, dripping, shivering, clinging to the shower door. There was a faint rash on her stomach and back, the skin raw and red as she cowered in the towel, too exhausted to argue about my helping her into clean clothes.

She leaned on me, her head resting on my shoulder as I helped her into bed. "I th-th-think I f-f-feel better," she chattered out, but her skin sizzled against mine. "I don't need a d-d-doctor, 'kay? C-can I have some more M-M-Motrin yet? My b-b-body hurts."

J.T. passed by in the hall, moving in a sleepy stupor as he cast a concerned look our way. "What's wrong with Zoey?"

"She's sick. You stay out of here, all right?" I crossed the room and stopped him at the door. Hopefully, whatever it was, he hadn't caught it and wouldn't. "Are you okay? You don't feel sick or hot or anything?"

"Huh-uh." He folded his arms behind his back, his collarbones poking out against the neck of his T-shirt. "She wasn't sick last night when she was in my room."

"When you two were playing Zago Wars, you mean? I think it started after that. Sometime during the night." There was no point in telling J.T. that his sister had apparently been on her way out the window to chase after a boy who'd dumped her once already.

His lip curled, compacting the freckles on his nose. "Zoey doesn't *play* Zago Wars." He rolled his eyes as if I should surely know better than to have made that assumption. "She e-mails people." He whispered the words, flicking a worried look that told me he'd been threatened with his life if he told.

"Who's she e-mailing? I didn't know you could e-mail on that thing." Not that it would have mattered, even if I'd known. I probably would have been afraid to check my old account to see if there were any messages from the reporter I'd sent Trammel's secret records to. I couldn't get over the feeling that any form of contact with my old life could lead Trammel to us.

J.T. turtled his neck between his shoulders. "Ssshhh."

We moved to the kitchen, and he folded his bare legs into a chair.

"Okay, now spill. Who's Zoey been e-mailing? Do you know where she was headed last night? Who has she been talking to online?" I'd thought the story about Rowdy and a beach party hadn't made sense.

Who had she been planning to meet?

"She . . . ummm . . . she . . . doesn't tell." J.T. was hedging. He always rolled his eyes upward and looked at the ceiling when he was pulling a story out of the air.

"You'd better tell me the truth, and you'd better tell me now." I leaned close, made him look at me. "J.T., if you know anything about who your sister has been talking to or why, I need to know."

"She wouldn't tell me who. I tried to see the password, but she told me to quit snooping on her. She texted Rowdy last night. I looked at it when she was in the bathroom. He was mad at her because she wouldn't give the cell phone back. She told him she was going on a road trip, and she needed it."

"A road trip?" This got stranger by the minute . . . and more frightening. How did all the pieces fit together? What did they add up to?

There was only one person who knew for sure.

I left J.T. at the table and ran back to Zoey's room. "Zoey, I want to know what's going on with you. All of it."

I leaned closer, touched her cheek. Felt the heat of her breath on my fingers, but Zoey wouldn't answer.

CHAPTER 19

"West Nile virus? How did she . . . ? How serious is . . . ?" The words were scrambled in my head.

The emergency room doctor pressed the clipboard to his chest, leaned forward sympathetically, and pulled the door closed, the sound echoing down the corridor where we'd been waiting for news.

Paul touched my arm, steadying me. Cords of muscle contracted, then relaxed inside the torn-off sleeve of a sweatshirt he must have thrown on after my frantic call this morning. When Zoey wouldn't wake up, he was the first person I thought of.

West Nile virus . . . The idea exploded inside my head, setting off a flash fire. West Nile was in the news every summer in Texas. When horses contracted it, the virus could be fatal. Cities sent out spray trucks with vats of insecticide to kill mosquito larvae in roadside ditches. Last year, the outbreak was so epidemic, there had been aerial spraying in Dallas.

"It's carried by mosquitoes and contracted through a bite." The doctor was calm, clinical. "There's no history of direct human-to-human transmission, so there isn't any reason to worry that family members or friends could have caught it from her. Mr. Chastain mentioned that your son went on to school today. There's no need to keep him home, as long as he's showing no symptoms."

I tried to catch my breath. Surely the doctor would be more concerned than this if it were really serious. Surely they'd be rushing around, giving her IVs, antibiotics . . . something. I took a step toward the door. I wanted to see her. I needed to touch her, to lay my head against hers and tell her everything would be all right.

"Typically human cases of West Nile are subclinical, but about 20 percent of the people infected will show mild to severe flu-like symptoms. Most often, those pass within a day or two, although on occasion the symptoms can linger. The real concern when WNV does produce a febrile illness, such as in Zoey's case, is the secondary development of meningitis, encephalitis, or both. Fortunately her case has been caught early. We've brought the fever down. There's some newer research that indicates the use of anti-virals, so we're going to start those with Zoey, just to be cautious. As with other viral illnesses, such as shingles, there can be a risk of flaccid paralysis, so it's important to make sure her treatment is continued at home and that she continues with her medications even after she feels better. Teenagers sometimes think they're fully healed before they really are. Keep an eye on her. Make sure she doesn't try to do too much for a while. No school, no working, no running around with friends."

Paul sighed, his shoulders sagging with relief.

"Home?" Had I heard that correctly? Just a couple hours ago, Paul was lifting Zoey's limp body from the perspiration-soaked sheets and carrying her to the SUV as she moaned on his shoulder. Was the doctor trying to shuffle us out of here because, by now, he knew we couldn't pay? We'd barely gotten in the hospital door before a woman with a clipboard had whisked me into an office to fill out forms. While Paul sat in the waiting room with my baby girl, I'd been forced to explain that I had no insurance and no money. "Are you sure it's okay for her to go home? She doesn't need to stay in the hospital?"

"We'll keep her for observation for the day, but at this point I don't think we'll have to admit her overnight. As long as there's someone home with her the next few days, monitoring her temperature, making sure she takes in plenty of fluids and doesn't exert herself, things should be fine. She'll recover more quickly at home, where she's comfortable, and at home there's less risk of her being exposed to any secondary pathogens while her immune system is compromised by WNV. It's really the best thing. Just don't leave her by herself."

"Oh . . . oh, okay," I stammered, still trying to process everything as the doctor walked away.

Paul tucked his hands in the pockets of his bleach-spotted camp pants and smiled, his eyes gentle and kind, tender. A rush of emotions filled me, and a mist clouded the image of Paul, standing there with his crooked, freckled grin.

"She's going to be okay," I breathed.

"She's going to be okay," he repeated. "Was there ever any doubt? She comes from tough stock."

Our gazes caught, and a hot flush replaced the coolness of the corridor. I purposely didn't analyze the meaning of it but stepped away instead, felt the heat in my cheeks as I watched the doctor disappear through another doorway.

"Thanks, Paul." There was a lump in my throat. "I just . . . I didn't know who to call. Ross is out of town, and . . . When she was so sick, I couldn't think of what to do. I just . . . panicked. If you hadn't answered the phone, I don't know . . ."

"It's okay." Without the ever-present fishing hat, his red hair fell in tangled strands over his forehead, curling slightly at the ends as he looked at me. "You would've handled the situation, Tandi. But I'm glad you called. It's not a problem."

"You're a good friend." It seemed important to say the word out loud for both of us. *Friend.* The relationship needed a label, a category. What did you call the person who dropped everything and came running to save your life? Paul had been so cool, so logical through this whole thing. He knew his way around the rigmarole of hospitals and medical forms. The reason hadn't occurred to me until now. Did being here among the clinical sights and smells bring back memories of his wife's illness, her death?

"I was a basket case." It was embarrassing now, thinking about how I'd babbled and sobbed out half of my life story — no medical insurance, no money, no family I could ask. It was a testament to Paul's character that he was still here. He'd even taken the morning off school so that he could stay with us. I'd heard the secretary joking on the phone that he'd ruined his perfect attendance record for the year.

"You love your daughter." He leaned across the space between us, his fingers still tucked in his pockets. "Don't worry about it, okay? But . . . if you really *are* worried about it, and you really feel the *need* to pay me back for all this trouble, you could make me some of those banana beignets." He lifted both shoulders. "I'm just sayin' . . . if that would lessen the guilt in any way, I will be happy to do my part and eat said beignets."

Then we were laughing again, and the strangest realization slipped by, stealthy and quick, like the breeze sliding around the leeward edge of a dune. I loved the way Paul made me laugh.

"I am *so* going to make you beignets," I sniffle-chuckled, and we moved to the chairs to wait for someone to tell us we could see Zoey.

Ideas circled in my head as time ticked by, news of Zoey coming a bit at a time.

Beignets in cute baskets, an assortment of beignets made with different fruits, chocolate beignets, beignets with homemade whipped cream like Meemaw used to serve, beignets in a fishing basket, beignets shaped like fish. I could surprise Paul at school with beignets for the whole class. . . .

The parade of inspirations was a good distraction from the question of hospital bills and how I could possibly stay home with Zoey for several days. I had to work, and in fact I needed to be at work today. But there was still the question of who Zoey had been e-mailing and why she was planning to sneak out the window in the middle of the night. What if she tried to run off again? What if whoever she was talking to came by the cottage?

"You're quiet," Paul said as we sat in the hospital cafeteria eating lukewarm sandwiches that he had insisted on paying for.

I glanced at the clock above the food service counter. "Sorry. I'm just trying to think things through. I guess I should call Sandy and let her know that I can't come today."

Paul handed me his phone.

I took it and rubbed my thumb back and forth across the screen. "This'll leave Sandy in such a bind. She has the building inspector coming on Monday. If the place isn't ready, it's like a month before she can get him out there again. The music festival starts Wednesday. She's counting on being open by then." Maybe I could leave J.T. home to help Zoey. If I called from the shop every hour to see that they were okay, made sure she took her medicine on time . . .

Paul was already stretching across the table, reaching for the phone. "You know what, let me call the school and —"

"No, Paul." The words were quick and sharp, stopping him halfway out of his chair. He hovered there, his brows peaking under tangles of hair. I closed my eyes, tried to gather my thoughts. "I just . . . You've already done enough. You can't take more time off work for us." *Watch out,* the voice in my head was whispering. *When people give something, they want something back. What is he after? What does he want?* The voice surprised me, although it shouldn't have. I'd understood that push-pull all my life. I'd lived by it, learned the lesson over and over and over again. When people showed unusual interest — teachers, neighbors, other kids' parents, foster parents — they wanted to get close to you for some reason, and those reasons usually led to pain. Those people wanted you or they wanted your secrets. Either way, you were safer on your own.

"I don't mind." Paul's eyes were so earnest, the welcoming brown of damp earth. I could sink my feet in, fall right into him. But this, exactly this, was how I'd gotten in such a mess with Trammel — a crisis, a desperate moment, a slow building of dependence. After the accident, Trammel had been so kind, so helpful and generous, I couldn't say no.

I felt the hardness around my body like an extra layer of skin. Iola had softened it. She'd eased it with her letters. She'd whittled away at it with donated Tiffany lamps and shrimp boats washed ashore and fifty-dollar bills in envelopes for the grocery boy.

And look what happened to her. Look how things turned out. A crazy lady, locked in her house. Dead, and not one of those people cared. She could have bought anything she wanted with the money from that lamp. . . .

Then there was Paul, slowly settling back into his chair across from me, a crease forming between his brows as he tried to bore through my forehead and get at my thoughts.

"I just need to do this myself." What else was there to say really? It was the truth.

Before I could lose my nerve, I dialed the number for Sandy's shop. She answered on the first ring, and I stumbled through an explanation.

I hadn't even finished and she was trying to shut me down. "Wait. Now, just a minute."

My stomach started churning, the taste of roast beef on rye bubbling up. She was upset with me, of course. I couldn't blame her. "Listen, I know what a mess this will put you in. I'm so sorry, but I just . . . Zoey can't be home by herself right now."

Across the table, Paul was once again trying to offer himself up, in sign language this time. I pretended to be focused on the phone conversation.

"Okay, now *listen.*" Sandy's voice was flat, determined. I prepared myself to face that side of her I'd only heard about — the one that was reserved for building inspectors, teenagers showing too much PDA on the boardwalk, and rowdy drunks who wandered in off the beach. "There are two of us here, and with you, that makes three. The rest of us can't finish the drywall, but we sure can look after a sick little girl, so *I'll* tell *you* how this is going to work. The minute they let Zoey out of there, you call me. Sharon or I, or maybe even Teresa and Cassie, will be at your house by the time you get there, *with* chicken soup in hand. I'll even make the chicken soup from scratch. I'll run out and pick up the stuff right now. I've been home with sick kids more than you can count. What time do you think we'll need to be there?"

Color prickled into my cheeks and emotion choked my throat. Why so much more kindness than I really deserved? They made me wish that I were a better person, that I weren't hiding so much about myself. "I can't ask you to do that, Sandy. I . . ."

Across the table, Paul rolled his eyes and threw his palms up.

"You're not *asking.* I'm *telling.* Right now, I wouldn't care if you were the Octomom — if you'd have my wall ready by Monday, I'd watch after eight sick babies. I'm a grandma. I know how to do these things. You don't argue with a grandma when she's got her mind made up. You won't win."

"No, I guess not." I laughed and sniffled. This day was breaking me down and building me in so many ways that I didn't recognize my own shape anymore. "Thank you, Sandy. This is . . . I don't know how to . . ."

"There's no need. You're in the Sisterhood of the Seashell Shop now. We Shell Shop girls look after each other. That's how it

354

works. What God puts together, no building inspector nor nasty virus nor category 2 hurricane can tear apart. It's like being married, only without the hanky-panky. Once you're ours, you're ours forever."

I couldn't even answer. I just nodded as Sandy went on.

"You call me the minute you know anything. I'm headed out for chicken and celery." She gave me her mobile number. Paul slid a pen from his shirt pocket and wrote it on a napkin as I repeated it.

There was a knowing look in his eyes when he handed me the napkin. His lips pulled sideways into a self-satisfied smirk.

"See?" His smirk added, *You should have listened to me in the first place.*

The strangest feeling came over me when we were finally notified that we could go upstairs to see Zoey. It was like the light from my dream — a fully enveloping warmth that surrounded my body from outside but came from inside me as well. I'd never known anything like it. As we stood in the elevator, I closed my eyes, let my head fall against the wall, felt it around me and through me. For a moment, there seemed to be nothing in the world to fear. Nothing more powerful than this.

The door chimed, I opened my eyes, and

the spell was broken. Tension crackled through me like an electrical current as I left Paul outside the room of curtained beds and followed a nurse back to the one that was hiding Zoey. She opened her eyes drowsily at the sound of my voice.

"Mama?" A whisper was all she could manage. She looked so pale and drained, her skin ashen alongside her dark hair, her eyes luminously blue against the pallor.

"Hi, sweetheart," I said and kissed her. "How are you feeling?"

"What happened?" she murmured, seeming confused by the curtain, the stainless steel trays, the tubes and monitors sitting idle in the corners.

"You've got a virus. You were really sick last night." She didn't remember any of it, I guessed. Maybe that was just as well.

"Did I go to Aunt . . . Aunt Gina's?" She pushed an arm against the mattress, trying to lift herself.

"Ssshhh. Lie still, okay?" *Aunt Gina's?* What in the world . . . ?

I hadn't heard from Gina in months. Six weeks after Trammel threw her off his place, she blew through town with a carful of cosmetic samples and wanted to pick up the clothes she'd left behind. Somehow, she'd landed a job selling makeup to drugstores. Gina had always been tall, willowy, beautiful like our mother. And like Mama, she knew exactly how to use it.

"Are we in Tex . . . Texas?" Zoey's hair bunched against the pillow as she looked for clues in the room.

A picture began sketching itself in my mind, the lines slowly filling in. Zoey had been trying to run away, and it had something to do with my sister. All that secret e-mailing had been about making plans. "Were you trying to go back to Dallas? Is that what's been going on?"

She turned her face away, closed her eyes, and tried to lose herself in the pillow. She was so tired, so weak, but I needed to know what she'd gotten herself into. "Zoey, were you trying to run away?"

Tears seeped beneath her lashes, and I was sorry I'd asked. "Why do *you* care?"

"Zoey, of course I care." Suddenly her illness was a blessing, the virus like an instrument of salvation. Instead of lying in a hospital bed, she could be . . . anywhere right now. How in the world did she plan to get all the way back to Texas? "Did Aunt Gina have anything to do with this?"

Even exhausted, her face revealed the truth.

CHAPTER 20

On Monday, when I stepped out the door to leave for the Shell Shop, Geneva Bink, of all people, was pulling into the cottage driveway in the little golf cart she kept next to the grocery store. She held up a casserole dish covered in a gingham napkin, smiling over the top of it as she exited the golf cart.

"I was just making our famous crunchy-sausage-and-crab balls for the ladies' lunch at church tomorrow. I thought I'd bring a plate over," she said as if it were the most natural thing in the world for her to be showing up on my doorstep.

Zoey bumped into me from behind, surprised when I stopped in the doorway. I'd made the command decision to take Zoey to work with me instead of leaving her home alone. The grandmothering from the Shell Shop girls had worked wonders in the last few days. Zoey was better physically, but not at all enthusiastic about returning to school sometime in the near future. With Rowdy and his crowd ignoring her, she felt hopeless and lonely, and there wasn't much the Shell Shop Sisters or I could do to help that issue.

Zoey threaded her way around me as Geneva came up the steps, holding the gingham napkin in place with her thumbs as the wind toyed with it. "Well, my goodness, look at you!" Geneva twittered when she saw Zoey. "Glad you're up and around. I hope that brother of yours hasn't been stuffing you too full of doughnuts these last couple days." With Zoey sick and me working like a banshee to piece Sandy's shop back together for inspection, J.T. had been hanging around at Bink's more than ever. He'd been coming home with little baskets of goodies packed by Geneva, in addition to the leftover doughnuts.

"Thanks for the cookies and stuff." Zoey's voice was lifeless and flat. Recovering or not, she still had misery written all over her.

"Well, sure. It's my pleasure." Geneva balanced the dish in one hand and touched Zoey's arm as she passed. "You just feel better, all right? That brother of yours has been worried about you."

Zoey forced a sad, tired smile and went on to the car.

Geneva and I stood in awkward silence, the scent of crab balls wafting up. "Those smell really good," I said finally, thinking I would take the dish to the Shell Shop. We'd all be working like crazy, getting everything in place for the inspection today and hopefully an opening before the music festival started. I'd finished the second coat of paint on the wall last night, while Teresa and Cassie sat at the house with Zoey and Paul took J.T. night fishing.

"One of my specialties." Geneva reached across the space between us and helped me capture the fluttering napkin. Her hand lingered there a moment. "I'm sorry we haven't been better neighbors. We're usually a friendly bunch, here in Fairhope. But it's always been a strange situation . . . with Iola and the house. I'm sorry you got caught in the middle of it. It has nothing to do with you and your precious kids. We're glad to have you here. We don't get new families all that often."

It has nothing to do with you . . . The muscles in my neck stiffened. "What, exactly, did I get caught in the middle of? I've wondered."

Geneva's lips pursed, her gaze flicking away. "Well . . . I never really understood all of it myself, not being from Fairhope. Bink and I didn't move back here until his parents gave up the store and retired about ten years ago. I mean, I'd heard a little chatter over the years when we visited — it's hard to come to Fairhope and not wonder about this big house. The whole patch of woods back there is part of the estate. It runs right behind our cottage. I'd heard Iola Anne Poole's name muttered around, but folks don't like to talk about it. But they haven't forgotten, either."

Geneva's gaze darted nervously toward the big white house. Then she leaned close and whispered, "She *stole* this place when old Mr. Benoit died. His mind wasn't good, and she took advantage of it — at least that's how the story goes. I try not to tell things as true, if I wasn't there. And I wasn't. But Girard Benoit's family members expected to inherit the estate, and there was an agreement to sell it to a group of local folks and repurpose it for a resort — sort of the bygone era of shipping tycoons, the grace and grandeur of *Titanic* and all that kind of thing. They'd already put quite a bit into forming the corporation and having all the legal work done. Almost everyone in Fairhope had money invested, and these weren't rich people. Then, next thing they knew, old Mr. Benoit died, and it all belonged to Iola, not the rightful heirs — his nephews. She wouldn't hear of selling it. Folks feel like she took advantage of the old man when he was bedridden and out of his mind — maybe threatened him with that nonsense about a voodoo curse and who knows what else. It set a lot of people back financially, and of course it kept all the new tourist business from coming to Fairhope."

Glancing toward the house again, she held her hands up at her sides. "Like I said, I don't know what's true, and Matthew 12 says that the things that come out of the mouth come from the heart, and that's not the kind of heart I want to have. I wish I'd tried harder to be a neighbor to Iola in the ten years we've been here, but it always started trouble with Bink, and to tell you the truth, I hated to see her just letting this house go downhill. She couldn't take care of the place, but she wouldn't turn loose of it."

"She loved this place," I said quietly, thinking of her letters. *You have brought me one step short of heaven. . . .* "People have no idea how much she loved the island. She'd been here most of her life." But Geneva was right. By clinging to the house, she'd come close to destroying it.

"I know the church has some hope of taking over ownership of it, but I'm afraid that's not what's going to happen." Geneva sighed. "Bink keeps an ear to the ground, and he's heard that the county commission is bound and determined to have this property for an eventual storm-water-management site. Since the hurricane, they've gotten a lot of pressure and support from high-dollar homeowners farther up the island, who are tired of their houses sitting in water every time a rain comes along. Bink believes that they'll make Fairhope into one big holding pond, if they can. It's David and Goliath, and I hate to say it, but we're David. The only slingshot that's kept this thing at bay was the fact that Benoit House was a historic landmark, and thanks to Iola, that may be ruined. If the house isn't viable, there is no landmark. Of course people are mad. Anyway, you asked, and that's the story as I know it. I'd better get back to the store."

I said good-bye to Geneva with a singular, terrible image in my mind — the little village of Fairhope, Iola's grand old house and the ancient maritime forest behind it, reduced to a holding pond.

In the car, Zoey was slumped in her seat, her head resting against the window, her face a picture of unhappiness. "You didn't have to bring me with you. I'm not gonna run away. I don't have any place to go, anyway." She'd refused to explain how she'd planned to get back to Texas, other than that she'd hoped to pawn the phone Rowdy had bought her and return some of the clothes that still had tags on. She thought that would be enough to buy a bus ticket.

Her problems inched into my mind, elbowing out Iola and her house. I wanted to make everything better for my little girl, take away all the pain, but nothing seemed to help. No matter how many times I told her that Rowdy wasn't worth all this heartbreak, and no matter how kind Sandy and the Shell Shop girls were to her, Zoey couldn't seem to break out of the gloom.

"I didn't decide to bring you along because I don't trust you, Zoey. I just thought . . . it might be a nice day for you. Different scenery, you know? If you feel like it, you can help Sandy with displays or something in the shop, and if you don't feel like doing anything, there are plenty of sofas and books and a couple computers with Internet service in the coffee bar." I instantly wished I hadn't brought that up. I didn't want her to think of contacting Gina. I'd hidden J.T.'s game box in Iola's house. The strange thing was that J.T. didn't seem to mind. He was more interested in hanging out at Bink's or with Brother Guilbeau or going fishing with Paul. Where his skin had always been sallow and pale, now he was ruddy and sun-kissed, an island boy with freckles under a tan, his hair bleaching to a soft gold on the ends. Brother Guilbeau had bought him a fishing hat so his nose wouldn't burn anymore.

I wished things were going so well for Zoey. "Not like that'll do me any good," she sighed. "Aunt Gina never even answered me when I told her I was coming down there. I guess she didn't really mean it about the extra room I could stay in." The truck bounced over a chuckhole, and her head rattled against the window. She didn't seem to care.

"Zoey, you never know what Aunt Gina means. She just . . . says the things she thinks people want to hear. Whatever's easy at the moment. Maybe she means it when she says it; I don't know. But she never should have told you anything like that." If I had the first idea where to find my sister, I'd snatch every hair from her pretty blonde head.

"Yeah." Zoey crumpled against the door again, watching without interest as hedges, hotels, and beach homes drifted by. She barely bothered to look when I pointed to the roof of Sandy's Seashell Shop, ahead on the right. As the place came fully into view, she sat up slightly, taking in the bright-yellow exterior, the colorful chairs and tables on the deck outside.

"Pretty neat, huh?" A sense of pride warmed me. I felt like a piece of Sandy's Seashell Shop was mine. My own little Ocean of Possibilities.

Zoey craned forward. "Yeah." She had a little more enthusiasm now. Once we were inside, hopefully Sandy, Sharon, and all their treasures would help. The Seashell Shop was like Iola's house. It had a magic all its own.

Inside, Sandy was already red-faced and sweating. She was bustling around the shop, pressing the end of a pen against different areas of the drywall. Before we'd painted yesterday, I'd fixed old termite-eaten areas we'd discovered in several other places, including a couple in the ceiling. The patches weren't perfect, but they were close. There wasn't any way the building inspector would find them.

"I'm just making sure," Sandy said without stopping to look at us as I carried the dish of crab balls to the coffee counter. "When that nasty inspector gets here, there is not going to be one thing he can find to fail us." She lifted the pen into the air, posing momentarily, her short blonde hair falling in sweaty strings over her forehead. "As God is my witness, we shall never be red-tagged again!"

Zoey gave me the sideways fish-eye, as in, *Is this what you people do around here?*

"No, we won't!" I pumped a fist in agreement. I'd gotten used to Sandy's rabid enthusiasm. The woman was part pit bull, part Energizer Bunny, and part tent preacher. For her, nothing was beyond the realm of prayer and possibility.

"Youth music festival starts this week," she reminded, then noticed Zoey trailing behind me. "Oh, hey, Zoey. You look like you're a whole sight better today. That's good. You can sort jewelry for me and put together some Build Your Own Beach kits — I want to have plenty in stock in the glass globes and also the little ones in the clamshells. Tourists love those for take-home gifts. No time to loll around. We've got to be up and running, fully stocked, and back in the swing before the first day of the festival. George is going to stop by Sam's Club on his way home from the airport to pick up supplies for the coffee bar. If we don't pass inspection and get the place open, all will be lost and the food George brings home will go to rot, but no pressure or anything. Help me check these walls one more time. Just to make sure. Not that I don't trust you. But you don't know what that new inspector's like. Not you, Zoey. You get those crates off the counter and sort out the jewelry for the Peg-Boards and then get to work on some BYOB kits. Ask Sharon to show you the stuff, and you can pick what to put in each one. It's all in a big jumble back there. We just threw it in boxes last fall. Don't work too much. You should be resting. But get the jewelry sorted and the kits made, okay?"

Sandy paused for a breath, and Zoey looked at me, blinking wide.

"Welcome to the Sisterhood of the Seashell Shop," I laughed, then slipped behind the counter for my putty knife. I wouldn't need it, I knew. These walls were right as rain. I'd been over every single solitary inch.

We were checking the walls, and Zoey was sorting jewelry, when the phone rang on the coffee counter.

Sandy answered, then handed it to me. "It's *Lover Boy.*"

Ross had called me at the shop yesterday. He was sitting at a hotel, bored and stuck somewhere in Mississippi, waiting for repairs on the lumber truck. I'd yakked as long as I thought I could get away with, holding the phone to my ear and commiserating while Ross ranted about his father being too cheap to buy new trucks. He was going to miss an amateur surf competition after he'd already paid the entry fee.

Sorry, I mouthed as I reached for the phone. Sandy clearly wasn't in the mood for distractions today.

I let Ross spill the latest in the saga of the broken truck for a minute, then tried to gently tell him I needed to go. "It's inspection day, so we're really cramming right now," I added. "Call me this evening, 'kay? I'm sorry you're stuck on the road."

"Yeah . . . well, it stinks. But I'm keeping my fingers crossed that the part comes in today. I could drive all night and get back to Hatteras in time to still make it before sign-in. I need my board, though. I left it down at the house on Ocracoke, so if you can catch the ferry down today, then bring it back, I'll pick it up at your place and be good to go. There's a key under the dead plant on the porch. I'll give you directions to the house. It's not hard to find."

"What? Ross, I can't go —"

"And the dog's there too. I didn't get a

369

chance to take him over to Mom and Dad's before I left, and he's probably out of food by now. I left a bucketful, but he eats like a horse. There's extra in the garage." His voice echoed into the room.

Zoey snorted, sorting jewelry on the coffee table. I realized that everyone else was catching at least the gist of this.

"Ross, I can't go down to Ocracoke today." Balancing the phone on my shoulder, I squatted by the baseboard to pull off the painter's tape from last night. "It's a forty-minute ferry ride, one way, and we're trying to get the shop ready for inspection today. I can't leave."

Ross made a sound that was somewhere between a groan and a whimper. "Well, okay . . . all right, Zoey can go after school. Tell her that as soon as I get back, I'll give her fifty bucks for doing it. She can get Romeo to ride along. They can take his car across with them."

"Zoey can't go. She's had West Nile virus, remember?" What world did Ross live in sometimes?

Zoey sneered at the phone. "Of course he doesn't remember."

Across the room, Sandy smacked her lips apart.

"Ross, I have to go."

"But the dog needs food and water, Tandi, and I need my board." All of a sudden, he sounded like a lost little boy.

"I *can't* take care of it. I'm sorry. You'll have to call Gumby or a neighbor down on Ocracoke or somebody else to feed your dog at least, okay?"

"Yeah . . . well . . . fine."

He said good-bye and we hung up.

"He's such a jerk." Zoey was untangling one pearl necklace from another. "I feel sorry for the dog."

Sandy scooped up Chum and gave him a noogie while he snorted and tried to lick her. "I'd never lock *you* in a yard and leave you without food while I went out of town." She started toward the back door without saying anything more, but clearly Sandy didn't have a high opinion of Ross so far.

I was glad when the morning passed and he didn't call again. Hopefully that meant he'd found someone to take care of the dog.

Zoey fell asleep on the sofa before lunch. By then, Sharon and Teresa had shown up, and the four of us had the shop ready for inspection. I left Zoey on the sofa and went outside to join the Shell Shop girls at a table on the deck. Sandy had decreed that there wasn't one more thing we could possibly do to prepare, and so we should take a break for crab balls and coffee. The inspector wasn't due for two hours yet.

I lost track of the chatter at lunch. I was thinking of Zoey and how monumentally sad she'd looked, sitting there sorting the jewelry, her movements robotic and disinterested. This fairy tale of an empty bedroom at Aunt Gina's was just one more blow, one more rejection when she was already hurting. I wanted to make everything better, but I didn't know how.

A pile of driftwood in back of the workshop caught my eye as Teresa and her mother said good-bye and Sharon got up to walk around front with them.

"You're in another world," Sandy remarked.

Chum hopped into one of the recently emptied chairs and sat down, his bug eyes shifting back and forth between Sandy and me as if he were looking for a chance to break into the conversation.

"I was just thinking about Zoey. She's having such a hard time getting over the breakup with Rowdy. She doesn't want to go back to school."

Sandy reclined in her chair, watching two kids in kayaks pass by on the sound. "Well, she's young. Rejection is hard to deal with when you're young. Give her time. She'll be stronger for it in the long run." Chum bounded into Sandy's lap and tried to kiss her, and she pushed his little snout away. "Stop that. I'll throw you to the sharks. You'll end up somewhere out to sea with my picture frame and the rest of my glass boxes."

An idea lit in my mind, sudden and alluring. "Sandy, could I have a piece of that driftwood that's piled behind the shop?"

Leaning around me, she looked at the wood. "Well, sure, if you want it. We just threw it there after the storm to get it out of the way. What've you got in mind?"

"I want to make something for Zoey. Would you mind if I used the tools out in the workshop? I mean, if there's nothing else you need me to do inside right now, that is. I'm too nervous to sit and wait for the inspector to show up, but I don't want to go home, either. I want to be here when he can't find one thing to complain about."

Sandy winked, then pointed a finger at me. "I like your confidence, and of course you can use anything you need in the workshop. My place is your place." Bracing her hands, she pushed to her feet, groaning. "I've gotta go sweep the porch or something. I'm a wreck."

She patted my shoulder as she circled the

table, then walked back into the store. Chum started after her but decided to follow me instead. Together, we selected just the right piece of driftwood from the pile — one grayed and cracked from the salt water, twisted and knotted in a way that spoke of struggle and strength. Chum helped himself to an empty stool near the workbench, watching as I measured and planned. Sometime later, he fell asleep to the hum and whine of the band saw.

All else seemed to fade away as I worked. I forgot about Zoey's problems and my own and the store inspection. There was only the bit of driftwood, slowly changing as I worked, slowly becoming something new.

Its intended form was taking shape when Zoey's voice traveled in from the back deck. "Mama! Mama!"

I hadn't heard that much emotion in her voice in so long. My heart sped up, and I wondered if something was wrong.

I covered my driftwood creation just in time. Zoey burst through the door, and Chum met her, yipping and wagging. They skidded into each other on the sawdust and nearly toppled a plastic container filled with sheet glass.

"Mama!" Zoey wheezed, catching her breath.

"Zoey, what's the matter?"

Her eyes glittered, her cheeks flushing as her lips parted in a smile. "We passed! The inspection. The guy showed up early, and I walked around with him and Sandy, and I was coughing a little, and I told him I had West Nile, and he didn't stay here very long *at all* — I think he thought I was, like, Typhoid Mary — and we *passed*!"

CHAPTER 21

A storm was slated to roll onto the island during the grand reopening day of the Seashell Shop. We watched the prediction on the news before finally locking the doors and leaving on Tuesday. The shop was cleaned and organized, fully stocked and waiting for the music festival customers to arrive. After working on inventory and sorting, polishing, and washing mud-covered pottery that had been stored in the shed after the last hurricane, the shopgirls were exhausted. We'd been like sailors on a ship making ready for the wild waters around Cape Hatteras, Sandy at the helm issuing orders and the rest of us scurrying.

Before we left, Sandy had rounded us up on the porch — all the Seashell Shop Sisters, Sandy's husband, George, Greg and Crystal from the restaurant next door, Paul and J.T., who'd come by after school, and Zoey, who made excuses not to go to school that day, complaining that she still didn't feel well. Watching her work at the shop, it was obvious that she wasn't really sick anymore. I was dreading forcing her to finally get on the bus with J.T. It would be an ugly battle of wills. Spending time with her at Sandy's the past couple days had been nice, more relaxed. The shopgirls fawned over her like a gaggle of grandmas, giving her and the West Nile virus credit for chasing away the inspector. Zoey laughed and talked and seemed more like her old self. It was good to see her happy.

Sandy wanted us to pray for tomorrow's reopening — right there outside the shop, with the cars rushing by. Zoey glanced at me, probably thinking I'd find some way to make a run for the car before the prayer circle could form, but I didn't. After weeks of sharing Iola's prayers, journeying along as she offered up her hopes, her pain, her helplessness and confusion when life didn't happen according to plan, it seemed natural. I'd started to write notes of my own and tuck them into a rusty cracker tin I'd unearthed in Iola's pantry and taken back to the cottage. A prayer box for myself. My first.

Someday, when I could afford it, I'd buy the lighthouse box from Sandy — the one that had survived the storm — and make things more official. Sandy had offered to give it to me, but I told her I'd rather pay for it. She'd agreed to put it in the storeroom until I was ready.

For now, my notes were simple, a fledgling effort at conversation, but committing them to the cracker tin somehow helped me to let the thoughts go and stop spinning them round and round in my head.

Thank you for Zoey's smile. Help me to help her, to show her how amazing she is. . . .

Thank you for Sandy and the Sisterhood of the Shell Shop. . . .

Please protect Iola's house. Show me what I should do. Stop them from tearing it down. Help me to save it somehow. There must be a way. . . .

Send good weather. No more rain. There's so much plaster falling in. . . .

Sandy and the Shell Shop girls were praying for good weather too. I felt the urgency of that prayer through our clasped hands, Zoey's on one side and J.T.'s on the other, linking to Paul. Each of us knew the high stakes of the days ahead. Hatteras had pieced itself back together again, and if the music festival didn't bring in a crowd, it would be a blow to the local businesses — an indication that tourists had decided to stay farther north on the Banks for now, rather than returning to Hatteras, where the streets were still dotted with ravaged houses and the remnants of storm damage.

When the prayer was over, we left quietly, like parishioners exiting church. Even Chum walked soberly off the porch rather than doing his usual crazy-dog figure eights.

J.T. asked if he could go by the classroom with Paul to get some things ready for tomorrow's lab project, and I let him. I knew that when Paul dropped J.T. off later, he would probably sit in his truck a minute before he backed out, and I would probably go outside. We would linger and talk about the day or Zoey's issues or some funny question J.T. had come up with while he and Paul were out and about. The routine had become an unspoken thing that both of us looked forward to.

Zoey and I drove home without saying much. I tried talking to her about going back to school tomorrow. She went into avoidance mode.

"Not tomorrow. It's opening day." A desperate look slanted my way, her bottom lip unconsciously pooching out in a pout, then trembling a little. "I'm caught up on all my homework, anyway." Paul had been helping by gathering Zoey's work and sending it home with J.T.

I caved. "Okay. One more day. But, Zoey, you're going to have to face this. You can't let other people decide your life for you. Who cares what Rowdy and his friends say about you or think about you? Other people's judgment doesn't have any power unless you offer yourself up for trial, so don't."

Zoey blinked and looked at me like I had two heads. That last part didn't sound like anything that would've come from my mouth. It was a quote directly from one of Iola's letters — a bit of parting advice from Sister Marguerite. Something I was trying to remember. I'd been offering myself up for trial my whole life, determining myself by what my parents said about me, whether men wanted me, whether the wives in Trammel's circle accepted me. It had never even crossed my mind that I had a choice in the matter.

Remember that you are God's, not theirs. Sister Marguerite's final words to Iola as she walked through the gates of the orphanage for the last time.

I wrote it down that night and tucked it into my box. *Please help Zoey to see that she isn't theirs.*

Thunder was rumbling outside when I closed the box and went to bed. I was tempted to sneak over to Iola's house to check the drip buckets, but that would only lure me into staying. I'd been keeping close to the cottage since Zoey's illness, just making sure the running-away idea didn't resurface. With Ross still stuck out of town, it was easy to hang around home without it being obvious to Zoey.

I hadn't given much thought to the fact that I wasn't really sorry Ross's mechanical problems had delayed him a few more days. I was afraid to analyze the reasons for that too deeply, but the question nagged as I closed my eyes and went to sleep, bone-weary but happy.

Just before dawn, I woke to the sound of a bird singing outside the window. I lay awake, listening, looking into the misty morning haze, the beginnings of a perfect day. After all our hard work, I'd prayed that it would be.

This day, the bird singing, the blushing sky felt like an answer.

In committing these prayers to you, I have come to see the answers in everything. Words from Iola's letters, now tucked in the closets of my mind. By asking the questions, I'd begun to see answers in the simple things that happened each day — like a pile of driftwood left stacked behind a building.

Zoey's birthday was coming up. I hadn't even thought of that when I'd started the box for her.

I took a blanket and a cup of coffee and went out on the porch, watching as fingers of morning sunlight stretched through the loblolly pines and touched the wet grass, outlining each strand in a silver hue. Just out of sight beyond the salt meadow and the trees, the marina came to life as fishermen rigged their nets and crews made ready for the day. Metal rang against metal. Motors rumbled. Tires grated against gravel. On the road, Geneva Bink passed by in her golf cart. She waved at me as if we were old friends, and I waved back with my coffee mug.

Closing my eyes, I rested my head on my knees, lulled by the music of early morning. Was it possible for life to really be this good, this peaceful? For everything to be so beautiful all at once?

Thank you. Everything in my soul was whispering it.

"I guess our big prayer worked."

I opened my eyes and J.T. was standing in the doorway, blinking drowsily under a bad case of bedhead.

"Guess it did. It's a perfect morning." I purposely didn't look toward Iola's house. I didn't want to be reminded of the problems with it. Not today. Instead, I stood, fanned out my blanket, and folded J.T. in for a hug. Then we walked backward through the door like a pair of clumsy dancers. "We'd better get ready, huh? Paul said if you wanted to come to the Seashell Shop with me this morning, he would pick you up there and give you a ride to school."

"Awww, man!" J.T. complained, and I was surprised. Usually he wanted to go any-where with Paul. "Why can't I stay home from school like Zoey?"

Don't remind me. "Oh no. Somebody as smart as you shouldn't miss school. Ever."

J.T. skewed his brows, one up and one down, tipping his head back against the circle of the blanket to look at me. "Does that mean I'm smarter than Zoey . . . because she's skippin' . . . ?"

"That means you're not skipping school." I tweaked the end of his nose. He was such a great kid. How could I have ever left him to shift for himself for hours and days on end, his best friends the characters on some video game? "And Zoey's only getting off one more day. And that's only because Sandy might need her. We have to make sure the shop has a smooth opening day." In the bedroom, Zoey was moving around.

The bed squeaked as she rolled over, probably flopping onto her stomach and covering her head with the pillow to shut out our noise.

"So if Sandy needs *me* when we get there this morning, can I ditch school? We used to ditch all the . . ." J.T. gathered the answer from my expression. "Sheesh. Okay."

Sheesh. He'd gotten that from Paul.

I ruffled his hair with the blanket, and it stood on end, clinging to the fabric. "Go get ready. Let's see if we can beat everyone else to the Seashell Shop."

But by the time we finally dragged Zoey out of bed and made it to the shop, Sandy was already there, bustling around the interior, checking and double-checking and triple-quadruple-quintuple-checking everything. The rest of us filed in one by one, and when Paul stopped by to pick up J.T., everything in the store was practically glistening — every candle, seagull statue, bit of shell art, and piece of jewelry placed, polished, and arranged to perfection. J.T. had even raked the surface of the sandbox to idyllic smoothness. He and Zoey had arranged the toys so that the play area was just waiting for kids to wander in and discover a mini wonderland while their mothers shopped.

"Whoa," Paul said when he stepped in the door. "This place looks awesome." He crossed the room and bellied up to the coffee bar, where I was working on Sandy's massive stainless steel warmer. It wouldn't come on, and we'd decided it might be the switch. It was our first hitch of the day. "What's a guy gotta do to get a cup of coffee around here?"

"Just ask." I smiled over my shoulder at him. Today he was wearing baggy cargo pants with a dress shirt that looked a size too big. The pants were burnt orange and the shirt was kelly green. He'd topped off the ensemble with a tie that had beakers, test tubes, and a chemistry joke printed on it in bold letters: *If you're not part of the solution, you're part of the precipitate.* The tie was red.

"What?" He lifted his hands innocently when he caught me studying the outfit.

I wondered if he really had a mother somewhere, and if so, did she know how her son was dressing? "You look like a giant carrot."

Frowning, he tipped his head forward and studied himself. Clearly the vegetable scenario hadn't occurred to him. A shrug and a wink testified to the fact that he really didn't care. "It's all part of my magic." He

385

added a goofy smile, and I stifled a laugh in the crook of my elbow.

"It's working, isn't it?" he asked.

"In its own special way." Turning back to the coffeemaker, I realized how natural it had become to joke around with Paul. He was like the nerdy-but-fun brother I never had, the coolest of all possible grown-up friends for J.T. I couldn't imagine what we'd done to get so lucky.

I fixed his coffee without having to ask how he liked it. I didn't realize I'd done that until I was handing him the cup. He blew noisily over the surface, then sipped and looked at me with a little foam mustache on his lip. "Perfect."

"Sandy's been training me. I'm going to help around the shop for a few weeks until she gets her new teenage help up to speed." I grabbed a napkin for Paul's coffee mustache, then leaned across the bar to hand it to him. "Here."

Craning away from me, he looked at himself in the foggy antique bar mirror. "I might want to keep it. I've never been able to grow one of these."

I laughed. "It spoils the whole Peter Pan thing. You'll lose your boyish charm." I was strangely aware of Sandy watching us from across the room. Maybe I was annoying her by goofing around. She was seriously up-tight this morning.

"Well, if you put it *that* way." Paul turned his face side to side, admiring the mustache in the mirror before reluctantly dabbing it away.

"You're such a goofball."

"I try." Grabbing a lid for his coffee, he pushed off the bar. "C'mon, J.T., let's get going. It's bad when the teacher's late for class." Taking another sip of his coffee, he smiled at me over the cup just before turning away. "Knock 'em dead today." His eyes met mine as he saluted me with his coffee, and I felt warm all over.

The feeling stayed with me through the morning, although there wasn't much time to focus on it. The weather was beautiful, and based on all evidence, Hatteras, even in its current shell-shocked condition, was still Hatteras. The road through the village and down to the ferry landing was crowded with cars, bicycles, and pedestrians strolling from shop to shop and enjoying the activities offered in outdoor booths and the giant tent in front of the Hatteras Village Welcome Center. Sandy's Seashell Shop was wall-to-wall, the deck filled with tourists. Merchandise and coffee were walking out the door as fast as we could ring it up. Zoey got a crash course in operating the cash register, and Sandy offered her an after-school job if she wanted it.

When business finally hit a lull in the afternoon and Sandy's teenage help showed up, the rest of us walked outside and sat on the deck, gazing toward the water and listening to the music wafting over from the ferry landing. Overhead, cabbage palms fluttered gently against a wispy sky that stretched toward the edge of the world. I could see why sailors had once thought they would fall off into nothingness when they reached those watery horizons.

"Oh, I forgot to tell you that a woman called for you yesterday when you were out in the glass shop working." Sharon rolled her head my way but didn't lift it from the chair. If a customer happened to come by and the teenagers couldn't handle it, I wasn't sure any of us would be able to get up and tend to business. I'd thought fixing walls and mucking horse stalls was hard work, but today really took the cake. Dealing with people's needs for hours on end was both exhausting and exhilarating.

"For me?" I couldn't imagine who would be calling me. We hardly knew anyone here. It could be somebody from the school checking on Zoey. I hadn't told them I was working at Sandy's, but word might've gotten around.

Or maybe someone from the hospital trying to track me down about the bills? That idea was a black cloud in an otherwise-perfect day. I'd been trying not to think about the hospital bills. With my handywoman paycheck from Sandy, I'd finally gained a little breathing room, but I had a feeling that the hospital bills would eat that up and more.

"Did she say who she was or what she wanted?"

Sharon blew strands of auburn hair out of her eyes. "Didn't say. I told her you'd be here today and that we'd be having our grand reopening. She wanted to know our hours and whatnot. I got the impression she might come by."

"Huh . . ." A muscle contracted in my neck, the tension slowly moving down my back, like a ratchet tightening a cable from one end of my body to the other.

"Well, guess she didn't come by today," Sandy added. "Or else she got lost in the crowd, whoever she was."

Suddenly I felt like I couldn't sit there another minute. "I think I'll go out back and work in the shop while things are quieter around here, if it's okay." Zoey's box was almost done. Paul and J.T. had combed the beach, picking up tiny bits of mother-of-pearl and sea glass from deposits of shell hash so I could inlay the cracks in the wood. They'd even found a good-size piece of pale-blue sea glass — rare for the Outer Banks, where the force of the waves broke shells and other treasures into tiny shards before leaving them on the shore.

Just one more coat of lacquer, and Zoey's box would be ready to give to her. If I could get Sharon or Sandy to help me with the piece of sea glass today, I would make a pendant to go inside, like the one Pap-pap had given me. Maybe when the negative came at Zoey as she struggled through her return to school, the mermaid's tear necklace would remind her of how precious she really was.

"Can't imagine where you get all that energy, but go for it. The only way I'm moving from this spot is if things get crazy inside, or the sun goes down and the mosquitoes get bad . . . unless, of course, the concert lets out at the music fest and everyone comes here for coffee. Which they probably will. Better get your workshop time in while you can." Sandy gave me a conspiratorial look. She knew why I wanted workshop time, of course. "We'll just sit here and hold the deck down, won't we, Zoey?"

"Mmm-hmm," Zoey answered with a weary smile. Fortunately she didn't look like she wanted to go to the workshop with me. "This morning was crazy. Is it always like that?"

Sandy nodded. "During the season, it is. The rest of the year, it's just locals wandering by for coffee and us girls working in the shop or curled up by the fireplace." She backhanded Zoey's arm lightly. "You'll see this winter."

A truck passed by, and Zoey didn't have to answer. I knew without looking at her that the idea of still being here by winter was almost more than she could stand.

The problem consumed my mind as I worked in the glass shop, lightly sanding the latest coat of varnish on Zoey's treasure box, then adding a new coat, watching it flow over the bits of glass and mother-of-pearl tucked into the network of cracks created by the sea and the sun. Like the beach glass, the wood was more beautiful because of its journey, because of the things it had been through. Holding it up to the window, I watched the light press through the cracks, gathering the colors of glass and mother-of-pearl.

Inside the perfect shells is dim,
It's through the cracks, the light comes in.

My life was like that box. The best things in all the imperfections. A college girl's unexpected pregnancy — a daughter who was almost a young woman now. A failed relationship I thought was love — a son who wanted to grow up and be a sea turtle researcher. A frantic flight from Texas — a hiding place by the sea. A healing place. A house filled with an old woman's clutter — prayer boxes in a closet.

The journey itself was the architect of the wood. The interior would never be fully dark because the struggle had cracked it, providing an avenue for the light.

Impulsively I grabbed a sawdust-covered notepad and pen from the workbench, wrote the story of the box next to a black-and-white etching of the lightkeeper's house at Currituck. I told about Pap-pap and the box he'd built for me, how much it had meant, and why I'd made this one for Zoey. I told her that she was beautiful and trea-sured and that I loved her in a way for which there were no words.

Hold the box up to the light, *I finished.* See what happens to the cracks. Some of the hardest things you go through will teach you the most. Don't let other people tell you who to be, Zoey.

You are loved just the way you are.

Happy fifteenth birthday,

Mom

When I was finished, I tore out the paper, folded it, and put it in my pocket. When Zoey's box was ready, I would tuck it inside for her to read.

The chime went off overhead once, then a second and a third time, alerting me to the fact that the front end was busy again. Tucking the driftwood box high on a shelf to dry, I hurried off to join the crew.

An hour whirled by in a rush of coffee, souvenirs, sandwiches, soup bowls, and jewelry sales. Kids played in the sandbox while women in sarongs and sundresses shopped, tried on straw hats, experimented with the necklaces and earrings, and picked out T-shirts for people back home. Men sat on the sofas and watched TV or pulled out laptops and iPads to check e-mail or monitor the stock market. The deck outside drew a crowd again, now that there was a break between concerts. Sandy's desserts and sandwiches were selling like hotcakes, and other customers carried plates over from Boathouse Barbecue next door.

Sandy asked Zoey to bicycle down to Burrus Market for an emergency bread run. "You're a lifesaver," she said as she tucked money into my daughter's palm. "Watch out for the traffic. And don't get distracted, smiling at some cute boy. You'll run into a signpost like one of my shopgirls did last year."

"I won't." Zoey smiled and rolled her eyes as she slipped out the door, temporarily too busy to be depressed.

Three more groups came in as soon as she was gone. In the flurry of human activity around the coffee counter, I was eventually aware of someone watching me. I looked up, scanned the crowd, and suddenly there she was, a blingy bandanna tied around her platinum-streaked hair, her tall frame willowy and alluring in a white sundress and cowboy boots. My mouth fell open. I froze. She smiled at me. She'd been waiting by the display of quirky shell art near the door — waiting for me to notice her.

My sister.

She smiled now, swept across the room as if there were no one else in it. Circling the end of the coffee bar, she opened her arms, exposing the tiny vine of red roses tattooed on the inside of one wrist. Her voice came in an excited squeal — "I found you!" — as if we'd been playing some sort of game and she'd unearthed the winning card.

I stood with a pot of hot tea in hand. Protection, a barrier. I blinked. Blinked again, had the odd thought that perhaps I was still sitting on the blue chair out back, rocked to sleep by the lull of the water. Only dreaming. She couldn't really be here.

How? Why?

An impatient wag of her head instantly reminded me of Zoey's teenage angst. "Well, give me a hug, stupid! I drove all this way. I had to get a hotel in Buxton last night because I didn't have a *clue* where to find you. Have you got a place? All Zoey mentioned was that you were working at Sandy's Seashell Shop. So you're a coffee lady now? Seems like kind of a step down from living on the hacienda with Dr. Strangelove, Little Sis." Heavily cloaked lashes lowered, a smirk lifting her ruby mouth on one side. The skin below her blue eyes was smooth and tight. She'd had some minor nip-tuck since I'd seen her. Wonder who'd paid for that? A boob job, too. They were larger and . . . evident. Well-displayed in the sundress.

Zoey . . . the e-mails . . . the call to the Seashell Shop yesterday from a woman looking for me. It all made sense now. For whatever reason, Gina had tracked us down. "Gina . . . what are you doing . . . ?"

At the counter behind me, a woman tapped her credit card against the wood, impatient for two glasses of iced tea to go. Sandy glanced over from the main register. I was conscious of past colliding with present, the pileup of two speeding trains on the same track, reaching the same point at the same time, going opposite directions.

"Hello-oh?" Gina's voice clattered above the din of activity. She stiffened her arms in the air, presented them again. "Give me a hug already."

I hugged her, taking in the cloying scents of perfume and cigarette smoke. Her body was thin, the muscles and bones tight beneath the surface. "I . . . I can't talk right now."

"Oh, no problem." She held on to me a moment, then let go when she was ready, the way a business executive clenches a handshake just an instant longer to let an underling know who's in control. "I'll just go hang over there on the sofas. I'm wiped out after that concert. I've been backstage. I met the guys last night when I couldn't find *you.*" Pulling a wadded-up five-dollar bill from her small straw purse and setting it on the counter, she added, "Bring me a chai

396

latte when you get a chance, 'kay?"

"Okay." I nudged the money aside. I just wanted Gina as far away from me as possible. I needed to think, but I didn't have time to figure her out right now. There was too much work to do. Sandy was clearly wondering what was going on. Letting customers come behind the counter was against her rules and the health department's. We'd all been warned to mind our p's and q's, in case anyone official happened by. I couldn't let Gina mess things up for me or for Sandy. Or for the kids.

Ohhh . . . the kids. The last thing my daughter needed was more of Gina's pipe dreams. Zoey was so fragile right now.

I grabbed the shop phone, dialed Paul's number, and braced the receiver on my shoulder while I finished the tea and delivered the customer's order, then helped the next person in line.

The wind was buffeting Paul's phone as he answered. "Hey, I was just thinking about you," he said without waiting for me to tell him why I'd called. "Wondered how opening day was going. There's a report on the Stranding Network about a manatee cow and calf, stuck in Dough Creek up in Manteo. I'm just picking up J.T. from the school. I don't know how the parents survive this carpool lane, by the way. It's like demolition derby. I think some lady in a minivan just gave me the ugly finger. Anyway, I'm headed up to Manteo. I thought maybe the kids — well, and you if you can get away — might want to go along and see the manatees, watch the Stranding Network in action."

"Thanks, Paul." How was it that he was always there, saving my life before I even knew I needed it? He was like Superman in a Hawaiian shirt and mismatched shorts. "I can't go, but it'd be great if you could take the kids. I know they'd love it. We've been really busy here at the shop." *And my sister's sitting there, taking up space on one of Sandy's sofas while she waits on a chai latte.* "It comes and goes in waves. The crowd thins out a little, then it gets busy again. More of Sandy's high school help should be showing up any minute, which means she won't need Zoey." With any luck, Paul would get here before Zoey made it back from the grocery store, and he could wait for her outside. I didn't want her to see Gina until I could figure out what angle my sister was playing this time.

"Be there in a wink," Paul said.

"Thanks." He couldn't imagine how much I really meant that.

I continued with the rush of customers, all the while watching the door and hoping to intercept Paul or Zoey or both. Things had calmed and I was up to my elbows in the dishwater when Paul came in the door. J.T. trotted in behind him and threaded his way to the coffee bar, carrying a DNA model he'd made from toothpicks and gumdrops in science class. Across the room, Gina was busy flirting with someone's husband. I was glad when she didn't seem to notice J.T.

Sandy walked to the counter to admire J.T.'s model. "You all go talk a minute," she said, shooing me off, then casting a curious glance toward Gina, who was entertaining the guy on the sofa with something on her cell phone. They were shoulder-to-shoulder, laughing, all the signals of flirtation traveling back and forth.

I guided Paul and J.T. toward the front door, anxious to get them out of the place and away from Gina.

"You should just blow this joint and come with us." Paul wagged an eyebrow as we stepped onto the porch. "Stranded manatees — you don't see that every day."

"Can't." I paced to the edge of the porch, distracted as J.T. followed me, trying to explain the pieces of his DNA model. "J.T., not right now, okay? We'll look at it tonight."

Zoey was coming up the road on the bike. I blew out a tension breath, stretched the knots from my neck.

Paul frowned at me. "You okay?"

Nodding, I moved toward the steps to catch Zoey in the parking lot. "Thanks for letting the kids come with you."

"Sure. No problem. I'll just drop them by your house when we're done." Paul helped unload the groceries from Zoey's basket and put the bike in the rack. A few minutes later, they were driving away in his pickup.

Inside the shop, the crowd had thinned, the music fans heading for yet another free concert. Gina moved toward the coffee bar as her person of interest disembarked from the sofa and walked out the door with an annoyed wife.

"So who's the nerd?" She shrugged vaguely toward the front window, where Iola's hummingbirds were slowly disappearing, dispersing to the winds with customers from everywhere.

"What . . . ? Who?" I ran water in the sink and started washing the parts of the blender. The whole area was one big sticky mess. A coffee carafe slipped from my hands and landed in the soapy water, hitting the other dishes with a clink. Having Gina nearby made me as nervous as a squirrel crossing eight lanes of traffic. I didn't know which way to run.

She rolled a look at me. "C'mon, the one you ditched your kids with just now. The Don Ho wannabe. Looks like he's stuck in the seventies."

"You know what, Gina? Shut up." A spatula clattered against the counter, and Sandy took notice as she walked out the back door with a tray of sweetener packs. "He's a nice guy. And he's just a friend."

Gina lifted her hands in mock surrender. "Well, *sor-reee*. My bad. Just saying, he doesn't seem like your type, that's all. You usually go for tall, dark, and . . . hard to get along with. That one doesn't look like he's got any money, either. Dr. Strangelove was a jerk, but at least he was loaded. I never liked him, though. Too controlling. Sometimes it's like I didn't teach you anything."

"You . . ." I pressed my lips together, reining myself in. I didn't want Sandy to hear our family drama. Fortunately my new boss was still out back. "Why are you *here*?"

Gina's eyes turned the tinny blue-gray of a storm cloud just looking for a place to rain. "What? I come all this way to make *sure* you're all right, and *that's* what you have to say to me? I was worried about you,

you know. I hear on the news that Trammel Clarke has been arrested — which made my day — and I go looking for you, and the gardener tells me you've split. He let me in, by the way — you know the gardener always liked me. Anyway, I picked up some things for you. Clothes, a little jewelry." Slick white-blonde strands fell forward over her gold hoop earrings as she bent and pulled something from her purse — a ziplock bag with pieces of jewelry that Trammel had hidden away so I couldn't use them to buy an escape. Some of it had been mine before I came to Trammel's place — awards I'd won at shows, jewelry that had been given to me by horse owners grateful after a big win.

Gina held the bag between two fingers and smiled. "Yours, I believe. It helps to know people, Little Sister. Actually, you ought to get half of everything that jerk owns, but I have a feeling the Texas Medicaid system and the injury lawyers are going to beat you to it."

"Oh . . . wow." I reached for the bag, and Gina held it out of reach playfully. Trammel was gone from our lives for good. He couldn't hurt us anymore, and that jewelry would make everything so much easier, including paying the medical bills. *Thank God.*

Could God use someone like my sister to work a miracle? After so many weeks of scraping by, this felt like a miracle. If I was careful, I could start buying the tools I would need to take on some handywoman jobs. Meanwhile, I could work at Sandy's however much she needed me, maybe make some driftwood boxes to sell in the shop, as Sandy had suggested. The one for Zoey had come out beautifully.

I had the strangest temptation to show it to Gina, to see if she remembered when Pap-pap had given me the treasure box.

"Who's your favorite sister *now*?" She grinned smoothly, the skin around her smile as tight as a drum in a Mexican tourist shop, her lips artificially plump, her teeth three shades beyond white.

"Okay, right now you are." I grinned back at her, and for just a moment it felt like we were kids again, playing *Top Cops* or *Cagney & Lacey* in the orchard beside Meemaw and Pap-pap's place, picking rotten mulberries off the ground and throwing them at bad guys. "You have no idea how much this is going to help."

"What are big sisters for?"

"This is your *sister*?" Sandy was on her

way into the shop again. I had no choice but to make introductions. As usual, Gina was all smiles. She could turn on the charm when she wanted to. She praised the store, gushed about how beautiful the island was, lamented the lingering evidence of hurricane damage, and complimented one of the teenage helpers' jeans and the other one's haircut. The girls, Stephanie and Megan, were clearly impressed. Gina could be larger than life sometimes.

"So you're here visiting?" Sandy was pumping for information, not so easily wooed, clearly. She looked like she wanted to check Gina's purse and make sure there wasn't anything from the shop tucked in there.

As usual, my sister remained completely cool, dancing around answers with a practiced ease, until a customer came in and required attention. Sandy hugged me before going to help. "Well, listen, thanks for everything you did to help out today and for all the hard work to get the shop open. There's no way we could have done it without you." She turned to Gina. "Your sister's a wonder."

"Yes . . . she is." Gina's lips stretched into a thin smile.

"You two go on." Sandy shooed us toward

the door. "Go enjoy the music and the rest of the day. The girls, and Sharon and I, can handle things."

"Are you sure?" Part of me wanted to stay here, where the magic of the Shell Shop would keep me safe. Once we were out the door, I had a feeling that Gina would unleash some plan on me. She hadn't come all this way for nothing. She could have gotten an address for the shop and mailed the jewelry.

"Awesome!" Gina said. "C'mon, I'll introduce you to the band."

I didn't argue until we were outside, Gina turning and starting in the direction of the music, the filmy white dress floating around her legs, the sunlight tracing the outline of her body. She had a bikini on underneath. A very small one.

I stayed where I was. "Listen, I'm wiped out. It's been a really long day. Besides, I don't know when the kids will be home."

"Oh, come *on,*" she whined. "When did you get so domestic? Give the kids twenty bucks for a pizza, and let's *go.* My treat. We won't stay out late, I promise."

"Gina, I said *I can't.*" The sad thing was that there was a time when I would've been jumping in the car with her and taking off in search of guys or thrills or anything that would make me feel like I mattered. "Zoey's really been going through some things, and . . . it's complicated. You know what, as a matter of fact, I'd like to ask why you were e-mailing back and forth with her and why in the world you told her she could come live with you."

Gina's eyes narrowed in a look of confusion, then widened with convincing innocence. "What? When I found out you weren't at Dr. Strangelove's anymore, I tracked Zoey down through Facebook. I wanted to make sure he hadn't dumped you in a ditch somewhere, for one thing. Anyway, I felt sorry for Zoey because she was so upset about leaving Texas. I didn't say anything about her coming to live with me."

I studied my sister, trying to separate truth from good acting. With Gina, it was hard to tell the difference. She could spin a story so fast that reality and fiction were nothing but a blur. "She tried to run away, Gina. If she hadn't been too sick to get out the window, she could be heaven knows where by now."

"I might've said that you guys could live with me . . . or something like that. But *of course* I didn't mean for Zoey to hit the road. What kind of an aunt do you think I am?" Her hips jutted to one side, her arms crossing.

We stood momentarily at a stalemate. Who could say where the truth was hiding? Zoey was emotional right now. She could have misinterpreted whatever Gina had said to her. . . .

Someone catcalled from a passing car, and Gina tossed her hair over her shoulder, watching the vehicle go by before giving me a beseeching look. "Come on, Tandi. We haven't seen each other in forever. Let's not fight. With Trammel finally out of the picture, we can go have some fun — do sister stuff. We'll just hit the concert a few minutes. The kids are gone with your nerdy friend, and the weather's perfect." Tipping her head back and closing her eyes, she drank in the air, let it flow over the sunlit curves of her body, molding the dress. "Man, I'd forgotten how amazing this place is. And have you seen the beefcake around here? We're gonna have such a good time!" She started down the street without waiting to see if I was following.

Before I could decide one way or the other, a delivery truck rumbled into the parking lot. The horn honked, and I jumped back out of reflex. When I caught my balance, I recognized Ross behind the wheel, laughing. He left the engine running and exited the vehicle in one smooth maneuver, swinging to the ground with a hand wrapped around the metal grab bar.

"You scared me to death." I'd completely forgotten he was hoping to make it home so soon.

A wide white smile told me how glad he really was. "Got you something." He held up a white gift bag with a logo on the side.

"What?" I reached for the bag, but he scooped me up with one arm and kissed me instead.

"It's a cell phone. I told you I'd buy you one. Believe me, I had plenty of dead time walking around shopping malls and watching movies while I was on the road. Not a beach within four hundred miles. It stunk." He kissed me again and set me on my feet, giving me the bag. "Gotta go. Still need to dump some lumber at one of Dad's houses, then beat it back with this truck. Tomorrow, I'm hittin' the beach, no matter what the waves are like. Be ready."

He turned, jogged to the truck, and was gone before Gina could make her way back to the parking lot.

She shaded her eyes as the truck turned onto Highway 12. "Well, well, well, Little Sister. You're doing better here than I thought. No wonder you don't want to go

scope out the local hotties with me. Who
was *that*?"

CHAPTER 22

I woke to the sound of Gina coming in the door, again. As usual, she was staggering and laughing, making way too much noise. She'd been out every night for the past week, other than the one night she'd stayed home with the kids so I could go to Ross's birthday party. Gina had come down with some kind of food poisoning that night and she'd been flat on her back on the sofa, feeling too lousy to go anywhere. She wasn't happy about missing the party. When I got back, she made sure to let me know that staying home was a big sacrifice.

"I wouldn't do that for anybody but my little sis," she cooed when I came through the door afterward.

I didn't bother to tell her that she hadn't missed anything. By midnight, the party had moved to the beach, but it was pretty much over. Ross passed out on the leeward hollow of a dune, leaving me stuck there until some of the guys finally loaded him into the passenger side of the truck. I drove him back to one of his dad's empty rental houses, left him to sleep it off, and had Gumby give me a ride home. All in all, the evening stank. Ross had been trying to make it up to me ever since, bringing me little gifts and being sweet. He'd even picked up pizza last night and shown up at the house after I got off work.

"All the man did was have a little fun with his friends, and that's a crime?" Gina had whispered in my ear as she headed out the door to meet up with a guy I'd only seen from a distance. The date must have been particularly good. At 3 a.m., she was giggling as she came in. Instead of crashing on the sofa in her clothes, she put on her sweats and shimmied into bed next to me. She wasn't as wasted as I'd thought.

"Hey." Her voice was soft, intimate. She bunched the pillow under her head, turning toward me in a way that was familiar. Most of our childhood, we'd shared a bed or a bedroom, or a mattress on the floor, depending on where we were living. "Just like old times, huh?"

A wave of tenderness washed over me. Gina was the only family I had in the world, other than the kids. Without her, I would never have survived those first months in foster care. She'd made sure the predator next door knew he would be sorry if he ever touched me. I owed Gina. I wanted the two of us to be close. "Yeah."

Her hand found mine atop the quilt, our fingers threading. I thought of Iola and Isabelle. I'd managed to read from the boxes a few times since Gina had moved in, but having one more person in the cottage made it harder to slip away.

My sister's hand in mine reminded me of the last letter I'd read, a note written the night before Isabelle planned to leave Hatteras for good. Isabelle and Iola had curled up together on the big bed in the turret room, the blue wedding ring quilt from Isabelle's hope chest spread beneath them.

Isabelle had fallen in love with a dashing young aviator she'd met during the summer term at college. Girard Benoit had forbidden the relationship as unsuitable for a young woman of Isabelle's social standing, but after years of freedom while her father was away, Isabelle would not be denied. She planned to meet Andrew Embry on the beach the next morning, elope with him, and travel to his new duty station in idyllic Hawaii. Her mind was filled with romantic dreams of island life as an aviator's wife, finally free of her father's control and the family name that seemed to bring both expectation and a lingering darkness with it.

Iola was filled with sadness as she poured out her heart in her prayer box.

Father, what will I do without Isabelle? My sweet and truest friend, this other half of my soul? She, the one who knew my same loneliness when Madame sent me away to the mission school. She who saw to it that I would be brought here to these beautiful shores, with Maman and Mama Tee, rather than given a position in a cotton mill or a tobacco house. She who comforted me as we laid Mama Tee's body in the ground. "She's seeing the face of God, Iola. Imagine how grand that must be!" It was Isabelle who brought the preacher to Mama Tee before her passing so that my grandmother might finally know the fragrance of heaven.

How can we live on opposite sides of the ocean, Isabelle walking one shore while I walk another? Isabelle says it will not be for long. She promises this to me, as we lie atop the bed together, her heart buoyant and mine foundering so.

"You must take care of my father. You're needed here, Iola Anne, even more now that he is so alone. Andrew and I will return soon enough. His station in Hawaii is only for October '41 through October '42, and then he will return here to teach. We'll be back in time for Christmas, and we can celebrate together, I promise. We'll bundle up and watch the sunrise on a new year, as we always do."

I say nothing as she goes on. "After a few months pass, my father will have accepted the marriage. What choice will there be by then? In the meanwhile, you must look after him. See that he goes out fishing and gets around town in the car with Old Rupert. See that he doesn't worry about me. I know that what he does, he does out of fear that some disaster will befall me, that I'll meet the same ending as my half brothers. But I don't believe in curses, Iola. There is no curse stronger than the power of love."

I think of those sons whose photographs hang on the downstairs walls. Those young men dead while Isabelle and I were still so small. They are not gone. They have haunted Monsieur like ghosts. Always.

"If they had not gone out on the sea, they wouldn't have died on those ships," I say and clutch Isabelle's hand so tightly. "Stay here. Stay until Andrew comes home. You've only known him a semester's term. If you go, you'll never come back. I know it. We will never walk the shore again."

Isabelle's green eyes sparkle with adventure, her hair tumbling about the pillow in soft spirals. She is already lost.

"Fear builds walls instead of bridges. I want a life of bridges, not walls."

I close my eyes, pray hard, open them again. I am afraid in every part of me. "Take me with you. Take me to this place . . . this Pearl Harbor." The idea pushes my stomach, squeezing on every side, cutting in like ham netting. "I hear it's a good place to be colored."

"There isn't room for you to stay with us, Iola. We have only a tiny officer's quarters," she says. "And we've only an officer's pay. I'll be doing my own washing and mending and ironing. Just like a regular wife."

"Mercy! You do need me, then. You'll burn that man's uniforms," I say, and we, both of us, laugh, but I taste salt in my mouth, bitter against the sweet.

Isabelle takes the corner of the wedding quilt and dries my tears with it. "Now this blanket is part of the two of us," she says.

I am to send the quilt to her once she is settled.

"And Maman," I remind. Maman made the quilt from scraps of our old dresses. I'll stitch Isabelle's wedding date in the corner before I post the quilt for shipping. Now it carries the water of my sorrow, the proof of my love for this one person who has loved me most.

I imagine that I will wrap myself in the quilt and stow away, but I know it is only a dream, like Dorothy being swept off to Oz as Isabelle and I sat watching side by side, my heart pounding because the theater was not for coloreds. I worried that surely someone would look at me and know, but Isabelle had no fear.

"I'd send you away with a pair of ruby slippers, if I could," I say to her now as we lie with our hands intertwined. "Click your heels three times and you would be home."

"I'll be home soon enough. You'll see."

We smile at one another, but Isabelle's is happiness and mine is pain. She dries my tears again.

"I want you to find someone you love, Iola Anne. Someone you love in the way I love Andrew. You are eighteen. That's old enough. Your beau could work here for Papa. Or what about a soldier boy? There are the new bases at Holly Ridge and Wilmington. Andrew says they'll be bringing in units of colored soldiers for training. When you fall in love, you won't even think of anything else. These are changing times. When all this rumble of war is over, we'll settle in and raise our babies side by side, and we'll take them right into the theater together — just like Futurama at the World's Fair. Can't you imagine it?" She closes her eyes and rolls back against the pillow, drinking in air as her curls spill wild. "I want you to be happy, Iola. You're the closest I've ever had to a sister." Her lips spread into a smile as if her very soul is fair to bursting.

But my soul knows something else. I feel it, heavy like a stone. My Isabelle, my sister-girl who sees in me what I do not see in myself, is gone away already, and nothing will ever be the same again.

Please, Father, send the angels to watch over her. Keep this sister of my heart from harm and keep me as I wait on my side of the ocean.

Your loving daughter,

Iola Anne

Iola's story teased my thoughts, preventing me from drifting off as Gina fell asleep beside me, her breaths long and even, her fingers relaxing against mine.

Could it ever be that way between us? Could we get beyond all the wounds of the past — all the hurts and disappointments — and just love each other? I wanted to believe it was possible. I wanted to believe that, in some way, Gina was hoping for the same thing, and that was the reason she'd come here. She seemed lost right now, as lost as I was when I'd moved back to the Outer Banks. Maybe this place could work its magic on her, too. Yesterday when I'd come home from work, I'd seen Gina standing in Bink's parking lot with Brother Guilbeau. Maybe she was seeking something here, and I just needed to give her time to find it.

In the morning, I was up early again. Lately there had been so much on my mind that I was wide awake, my thoughts moving the first time I shifted in bed. Beside me, Gina was flat on her back, snoring, a nest of blonde hair flopped over her face. Not a pretty picture. I was tempted to snap a photo with the cell phone Ross had given me and keep it for all those times my inferiority complex flared up, making me feel like the ugly sister.

The thought made me giggle as I got up and woke the kids for school. Since we were awake early, I made pancakes to get Zoey's day started off right. She'd been doing better than I'd thought she might with the return to school. Sandy's shopgirls, Stephanie and Megan, had been friendly to her, which made some difference. That wasn't a substitute for having a popular boyfriend and a crowd to hang out with, but it helped repair the damage Rowdy had done by dumping Zoey and then telling lies about her around school. I'd told her to ignore him and not give him the satisfaction of reacting. Aunt Gina's approach was different. She'd shown Zoey a karate maneuver designed to incapacitate people of the male variety. No telling where she'd learned that, but if the karate didn't work, Gina had offered to run Rowdy over with her slick, silver Acura sedan. No telling where she'd gotten the car or who'd paid for it, either. My sister had never saved up that much money in her life.

Zoey was quiet during breakfast. She looked tired as she and J.T. started out the door to catch the bus.

"No punching anyone's lights out . . . or anything else Aunt Gina told you to do." I held her head between my hands before letting her off the porch. The last thing we needed was Zoey ending up in detention.

"You told me that already."

"I know."

As much as I wanted to be the one to help my sister find the same thing I'd found here on Hatteras, life in close quarters with Gina was a challenge, especially with Zoey at an age where she was struggling to define herself. Gina's beauty, her clothes, her nice car, even her irreverence lured Zoey in — I could see it. Zoey's birthday was coming up on Friday. Gina had already promised to take her out shopping. Where in the world Gina had managed to come up with all this money, and when it would run out, I couldn't say, but a homemade driftwood box and sea glass necklace would probably pale in comparison to whatever Zoey and Gina picked up on their shopping trip.

"At least it's Wednesday already," Zoey sighed. "I'm almost halfway through the stupid week."

I kissed J.T., and then they were gone, off

across the salt meadow in the ribbons of morning fog.

Gina wouldn't be up for hours yet, and I wasn't due at Sandy's until lunchtime, so I took advantage of the chance to go over to Iola's house. I'd been dreaming about Iola and Isabelle all night, but in a way, I was dreading opening the boxes again. I'd paid attention in history class enough to know that the bombing of Pearl Harbor was imminent, and because of the historic-homes booklet I'd found downstairs, I knew that Isabelle died young. At some point, Iola would lose her sister-friend to a home much more distant than Hawaii. As far away as earth is from heaven.

But still I had to know the story.

The one-eared tomcat greeted me on Iola's porch. He'd been lying low lately. Gina hated the cat, and the feeling seemed to be mutual. For several days now, he'd taken advantage of the opportunity to leave sandy tracks all over Gina's Acura in the middle of the night. Two days ago, he'd left a dead rat on the ground by her driver's side door. She was convinced that the cat was out to get her.

He skittered off the porch and darted into the flower bed, disappearing as I opened the door and went inside.

A rhythmic knocking caught my attention when I started toward the stairs, the sound drawing me past the piano room and down the long hall to the kitchen. Above the sink, a bird was beating against the window, trying to get in. I shooed it away, then heard something else — a faint slithering and scratching coming from Iola's ancient-looking washer and dryer in the utility. Something was back there.

I pictured snakes, raccoons, squirrels. Over the years, living near stables and horse pastures, I'd done battle with all of those and more.

Grabbing a broom for protection, I crept across the floor, moving at an angle, trying to get a view of the area behind the cockeyed dryer. *If something's back there right now, other things could've crawled in earlier . . . or yesterday . . . or the day before.* A shudder ran through me all the way to the bone, and the next thing I knew, I was running to the dryer and crawling on top, then peering over the edge.

In the shadow of the wall, the accordion-like vent hose had a life of its own. Something was in there. Something large. The hose bulged like a snake's belly after a hen-house visit, the length of it wriggling on the floor. I watched with a combination of fascination and horror, thinking, *Now what? Do I call an exterminator? The humane society? The park service? The Ghost Hunters?*

Paul was the first person who came to mind. He would either know what to do or get a laugh out of this — me on top of the dryer, having an *I Love Lucy* moment.

Something protruded slowly from a slit in the dryer hose — something black, small, furry. A paw, the pads stretching out, grasping the slit and pushing it open, allowing another paw to press forth and touch the floor.

The dryer hose slowly birthed the point of a nose, a set of whiskers, a tattered ear, a familiar face.

"So that's how you do it." Setting the broom aside, I watched the tomcat emerge, then shake off the final traces of lint before strolling regally into the house.

Midway across the kitchen, he paused to cast a curious look over his shoulder, as in, *Why, pray tell, are you squatting atop the clothes dryer?*

"Now I know your secret." I pointed at him and smiled.

He blinked slowly, then turned away, the movement seeming to say, *Oh, there are so many secrets. You've only scratched the surface.*

He followed me upstairs to the blue room and lay in a stream of sunlight by Iola's black shoe as I opened the closet and reclaimed the box from 1941, piling the letters atop the quilt and sinking slowly into Iola's life. Changes were coming fast.

Isabelle's father was furious after her elopement. He'd tried to force her to return to Hatteras and petition that the marriage be annulled on the grounds that it was not conducted by a priest of the church and no dispensation had been granted. But Isabelle was determined, and she was of legal age. She refused to come home, even when her father threatened to disinherit her. Girard Benoit attempted to use his considerable political connections and his pull within the prewar shipping industry to prevent Isabelle's aviator husband from being restationed to Hawaii, but even he couldn't sever every tentacle of the Army's reach. Orders were issued, channels circumvented, and Isabelle got what she wanted.

In October of 1941, Isabelle and Andrew Embry moved to beautiful Pearl Harbor, Hawaii, where a revolution of sorts was taking place. The island was rife with young minds, adventurous spirits far from home for the first time, free from the social taboos of the mainland.

Iola's prayers were filled with her reactions to Isabelle's letters.

. . . and Isabelle writes to me, "Oh, Iola, this is that City of the Future we dreamed of. This is that place where everything is possible. I have joined a group of wives in auxiliary service at the hospital, although there is not much to be done there. The place is peaceful, save for the occasional results of a training accident on board ship or plane or the aftermath of a night of brawling with so many young soldiers and sailors nearby. I want you to come here, Iola. I know that Father won't provide the funds for it, but we will find a way."

How can I tell Isabelle that it isn't the City of the Future my heart wants, but the moments of yesterday? I wish for our long walks on the beach with the old horse, the days as endless as ocean and sand. How can I pray against Isabelle's dreams? Is it wrong, Father, that my heart says to you, *Don't bring me to Pearl Harbor. Bring Isabelle home, instead?*

And yet your Word whispers here also, as Sister Marguerite read to me from the Scriptures of the apostle Paul, "But this one thing I do, forgetting those things which are behind, and reaching forth unto those things which are before . . ."

My heart reaches back and back and back. All in this house reaches back and strains for seasons that cannot be again.

And I wonder, Father, if Isabelle is the wiser one when she says that the only way to look is forward.

But how to go forward, when I don't see good ahead? I think on this as I walk miles along the shore while Maman and Monsieur and Old Rupert sit silent in the shadows of this sad house.

How to go forward, always seeking, always in anticipation? Always a little more and a little more, just a few steps farther, a few moments longer. Something new may have washed up on the tide, just over there or beyond that dune or around that point or just out of sight, waiting in the next curl of a wave.

I desire to live my life this way, Father, as Isabelle has. Not caged by the walls of fear, but in anticipation of the bridges to magnificence.

Help me to find the way.

> Your loving daughter,
> Iola Anne

When the surprise bombing of Pearl Harbor reached the world through President Roosevelt's radio address, just two months after Isabelle's departure, Girard Benoit was inconsolable, raging through the house with a pistol, drunk on Southern whiskey, until finally he sank into a chair and wept, certain that he had lost another child to the curse on his family.

The words now come from Monsieur, wild like a flood. Maman runs to the kitchen room to hide, and I press myself cold and stiff against the wall. Only Rupert enters the study. He speaks softly, as if calming an animal, as he slides the whiskey and the pistol away.

"I have no one," sobs Monsieur. "The curse. The curse has taken them all. Each of my children. All that I have been, wiped from the earth . . ."

A shiver pulls through my bones, and my body quakes with fear and grief. I cover my mouth and press hard into the wall. I close my eyes, Father, and I call to you.

"No'sah, that ain't so." Old Rupert's voice seems far away. "You know that ain't so. Miss Isabelle, she gon' get a message through, you gon' see. She gon' get a message through, and she gon' be fine."

I pray, I pray, I pray. You, Father, hold the power of death and life.

"My blood shall not survive on this earth!" Monsieur's voice trembles the rafters. "It is the curse! This wicked curse on my blood!"

"Your blood be livin' right down there in that room off the kitchen!" Old Rupert's voice booms deep and loud. I lean closer, my heart pounding, the words loud and strange. My mind cannot take them in.

"Your blood been there all this time, and you know that be true. You know your son, Miss'uh Stephen, he the father of Iola Anne, and it was you what send him off on the ship when he been with Iola's mama, when they talkin' fool talk of love, like young folk do. Ain't no voodoo on this fam'ly. Ain't no voodoo nowhere but in yo' mind. You still got blood on this earth. You still got Iola Anne. And Isabelle, she gon' come home too. Ain't got nothin' to do with no blood curse. Nothin'." . . .

I stared at the letter in which Iola had poured out her heart, her pain and confusion as she tried to reconcile the truth of her parentage. She'd been told all her life that her father was a light-skinned groom who'd died after being trapped in a stall with an unruly young horse.

A week after the revelation, when word came that Isabelle and Andrew had survived the attack on Pearl Harbor, Iola packed her belongings and left Benoit House under cover of darkness.

On the mainland in Norfolk, war fever was on. The attack on Pearl Harbor had brought America into the conflict, full force. With young men signing on to the war effort, there was work for young women. Iola took a job cleaning in a hotel filled with men preparing to ship out.

Months later, in the summer of 1942, with America still believing the war would quickly be won, Iola passed by a makeshift recruiting office on her walk home from the grocery store. At a table out front, she signed up to enter the Women's Army Auxiliary Corps. She'd been told that, as a WAAC, she could be sent to Hawaii to aid in the rebuilding of Pearl Harbor. With the single stroke of a pen, she left her old life behind.

I hand that form across the table, and

the college boy with the New York accent and the baby-smooth face frowns at it, then squints at me for a long time. "You've gotten in a hurry and checked the wrong box here," he says and looks close into my eyes in a way that is filled with hidden words. "I'm sure you meant to check WHITE. There is some plan to gather coloreds into a regiment, but they'll likely be sent to Fort Huachuca, Arizona, for training and service. It's no matter. Obviously you meant to check here." And he marks the box that reads WHITE. "Just initial the change. There's no need to rewrite the form."

As quickly as that, Father, I am a new thing. I sleep and wake and attend my training, where the soldier boys smile and the young women speak to me of their brothers and sweethearts, who will soon be off at war. I learn and study and become skilled with the radio. I keep to myself at first, then not as much.

I am an actor on a stage. Each day, I become less of myself and more of the clothing I have put on.

I send a letter to Maman, to tell her I have joined the war effort. Old Rupert will read it to her, I know. She cannot answer because I do not give her an address to write to me. I say nothing to her about the things I heard that night outside Monsieur's study. I say nothing about the college boy at the recruiting table or the single check mark with which I have both denied and accepted what has been.

All around Norfolk, there are stories of Pearl Harbor. Terrible stories of death and suffering and the disease that spreads when so many bodies are broken at once. I pray that Isabelle is well. Please look after her, Father. For now, there is no way I can know.

Always, I wonder if the choice I have made is the right choice, the one you would have me make. There seems to be no life for me that is not, in some way, wrapped inside a binding cloth of lies.

Your loving daughter,
Iola Anne

I finished reading Iola's box from 1942 before it was time to put the boxes away and head off to work at the Seashell Shop. Iola had been stationed in Europe rather than being sent to Pearl Harbor. As a skilled communications radio operator, and with the knowledge of French and Latin she had gained at the orphan school, she was needed in the European theater. She wrote to Isabelle, but no reply came. The last ties to Iola's old life had been severed, whether she was prepared to let go or not.

Before leaving the closet, I peeked into the box from 1943, turning the stack of letters over inside the box and reading the first one quickly.

Even though fraternization between WAACs and male soldiers was prohibited by post command, Iola had fallen in love with a young officer from Nevada. In the last line of her note written in January of 1943, despite her happiness, she still grappled with the lies that surrounded her.

The man she loved had no idea who she was.

Tears blurred my vision as I closed the box and put it back on the shelf, checking my watch. If I didn't hurry, I'd be late getting to Sandy's, and I was never late.

Iola's story whispered in my thoughts, trailing me down the stairs and out the back door. I slipped around the bayberry hedge — something I'd gotten in the habit of doing since Gina had arrived. If my sister happened to be awake, I didn't want her to know about Iola's house. Gina had a talent for turning random bits of knowledge to her own advantage.

She was on the cottage steps talking on her cell phone when I rounded the corner. She hung up, giving me a surprised look. "Where've you been? I woke up a few minutes ago and looked for you, and you were gone."

"I just wanted to get out awhile before it was time to go to work." I left it at that. Not a lie. Not the full truth, either. Gina seemed fine with it. She stretched her neck to one side, rubbing her shoulder. Last night must have been a doozy. She looked a little rough.

She shrugged. "Oh . . . well, whatever. Hey, I noticed that you've got a flat on your car. I'll give you a ride to work, if you'll make me a latte."

I looked at the SUV, sitting cockeyed with the left rear tire flat against the rim. I wished I'd noticed sooner; I could have put the spare on. Now there wasn't time. "Sure. Let me pull my hair up and grab my stuff for work, and then I'm ready." I hurried into the cottage and was back out almost before Gina had located her purse.

We were in the car and driving through Hatteras Village before I realized she had an agenda. "So listen, I've been thinking . . . I'm between things right now, and you could use some help with the kids, especially if you're going to do this handywoman business. Why don't we get a place together — something bigger, where there's space for all of us?"

I blinked at her, temporarily mute. Every time my sister and I moved in together, the arrangement ended in a nuclear meltdown.

Possible responses took a minute to percolate through the rubble of past disasters. "What's the rush? You just got here, and right now the kids and I are settled at the cottage. I really can't afford to do anything else. You could look for something for yourself, and if things change later, we can worry about it then."

My sister's disappointment was instant and evident enough to make me feel guilty. "Sounds like you'll have to make a change anyway. I talked to that preacher guy — Brother Bill-bo, or whatever his name is — and he said there's really no telling what'll happen with the place you're in — some sort of legal rigmarole. Anyway, so I came up with a plan. I can sell this car, get something more . . . right for the beach scene, and have money left over to rent us a place."

My mouth was hanging open as we pulled into Sandy's parking lot. I wasn't even sure what to say.

"Oh, don't look at me like that. I *have* the title to the car." Gina snorted, rolling her head to one side, her nose crinkling. She knew exactly what I was thinking — that whoever paid for the shiny new Acura might be out there looking for it.

"Let's talk about it later, okay?" I opened my door and took a breath like a diver escaping a malfunctioning air lock.

On the other side of the car, my sister was also climbing to her feet. "I try to do something to help you out, to make sure your kids have a place to come home to, and this is what I get? Thanks a lot."

"I didn't say no, Gina. I just said let's talk about it later." But I could feel my resolve thinning already. The usual load of guilt descended as my sister's shoulders sagged and moisture glittered in the corners of her eyes.

"I want it to be different between us now, Tandi."

Everything in me yearned to cross the space that separated us, hug my sister, and agree to all of it. I wanted to believe we could move beyond all the past hurts and disappointments, beyond all the patterns we'd learned from Mama and Daddy. I wanted to say, *Of course things can be different, Gina. We're family.*

Instead, I said, "Me too." Then I turned and rushed up the stairs into the Seashell Shop. I was glad when she decided to pick up her latte someplace else.

Sandy was standing near the front door, arranging a display of glass boxes in the bay window as I walked to the coffee counter to put away my purse. "You know," she said without looking at me, "it's none of my business, but dealing with the public for years gives you a sense of people. You and your kids are making a place for yourselves here. A life. I know that *is* your sister out there, and blood runs thick, but think long and hard before you jump into anything. If she means what she says, let her prove it over time. You can dress a toad in lace, but the minute you let it go, it'll still poop on your porch."

Sitting at Sandy's feet, Chum sneeze-nodded in agreement.

Sandy didn't wait for me to answer, just grabbed her feather duster and walked into the next room with Chum following behind her, the two of them leaving me to contemplate the image of my sister as a toad in lace.

A picture like that stays with you, and by the end of the day, when Sharon gave Zoey and me a ride home, I'd decided to tell Gina that I wasn't making any decisions right

436

now. Sandy was right. I couldn't expect things to change overnight, and getting a house together probably wasn't the best way to start working on our relationship. We would just be on each other's nerves. Aside from that, so far I hadn't seen a hint of her looking for a job or even beginning to think about what she would do with herself here on Hatteras, other than hang out in clubs.

When we reached the cottage, her car was nowhere in sight, and the clearest feeling I could identify was relief. Even that was an indication that Sandy was right. We needed time and space to find a new normal as sisters. Normal doesn't happen overnight when the world around and between you has always been off-balance.

By Friday, I wondered if any kind of normal would ever be possible with Gina around. Zoey's birthday wasn't starting out the way I wanted it to. Zoey was mad because I wouldn't let her take the day off school. Gina picked that moment to roust herself from sleeping on the sofa and lumber to Zoey's defense, and the morning started with an argument that felt weirdly typical. Fortunately Gina was too hungover to fight very hard, and really she just wanted everyone to stop making noise so early in the morning. Once Zoey and J.T. were out the door, she stumbled to my bed, pulled the comforter over her head, and went back to sleep.

I left for the Seashell Shop, limping along on a spare tire that needed air and feeling like a lousy mom. I was barely in the door when Sandy wheedled a confession out of me, and the next thing I knew, she and the sisterhood were deep in a plan to arrange a surprise party for Zoey that evening. Before long, we'd called everyone we could think of to make a crowd — Brother Guilbeau, Bink and Geneva, Greg and Crystal from Boathouse Barbecue, a couple other shopkeepers Zoey had gotten to know. I called Gina's cell, but she didn't answer, so I left a message inviting her to the party. Ross was headed to meet his buddies at the beach, but he promised he would show up at the shop in time. Sandy texted her afternoon shopgirls, Stephanie and Megan, and arranged for them to grab Zoey after school and tell her she was needed at Sandy's. On the way, they would delay a bit with a trip to the grocery store so that Paul and J.T. could get to the shop and join the party group.

When I tried to thank Sandy, she just smiled and said, "Are you kidding? We wouldn't even be open if it weren't for you." Then she pulled me into a shoulder hug and added, "Besides, this is how the sisterhood works. We take care of each other. There are all different kinds of sisters, Tandi. Not just the ones you're born with."

The phone rang, and she released me so she could cross the room and answer it. A minute later, she was laughing and saying, "Well, I think that sounds just great. I'll call some more people. We'll make it a combination birthday bash and grand reopening party. We haven't danced out on the deck since last fall before the hurricane. This will be a night to remember, to put all the bad times behind us and celebrate."

Sharon and I were watching her quizzically when she hung up the phone.

"Okay, what's going on?" Sharon paused with a necklace dangling from her fingers, the green beach glass twisting in the glow of display lights.

Sandy's eyes twinkled. "Brother Guilbeau just called. He wondered if we'd like a little zydeco music — said his band hasn't played anywhere in a while, and they need to tune up. I told him sure. If we're going to have a party, we might as well really make it a blowout celebration, right? It's Friday night, and heaven only knows it's time for some joy around here. Neither can flood nor pestilence nor building inspectors with attitude overcome those who labor justly. Amen?"

"A-men!" Sharon agreed and pumped a fist. She and I exchanged giddy looks before Sandy put us both to work. Zoey's birthday party was taking on a life of its own.

The rest of the day was taken up with party planning and wild preparations. When Sandy seized on an idea, the woman was a force of nature. By afternoon, Boathouse Barbecue was planning to open its doors for a five-dollar barbecue-and-boiled-shrimp buffet, and the bakery down the street was remaking a failed wedding cake into a birthday-slash-grand-reopening centerpiece. At the Seashell Shop, we baked cookies as fast as we could in the single oven that wasn't meant for large baking jobs.

"I don't know if you realize what you've gotten yourself into," I told Brother Guilbeau when he and his band arrived with equipment to set up on the patio.

"Hoo-eee! We gonna have us a good time tonight!" Brother Guilbeau laughed. "I got the information out to ever'body on my list. Half the island's gonna be here. We gonna celebrate this day!"

"It looks like we are." I handed him an

extension cord from Sandy and went back inside to try to call Gina again. I'd phoned the house and her cell, but she hadn't answered. Standing there with my hand on the button, I had the fleeting thought that it might be for the best if she didn't answer. When Gina partied, she really liked to *party,* and though mixed drinks weren't on the menu at Sandy's, there was a bar right down the street. What if my sister got lit and embarrassed Zoey and all the rest of us?

I didn't call her again and instead started hoping she wouldn't get my messages.

By three thirty, everything was in place. Paul had brought J.T. from school, our small crowd of friends was milling around in the shop, and we were just waiting for Zoey to arrive and kick off the celebration.

"What time did you say this shindig was supposed to happen?" Ross was impatient. He'd left the water to come. As soon as we blew out the candles and cut the cake, he was planning to head back to the beach for a couple hours, then return later, once the grand reopening party really cranked up.

"Any minute now. At least stay until Zoey gets here and opens her presents, okay?" Ross had even thought to bring a gift for Zoey — something wrapped in a surf shop bag. I wanted him to see the driftwood box.

Paul had seen it as I was working on it, but Ross hadn't. I was proud of the way the box had turned out. Watching Zoey unwrap it and find the note and sea glass necklace inside would be fun. I hoped she liked it.

"Okay, okay." Ross checked his watch again, then scanned the room, his gaze drawing a bead on J.T. and Paul, who were messing around in one corner of the sandbox, Paul sitting on his knees like a little kid. "You sure Zoey's gonna like this whole party thing? I mean, hanging out with a bunch of old people isn't exactly a teenager's idea of fun."

A sliver of worry needled me. Not that I hadn't thought of that possibility as the party morphed into something so elaborate, but I didn't need to hear it out loud.

The phone rang, and from the corner of my eye, I could see Sandy motioning me to the front counter. The look on her face told me instantly that something was wrong. My mind tripped, stumbled, and fell into action — *car wreck, trouble at school . . . Maybe Stephanie and Megan missed Zoey after classes let out. Maybe Rowdy or someone else gave her a ride. But why wouldn't she come on to the Shell Shop? She usually works in the afternoons . . .*

Sandy covered the phone when I reached

the counter. "It's Megan. She and Stephanie are in the administration office. Zoey's not at school. The secretary says your sister checked her out hours ago."

"What?"

Sandy handed me the phone, and I talked briefly to Megan and then to the school secretary. Gina had taken Zoey shopping for her birthday.

"I'm really sorry," the secretary pleaded. "Zoey didn't seem worried about it. I definitely got the idea that the shopping trip was something planned."

"It was, but not *today.*" When I did find my sister, I was going to choke her. I really was. How dare she pick up my daughter without even asking me. Didn't she even consider that I probably had plans, that this was Zoey's birthday and I wanted to be with her?

I knew the answer. Of course she didn't, because this was Gina, and she always did these things. Whatever felt good in the moment. Whatever she wanted.

As soon as I was off the phone with the school, I called her cell again. I was conscious of Sandy staring at me with fire in her eyes. If Gina did bring Zoey here, I wouldn't have to kill her. The sisterhood would do it for me.

Gina's line rang and went to voice mail. The message I left probably sizzled the air between the shop and the nearest cell tower.

Sandy announced a change of plans for the party. "Okay, little delay!" she chirped. "The birthday girl surprised *us,* I guess. She's out shopping with her aunt. We'll just go ahead with the Sandy's Seashell Shop grand reopening party, and when Zoey gets here, we'll break out the cake and candles."

When the crowd didn't immediately switch gears, Sandy fanned her hands, giving everyone the *shoo-shoo.* "Now, come on, everybody! Don't be shy. Greg and Crystal, you'd better get that buffet going. I sent out e-mails all over town, and I put it on the Facebook page. Before you can blink, people will be bubbling up on the deck like ghost crabs under a full moon. Brother Guilbeau, you and your boys grab a bite of food while you can. We'll be needing some good music pretty quick. I'm ready to dance! The storm came, the storm went, and we're still here. If that's not a reason to celebrate, I don't know what is!"

As the guests filed out to the patio, I called Gina's phone again. No answer.

CHAPTER 23

I was dozing on my sofa when Gina and Zoey finally came in. A storm had blown in around nine and chased the crowd off the patio at Sandy's. By then, the party was a huge success, if you didn't factor in Zoey's absence and the uneaten birthday cake . . . and the fact that I was seriously contemplating making myself an only child. The idea that Gina would take off with Zoey, without even asking, and then keep her out until after eleven o'clock on her birthday made me insane.

When I heard the cottage door unlocking, I whiplashed from drowsiness and anxiety to rage. Zoey appeared in the opening first. Gina probably planned it that way — using my daughter as a human shield.

"Where have you *been*?" The words were an angry hiss. I wanted to scream them, but J.T. had already gone to bed, exhausted after the big night at Sandy's.

Zoey was all smiles, and so far there was no sign of Gina, other than a car door closing outside. Zoey had a shopping bag in each hand, and her hair was hanging in glitter-sprayed curls, pulled away from her face by a rhinestone-studded headband. She was wearing way too much makeup. Long, red fingernails clutched the handles of her shopping bags, and she was dressed in a black miniskirt and impossibly high silver platform shoes. She looked twenty-five.

"Come see what we got!" she said, then trotted across the room, wobbling in the heels as she grabbed my hand and pulled me off the sofa. She was so giddy that for a minute I was afraid she and Gina had been out drinking together, but Zoey was sober under all that makeup. "It's, like, the cutest thing ever, and it's four-wheel drive. Now we can go on the beach without getting stuck, and Aunt Gina says that next year when I get my license, I can have it, and she'll get another car, and . . ."

Zoey didn't stop until she had me out the door. In the driveway, Gina was lounging on the hood of a vintage ragtop Jeep. In tight jeans, shoes that matched Zoey's, a silver tank top, and enough jewelry to choke a horse, she looked like an auto show model doing a night shot under the porch lights.

"Like it?" she asked. "I came out $6K ahead, too. That car dealer over in Norfolk didn't even know what hit him, did he, Zoey bear? We're gonna have some good times in this car, Baby Sister. I mean, does this say *I live in paradise,* or what?"

"Zoey, go inside." She didn't need to hear what I was about to say. Especially not on her birthday. *Norfolk.* Gina had dragged Zoey off to Norfolk to trade in the Acura. Between the three-hour drive over and rush-hour traffic later on, my sister had known full well that they would be gone all evening.

"Mama . . . ," Zoey protested.

"Just go inside, okay? I'm not mad at *you.*"

"But, Mama . . ."

"Zoey, *please.*"

Zoey ducked her head and slipped into the cottage, muttering, "Great," as the door closed behind her by itself. I felt the sting of instantly being made the bad guy, despite the fact that I hadn't done anything wrong. Gina was the guilty one here.

"What?" Gina unfolded from her sultry pose and slid off the Jeep. "Oh, *seriously?* You're mad. I do something to get some cash for us, and I take little Zoey bear birthday shopping, and you're mad at me."

"You didn't even ask me, Gina. You checked my daughter out of school without

447

making sure it was okay, and you just took off."

"You knew I told her I'd take her out for her birthday." My sister's chin jutted out, her hair flying in moon-platinum strings. Her face was in shadow, but I knew the self-righteous expression that would go with that posture. "We had fun. I showed her a good time. I spoiled her a little. What's so *wrong* with that? What? You don't trust me now?"

No, you know what? I don't. "I needed her to be here. *Here,* Gina. You never even thought about the fact that *I* wanted to spend my daughter's birthday with her? That I might have plans? We had a surprise party all ready for her at the Seashell Shop, and we couldn't even find her. She missed the whole thing."

Gina was momentarily silenced, frozen in stop-motion before coming to life with a return volley. "Well . . . just do it tomorrow. It'll be like double birthdays."

How did I answer that? It wasn't even worthy of an answer. "I've been calling you *all evening.* Why didn't you pick up the phone?" But I knew why. Gina wanted to do what she wanted to do, and she wasn't going to let me get in the way. If she didn't pick up the phone, she didn't have to answer to anyone.

She glanced at the Jeep as if it might hold the answers. "Oh, I think I left my phone. I didn't realize it until we were on the road. . . ." She started toward the cottage, indicating that I'd reminded her of the loss of her cell, and now she needed to conduct an emergency search. When she got in there, she would magically come up with it under the bed or someplace and pretend it'd been there all along. She probably had it in her pocket or her purse right now.

"It's not here, Gina. There's no cell phone in here. I should know. I've been calling it enough."

"Off, I mean," she finished smoothly. "I wondered why I hadn't had any calls all afternoon." She burrowed in her purse, pulled out the phone, checked it, and added, "Yep. Turned off. Sorry about that. This stupid smartphone — half the time it's —"

"Stop it!" The echo reverberated across the yard, stealing through the trees and the climbing roses and bouncing off Iola's house. "Just stop it, Gina. Don't you ever, *ever* take my kids anywhere again, do you hear me? You ruined *everything* tonight."

Disappointment, pain, bitterness welled in my throat. Why did it always have to be this way? Why couldn't we be like sisters were

449

supposed to be? Why couldn't we have what Iola and Isabelle had? Why did anything we felt for each other, any interaction we had, have to be crisscrossed by scabs of pain and misunderstanding? Couldn't the wounds ever heal?

I went into the cottage without waiting for her to answer the spoken question or the unspoken ones. What was the point? Closing the door hard, I let my forehead rest against it. Outside, the Jeep rumbled to life and backed out of the drive, then sped away.

"Mama?" Zoey's voice was a thin ribbon in the storm of anger and disappointment. When I turned around, she was standing by the kitchen table next to the pile of gifts and the remodeled wedding cake that still read:

Happy Birthday Zoey
From the Seashell Shop Gang!

In her hands, Zoey was holding the driftwood box, the folded note open against her thumb, wrapping paper lying at her feet. "I'm sorry, Mama." A tear spilled from the deep-blue ocean of one eye and trailed down her cheek as I crossed the room, opening my arms to her.

"I love you, baby," I whispered, taking in

the scents of hair spray and perfume at first, but beneath those, the scents of the little girl who had come from the body of a lost, lonely, terrified nineteen-year-old. "Happy birthday, Zoey."

We held each other and rocked back and forth, swaying to a rhythm the two of us were only now beginning to understand. The dance of mother and daughter.

The birthday celebration was just Zoey and me, the recycled cake, and a tub of ice cream. Zoey kicked off her platform shoes and opened her gifts from the Shell Shop crowd, and before she went to bed, I hung the blue mermaid's tear necklace around her neck.

When I finally turned out the cottage lights, there was still no sign of Gina, and I wasn't sorry. She would show up when she figured things had cooled off, and unless I brought it up, she would act like the whole thing had never happened. Gina had always been that way. She didn't apologize; she just moved on.

We needed to have a talk about boundaries, if she was going to stay here on Hatteras. But I wondered if talking would do any good.

Sitting on the edge of my bed, I took a pad of paper from the night table and wrote down my hopes, then put them in my prayer box and tucked it in the drawer beside my bed. The vision of a future with my sister was still murky and uncertain, but one thing I'd learned from Iola's letters was that miraculous answers to prayer were possible. The other thing I'd learned was that prayers aren't always answered the way you expect.

On Saturday morning, Zoey was up early on her own and waiting to go to work with me. She wanted to tell everyone at the Seashell Shop that she was sorry she'd missed the party. She'd showered off the makeup and washed the glitter from her hair, and she looked fifteen again. J.T. had plans to go fishing with Paul. Gina hadn't reappeared during the night, and maybe I should have been worried, but I wasn't. I knew Gina too well.

"She didn't mean anything bad by it, you know. She sold her car to get money for all of us," Zoey pointed out as we pulled into the shop parking lot. The mermaid's tear dangled around her neck, a reminder of the two-person birthday party that turned out just right.

Her lips trembled downward at the edges as she reached for her door handle, then stopped. "I wish you wouldn't be mad at

Aunt Gina, okay? Everybody doesn't like her already."

"I'm just . . . disappointed." Zoey's eyes were filled with so much hope right now, so much faith in my sister. I didn't want her to be hurt if Gina changed directions and took off with her sights set on something new. "Let's not talk about it, okay? Let's just have a good day."

I leaned over the console and smoothed Zoey's hair. It *was* a good day. Zoey looked adorable in her new birthday dress from Sandy's shop. The sun was out. The tourist crowd looked promising. I wanted to just enjoy all that was good and right, to forget about Gina, at least for now, and just live in the bliss.

Unfortunately we were only halfway through the day before Gina showed up at the shop, and my bliss came crashing back to earth. Gina was all smiles and gifts. She'd bought silver necklaces, two halves of a heart with *My Sister, My Friend* printed on them. One for me. One for her. Our names were engraved on the backs.

"Friends again?" she said as she dangled mine in front of me.

I tucked it into my pocket. "I'm not supposed to wear jewelry here, unless it's from the shop."

"Well, that's a stupid rule."

Sandy gave her a dirty look. Whether I chose to forgive Gina or not, it was fairly clear that she wouldn't be invited into the Sisterhood of the Seashell Shop anytime soon.

"But . . . okay," Gina added, smiling at me. "You guys here for the whole day? Because I was thinking we could take the Jeep out, drive down the beach . . ."

"We're here for the day." I was careful to indicate that Zoey would be staying too. She, Megan, and Stephanie were enjoying themselves, making sale posters and shell-based decorations for a sidewalk display out front. "J.T.'s gone fishing with Paul." *So don't try to kidnap him, either.*

Gina yawned behind her hand. She looked warmed-over this morning. "Think I'll mosey on home and catch a few winks, then. I'm beat."

I didn't argue with her. I just let her go. Sandy gave me a dirty look for that too. Not long after Gina was gone, she caught me in a corner and told me I should kick my sister to the curb. "Not that I'm trying to tell you your business," she added.

"I just . . . need time to think it all through." I didn't want to be a wimp, but Sandy had no idea how Gina could be when you made her mad. "She's the only family I have."

"You've got us." Sandy's gaze met mine, and she sighed, her shoulders slumping. "But I know you're a big girl. You can make your own decisions, and I need to butt out." I had a feeling she'd been told that more than once before. The line had a practiced quality to it.

"I love it that you care." I turned back to making coffee. After so many years of dysfunctional relationships that masqueraded as love, having someone offer real love and ask nothing for it in return was startling, sometimes too much to handle. I wasn't sure I could trust it or was worthy of it.

"Well, just remember, we're here if you need a friend . . . a bouncer . . . anything." Sandy circled the counter and went out the back door to the glass shop. After a busy week, she and Sharon were working on more boxes, wind chimes, and suncatchers. During the un-birthday party last night, she'd asked me again to make more driftwood boxes. She especially liked the technique of filling the cracks with shell hash and lacquering over it. She was sure that my boxes would sell for big dollars in the shop. She described them as "sea art." I'd never thought of myself as an artist, but I guessed I was.

A while later the shop phone rang, and it was Paul. I'd noticed that, so far, he had subtly refused to call me on the cell that Ross had given me. Paul hadn't come right out and said it, but he didn't like Ross or my sister any more than Sandy did.

"Hey, so how was the fishing?" I asked. "Did you and J.T. catch anything?"

There was a strange pause on the other end. "Listen, Tandi, I've got some bad news — I mean, not about J.T. or anything. He's fine, but earlier today we were fishing the Boiler up at Pea Island, and I got to talking to a couple guys who were there. Anyway, Fairhope came up, and they said they'd heard that some property had been condemned in Fairhope for flood retention and a borrow pit. I told them I didn't know anything about it, but it's been bothering me all day. So I finally made a few calls . . . and . . . well . . . as far as I can tell, they're talking about Iola's house. We've got to reel in the lines here and pack things up, but I'm headed to Bink's to see if they've heard anything. This doesn't sound good, though."

The fear that had been lingering in the back of my mind for weeks now bubbled to the surface. In some way, I'd known this was coming, but in another way, I'd been living in total denial — pretending Iola's big white house would always be there. If the situation was about to change, I had to get there first, to at least take care of the boxes before Iola's letters could become fodder for public discussion.

"Paul, I'm headed home. There's something I have to do there. I'll need help, and I need the ladder — the tall one, okay?"

"No problem. Whatever you need. I'll go by Bink's and then meet you there."

We hung up, and I hurried to the workshop to find Sandy. Zoey was out there with her, learning to solder the leading on sea glass picture frames.

Sandy pushed her goggles up and beamed at me when I came through the door. "I'll tell you, we're going to have to keep this girl a . . ." The smile faded midsentence. "What in the world is wrong? You look like you've seen a ghost."

I explained the situation with Iola's house, and within a few minutes, Zoey and I were hurrying out the door. "Anything you need, you just call me!" Sandy yelled after us. I realized it was the second time I'd heard that in less than fifteen minutes. *Anything you need.* What could I possibly have done to deserve people like Paul and Sandy?

And Iola.

I couldn't let the house be demolished. Somehow, I had to find a way. Yes, there was storm damage, but the place could still be saved. It had withstood a hundred years of storms. It shouldn't be taken down by a wrecking ball, by someone's random decision that the property should be used for something else.

Adrenaline surged through my body as we drove home, and with it came determination, a sense of focus. Just as quickly, I felt it draining like a wave retreating into the sea. My skin went cold and clammy as we pulled into the driveway. Gina's new Jeep was parked in front of the cottage and beside it a tricked-out four-wheel-drive truck that I recognized. Ross's.

Zoey slanted a glance my way as we drifted to a stop without pulling into the cottage parking nook. All of a sudden, I wished I'd left my daughter behind.

"Zoey, go over to Bink's and see if Paul and J.T. are there, okay? Tell them we're home."

"But, Mama . . ."

"Just go." My stomach was churning, my mind racing ahead, dashing back and forth between harmless explanations for those two vehicles being parked together and terrible visions of why they probably were.

Zoey slid from the truck and jogged off across the yard, casting nervous backward glances as I crossed the driveway and walked up the steps to the cottage. I waited until she was out of sight before going in. The door was unlocked, but no one was inside.

Maybe Gina had some kind of trouble with the new Jeep, and . . . and she called Ross. Maybe the obnoxious man from the county came back, and . . . and Gina was worried, and . . .

So many logical scenarios, but none seemed to fit. There had never been logic where my sister was concerned. Only impulse and a constant, wild changing of direction, like the sails on an unmanned boat, the boom swinging dangerously in the wind.

A part of me knew. I felt it as I walked out the door of the cottage again, looked around the yard, toward the hedges, toward the barn, toward Iola's house. Something moved beyond the glass — just a transient form, a ghost, a specter from the past, from all the other times that I'd hoped and believed and yearned and wanted . . . and been disappointed.

Dread flowed cold inside me as I crossed the yard, tiptoed up the porch steps, settled my hand on the doorknob, heard Gina's raucous laughter, high and light. They didn't even notice me when I stepped inside. They were too busy on the rug in front of the parlor fireplace — Gina slipping out of her sundress seductively, Ross with his shirt off, one arm braced, his flesh ruddy and tan against hers.

I felt sick, then wounded, then filled with rage. "Get. *Out!*" I screamed, grabbing a cheap ceramic flowerpot from the hallway table. I flung it at them, and it shattered against the hearth. "How *dare* you come in here? You have no right! Get *out*! Both of you get out!"

Ross stood first, grabbing the loose ends of his belt. "Tandi, wait a minute. I . . ."

Gina blinked in surprise, looked from me to Ross and back as she pulled her sundress into place. "Tandi, it's not what it looks —"

"So is *this* where you were last night?" I spat. "First my daughter and now Ross. If I *have* it, you want to get your hands on it . . . just to prove you can. That's how it's always been, right? I was an idiot to think things could be any different."

"Tandi, I didn't mean for this to . . ." Gina stood, faced me. "It wasn't any . . . Nothing happened, okay? I wasn't with him last night, I swear. Just calm down, okay?"

"Leave," I growled.

Her lips pressed into a thin line, her nostrils flaring. "You know what? You're the same brat you always were. I sold my car for you — to help you out, to get us a place. And if we're going to talk about people keeping *secrets,* why don't we talk about *yours*? I've seen you over here with the lights on at night, sneaking around when you think no one's watching. What are you doing in this house all the time, Tandi?" She rammed her hands onto her hips, glared at the walls. Beside her, Ross looked completely confused, but Gina had homed in. "Maybe making a few bucks on the side, because there's *lots* of stuff around here that's worth some *money.* Wonder what Brother Bill-bo next door would say if I told him you're in here all the time — that you come over here for *hours* sometimes. No telling what you've *stolen* out of this place, because that's *who you are,* Tandi. You're going around trying to make these people think you're so good. You think they really *love* you? You think they won't figure it out? You're *nothing.* We're just like Mama and Daddy, and we always will be. Once these people find out who you *really* are, you'll be out on the street, and you'll come crawling back, looking for somebody to make it okay.

461

Blood runs thicker than water, Little Sister."

Fear made me hesitate, freeze up just long enough for Gina to narrow her sights, put me in her crosshairs. *Blood runs thicker than water* . . .

Her posture softened, her head tilting to one side, the strap of the sundress sliding down her shoulder. Her lips curved upward at the corners, the expression almost tender, alluring. "You should see yourself. You look like a deer caught in the headlights. *Relax.* It's okay. Hey, it's not like the old lady can use this stuff anymore. Why shouldn't somebody have it? Come on, we could look around, and —"

My anger exploded in a white-hot flash, and before I knew it, I was crossing the room, grabbing the fireplace poker, brandishing it at my sister. "You get out of this house! I'm not anything like you and Mama . . . and Daddy, and I never will be. You get out and don't come back!"

"Right *now.*" The voice came from behind me, and I realized it was Paul's. He was standing in the entry hall, his face deadly serious. In his hand, he was holding a heavy wooden spindle from the porch railing, tapping it against his palm like a baseball bat. His red hair was wild around his head, his face flushed beneath the freckles as if he'd been running. "If Tandi wants you out, then get *out*. Both of you."

Gina coughed indignantly, drawing her head upward.

Ross lifted his hands, palms out, and sidestepped toward the door. "Look, dude, this isn't worth it, okay? I didn't come for a fight. I'm gone." He turned and quit the room.

Gina flashed a look filled with resentment and anger, and even though we'd played this scene out so many times before, it still stung.

She stormed after Ross, her heels clicking through the entry hall and across the porch.

Tears filled my eyes, and I wiped them impatiently, then turned away from Paul, filled with pain and shame. *You're* nothing. *We're just like Mama and Daddy, and we always will be. Once these people find out who you really are, you'll be out on the street, and you'll come crawling back. . . .* Gina knew me. She knew my life from the very beginning.

"I'm sorry, Paul." I swallowed the acidic mix inside me, stuffed it down, and pulled a hard covering over it. "You should leave too." Why wait for it to happen on its own? Who was I fooling, thinking I could change my life, change everything about me? I was like Iola — an actress on a stage, playing a part for the rest of the world to see, denying who I was.

If Paul knew where I'd come from, he wouldn't want a thing to do with me. Neither would Sandy or Brother Guilbeau or the rest of the Seashell Shop girls. It was easier, less painful to just speed up the natural progression of things. I could do Iola this last favor, clean out the letters and throw them away, and then leave. If Trammel was a big story in Texas now, there might be some money to be made telling my side, letting the world know what it was really like, living in his house . . .

"I'm going," Paul said, and the hard place inside me clenched tighter, the skin ripening, preparing for harvest, a bitter fruit.

He lowered the wooden spindle, his fingers relaxing against the cracked surface and peeling paint. I nodded, closed my eyes. I didn't want to watch him walk out, to see the beginning of the end of this life.

"But just to get my hat. It blew off as I was running over here."

I looked at him standing there, thumbing over his shoulder in a ridiculous peach-colored shirt with dancing geckos on it. I couldn't speak.

". . . and the kids, I guess," he went on. "I

left them at Bink's. I was afraid there might be trouble here." Outside, vehicles started and roared away, and Paul turned an ear to the sound, listening until they were both gone before he looked at me again. "Besides, if I leave, my long ladder's going with me. I priced new ones at Home Depot the other day, and do you know how much those things cost?"

A puff of laughter pushed past the mountain of pain — impossible laughter that came from somewhere new, somewhere soft and bright, far from all the old wounds. I wanted to step into it, but I was afraid. That place was wide open, vulnerable. "Paul, you don't have to . . ."

He smiled and shook his head, met my eyes. "Not everyone's the same, Tandi. Not everyone is working the angles, looking for something. People can care about you just for *you*. Just because you're worth caring about."

I felt the warmth inside, the explosion of the light I'd seen in my dream flowing over me, enveloping me. I wanted to step into it, to be covered by it, blinded by it. The only thing stopping me was fear. It clenched my throat, made words impossible to find. I could only stand there, silent.

"Anyway, we've got work to do." Paul

straightened, suddenly all business. "We have to come up with a plan. I just found out there's a county commission meeting on Monday. They want to condemn this house and the property around it as a flood-control zone, then dig a borrow pit here to excavate sand to restore the beaches around those multimillion-dollar homes that are sitting in water since the storm. In the end, they'll turn this whole place into a holding pond for flood retention. If they do that, not only is this house finished, but there won't be anything left of Fairhope that's worth having."

He walked out the door, and I stood looking around the house, thinking of everything that had happened here, the way this place had changed my life. Changed me.

It wasn't right that Iola's house be destroyed in order to save homes that had been built only a few years ago. This couldn't happen.

"It's wrong," I whispered. "If people knew how much you loved this island . . . If they knew everything you did for them . . . If they knew who you really were . . ."

It came to me then. The answer. If we were to have any chance of saving Iola's house, we had to tell the people her story.

CHAPTER 24

Is there, in you, a forgiveness for sins of the father or the mother? Is there an absolution for the innocent? For the fragile life that had no say in its beginnings? For a wife who carries secrets to the wedding bed?

Forgive me, Father, for I have sinned. I have sinned the sin of lies and love. I have hidden all the parts of me he does not know. For him, I have become the mask. The mask of passion, of love. I have entered into this sacrament a shell with nothing inside that does not hide in the shadows, and now there is life growing, and it is loved, yet it lives so near the darkness.

Will you forgive me, Father? Will you forgive this child?

I yearn to cast aside the fear, to tell.

And I fear I can never tell.

I wonder at this web of lies, and I feel

it tightening. Love cannot live in the darkness, in the shadows. It is a growing thing, a thing of light.

I, a child of lies, know this so well.

But I come before you, and I fall on my knees, and I beg of you, Father. Show mercy. . . .

Iola was a wife, a newly expectant mother traveling home to stay with her husband's family. Two months after their secret marriage in a tiny church on the Swiss border, her husband, Marcus, had been injured in a land mine explosion, and she found herself en route to Nevada with him. She'd discovered her pregnancy only weeks before, and she was filled with fear. The life she'd built after joining the WAACs suddenly seemed to be compressing around her. She'd told her husband nothing about her history, other than that she'd grown up in a convent school and had no family. She'd kept her pregnancy secret so far. . . .

Paul's cell phone rang in the closet, and I jumped. Deep in Iola's letters, I'd forgotten there was anyone else in the house, much less in the room. Paul had been moving boxes down from the upper shelves and searching through them, ferreting out Iola's connections with others on the island —

the people she'd included in her prayer letters, the causes she'd secretly supported. Paul was discovering Iola's life from the top down, while I worked from the bottom up.

We photographed bits of her history with Paul's phone, slowly compiling her story, documenting all the ways she had used the Benoit money to change lives on the Outer Banks and far beyond. Over the years, she'd given the Benoit shipping company over to its employees, allowing the board of directors to create stock-option plans, retirement funds, medical plans, and college scholarships for employees' children. She'd helped fund libraries, schools, churches, and parks intended to preserve the wild spaces of the Outer Banks for future generations.

She'd helped new businesses like Sandy's, often making purchases from local shops and then donating the items to charity auctions and nonprofit programs. She'd aided families in need, sent anonymous donations to pay for cancer treatments, bone marrow drives, a motorized wheelchair for a woman who'd lost her legs in an accident on the docks. As her cash resources slowly dwindled, she began using items of value in the house to continue to do the work she felt compelled to do. There had been other Tiffany lamps before the Magnolia left the blue room. Lamps and paintings and statues and jewelry. Symbols of opulence, slowly given away.

Downstairs, Zoey and J.T. were going through the stacks of newspapers that had been stored among the clutter. As I'd suspected, the newspapers weren't there at random. They were a record — a paper trail of all the needs to which Iola had devoted herself. She'd been an angel of mercy for so many people. Always in secret.

She'd changed so many lives before she'd changed mine. The only difference being that I was the last.

"This woman was everywhere," Paul commented, coming out of the closet, already reading a letter from a box pulled off the shelf second to the top. "It's amazing. This is from a tanker spill in 2008. There was a group of students down in Florida trying to help transport a pod of beached dolphins back out to sea. She sent a massive donation to pay for equipment, along with a copy of an old newspaper article about the whales that were rescued from the ice cover in Barrow, Alaska, twenty years before — there was a movie about it a couple years ago, remember that? Iola sent money to help fund that rescue too. She wanted to share the whales' story with the college kids rescuing the dolphins in Florida, to inspire them to believe it could be done. I love this woman! Listen to this: 'Father, help these young people to see. Help them to show the world that our greatness is not in things we do for ourselves, but in things we do for others. In power that channels itself into kindness, in a hand outstretched in love. Be with these determined students. Help them to believe, when the naysayers come, that you make all things possible.

" 'And, Father, touch your fingertip again to the life of the Mulberry Girl, that she might be well. I've not mentioned her in some time, but I know you are mindful of her, as you are mindful of each sparrow of the field. . . .' " Paul set the letter atop the box and continued to the desk, smiling at me as he passed. "That is magnificent. This woman is like a tiny St. Francis — whales, dolphins, cancer patients, mulberry girls . . . whatever that means."

"Mama! She bought computers for the library, I think!" Zoey yelled from the bottom of the stairs. "J.T.'s taking a picture of the article!"

"Good!" I called. "Keep going through the papers. Save everything we can use. We'll print it all at Bink's later." The cell phone from Ross was coming to good use after all.

I went back to Iola's letters, sank into her life again as the night ticked by. A squall blew onto the Outer Banks, and we added emptying drip buckets to our tasks as the hours wore on. The water was coming through the ceiling in streams now, seeping down walls, dampening floors and carpets, leaching through to the lower floor. Paul gave the ceiling in the blue room a worried look as he passed by the bed where I was reading. I knew what he was thinking.

What if the place was too far gone?

I focused, instead, on Iola's life.

On the other side of the room, Paul muttered to himself, cataloging letters. ". . . prayed for the new pastor at the church, prayed for the UPS guy and the Mulberry Girl . . . Oop, helped fund playground equipment at a new community center. Here's a good one." He grabbed the cell phone from the bed and snapped a photo.

I moved through another letter and another.

Water plinked into buckets.

Paul snapped pictures.

"Mama, we're making some Jiffy Pop, 'kay?" J.T. yelled from downstairs. "We're hungry and it smells yucky down here."

"Okay. Yes," I called back, frustrated by

472

the distraction as I followed the trail of Iola's life. She'd lost the initial pregnancy after the marriage, and with Marcus redeployed to the war front after recovering from his injuries, she'd waited out the war with his family, learning the life of a ranch wife out west. The Jane Russell–style photo she'd shown to the UPS man had been taken there. There were several shots of Iola in the box, all snapped when she'd gathered with local wives and sweethearts to take photos that would be sent to husbands and beaus overseas — something to boost the morale of the boys fighting far from home.

The UPS man was right. Iola had been a beautiful young woman — olive-skinned, bright-eyed, exotic, her hair flowing over the haystack in rich, dark curls. She looked happy, laughing as the horse nuzzled her, stealing hay from the stack. The photographs captured the moment perfectly. A moment of youth and innocence. Of joy.

Then the war was over, victory declared in Europe and in Japan, the Allied occupation forces turning to the rebuilding of liberated countries, as the box from 1946 began. Marcus's duty was ending, and he was coming home. He and Iola could finally be together again. A promise of prosperity, peace, and abundance was ahead. They would build a home of their own.

Iola's joy had been tempered once more by fear. A new home was a place for a growing family. Marcus, his parents, his brothers and sisters and aunts and uncles expected it. But Iola had heard stories about women of mixed race who entered marriages while keeping secrets, women whose hidden heritage was revealed in the births of their children. She'd heard of illicit ways that a woman could make certain she was never able to conceive.

She was afraid. . . .

I sat staring at her words, thinking of that moment when I stood outside the abortion clinic, alone, terrified, pregnant by a man who promised to love me, then didn't. *This is the only way, Tandi,* he'd told me. *I'll take care of you once it's finished. Surely you understand, I have a career to think about, a reputation to protect. Just give me time to work it all out, and we can be together. We won't have to hide forever. . . .*

I understood the fear inside Iola Anne, the desperation, the consuming need to be loved.

And then, as she sat on the porch of the ranch house, contemplating her future, a neighbor boy came by on his pony, carrying a letter, saving the postman a trip. The

handwriting on the envelope was unmistak-
able, the return address a link to the past
she'd left behind before the war.

Isabelle had found her.

Wrapped inside Iola's prayer letter was
the letter she had received from Isabelle in
March 1946. Isabelle had returned home to
the Outer Banks, her husband dead at
Normandy, and she herself weakened by a
bout of polio.

. . . but there is joy also! My child has
survived. Christina is beautiful, though
small for an infant her age and frail, having suffered such trauma in the womb.
But the air here by the sea is good for
her. She grows stronger each day.

Even Papa dotes on her. She has become the joy of his old age in these
recent months, and if he in any way
resents the circumstances of her enter-
ing this world, he does not show it.
Eventually the past must be buried and
all must be forgiven if life is to go on.
While the circumstances of my returning home, the loss of my dear Andrew,
sadden me, I count it gain that there has
been the opportunity for rebuilding
bonds with my father before it is too
late. Andrew's death and my long hours

in the iron lung have taught me that not one day of our lives is a given, Iola Anne. There comes a moment when time stops, and to each of us that moment is a mystery. It so often slips around a blind corner.

I do not speak of this idly, Iola Anne. It is with a dire purpose that I have gone through the effort of using Papa's considerable contacts with the War Department to find you and send this letter. I must tell you of your Maman. The doctors say that she is not much longer for this world. Her fondest wish is that she would see you again. I do not know your financial circumstances, so I have taken the liberty of including train tickets in this envelope. I hope that you and your husband will use them to come to us.

Please know also that I love you and have missed you dearly these years since you left.

Please come home to us. . . .

I realized I was reading the letter out loud to Paul. I hadn't meant to, but I was.

"Wow," he breathed. "What a decision, huh?"

"Yes," I said and silently returned to the

box. "I'm afraid to even look at the next one."

Paul rubbed his eyes and blinked hard, yawning. It was after eleven already. "Well, surely when she told her husband the truth, he stuck by her." Hooking a hand over the back of the chair, he rested his chin on it and watched me as I unfolded the next letter and then another, skimmed the words, shook my head.

"She came home alone. And she came home for good."

"So he left her when he found out . . . ," Paul whispered.

"He did." I turned back to the letters as Paul went downstairs to check on the kids.

The trail of Iola's words led me on a train ride across the country and finally a ferry back to Hatteras on a stormy March day, where Isabelle was waiting, her legs in braces, her infant daughter nearby in Old Rupert's arms.

Tears blurred the page as Iola recounted Isabelle's words at their reunion.

"Oh, Iola Anne, Old Rupert told me what he supposes to be the reason for your leaving. Don't you know that sisters are created not by blood but by love? In my heart, you have not been my niece,

477

but you have always been my sister. . . ."

Closing my eyes, I brought the letter to my lips, breathed in the scents of ink and aging paper and truth. *Sisters are created not by blood but by love.* All my life, I'd let the ties of blood control me, limit me, define me, yet I'd ignored the ties of love. I'd shielded myself from the people who tried to slip inside the armor, who told me that I was worthy.

Paul came into the room again, giving me an uncertain look as he passed by. "Everything okay?" he asked tentatively.

"Yes. It's more than okay."

A new sense of joy filled me as I returned to the letters, the late-night hours slowly giving way to the early hours of morning. J.T. fell asleep on a fainting couch downstairs. Zoey made coffee and continued digging through newspapers, refusing to quit the task and go to bed. Paul and I worked closer to the center of the boxes, narrowing the open window on Iola's life.

She'd lived on the island the rest of her years, moving back to Benoit House, first to nurse her maman, then caring for Isabelle and little Christina and for the grandfather who refused to claim her as his own.

Isabelle, eventually weakened by a bout of

influenza that claimed the life of Christina, became bound to a wheelchair, her frame thin and frail, but her spirit undimmed. She discovered a love of photography and became an advocate for the wild Banker ponies living on the islands. With Iola's help, she took countless photographs of the horses in their natural habitat, wrote articles for magazines, petitioned the park service for care of the horses, and argued against the wholesale roundup and removal of the horses that had survived on the islands for hundreds of years since swimming ashore from shipwrecked Spanish galleons. Even as Isabelle's body began to fail, she and Iola fought to preserve the unspoiled beauty of the place that they loved.

I drive the car close to the dunes, as far as we dare go, so as to avoid becoming trapped in the sand. Isabelle recounts the last time we mired our vehicle, and we laugh together about our escapades, our life a grand adventure. We've traveled up to see the Banker ponies again today, to take photographs.

"Remember our rides on the old horse?" she asks. "And the day we discovered the shipwreck? It was a magnificent day."

"Yes, it was," I say, and for a moment I see the light of that young girl with dream-filled eyes. I find her inside the body that grows thin and rebels and refuses.

"I had the life I wanted," she says. "I had my adventure. It was shorter than I'd planned."

"I wonder if it is ever what we plan." I squeeze her hand, then slip out my door and circle the car to hers.

"I hope we've done some good . . . for the horses and the people . . . and the islands." For a moment, her gaze is far away. "There was no other place I loved so well as this one."

"Me as well," I say, and I know it is true. For all the places I've loved, there have been none like this. This place is a deeper love, a sisterhood of water and sand and soul. A place where you fill me through my eyes and my ears, Father.

I lift Isabelle onto my back to carry her over the dunes. She is as light as a child. The camera swings from her hand as I walk.

Isabelle chatters. This wasting of the body has done nothing to dull her mind. "I read that in five years, there will be a bridge connecting Hatteras from Pea

Island to Nags Head. There will be a paved highway from one end of the Banks to the other. No need for the ferry, except perhaps for Ocracoke."

"Well, I don't know. They say anything in those newspapers." I heave and groan as we pass through the dunes.

"You sound like the old horse," Isabelle teases.

I laugh and snort and toss my mane. "Be careful, or I'll dump you in the sand. Remember when you let the picnic blanket dangle against the old horse's flanks, and he threw us both?"

"I think that was you who let the picnic blanket dangle."

I snort again. We, both of us, know who insisted on the blanket with the fancy silk fringe that day so long ago. Isabelle was always the one with the grand ideas.

"They could save themselves the trouble of a bridge, you know," I tell her. "In five years, it will be 1960, and we'll be living in Futurama." I think of that tiny city at the World's Fair, almost twenty years past now. That miniature, perfect life with its plastic people. "And we'll be coming here by dirigible and autogiro, remember?"

When we reach the shore, Isabelle tosses the blanket off her shoulder, and it lands in the sand. I spread it with my foot, lower her onto it, and sit beside her. The Banker ponies are nowhere in sight, but they'll be along in their own time.

For now, we watch the sea, my sister and I, and the sea is always enough.

"They say we'll put a man on the moon in not so many years," she tells me. Isabelle is taken with *Life* magazine and *National Geographic.*

"I don't believe it," I answer. "Men are always trying to solve the mysteries of God, but they never will."

She plucks a whelk shell from the sand, contemplates it, turning it over with her bone-thin fingers. "There will always be another mystery. God is infinite."

She hands the shell to me, and I hold it up, letting the sun shine through it. I think of the creature that once lived here. Perhaps he has outgrown his old home. "You tie my mind like knitting thread. In very small knots," I complain to Isabelle. "You always have." I wonder what I will do when she is gone, when the thread runs out and its end drifts beyond my reach.

"You've always been the wiser one." She lays her tired head on my shoulder and looks through the shell with me, into the great mystery. I think again that heaven must be like this place, and I say that to Isabelle. I wonder, When she is in heaven and I am not, how far away will she be?

"It's just another journey," she whispers, the long, strawberry-gold strands of her hair teasing my skin. "Heaven. It's one more beautiful adventure. I'm not afraid. Don't worry about me. Christina waits for me there. My little girl. And Andrew."

"And Maman and Mama Tee and Old Rupert," I remind her.

"Yes, and all of them." She laughs softly. "I think the first thing I'll hear is Mama Tee singing and Christina's laughter."

"I think so too."

Her fingers hold mine, and we rest them on the sand.

"You'll take care of Papa?" she asks. Somewhere in the distance, I hear the ponies call out. They're coming down to the water. Anytime now, the herd leader will appear on the dunes to watch over the smaller and the weaker as they gallop to the shore.

I tell Isabelle that I will care for Monsieur until he is gone. It won't be many years. He is old and lame, and he has outlived all the ones he loved, except for Isabelle.

"He comes from a different time, Iola Anne," she pleads. "He doesn't know another way. Forgive him for what he is."

"I do," I say as the ponies appear on the hill, wild and unbridled.

Isabelle rouses herself and takes up the camera to preserve yet one more day in this place. One more day together with the sister that love has given me.

Forgive me, Father, for asking for another day yet, and another beyond that, when this one is so very beautiful. We, in our humanness, cannot help but foolishly desire eternity in this life.

Your loving daughter,
Iola Anne

I set the letter aside, swallowed tears, and stood to stretch. Outside, the skies had dried up, a heavy moon casting a silver lining around the clouds above the loblolly pines. Paul had fallen asleep at the desk after finishing the last box before the one I'd opened on the bed. We'd finally come together in the middle.

Downstairs, the kids were both sleeping now. In a few hours, the church bells in Fairhope would ring out their morning call to worship. Desperate prayers would be offered up, conversations played out, and legal chatter kicked back and forth in search of some means of saving Iola's house and Fairhope. In a strange way, Iola and the town were finally united.

I looked over Paul's shoulder at the letters scattered on the desk. Girard Benoit, Iola's grandfather and Isabelle's father, had died in 1963, just after the Herbert C. Bonner Bridge connected Hatteras to the northern Outer Banks, opening Hatteras to drive-on tourism and changing it forever. The era of quiet, remote life in saltbox houses was over. Girard Benoit had never acknowledged Iola's blood relation, other than in leaving her the family inheritance that caused her neighbors to accuse her of taking advantage of an old man whose mind was gone. Why she'd kept her secret all her life, I still didn't know, and I guessed no one ever would.

I laid a hand on Paul's shoulder and woke him. "You don't look very comfortable there," I said. "There's a bed downstairs in the room off the kitchen. Why don't you go catch a little sleep? I think I'll curl up in the parlor with the kids for a while. In the morning we can go to Bink's and print out all the sections we photographed, make the displays with the newspaper articles and whatnot." The poster boards were J.T.'s idea — something resembling the science fair project he was working on in Paul's class, but this display would be about Iola's life. A visual catalog of all that she'd done for the Outer Banks. We planned to include some of Isabelle's photographs and her magazine articles. Zoey had unearthed a pile of old *Ladies' Home Journal, McCall's,* and *Life* magazines in the storage closet under the stairs, all featuring Isabelle's works about the islands.

Paul blinked, seeming confused at first about where he was.

"You were really asleep," I said, a drowsy chuckle teasing my throat as I peeled back a piece of stationery that was stuck to his arm. There was a sketch on it, a little girl sitting in a metal porch chair, her face buried in her hair.

"I thought we'd put that one on the display boards," he said. "I just like the feel of it . . . sort of conveys a moment when all hope seems lost, you know?"

486

"Feels like it fits the mood," I admitted. Now that we'd gone through the boxes, I wondered if anything we were doing would make a difference. There was money and power on the other end of this struggle. Fairhope was a tiny community of fishermen and working people. There was no political pull here.

Paul squeezed my fingers. "We can do this," he promised, and then we walked from the blue room together.

CHAPTER 25

Two steps outside the county commissioners' court, I was filled with righteous anger and determination. In my hand, I held a notebook with my speech about Benoit House. Beside me, Paul carried the poster boards on which we'd gathered parts of Iola's story — paragraphs copied from her letters, articles we'd taken from the newspapers stacked among Iola's things, a smattering of Isabelle's writings and photography, scraps about the historic value of Benoit House. Like a warrior's armor, they made me feel strong — a shield, a sword. A cause that was worth fighting for.

This entire community would hear Iola's story now. They would know her as I had come to know her. Secrets would be revealed, and people would finally understand who she was and what she had done. She wasn't a thief, a squatter in Benoit House. She was a daughter of it. She was a small, humble woman who had made her life a gift of service and never asked for anything in return — not recognition, not fame, not even the gratitude of those she'd helped. A quiet angel, a woman who served a calling first learned from a gentle nun in an orphans' home. If not for the boxes, no one would ever have known. Iola Anne Poole would've disappeared from this place, silent and invisible. Forgotten.

If I had anything to say about it, she wouldn't be. Her neighbors here on these narrow strips of sand would see that they owed her the debt of granting her final wish, the only thing she'd ever desired for herself — that her family home, the place she treasured, be preserved.

Paul and I had worked all day Sunday and Monday on the speech, honing and refining it while Zoey, J.T., and the Binks printed photos of Iola's writings, then clipped and laminated and arranged them with old pictures of the house and Isabelle's magazine works. Geneva Bink had done an e-blast of an electronic postcard that Zoey helped design. At the Seashell Shop, Sandy had shared the information with every business owner on the island and with her list of customers. Mike Mullins, the UPS driver, had taken flyers and given them to his contacts. The hope was that even people who loved to vacation in the Outer Banks might show up at the meeting, flood the commissioners' court with citizens who were more concerned about preserving the island's history and character than satisfying land developers anxious to support rampant construction along the shore.

I'd imagined the scene over and over as I practiced the speech, Paul giving me encouraging looks while running a stopwatch. Three minutes. That's all that was allowed for each person in the public comments forum.

Three minutes. Was it possible to encapsulate an entire life in such a small scrap of time?

Geneva Bink would speak before me, talking about the history of Fairhope and its importance to the citizens who lived there. I would follow with my speech about Iola's life and Benoit House, and several other Hatteras residents, including Sandy, would speak after me, with the intent of driving the point home. Our names were on the public comments list. The only question now was whether anyone would listen.

"Here we go," Paul said as we neared the doors to the building. "If anyone can make Iola come alive for these people, you can."

I looked into his eyes and was momentarily convinced that I could do anything. Paul made me feel larger than I was, invincible. He believed in me in a way that made me believe in myself. Sometime in the middle of the night, as we sat in the blue room, the soft light of the Tiffany Magnolia lamp bathing dozens of failed attempts at speech writing wadded on the floor, I'd looked at Paul, bent over one of Iola's prayer boxes, and realized that I didn't know what I would do without him. His was the smile I looked forward to most in the day, his and Zoey's and J.T.'s. His was the voice that fell softly on my ear, that built me up rather than tearing me down. I'd never known anyone like Paul Chastain.

I hadn't told him that — how much he meant to me. I wasn't sure why, but the words weren't there. I didn't have a definition for Paul and me. I didn't have words for what this was. Maybe he didn't either, and that was part of the problem. I wasn't sure what I was to him — a project, a way to fill a gap in his life, part of a fractured family he felt the need to reroot and repair, rebuild like he rebuilt storm-damaged beaches?

What could I possibly be to someone like him, other than a project?

Two steps inside the commissioners' court, I panicked. Completely. The room was filled to capacity, even though the meeting wasn't to begin for twenty minutes yet. People stood along the walls, sat on the floor in the center aisle. In the semicircular rows of seats, some attendees were already sitting two to a chair.

"I can't do this," I whispered and tried to hand the notebook to Paul. I wasn't sure what I'd expected, but the interior looked like a courtroom: dark wooden walls, gallery seating filled with onlookers, a heavy U-shaped stand where the commissioners sat behind marble countertops on a raised dais. My mind rushed back to countless visits to family court, adults asking questions, making decisions, casting looks of pity our way. Suddenly I was a little girl again, powerless, afraid. "I think I'm going to be sick."

I tried to turn and run out the door. Paul caught me before I could escape. His arm formed a firm, strong circle around my waist.

"Let go!" I protested, loudly enough that a uniformed officer glanced my way. I lowered my voice. "Just take the notebook, Paul. You know everything we were planning to say. I can't go in there." I couldn't breathe. I couldn't think.

Paul's skin pressed warm against mine. "Yes, you can, Tandi. You can." His gaze grabbed me, held on. "You're the one who lived it. You're the one who needs to tell the story of the boxes and that house." He set the poster boards beside the wall, took my face in both of his hands, stared hard at me like a rescue diver trying to convince a shipwreck victim to stop floundering and start swimming. "Come on, just like we practiced. Don't let these people intimidate you. You're stronger than that."

"Paul, I —"

"I'm right here. I'm not going anywhere." He leaned close, his forehead almost touching mine. His nearness blocking out the sounds of people whispering, bodies shifting impatiently, chairs scraping the floor.

For a moment, I saw only Paul, heard only his voice. "When you get your turn to talk, don't think about the commissioners. Just tell *me* the story, like you did last night when we practiced at Iola's house. Now remember, they'll go through all the people who signed up earlier on the agenda first, so there will be a bunch of talk about different issues. Then Geneva comes up and then you. Geneva will prep the court with the list of complaints she's gathered about more

493

borrow pits and a holding pond going in, and then it's you. You show them, Tandi. Show them what they're talking about destroying so that they can dig sand and drain water to save houses that've been built where they shouldn't have been in the first place. Houses that likely won't survive another storm or two. You ask those commissioners, and the audience, which house has the right to be here — the ones that are sliding off into the water or the one that has made it through every storm? You show them who Iola was and what that house meant and everything she did for the Banks."

Which house has the right to be here . . .

I heard my grandfather's voice. *What do they think — the storms will never come? You build a house on the sand, the sand shifts eventually, Tandi Jo. You remember that.*

I heard Isabelle. *Fear builds walls instead of bridges. I want a life of bridges, not walls.*

Swallowing the pulsating lump in my chest, I pulled in air, nodded because I couldn't find my voice, and let Paul lead me forward. Geneva, Bink, Zoey, J.T., and Brother Guilbeau were sitting in a row near the middle. I recognized many of the faces around them. The fishermen of Fairhope had turned out in force.

Zoey and J.T. wiggled out of a single seat by the aisle.

"Here," J.T. offered, grabbing his jacket from the back of the chair. "We saved you a seat."

Zoey nodded, her face filled with tenderness and something else I'd never seen in her before, or at least not in a long time. Admiration. "Go get 'em, Mama." She hugged me, then pressed the mermaid's tear necklace into my palm.

I closed my fingers around it and let her faith seep into me. We'd been brought here, back to these islands, for a reason. For so many reasons that I was only now beginning to see.

"I will," I promised, holding the necklace as I slipped into my seat. "I will, Zoey. Don't worry."

J.T. folded himself into the space in front of my chair, sitting on my feet, while Zoey moved to the back to stand by the wall where Sandy and the girls had staked out a corner. Paul sat beside me on the floor, holding the poster boards on his crossed legs as the meeting came to order with all the normal proceedings — announcements, prayer, Pledge of Allegiance. I tried to take in air and let it out, to still the trembling in my hands. I needed to appear confident when it was my turn to speak. I had to be convincing. I had to be worthy.

After the court's opening program, the agenda moved on with a short ceremony, giving several county workers their five- and ten-year service pins. In spite of the routine proceedings, the room was filled with tension and expectation, with a sense that everyone was waiting for what would come later.

I closed my eyes and turned a page in my head, imagined this moment as if it had already passed, as if I were reading it in one of Iola's prayer letters. How would she write this? What would she say? What would she ask for just before those closing words, *Your loving daughter*?

Wisdom? Strength? A steady voice?

The presentation of the pins concluded, and the opening of the podium was announced. "Ladies and gentlemen, this is the time that has been set aside for public comments. If you have a public comment this evening and you have not signed up, in a moment, please raise your hand, and I will recognize you. When I do, please go to the podium, state your name, and tell us where you are from. Please limit your comments to three minutes. There's a green light on the podium that will come on when your time begins. A yellow light will come on when you have about thirty seconds left, and a red light will come on when you need to conclude your comments."

Three minutes. Just three minutes. So short a time. How could I possibly make them see?

I opened the notebook, looked down at it, but the words were a jumble in my mind. At the podium, a man was talking about a change in the regulation of lot sizes in Manteo and how it would lead to overdevelopment. From behind the marble counter, the county commissioners watched, polite yet emotionless, giving no hints as to what they were thinking.

Would they even hear me? Who was I to talk to them? I'd only been here a few months. The man petitioning the court right now had lived here twenty-seven years, and no one had protected *him* when a developer bought the land next door and made plans to stack it full of condos and retail shops.

Why would anyone care about Iola's story?

Movement on the opposite end of the room caught my attention. Someone was threading a path through the crowded side aisle. Slick blonde hair swayed over the shoulders of a tight red dress.

"Gina," I whispered. Paul looked up, then

turned a wary look my way.

Another familiar face towered over the crowd behind her. Ross.

"Oh no," I whispered. If Gina was here, it was a given that she knew about our plan and had come to derail it if she could. I should've known she wouldn't quietly disappear after our confrontation in Iola's house. Anytime shots were fired, Gina made sure she won the war, whether she really cared about the spoils or not. Just the fight was motivation enough.

"Steady now." Paul winked at me.

I focused on the podium again, staring straight ahead as one speaker and then another came and went, airing grievances and concerns having to do with everything from school funding to noise control ordinances. Everyone had problems and needs, and every need seemed important. A building contractor spoke about the cost-effectiveness of having borrow pits nearby, to provide fill for construction and sand for waterfront homes. A couple whose life savings were tied up in a beach house that now had runoff sitting underneath it pleaded for new measures in flood control and stormwater retention.

My head was spinning by the time Geneva's name was finally called and she walked calmly to the podium. I could feel Gina's laser focus from across the room as Geneva talked about the community of Fairhope and the fact that the town and its residents were already struggling to recover from the effects of multiple storms. "And we in Fairhope are no strangers to the experience of living next door to borrow pits. In the past, many of us have lived with trucks rumbling in and out at all hours, and dust and fumes, as well as the noise of drag-lines and dredging equipment endlessly removing sand and fill dirt so that it can be used to satisfy the needs of others. But I would like to tell you that in Fairhope, we love our community. We don't want it to be pillaged." She punctuated with a nod and a pause, and in the room, murmurs of agreement went up.

Audience members shifted forward in their seats as Geneva continued. "My mother-in-law is eighty-seven years old. She has lived in Fairhope all her life. Her greatest joy at this advanced age is sitting on her screened porch with her coffee and watching her birds. If the proposed property, the Benoit estate, is used as has been suggested, she will have a mining operation less than thirty yards from her back door. Our daughter's house is next to hers, on property that has been in our family for over one hundred years. If these pits go in, trucks and equipment will be rolling past, literally feet from where her children play. Now I ask you, close your eyes for a minute and picture that it's your mother, your daughter, your grandchildren, your house. Fairhope is a community, a place where fishermen have raised their families since before the Civil War. Like every community, it has flaws, but it is *our* community."

Geneva glanced down at the podium as the warning light went on. "I know my time is almost up, and I know there are others who wish to speak to this issue, so I'm going to stop here and trust that you on the commissioners' court will do what is just and fair. If other towns need sand or fill or retention sites for storm water, let them truck in their fill dirt or find the space in their own communities. We should not, because we are a small community tucked back in the maritime woods, be railroaded by moneyed interests seeking to condemn a historic property. I'd like to request that, before any digging can take place in Fairhope, a public hearing be held to discuss a moratorium on borrow pits of any kind until the community can look at zoning changes to prevent such activity in the future."

Cheers erupted around the room as she left the podium and walked down the aisle. Patting my shoulder, she leaned close to me. "Go get 'em, tiger. You tell them what Iola would think of them dozing her house under and digging a hole in her woods."

"The next person I have is Tandi Reese." The man with the clipboard looked expectantly toward the gallery, and every eye in the room turned my way as I stood. My heart pounded wildly in my chest. The aisle seemed impossibly long, like the distance to Iola's house in my dream, when my legs wouldn't carry me. The room, the voices, the people shifting forward in their chairs, Paul passing the poster boards down the row, the commissioners shuffling papers on the dais, the air conditioner kicking on overhead . . .

Everything seemed far away. As I set the notebook on the podium, opened it, shuffled the pages, there was a strange silence in my mind. *Please help me do this,* I whispered into it. *Please help me be good enough.*

"My name is . . ." My voice cracked and the microphone squealed, getting feedback from somewhere. In the periphery of my vision, Gina scoffed, pushing off the wall and tossing her hair, then slipping her hand over Ross's bicep and whispering something in his ear.

The green light on the podium blinked on, and I started again. "My name is Tandi Reese. I live in the cottage at Benoit House in Fairhope." The voice seemed to come from outside me, but it was strong and clear. I heard the words as if they were someone else's. "I've been caring for the place since the death of Iola Anne Poole, the longtime owner of the property."

Gina coughed and one of the commissioners glanced her way. I straightened my shoulders and went on. For once, I would not let my sister or anyone beat me down. I wasn't that little girl hiding behind the sofa anymore, trying to keep myself hidden to survive. I was a woman ready to finally make her own life.

"I'm just across the salt meadow and through the woods from Bink's store. The back portion of the Benoit estate is the property in question for the borrow pits, and the historic home under threat of condemnation lies directly west of my cottage. My grandfather was an insurance adjuster who many times assessed storm damage to homes here on the Outer Banks, and my father ran his own construction company for years. I often helped with his jobs as I was growing up, and I recently completed repairs to water-damaged areas of Sandy's Seashell Shop, so I do know a bit about storm damage and structural renovation."

Gina sighed loudly, and my thoughts jumped.

Taking a breath, I focused on the notebook again. Somewhere on the dais, a pencil scratched against a piece of paper. Who was writing and what?

I closed my eyes, opened them again. "Benoit House can be saved. It deserves to be saved. Many of you have heard of the house. It's one of a few original Victorian-style homes remaining on Hatteras. If you know the Outer Banks well, you probably know of it. Before you consider condemning Benoit House, you should understand what you will really be tearing down."

"That house is a wreck, and she knows it is!" Gina moved from the wall, stepping toward the podium. "She's been trying to keep people out so they won't see that, but I was inside the place just the other day, and there were buckets full of water everywhere, the ceilings are falling in upstairs, and —"

"Sit down!" someone yelled from the gallery.

The judge hammered his gavel, attempting to bring order to the room. "Ma'am, you have *not* been recognized by this court." He pointed the gavel at Gina. "If you would like to speak, you may raise your hand when we ask if there are any more comments, and at that time you will be recognized by the court; however, if there are any further outbursts, I will ask that you be forcibly removed from the room."

Gina's nostrils flared and she bolted her arms, sulking against Ross.

At the dais, the commissioners leaned away cautiously, now fully sensing what a contentious issue we were dealing with. Where a moment ago they had seemed receptive, now they appeared reserved, careful.

I fumbled through my notes, trying to find my place again. How much time had gone by? How much did I have left?

A page of information about the current damage to Benoit House and the details of its historic value drifted to the floor. I didn't retrieve it.

"I'd like to read something to you," I said instead, taking one of Iola's letters from the side pocket of the notebook. "This was writ-

ten by the owner of the house, Iola An.
Poole, who, though it was never widely
known, was a blood relation of Girard
Benoit. She was the child of his eldest son
and a housekeeper of Creole heritage. Over
the course of her life, she not only cared for
the members of the Benoit family, but she
served this country in the Women's Army
Auxiliary Corps in World War II. She traveled the world, yet this island was the place
closest to her heart. She documented her
life in letters that she kept in boxes. They
were her prayer boxes — her letters to God
— but they should speak to all of us."

Closing the notebook, I unfolded the letter. "She wrote this just after the famous
Ash Wednesday storm lashed the eastern
coast for three days in 1962. The nor'easter
came without warning on the night of
March 7, and by the time it was over, it had
killed forty people on the Eastern Seaboard
and injured over a thousand. At that time,
Iola was struggling to care for her biological
grandfather, Girard Benoit, who was bedridden and stricken with dementia. She had
also suffered the recent loss of Isabelle, who
by blood relation was her aunt, but whom
she loved as a sister. Here is what she wrote
in the aftermath of that terrible storm:

mes lie toppled in the sea. Power
ean against wires that hang twisted
read. Boats sit upended and piled
ore. The road has been lifted and
broken. The storm has cut an inlet
through the island between Buxton and
Avon, separating the south from the
north. It seems as though our lives here
will never be whole again. There is too
much devastation to face.

"Yet we of this island slowly come
forth from the wreckage. There is no
other way for us, Father.

"Dawn comes after the darkness, and
with it the promise that what has been
torn by the sea is not lost. All of life is
breaking and mending, clipping and
stitching, gathering tatters and sewing
seams. All of life is quilted from the
scraps of what once was and is no more
— the places we have been, the memories we have made, the people we have
known, that which has been long loved
but has grown threadbare over time and
can be worn no longer. We keep only
pieces. All colors, all shapes, all sizes.

"All waiting to be stitched into the pattern only you can see.

"In the quiet after the storm, I hear
you whisper, 'Daughter, do not linger

where you are. Take up your needle and your thread, and go see to the mending. . . .' "

I stopped reading there, looked at the men and women on the dais, the people with the power to save or condemn Benoit House, the power to finally validate the hidden work of Iola's life.

On the podium, the yellow light blinked on. "A week after this letter was written, an original Remington bronze worth $900,000 was donated to a relief fund created to help rebuild the island and to close or bridge the new inlet. At the time, residents were so desperate to reunite the north and south ends of the island that they were dumping junk cars in the inlet, hoping to close it. The donation of the statue was made anonymously — you can see a newspaper article about it on the poster boards that are being held up in the back of the room.

"In fact, you can see a number of articles and photos and letters there. They tell the story of this island, but they also tell the story of a woman few people really knew. She devoted herself — her resources, her energy, her efforts, her prayers — to the Outer Banks and the people who live here, many of whom were strangers to her. She gave almost everything she had, and when this last storm came, when water began trickling through the roof of the home she had loved most of her life, instead of asking her neighbors to pick up their mending threads and help her save her house . . . instead, at ninety-one years old, frail in her body and alone in her home, she put buckets and pots and pans under the drops, and she served her neighbors. The Tiffany Magnolia lamp that caused such a stir, that created the fund to aid families displaced by the recent storms, came from the upstairs bedroom in Benoit House — the last untouched place in the house. The room where Iola Anne Poole died."

The red light came on. No one in the chamber moved. On the dais, the commissioners were gazing past me, looking at the posters, finally meeting the small, quiet woman so few people understood.

I finished with the last paragraph of what Paul and I had written. "By the world's standards, she might not have been a person who really mattered, who was noteworthy. But by all the standards that matter most, she was an incredible human being. She touched the lives of people who never knew her. She asked for nothing in return — no press coverage, no name on a plaque, no

TV interviews, no thank-you notes. We have the chance to honor her with this one final act of gratitude. We can save her house — the house she intended to leave in the hands of the church so that it would be cared for and used for something good. I hope . . . I pray that you who sit on this court, and all of you who are in this room today, will feel, as I do, that this is a cause worth fighting for."

Gathering my papers, I turned to leave. Behind me, members of the gallery were slowly rising to their feet. Near the back door, Gina threaded her way through the crowd, making a hasty exit with Ross in tow.

A man, a stranger with the ruddy look of a seaman, began to clap, the noise shattering the silence. Another set of hands joined, and another and another, the applause slowly growing as Iola's neighbors came out to meet her for the very first time.

CHAPTER 26

Outside, the tips of tree branches squealed as they scratched across the moving van. I walked to the window and looked, then noticed the suncatcher still hanging there on its green ribbon. The knot was just beyond my reach.

"Guess it's time." Paul walked out of the closet, glancing down at the moving van. "Here, I've got it." He stretched toward the ribbon, his body molding against mine, the sleeve of a shirt printed with turkeys in flip-flops and swim trunks tickling my ear.

"Where in the world do you find these things?" I grabbed the fabric, giving it a playful tug.

"What?" He coughed softly in his throat. "It's my Thanksgiving shirt."

"Thanksgiving's not until tomorrow."

His lips spread into a playful smile, his brown eyes catching the window light and turning the warm color of polished wood.

"I have something *better* in store for tomorrow."

"Your mom will love that." Paul's mother had already assured me, long-distance, that she was not in any way responsible for his fashion sense.

"My mom's going to love *you,*" he said, and I felt myself melting. Never, ever in my life had I imagined that there could be someone like Paul Chastain. The way I felt about him was the stuff of fairy tales. Yet each day it grew and became more real.

The suncatcher came loose unexpectedly, and I caught it as it tumbled toward the Tiffany Magnolia lamp.

"Watch the lamp!" Paul squeaked, sucking a breath through his teeth.

"Me?" I giggled, setting the suncatcher on the bare mattress. Isabelle's wedding quilt had already been carefully packed in a box, as had almost everything else in the house. The Tiffany Magnolia was waiting for a local antique dealer to come and expertly prepare it for transport.

Below on the lawn, a car pulled in and then another, followed by a Suburban with an antique store logo painted on the side. "Right on time, I guess." I touched the suncatcher, thinking of the first day I'd seen it, its colored light drawing me toward Iola's boxes.

"Right on time," Paul echoed. His eyes met mine for a moment. I thought of the night we'd spent traveling together through the prayer boxes, trying to save this house. "Guess we'd better go let them in."

"The door's not locked. Besides, the kids are downstairs." I sat on the edge of the bed, took the little hummingbird in my lap, fingered its glass wings.

Paul slipped in beside me, stretching an arm around my waist and hugging me close. I rested my head on his shoulder. "It's what has to happen, you know," he reminded.

"I know."

"You wanted to save this house."

"Yeah, I did."

The trail of his fingers was featherlight on my skin. "You know, some things are pretty much impossible."

I nodded, watched the hummingbird's wings cast color over my fingers, thought of Iola's belongings, now packed in cardboard cartons all through the house. "I just wonder how she would feel about it if she were here — all these people handling her stuff, moving her out."

Paul ruffled my hair, then kissed it. "Well, you've pretty much *done* the impossible here, but the fact is, now that the roof has been redone, the place has to be gutted if it's going to be saved."

"I know, I know." Despite all that had happened, despite the fact that this house really belonged to the island, there was still a part of me that didn't want to share it.

"And considering that everyone from the mayor to the kids in school have their pennies invested in the renovation fund, it's good that there's a competent handywoman right next door, making sure it's all done the way it should be. This house has another hundred good years in it. Who knows what it'll see."

"Well, quite a few weddings and lots of museum traffic." I turned to Paul, wondering again how Iola would feel about so many people tromping through her home. She'd been a private woman, but she and Benoit House had an extraordinary past, a story that should be shared. The attic had been filled with trunks containing photos, ledgers, and other bits of Outer Banks history from the Benoit shipping empire, dating all the way back to the mid–eighteen hundreds. Some had been ruined by the water leaks, but many had survived, and there was much to be sorted through yet.

"Relax." Paul slipped a finger under my

chin and kissed me, then whispered against my lips, "If anyone can make it all happen the way it's supposed to, you can."

There were footsteps downstairs now and voices.

"I can't believe all these people came to volunteer, especially right before Thanksgiving."

"They love this house and they love the island." Standing, he took one last look around the blue room. "Guess we'd better head down there before they start loading things without us." He crossed the room and grabbed a clipboard from the dresser. "Here's the list of which stuff goes to storage and which stuff goes to Norfolk for renovations and cleaning."

Nodding, I reached for the poster boards that had helped to save Benoit House. "I'm going to put these in the cottage for now, I think . . . and the suncatcher, too. I don't want them to be in the storage unit."

"We did work hard on these posters." Paul hooked a finger over the edge of one of the boards and opened it. "A masterful job, if I do say so myself. A little more island flair would have jazzed them up a bit, though — something in a Hawaiian print."

I laughed. Paul could always make me laugh. Even today. "With you, *everything* needs a little more island flair."

I laid the posters on the bed, and we stood a moment, looking at the photos of the house in its glory days, taking in the bits of copied prayer letters bearing Iola's words and her sketches. A whelk shell here, a lighthouse there. I hadn't looked at them since they'd been displayed at the public hearing.

I touched the drawing of the little girl in the porch chair. "I wonder who she was — Christina, maybe?" Was this Isabelle's daughter, who was born sickly and died so young?

Paul shook his head. "That's not Christina. That's the Mulberry Girl, the one who's mentioned at the end of so many of the later letters. She doesn't show up until the box from 1986 — the glass box. The only reason I remember that is because the box was different, being stained glass, and it was the only box out of order. For some reason, it was on the top shelf, at the very end of the line. That spot should have had the newest box, but it didn't."

"That's strange." I traced a fingertip along the outline of the girl, then thought about the box and how close I'd come to toppling it on my head when I'd tried to reach it with the short ladder and the broom handle.

"She came here to visit, and she had to stay outside on the porch because she had mulberry stains on her feet," Paul offered. "I don't remember the whole story, but I remember that part. To tell you the truth, by then I was skimming — just looking for stuff that would help us at the commissioners' court."

"Mulberry stains on her feet . . ." Something was happening in my mind. There was a reaching and straining, a grasping at threads. I closed my eyes, tried to pull them closer.

Paul's voice came from outside the rush of thought. "Yeah, I guess nobody told her you can get rid of the stains if you take the berries that aren't ripe yet, the —"

"The white berries and rub them on the stains." I pressed my hands to my mouth, drew in a breath, heard the words again in my mind.

Honey, just take the white berries and rub them on the stains. There's an old mulberry tree right out back. You can go on and pick some. It's all right.

A hand patted mine.

I pulled away. . . .

The snatch of memory was gone as quickly as it came.

"Paul, where's the box? The glass box?" I

516

grabbed my head, feeling like it might explode. "The glass box, where is it?"

He drew back, frowning. "It's safe. I packed it myself." His eyes looked for mine, but I couldn't focus. "Tandi . . . you all right?"

"The *box*, Paul. I need to see the glass box." What was there? What was there in the shadows, just beyond what I could pull from memory? It wasn't even a memory, really. Just a scrap. A few words . . . a voice . . . the touch of a hand.

"Okay. All right, hang on a minute." Paul shifted the clipboard, flipped the page. "Container B7. It's on the front porch already. I carried those down a while ago. I thought I'd take them in my pickup instead of putting them in the moving van. It seemed like the prayer boxes should get special treatment until we figure out what to do with them, you know?" His fingers cupped my elbow. "Tandi, what's going on? You look like you've seen a ghost."

"I have," I whispered. "I think I have." I spun around and ran for the door, with Paul calling after me.

My footsteps echoed through the house as I dashed past the nursery room, down the stairs, past the volunteers who were already bringing in dollies, talking about how to move the furniture, turning over tables so as to carefully remove the heavy bases. The noise, the activity seemed far away as I bolted onto the porch.

Startled, the cat sat up in the weathered rocker where he'd been sleeping. He arched and stretched, yawning and watching me curiously as I searched the containers on the porch, found the one with the right number, tugged the edge of the tape to pull it open.

"We're supposed to be putting stuff in, not taking it out!" the UPS driver joked as he passed by, wearing his civilian clothes today.

I didn't answer, just threw wads of newsprint out . . . until, nestled between four decorated shoe boxes, I found it, the tag from Sandy's Seashell Shop still visible through the stained-glass lid. Was this the box Iola had brought for repair when the shop first opened — the one that had helped to inspire so many of Sandy's creations?

I was lifting it out when Paul reached the porch. "See? The box is fine. I told you it was."

I moved to the old swing beside the cat's favorite chair, then opened the lid, checked one letter, then another, then another, until I found the one with the drawing of the

Mulberry Girl.

There on the next page was her story.

. . . the little girl, Father. The one who sits outside while her grandfather works upstairs, inspecting the damage done by the tree that's fallen into the second-floor balcony.

"She doesn't seem very happy today," I say to the man as he comes down with his notepad in hand. Outside, the cat is rubbing round the girl's little mulberry-stained feet. "I tried to interest her in some of my beignets, but she would have none of it. I've packed a few in a napkin for her. Maybe they will cheer her on the drive home. There's no need to fret over the mulberry stains. They come clean if you rub them with the white ber-ries — the ones that aren't yet ripe. I told her that."

The grandfather sighs, gazing outward in a way that is troubled yet kind. "The stains aren't the problem, I'm afraid," he says. "Child's seen too much of life for her age. Been dropped off again by her mama, no telling for how long. It's always hardest the first few days. Chil-dren don't understand. They're sure they did somethin' to deserve it. I never thought any daughter of mine would treat her babies like this." He sighs again and looks down at his hands, the weathered hands of a workingman. "You a prayin' woman, Mrs. Poole?"

"Why, yes. Yes, I am," I say.

"I thought so." He pauses as the church bells ring next door, the sound drifting across the field. "I'd appreciate it if you'd mention my granddaughters when you're talking to the Almighty. It's hard to know what to do when the parents won't take care of them, but they won't give them up, either." He holds away his emotions and swallows hard, then pulls the ticket from his pad. "Didn't mean to burden you. I'll get the report in to the insurance company so your railin' can be fixed. Until then, better stay off that balcony."

"Certainly." I fold the paper between my fingers, walk to the door with him. "It's no burden," I say, then give the beignets to him as he opens the door to leave. "I will keep your granddaughters in my prayers, especially this little one. Do let me know if things change for the better. It's hard for a child to be away from home."

"Yes, it is." He wipes the moisture

around his eye, and then he gathers the girl and is gone.

I never thought to ask her name, Father, but you know the little mulberry girl as you know each sparrow of the field.

You are the white berry that removes the stain.

Be with her, as you have been with me.

Your loving daughter,
Iola Anne

"That was me," I whispered, looking from the letter to Paul. "I came here with my grandfather when I was six. I don't even . . . remember it . . . except, someone's hand, someone's voice. Her voice. I didn't go inside because I had stains on my feet from hiding in the mulberry orchard when my mama left us." The memory was all around me now. Scraps of fear and comfort, loneliness and love, darkness and light. The quilt of who I had become.

Beside me, Paul frowned, cocked his head, and looked at the letter, an understanding slowly dawning as he studied the little girl in the sketch. "That was you?"

"It was." Joy filled me, sweet, overwhelming, rushing like a tide. Iola and I were not strangers. She had kept me in her boxes all these years. In her prayer letters. "I was the Mulberry Girl."

Paul's hand slipped over mine, our fingers intertwining as we fell silent in the knowledge, in the secret. No words can encompass the miracles of God.

None can contain the magnificence of a wave kissing sand or the perfect spiral of a shell drying translucent in the sun or the fire of morning rising over endless water.

Or the beauty of a hummingbird as it hovers just an arm's length away, mysteriously out of season on the day before Thanksgiving, its wings stroking air, rapid, invisible, powerful. Frozen in time for only an instant.

And then it flies away, growing smaller and smaller and smaller against the blue of an endless sky.

Until finally it disappears into heaven.

A NOTE FROM THE AUTHOR

DEAR READER,

This is how *The Prayer Box* came to be: by accident, if you believe in accidents. I glanced across the room one day, saw the small prayer box that had been gifted to me, and a story began to spin through my mind. What if that box contained many prayers accumulated over time? What if there were *dozens* of boxes? What if they contained the prayers of a lifetime?

What could more fully tell the truth about a person than words written to God in solitude?

Of course, Iola would say those random questions that popped into my mind, and *The Prayer Box* story itself, weren't accidents at all. She would say it was divine providence. Something that was meant to be.

I believe divine providence has brought this story into your hands too. I hope you enjoyed the journey through Iola's prayer boxes as much as I did. If the journey is still ahead of you, I hope that it takes you to far-off places . . . and into inner spaces as well. More than that, I hope it will inspire you to think about keeping a prayer box of your own and maybe giving one to somebody else.

The little box that was given to me was by no means unique. I'd heard of prayer boxes, and I knew what they were for. Either they're keeping places for favorite Scriptures, or they're similar to a prayer journal, only more flexible. Any scrap of paper will do, anywhere, anytime of the day or night. The important part, in a world of fractured thoughts, hurried moments, and scattershot prayers, is to take the time to think through, to write down, to clarify in your own mind the things you're asking for, the things you're grateful for, the things you're troubled about, the hopes you've been nurturing.

And then?

Put them in the box and . . .

Let. Them. Go.

That's what trust is. It's letting go of the worry. It's the way of peace and also the way of God. Such a hard road to travel for people like me, who are worriers. When I'm writing a story, I control the whole universe. In life . . . not so much. Actually, not at all. Things happen that I hadn't anticipated and wouldn't choose and can't change. That's the tough part.

Closing the lid on a prayer box is symbolic of so many things. When we give a prayer over to God, it's supposed to be in God's hands after that. I think that's what Sister Marguerite was trying to teach Iola when she gave her that very first prayer box. Life is, so often, beyond our control, just as it was for that little ten-year-old girl, far from home. I like to imagine that Sister Marguerite decorated that box herself, preparing it with young Iola in mind.

After studying more about prayer boxes and using them myself, I'm surprised we don't do this more often. Prayer boxes have a long-standing tradition, both among early Christians and among Jewish families. Jews and early Christians often wore small leather or carved bone boxes on the body. These phylacteries or tefillin were a means of keeping Scripture close to the wearer. Large boxes called mezuzah cases are still affixed to the doorposts of Jewish homes today.

It's a beautiful tradition, when you think about it, to surround our coming in and going out with a brush with God. It's also a reminder, as family members pass by, to pray and to trust that our prayers are being heard.

That's one of my favorite reasons for keeping a prayer box inside the home, or for giving one as a gift. When you see the box, you're reminded that things are *supposed* to go *in* it. In other words, the prayer box isn't meant to gather dust; it's meant to inspire a habit. That's the real idea behind making a prayer box attractive, and the reason I think Iola must have decorated so many of hers. I imagined that, as each year came, she prepared a box that represented her life at the time, and then she kept the box out where she would see it and be reminded that her Father was waiting to hear from her.

I wonder if Iola ever gave prayer boxes as gifts, just as that first box was given to her. Maybe that's what she did with those many glass boxes she purchased from Sandy's Seashell Shop. Do you think so? What better way to bind a family, help a friend struggle through an illness, start a just-married couple off right, celebrate a tiny new life just born, send a graduate into the world, than to give a prayer box and an explanation of what it's for? The box can be something you buy premade or something

526

you decorate yourself. If you're hand-decorating it, why not personalize it with photos or favorite Scriptures?

Are you inspired to consider spreading the tradition of prayer boxing yet? I hope so. I could go on and on with ideas and stories here, but that's another book in itself. If you'd like to learn more about how to use prayer boxes in your church, your study group, your family, your ministry, your community, or as gifts, drop by www.Lisa Wingate.com for more information about prayer boxes, some examples, sample notes to include with prayer box gifts, and other ideas for making, using, and giving them.

My wish for you is that, in this age-old tradition, you and others will find what Tandi found when she entered Iola's blue room in her dream. May the glorious light fill you and shine upon you and draw you ever closer.

We all know who waits inside the light.

DISCUSSION QUESTIONS

1. Iola's written prayers create a record of her life. Have you ever written down your prayers or considered writing them down? What advantages can you see to using a prayer box?

2. How do the prayer boxes change Tandi's perspective on faith? Do you think the simple display of everyday belief can change people, even change a community? Have you ever seen it happen?

3. Tandi wants a better life for Zoey and J.T., but she struggles with figuring out how to make that happen. What did you think of her choices about how to care for them? How did you feel about her parenting at the beginning of the story? At the end?

4. Iola sees the kindness of friends and

strangers as an extension of grace. Do you agree? Have you seen the "grace water" in your own life or in your community?

5. It seemed to be easier for Iola to give help than to accept it. Why might that be? Is it easier for you to serve others or to accept the gift of service?

6. Before Isabelle leaves for college, she and Iola have opposite goals for their future — Iola opting for a "safe" life and Isabelle seeking adventure. Isabelle notes that "fear builds walls rather than bridges." Do you think Iola, as a young woman, made her choices based on fear? Which woman's perspective is closest to your own?

7. Tandi finds herself so trapped by her past, by the need to replace the love she lacked growing up with something, that she consistently repeats the same mistakes with men. Yet when Ross comes into her life, she sees him as her "knight in shining armor." Why? Have you seen similar relationship patterns in your own life? What advice would you give to a woman trying to move beyond the wounds of her past and become fully whole?

8. Iola enters into her life as a WAAC and even into her marriage while keeping her heritage a secret. Have you ever maintained a family secret? Or have you ever discovered one in your family? Do you think Iola made the right choice when she ultimately decided to risk telling her husband the truth?

9. Tandi wonders how Iola could cast aside the word *anathema* rather than taking it on as a part of herself. How do you think Iola was able to do this? Is it possible to shed the labels given to us by others? How can we accept that one most important label — beloved?

10. Tandi and Zoey struggle as mother and daughter, particularly as Zoey navigates her teenage years. Is the relationship between all mothers and daughters a battle in some ways, or is this a result of Tandi's past mistakes? How can mothers guide their daughters without being overbearing? Do you think children can be prevented from repeating their parents' mistakes, or do they have to figure things out on their own?

11. Sandy seems to almost instantly recog-

nize that Tandi has been sent to the Seashell Shop for a reason and quickly welcomes her into the sisterhood, yet Sandy's reaction to Gina is very different. Why do you think that is? Have you ever had an intuition about someone that proved to be true? Or have you seen a first impression proven wrong?

12. Iola eventually desires to live her life "in anticipation of the bridges to magnificence." Some people seem to have a talent for doing this — for always seeing the positive and looking at the future with anticipation. Where do you think that ability comes from? Does this reflect your outlook on life? If not, how could you cultivate a spirit of anticipation?

13. Even when the community shunned her, Iola didn't reveal the truth about her relationship to the Benoit family. Why do you think she kept that secret all her life?

14. Despite the evidence stacking up to the contrary, Tandi can't quite give up on the dream of having a real relationship with her sister. Why do you think the bonds of family sometimes hold us, even when everyone around us is advising us to cut

the ties? Do you agree with Sandy that sometimes the family we find can be as powerful as the one we're born with? Do you think Tandi and Gina will ever reunite?

15. What did you take away from *The Prayer Box*? Did you relate more closely to Iola's story or to Tandi's?

ABOUT THE AUTHOR

Lisa Wingate is a former journalist, a speaker, and the author of twenty novels, including the national bestseller *Tending Roses,* now in its eighteenth printing. She is a seven-time ACFW Carol Award nominee, a Christy Award nominee, and a two-time Carol Award winner. Her novel *Blue Moon Bay* was a *Booklist* Top Ten of 2012 pick. Recently the group Americans for More Civility, a kindness watchdog organization, selected Lisa along with Bill Ford, Camille Cosby, and six others as recipients of the National Civies Award, which celebrates public figures who work to promote greater kindness and civility in American life. When not dreaming up stories, Lisa spends time on the road as a motivational speaker. Via Internet, she shares with readers as far away as India, where *Tending Roses* has been used to promote women's literacy, and as close to home as Tulsa, Oklahoma, where the county library system has used *Tending Roses* to help volunteers teach adults to read.

Lisa lives on a ranch in Texas, where she spoils the livestock, raises boys, and teaches Sunday school to high school seniors. She was inspired to become a writer by a first-grade teacher who said she expected to see Lisa's name in a magazine one day. Lisa also entertained childhood dreams of being an Olympic gymnast and winning the National Finals Rodeo but was stalled by the inability to do a backflip on the balance beam and parents who wouldn't finance a rodeo career. She was lucky enough to marry into a big family of cowboys and Southern storytellers who would inspire any lover of tall tales and interesting yet profound characters. She is a full-time writer and pens inspirational fiction for both the general and Christian markets. Of all the things she loves about her job, she loves connecting with people, both real and imaginary, the most. More information about Lisa's novels can be found at www.lisawingate.com.